THE KEYS
TO THE
TEMPLE

Also by David Furlong
The Complete Healer
Healing Your Family Patterns
Develop Your Intuition and Psychic Powers (Bloomsbury)

DAVID FURLONG

THE KEYS TO THE TEMPLE

UNRAVEL THE MYSTERIES OF THE ANCIENT WORLD

PIATKUS

© 1997 David Furlong

First published in 1997 by
Judy Piatkus (Publishers) Ltd
5 Windmill Street, London W1P 1HF

**The moral right of the author
has been asserted**

*A catalogue record for this book is available
from the British Library*

ISBN 0-7499-1745-8 hbk

Edited by Nigel Cawthorne and John Malem
Designed by Sue Ryall
Diagrams by David Furlong
Artworks by Zena Flax

Set in Garamond by
Phoenix Photosetting, Chatham, Kent
Printed and bound in Great Britain by
Mackays of Chatham PLC, Chatham, Kent

To Diane

ACKNOWLEDGEMENTS

The research for this book took place over a twenty-five year period. During that time many people have contributed ideas and constructive criticism, plus much encouragement to continue with my studies. I acknowledge and thank all those people who have helped in one way or another. There are a few individuals who deserve special mention.

Firstly I wish to thank Diane Furlong for joining me on the innumerable journeys of exploration to many different sacred sites, both in Britain and abroad, and for her valuable intuitive perceptions. I also thank my daughter Claire for helping with some of the practical research and photography of the Marlborough Downs sites and my son Maaten for checking some of the maths.

I especially thank Murry Hope and Jude Stammers for reading through the manuscript and for providing some valuable feedback.

Finally, I thank my editors, Nigel Cawthorne, John Malem, Gill Cormode and Anne Lawrance for their patience, constructive input and perseverance in bringing this book to fruition.

Credits

Plate Section: Photograph 1: English Monuments; Photograph 2: Collections/Fay Godwin; Photograph 3: Collections/Fay Godwin; Photograph 4: Collections/Robert Pilgrim; Photograph 5: David Furlong; Photograph 6: David Furlong; Photograph 7: Mick Sharp; Photograph 8: David Furlong; Photograph 9: David Furlong; Photograph 10: English Monuments; Photograph 11: Collections/Robert Hallman; Photograph 12: Collections/Fay Godwin; Photograph 13: Fortean Picture Library/Janet and Colin Bord; Photograph 14: Collections/Paul Watts; Photograph 15: Irish Picture Library; Photograph 16: Werner Forman Archive; Photograph 17: Travel Ink/Abbie Enock; Photograph 18: Werner Forman Archive; Photograph 19: Werner Forman Archive; Photograph 20: AKG London; Photograph 21: AKG London.

Maps and Plans: Plan of Hagar Quim (below photograph 21): from *The Prehistoric Antiquities of the Maltese Islands: A Survey* by J.D. Evans, 1971. Reproduced by kind permission of the Athlone Press. Ordnance Survey maps reproduced by kind permission of Ordnance Survey Copyrights. Map on p. 18 copyright Bartholomew 1972. Reproduced with permission of HarperCollins Cartographic MM-0997-34.

CONTENTS

INTRODUCTION

Patterns set out in the landscape are fragments of a forgotten science

This is a book of an extraordinary quest. It began more than twenty years ago in my discovery of a vast geometric pattern set out in the landscape in Wiltshire, England. Hidden within the rolling chalk uplands of the Marlborough Downs I found a pattern whose underlying symmetry is precisely the same as that embodied within the Great Pyramid of Khufu in Egypt. This dramatic finding points either to a direct communication between these two widely distant countries or, as I have come to believe, that the people responsible for these creations had a single, common origin.

The Great Pyramid of Khufu was erected about 2500BC. As one of the Seven Wonders of the Ancient World it is a pinnacle of unsurpassed architectural achievement. The roots of this awe-inspiring monument can be traced back to the beginnings of dynastic Egypt which, according to Egyptologists, emerged suddenly around 3100BC.

It is less well known that Britain too can boast of some amazing megalithic stone edifices, built at the same time as the pyramids. In the valley of the River Kennet that borders the Marlborough Downs, stands the conical mound of Silbury Hill. This is the largest man-made prehistoric structure of its kind in Europe. The angle of its slope is 30°. This is significant because 30° is one third of a right angle and the bisecting angle of an equilateral triangle. Its use tells us that the mound's builders knew about geometry. We also know that the work began in the late summer

season around 2750BC, because of the insect and plant remains found at
the base level of the mound. This organic material allows scientists to date
the work accurately using radiocarbon dating. A short walk from Silbury
Hill is the equally impressive henge monument of Avebury, with its huge
circular earth bank and ditch and massive stone circle rings. Avebury was
built around the same time as Silbury Hill.

Both of these monuments highlight key positions in a geometric pattern that overlays the Marlborough Downs. I will show that this pattern
was consciously created, deliberately surveyed and set out in the landscape
of ancient Britain – 5000 years ago. Silbury Hill, Avebury, and the many
other prehistoric monuments in this area, are positioned on a pre-
determined geometric plan. The question is simple: why?

Archaeological evidence tells us that the cultural movement in Britain
that led to the building of stone circles, tumuli (burial mounds) and
henges (circular banks and ditches) began, as the pyramids did in Egypt,
around 3100BC. The similarity of this date is surely more than
coincidence.

The body of my quest has been the search for the unifying link between
ancient Egyptian and ancient British culture, which I now firmly believe
lies rooted in a 'lost' civilisation. I also believe that the destruction of this
civilisation occurred on, or very close to, the 12 August 3114BC, the date
which, according to the ancient Mayan calendar, is when the present age
began, following a global catastrophe. Climatic evidence shows that this
was a time of massive disturbance and instability, commensurate with
some kind of cataclysm.

In the Alexander Keiller Museum, Avebury, situated near the medieval
church, stands a statue representing a Neolithic man. One half depicts a
coarse wild, unshaven, brutish person covered in ragged clothes; the other
shows a refined, well-dressed individual, with neatly trimmed beard and
hair. These images are the two faces of Neolithic man that have emerged
from archaeological excavations and the study of his monuments. On the
one hand, we have a brutish illiterate existence, and on the other a sophisticated understanding of astronomical, geometrical and architectural
principles. Which of these two more accurately portrays our ancient
British forebears? The answer may be both, as shown by two distinct types
of skeletal remains that date from this time.

The books *Fingerprints of the Gods*, written by Graham Hancock, and *Keeper of Genesis*, co-written with Robert Bauval, have argued that the destruction of an earlier advanced culture around 10,500BC laid the foundations of dynastic Egypt. I do not doubt that such a cataclysm occurred. Indeed, many myths, such as those of the Hopi Native American peoples of Arizona, indicate a number of previous global destructions. According to Mayan beliefs, 3114BC heralded the termination of the fourth age while the fifth, which we are now living in will complete its cycle on 22 December AD2012. Each previous age, we are told, was destroyed by either fire or flood which wiped out most of humanity. I believe that the Mayan date, 3114BC – rather than 10,500BC – is the most likely date of the destruction of an advanced culture that preceded the Egyptians.

My main argument for this more recent date is simple. Let us suppose that an island, or group of islands, perhaps not too dissimilar in size to the British Isles, existed somewhere in the Atlantic Ocean and was home to a society with considerable scientific knowledge. Let us also imagine that those who lived in the lands on either side of the Atlantic, still led a comparatively primitive existence. If some disaster overwhelmed that island race, giving just sufficient time for small groups of people to flee in their boats, what would be the result?

When these refugees made landfall, they would start to integrate into the local population. Their advanced ideas, where accepted, would be quickly absorbed, leading to a rapid acceleration in local cultural development. We would expect to see significant changes occurring within a relatively short period of time; perhaps one or two hundred years at most.

Attempting to link dynastic Egypt with the destruction of an advanced culture in 10,500BC, more than 7000 years earlier, does not make sense. But if the date of the cataclysm was closer to 3100BC, then the pieces of the jigsaw fit neatly together and the massive cultural shift that occurred simultaneously in Britain, Egypt and elsewhere can be readily explained.

Compelling evidence presented in this book lends further weight to this argument, showing that those who entered both Britain and Egypt at this time brought with them a sophisticated understanding of astronomy, surveying and geometry. The patterns set out in the landscape of the Marlborough Downs are fragments of a forgotten science – a science that incorporated geometric principles that are in direct harmonious relationship with the proportions of the Earth.

The initial discovery of the Marlborough Downs patterns occurred in 1975. It has taken more than twenty years of determined research to show how the ancient inhabitants of Britain were able to survey and set out their landscape patterns, sometimes over considerable distances. I wanted to know how they could have done this, and with what technology. The answer, when it came, was deceptively simple. Incredibly, it showed another link with ancient Egypt. The erection of enigmatic structures like Silbury Hill can now be understood in terms of surveying and geometry.

Ancient sites in Britain were linked together in a series of alignments, popularly known as 'leys'. This phenomenon was brought to the public's attention in the 1920s by Alfred Watkins, in his ground-breaking book *The Old Straight Track*. Working with a computer I have been able to advance our knowledge of leys, by demonstrating that these alignments form precise, interrelated geometric patterns.

Growing evidence also suggests that these landscape surveyors were adept at manipulating subtle forces which we are only now just beginning to discern. For many years, I have been interested in how the mind can channel subtle forms of energy that can benefit others. There is not the space in this book to present the evidence from different scientific studies which substantiate the psychic powers of our consciousness, but these powers certainly do exist. Computers are rapidly reaching a point of being able to replace the mechanical capabilities of our brains. But they will never surpass the ability of the human mind to link through intuition into higher fields of perception, or access into realms of inter-dimensional thought. Many people have had strong inner experiences at places like Avebury and other sacred sites. These can, on occasions, cause a shift in consciousness and produce a mystical awareness of other dimensions of being.

Travelling alongside my exoteric quest to unravel these mysteries, has also been an inner journey – an exploration of the spiritual power woven into the landscape more than 5000 years ago by those purveyors of a higher wisdom. Like time capsules from a distant age, this energy is now being re-activated by groups and individuals, seeking to connect back to this wisdom.

According to the Mayan calendar, we have come full circle once more, approaching, as we are, the end of another age. What has been lost is now being re-discovered. Individually and collectively we need to turn the keys, both within ourselves and at these sacred places because, I believe, the energy found within these landscape temples holds a power that can transform the human race.

1
THE MYSTERY LINES

The more I looked at it, the more it seemed they might
lie on the arc of a circle

One day in the summer of 1975, I made a startling discovery which changed my life and sent me on an incredible journey. It took me to Glastonbury, to Stonehenge, to Avebury – and to the Great Pyramid of Khufu, in Egypt. My quest transported me back through the mists of time, delving into ancient myths and searching for lost civilisations, particularly that of the fabled land of Atlantis. Like the pathways to the centre of a labyrinth, there were many false trails and blind alleys, but my quest always led me on to more tantalising revelations about our ancient past, and the enigmatic people who lived in Britain more than 5000 years ago.

At the time of my initial discovery I was living in Cheltenham, a pleasant Georgian town on the edge of the Cotswold Hills, in England, where I had recently set up my own architectural and planning consultancy. My business regularly took me out into the surrounding countryside and gave me the opportunity to visit old churches and archaeological sites. My professional work involved the use of maps of various scales. I had found maps fascinating since my school days. And so it was, that while I was looking at an old Ordnance Survey map of the area around the megalithic henge monument at Avebury, I noticed something that seemed totally improbable. Something that puzzled me. Something I knew I had to investigate.

Maps are a pictorial two-dimensional way of conveying information about what lies on the ground. Different scale maps provide various tiers of information – only the broadest general features can be shown on a map depicting the whole world, while a high level of detail can be shown on a map covering a small area. Maps of varying scales are rather like a series of snapshots which zoom in on a three-dimensional subject in greater and greater detail.

Because they are flat, maps have to be adjusted to take into account the curvature of the Earth. Mountains and valleys are, effectively, flattened so that on a map the distance between any two points assumes everything has been levelled down to the same datum level. The distance you walk on the ground, particularly in a hilly area, can be very different from what is shown on the map.

The old one-inch-to-the-mile OS maps of Britain, which I originally used, have been superseded by the 1:50,000 series, each of which covers an area of 160 sq. kilometres (about 62 sq. miles). The Ordnance Survey Sheet 157*, covering the Swindon and Devizes area, was the starting point for much of my research. The region of Wiltshire it shows is rich in archaeological sites, with many prehistoric burial mounds, stone circles, standing stones and other places of antiquity. There is much for the visitor to explore. However, I was not studying the map out of idle curiosity. I wanted to see if I could find any alignments of churches or ancient sites.

Leys and site alignments

The alignment of various historic and prehistoric sites in straight lines across the countryside was first noted in the nineteenth century. But it was Alfred Watkins' book *The Old Straight Track*, published in 1925, that brought this phenomenon to a wider public. Watkins had discovered an extensive network of alignments, involving prehistoric earthworks, standing stones, henge monuments, stone circles, medieval churches and the like. He called these alignments, which generally run for several miles, 'leys'.

Watkins presented evidence for the existence of leys from many different parts of England and Wales. Since his time, other researchers have shown that alignments occur throughout Britain and Ireland. Indeed,

*New OS Landranger Series sheet 173

there are indications of similar phenomena in other parts of the world, such as the famous Nazca lines in Peru and alignments to Pueblo Alto in the Chaco Canyon, New Mexico.

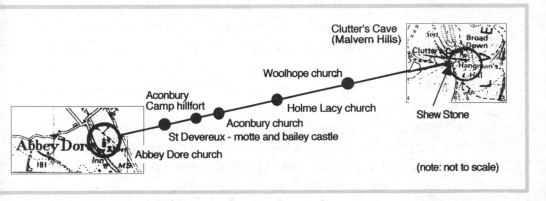

Fig. 1. Abbey Dore to Malvern Hills alignment

One example of a typical Watkins ley runs from a point on the side of the Malvern Hills, called Clutter's Cave, to the old church of Abbey Dore, a distance of just over 38 kilometres (23.66 miles). On this ley lies the Shew Stone, an ancient mark stone just below the cave, and the churches of Woolhope, Holme Lacy and Aconbury. The ley also clips the edge of Aconbury Camp hillfort at its highest point and passes through the medieval motte and bailey castle at St Devereux before reaching Abbey Dore church (Fig. 1). Watkins claimed that this alignment points to the place where the sun rises over the Malvern Hills on midsummer day, when viewed from the Shew Stone. Having spent many hours wandering across the Malverns, it is easy to imagine that many alignments could have been made to these prominent beacon hills.

The key points on this, and other Watkins leys, are monuments built at different periods, often thousands of years apart. At least a millennium separated the construction of the Iron Age hillfort of Aconbury and the churches at Woolhope, Holme Lacy and Aconbury, which were built in the eleventh and twelfth centuries. Indeed, Christianity came to British shores more than 4000 years after the first megalithic structures were put up. However, Watkins had spotted that old churches were often built alongside or on top of ancient monuments. In a letter to St Augustine in AD601, Pope Gregory I had specifically urged that 'pagan temples' should not be destroyed but sought out, purified and converted to churches.

Watkins was not the first to suggest that ancient monuments were erected to highlight significant positions of the sun and moon, or that several sites were aligned. Sir Norman Lockyer in the early 1900s had studied the orientation of ancient buildings in different parts of the world. In his book *Stonehenge and Other British Stone Monuments Astronomically Considered* (revised edition, 1909), he pointed out the alignment between Stonehenge, Old Sarum, Salisbury Cathedral and Clearbury Ring (see **photograph 9**). He also spotted how the site of Grovely Castle formed an equilateral triangle with Stonehenge and the Old Sarum hillfort. The distance between these sites is about 9.6 kilometres (6 miles). In my research, this distance came to assume great significance (Fig. 2).

To try and make sense of his discoveries, Watkins postulated that prehistoric people, for reasons never satisfactorily explained, created straight trackways across the countryside which they marked with standing stones and other ancient monuments. Although Watkins presented ample evidence to show that these leys were not just the product of his fertile imagination, orthodox archaeologists gave scant regard to his ideas. Leys did not fit with their perceptions of Neolithic and Bronze Age culture. Nor were they convinced by Watkins' hypothesis that Christians took over pagan sites. Purists argued that only pre-Christian sites should be considered, and as churches form a significant part of many alignments, discounting them seriously dented Watkins' argument. However, his book caught the public imagination and in the late 1920s and early 1930s ley hunting became a popular pastime, and branches of the Old Straight Track Club sprang up across the country.

The central question has always been whether alignments were created deliberately or whether they were just chance events. In recent years, statisticians have set up a number of mathematical models to analyse this problem, but the jury is still out. Some alignments do show a probability greater than chance, but they have not been found in sufficient numbers to prove that the alignments were deliberate.

The least satisfactory part of Watkins' theory was the idea of trackways, which link fixed points in the landscape, particularly as, in some places,

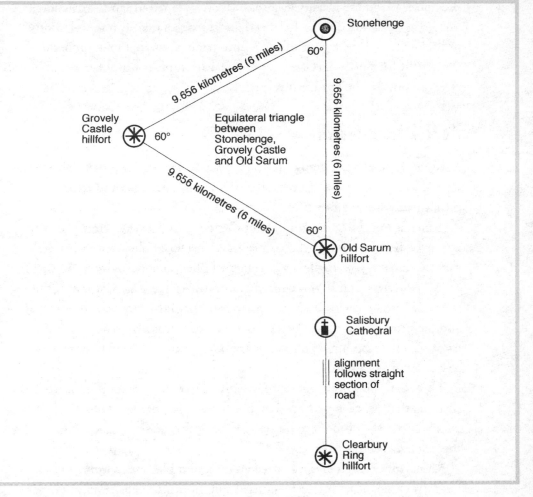

Fig. 2. Stonehenge to Clearbury Ring alignment

leys cross inhospitable terrain. Again such concepts did not fit into any orthodox archaeological view of the past. The outbreak of the Second World War brought an end to much of the interest in leys. It was not to be revived again until the late 1960s when the era of the Beatles, hippies and 'flower-power' saw a renewed interest in the mysteries of the landscape. Watkins' work was re-discovered.

In his book *View Over Atlantis*, published in 1969, John Michell took Watkins' ideas a step further by suggesting that these alignments hold some hidden and, as yet, undetected terrestrial energy. He linked leys with the ancient Chinese idea of *feng shui*, where patterns of landscape energy known as *ch'i* needed to be balanced and incorporated into the planning of buildings and the layout of the countryside. Certainly many individuals, myself included, have been aware of a form of 'atmosphere' or 'presence' at some of the key ley sites.

Modern ley research

Modern ley research has now split into two distinct camps: those who see leys as manifestations of some form of terrestrial energy; and those who purely study site alignments.

Adherents of the latter camp, led principally by Paul Devereux, former editor of the *Ley Hunter* magazine, have distanced themselves from all notions of energy, seeing leys as a religious phenomenon more to do with 'spirit' pathways. But in the United States, where there are few megalithic sites, leys are perceived as bands of energy that criss-cross the landscape and are principally studied using dowsing rods. It is also true to say that most people in Britain who have heard of or read about leys believe them to be energy pathways.

The chasm between these divergent views has become enormous, rivalling that between orthodox archaeologists and the proponents of site alignments. One of my intentions in writing this book is to try to bridge the gap between the two camps.

My curiosity about leys was sparked by reading Michell's work. It fitted neatly with my other interests – megalithic sites and maps. And my business trips into the Cotswold countryside in the mid-1970s allowed me to indulge these pastimes to the full. Soon my maps were covered with pencil lines linking churches, earthworks, abbeys and standing stones, creating a confusing jumble of possible alignments.

This map work led me to visit places that were indicated as key sites on the alignments: churches, standing stones, ancient burial mounds and, sometimes, the crossing point of several alignments. It was on these trips that I noticed that some places had a strong 'atmosphere'. I would normally experience this as a tingling sensation throughout my body, although it was particularly focused in my arms and up the back of my neck. As I walked on to a ley site I would note down where on the site this sensation occurred, if at all. I had read several books on dowsing and, although I do not use divining instruments myself, I imagine that this atmosphere or body sensation is akin to what dowsers experience through their rods or pendulum.

This type of sensation was not new to me. I had experienced it in a very different context. For a number of years I had practised as a spiritual healer. In the mid-1970s healing stood at the very fringe of what is now called complementary medicine. In recent years, through a number of scientific studies, it has gained much wider acceptance, even among medical doctors.

The tingling sensations I felt when visiting certain sites were the same as those I felt while giving or receiving healing – although then it was generally restricted to my hands or feet. Many healers I know have had similar experiences and the consensus is that these sensations are caused by the flow of 'psychic' energy between the healer and patient. My experiences at a number of different ley sites suggested that some form of latent 'healing power' or psychic energy was manifesting itself at these places.

Sceptics might argue, with some justification, that this is a totally subjective phenomenon and that a belief in something is likely to induce an experience of it. I was very mindful of this possibility. But eventually the evidence I accumulated led me to believe that this was not the case here. I am now convinced that an independent energy, accessible through the human consciousness, permeates certain sacred sites such as Avebury and Stonehenge.

Not every site I visited produced such sensations or had an 'atmosphere' and, in some churches, the strongest reaction came, not within the church, but in the churchyard. I decided to mark on the map those places where I had registered a strong reaction. In doing so, I made an interesting discovery: many supposed alignments had no markings, while others were heavily highlighted. I decided to analyse these further.

Bredon Hill alignments

My initial researches focused on the area around Bredon Hill, Worcestershire, which contains many church sites. Slowly, a pattern started to emerge (Fig. 3). Set distances occurred with some regularity.

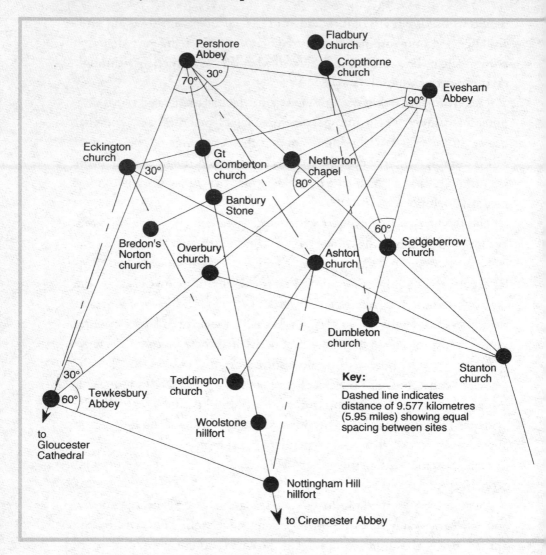

Fig. 3. Bredon Hill alignments and angles

Precise angles of 30°, 60° and 70° were often repeated. These suggested that, far from being random, some order lay behind the siting of the places. Nothing within the writings of Watkins or others suggested that geometric landscape patterns existed in the way that they were starting to appear to me. This was a radical departure from all that I had read. It was a tantalising mystery. One that I had to understand and explain.

On that momentous day in the summer of 1975, when my quest truly began, I was studying the map of the Avebury region to see whether I could discover any alignments. This area is on the edge of the Marlborough Downs. It is sparsely populated with extensive farmland and few churches. In recent years the area has become known for its crop circles, with some of the most fascinating patterns occurring within a few miles of Avebury itself. But 1975 was long before the era of crop circles.

I was studying the map for alignments when my attention was drawn to the churches in the villages of Winterbourne Monkton, Berwick Bassett (see **photograph 8**), Winterbourne Bassett and Broad Hinton, which lie just north of Avebury. Something about those four churches and their relationship to the Avebury henge nagged at me (Fig. 4).

Avebury

The Avebury henge is not as well known as Stonehenge, although it dwarfs its more famous cousin in size and structure (see **photographs 1–3**). Antiquarian John Aubrey, writing around 1665, stated that Avebury 'did as much excel Stonehenge, as a Cathedral does a Parish Church'. Built from around 2700BC, it covers a circular levelled area of some 11.53 hectares (28.5 acres) with a diameter of over a quarter of a mile, littered with numerous massive Sarsen stones weighing up to ninety tonnes. Sarsen is a type of sandstone, occurring as large boulders and blocks on the surface of the Wiltshire chalk downs. Avebury's circles and avenues originally boasted more than 600 large stones. Few now remain. Modern reconstruction work has restored something of Avebury's original grandeur and, despite the missing stones, it is still an impressive place to visit.

Such henge monuments are distributed throughout Britain, although they are mainly found on the west side of the country. The first were built around 3000BC. They have a circular earth bank with a ditch on the inside, making the structure useless for defence purposes. So it is inferred that they must have been built for religious purposes.

In most cases the bank and ditch would have been no more than a few feet in height. But at Avebury, where the earthworks are still prominent, the ditch was originally around 10 metres (33 feet) deep, and the bank rose to a height of about 6 metres (20 feet). Aubrey Burl, in his book

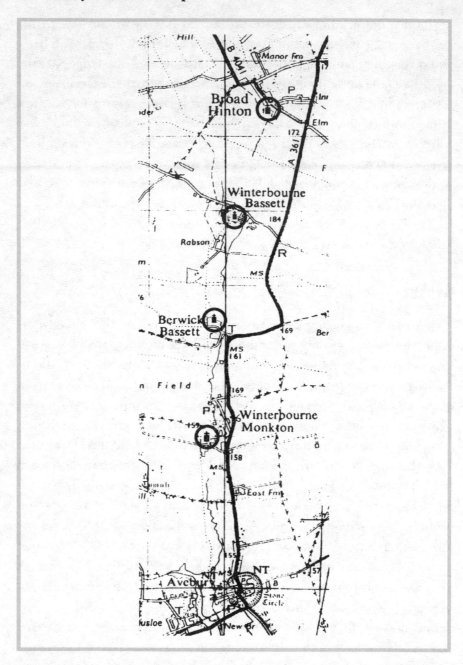

Fig. 4. Church sites north of Avebury

Prehistoric Avebury, has estimated that 90,000 cubic metres (97,000 cubic yards) of chalk were removed from the ditch, which is more than one kilometre (half a mile) in length. This is about the same volume as the seven pyramids erected by the Egyptian pharaohs of the 5th Dynasty, between 2494BC and 2345BC – around the same time as the henge at Avebury was being built.

It has been calculated that the bank and ditch alone at Avebury would have taken 250 people more than twenty years to complete. This would have been an enormous undertaking for the small communities that were thought to have lived in the area at the time.

The erection of the Sarsen stones was an equally monumental undertaking. These giant blocks would have had to have been dragged for several miles before being erected. In 1934, an experienced foreman and twelve workmen re-erected a relatively small eight-tonne stone in one of the two avenues of the standing stones on the approach to the great circle itself. It took them five days.

When the henge at Avebury was finished, it was the premier megalithic site in Britain, and it remains so today. On many occasions, and at different seasons, I have stood within the precincts of this mysterious place, my body tingling with the atmosphere that I have sensed there. I have often leant against one of the giant Sarsens and wondered at the people who built this edifice. What was its purpose? Why would they have spent so much time and effort on it unless they had a powerful reason? What secrets had this place to reveal?

The church sites and Avebury

Ley hunting from maps takes time, thought and experimentation. On that day back in 1975, I was sitting at my desk with a ruler, a pencil and the map, searching for some relationship between the church sites at Winterbourne Monkton, Berwick Bassett, Winterbourne Bassett and Broad Hinton, and Avebury itself. Several attempts to discover a straight alignment produced no satisfactory results. Yet something about their positioning bothered me. I felt intuitively there was a relationship between them and, the more I looked at it, the more it seemed they might lie on the arc of a circle. Could this be so? And for what purpose?

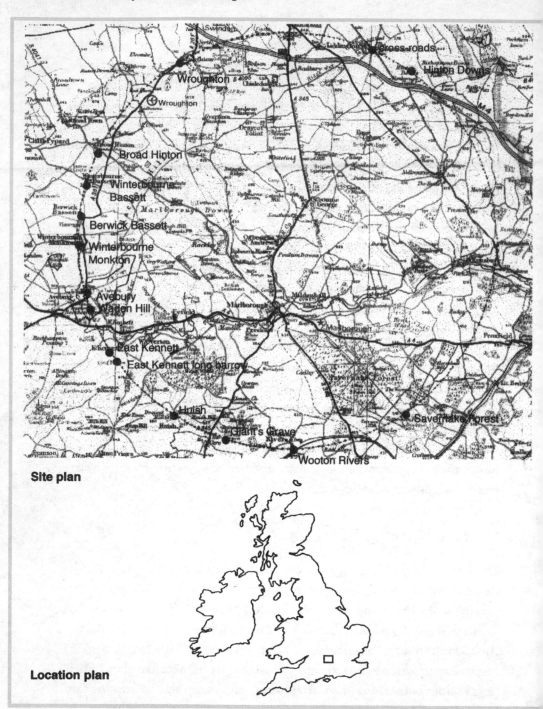

Site plan

Location plan

Fig. 5. Site and location plan

Leys or site alignments are, by definition, always straight. I had never come across any suggestion that circular landscape patterns might exist. Nevertheless, whether out of curiosity or perversity, I decided to draw a circle on a piece of tracing paper to check and make sure. The size of the circle I drew was not arbitrary, but based upon a shrewd guess and my researches to date. Its radius, on the ground, was a fraction under 9.6 kilometres (6 miles), the same distance Sir Norman Lockyer had found in the triangle of Stonehenge, Old Sarum and Grovely Castle.

What happened next left me in a state of stunned disbelief. I seemed to have hit the bull's eye at my first attempt (Fig. 5). The circle not only passed through the four churches *and* the Avebury henge, but its 60-kilometre (37-mile) circumference also ran through another ten prominent sites. Even the axis of the East Kennett long barrow had been aligned along the edge of this circle (Fig. 6).

If these sites had been aligned across the countryside in a straight line, they would undoubtedly have been regarded as a well established ley. To this day I have never found, nor heard of, a ley with fifteen sites aligned over so short a distance.

Mathematically, a circle can be drawn through any three points not in a straight line. Theoretically, it is possible for eight to ten random points to lie on the circumference of a circle with a radius of 9.6 kilometres (6 miles) merely by a statistical quirk. But increase the number of points and the odds against this happening by chance grow exponentially. Having fifteen points on the circumference of a 9.6-kilometre (6-mile) radius circle by chance is well nigh impossible.

Also, the creation of a 60 kilometre (37 mile) straight-line alignment across the countryside is relatively easy using siting poles and a little ingenuity. Creating a large circle is a much more complex task. It would require, at the very least, a much deeper understanding of mathematical principles and far more advanced surveying techniques.

Drawing a small circle on the ground with a diameter of several feet is easy. You can do it using nothing more than a peg and a piece of string. But creating a circle with a diameter of nearly 19.3 kilometres (12 miles) is a major undertaking that would challenge even the best modern surveyors. Yet there it was, staring out at me from the map.

As the consequences of this discovery slowly filtered through to my mind, disbelief gave way to exhilaration. Straight-line site alignments using basic equipment and simple surveying techniques were quite possible for primitive people. The construction of a circle of this magnitude was a totally different proposition. If it could be substantiated, there could be only one conclusion – that a highly sophisticated culture existed in the British Isles at least 5000 years ago.

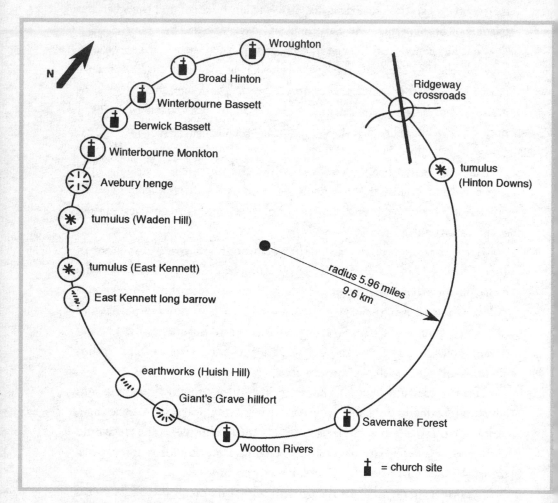

Fig. 6. Plan of Marlborough Downs circle

2

RIPPLES OF A CIRCLE

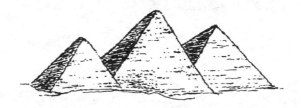

Something deep and ancient lies sleeping in these hills

I had made the startling discovery of a massive circle laid out in the landscape of southern Britain which posed many intriguing questions about
its creation. However improbable, it did not seem that the sites on the
circle could have been located on its circumference merely by chance.
Only further research would tell. But if this circle had been created deliberately, it would have to be contemporary with the earliest sites there.
This implies that an advanced people, capable of setting out such a pattern in the landscape, must have existed in Britain at the start of the third
millennium BC.

The circle drawn on the map looked convincing to me, but before I
could go any further I had to be sure that the sites were not an illusion and
that the circle really did exist. This could only be achieved by more exact-
ing research combined with some complicated mathematics.

1:50,000 scale maps are ideal for picking up general features in an area,
but not of sufficient detail to assess the accuracy of a circle 19.3 kilometres
(12 miles) in diameter. Larger scale maps, ranging down from 1:25,000 to
1:2500 would be necessary. And while the circumference of the circle was
highlighted by the various churches and ancient earthworks, there was no
obvious marker point at the centre. I would have to investigate the various
sites on the ground before I could have any confidence in what I believed
I had discovered.

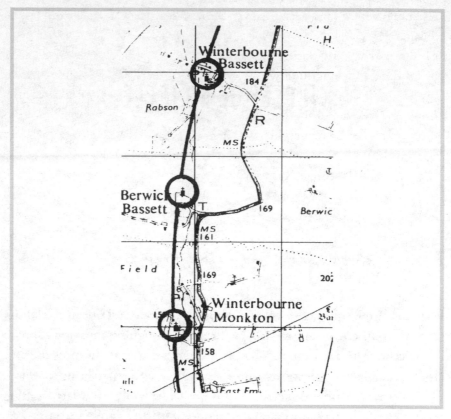

Fig. 7. Section of the Marlborough circle from the 1:50,000 scale OS sheet showing the churches of Winterbourne Bassett, Berwick Bassett and Winterbourne Monkton highlighted by a small circle

The grid system

Ordnance Survey maps are based on a grid system which allows every point in the British landscape to be given a specific numeric reference. On the 1:50,000 scale maps these references, or co-ordinates, are set at one kilometre intervals, with the provision of subdividing the squares down to 100 metres. For example, the grid reference of the church at Berwick Bassett is 098 735, which is correct to within 100 metres. The most detailed OS town maps available are scaled at 1:1250 and these can show accurately positions correct to within one metre. Using this system, the desk at which I am writing this book can be given an exact grid reference which any person using the appropriate OS map could then locate.

Alternatively, my position could be given using the global co-ordinates of latitude and longitude which are more generally used for navigation by sea or air. The problem with using these co-ordinates is that calculations are derived from complex geometry of spheres, which requires more complicated equations when working out distances and angular relationships.

Over relatively small areas such as the British Isles, cartographers have found it much easier to make adjustments for the Earth's curvature and establish a locally based grid system where both sets of co-ordinates are of equal length. This makes calculating the distances and angular relationships between any two or three sites easier. The methods used are based on trigonometry, which I had learned at school.

Mathematical calculation working from OS grid references has been very important in my research, as it takes the guesswork out of measuring from scaled maps. It might look as though a circle can be drawn through a number of points, but this can only be verified by showing that they are the same distance from a common centre. The trigonometrical method, working from grid references, is also the most reliable way of plotting alignments across adjoining maps. All other procedures lack the same precision, even when extreme care is taken.

The maths needed to do the calculations is not difficult, but it can be lengthy and time consuming. Fortunately, this is the sort of task that computers are very good at. But my earliest discoveries were made even before the humble pocket calculator came into common usage, so the original trigonometrical calculations were done the old-fashioned way by using printed tables.

The first step was to establish an exact grid reference for each site. To do this, I went to the Ordnance Survey's headquarters in Southampton where I worked from their extensive library of detailed County Series maps, scaled at 1:2500. The Ordnance Survey also held cartographic information on all the archaeological discoveries made in this part of Wiltshire.

After studying the maps – and to ease the calculations – I decided to work to an accuracy of 10 metres (33 feet). Even the smallest church building is at least 30 metres (98 feet) long; some are much larger. For the churches, I chose as my datum point the crossing of the aisle and the transept; with the megalithic sites, such as the tumuli and other earthworks, I worked from what I assessed to be the centre.

Avebury posed a problem because of its size – it has a diameter of 421 metres (1381 feet). I could see that the circumference of my landscape circle passed through the western side of the henge, but determining which point to use was a problem, for there was no reason why I should use one datum point rather than another for my calculations. So I decided to leave it out.

Having established the grid reference for the other fourteen sites, it then took many hours of detailed calculation to work out the centre of the landscape circle. To find the common centre of all the points, I began by selecting three points on the circumference and then calculated the common centre between them. Then I repeated the process for another three sites, and so on. This method produced a series of possible centres which I then averaged out.

For complete accuracy I should have carried out these calculations for all possible combinations of three sites. This would have necessitated many thousands of calculations. In practice, about twenty combinations was enough to find a common centre with sufficient accuracy. Once the centre had been established, I then set about calculating the distances of each of the fourteen points from it. From these distances, I could work out the mean, or average, radius and how far each site deviated from the mean circumference line (see Table 1).

The mean radius turned out to be 9588 metres (31,449 feet) or 5.9577 miles. The statistical error on this mean was only 8.07 metres (26 feet), which is less than the accuracy of the co-ordinates I had started from. The maximum deviation from the circumference was at the church at Broad Hinton, which lay 72 metres (236 feet) outside the circumference, with the church at Wootton Rivers falling 53 metres (174 feet) inside. Although in both these cases the circumference passed outside the church building itself, it was still close enough to cross the church grounds and the mathematics demonstrated that a circle could be drawn through the fifteen sites, confirming my original discovery.

Site	OS grid ref.	Distance from centre in metres	Variance from circumference	Type of site and remarks
Centre of circle	1938 7248	–	9588	–
Avebury	–	–	not included	henge and circle
Winterbourne Monkton	0978 7198	9613	+25m	church
Berwick Bassett	0985 7354	9588	0m	church
Winterbourne Bassett	1013 7490	9561	–27m	church
Broad Hinton	1052 7633	9660	+72m	church
Wroughton	1376 8025	9589	+1m	church and cross
Ridgeway crossroads	2310 8130	9572	–16m	crossroads
Hinton Downs	2531 8003	9600	+12m	tumulus
Savernake Forest	2520 6490	9557	–31m	church
Wootton Rivers	1969 6295	9535	–53m	church
Giant's Grave	1670 6328	9582	–6m	hillfort
Huish Hill	1433 6430	9613	+25m	earthwork
East Kennett	1163 6685	9579	–9m	long barrow
East Kennett	1127 6733	9607	+19m	tumulus
Waden Hill	1036 6925	9580	–8m	tumuli

Mean of measured radii from postulated centre	9588 metres
Variance (N Weighting)	841
Standard deviation (N – 1 Weighting)	30.22
Error on Mean (Standard deviation)	8.07 metres

Table 1. Statistical analysis of Marlborough Downs Eastern Circle

On the ground

Whether this was just a coincidence – a chance in several million – or whether this circle had been created deliberately I had yet to determine. I still found it hard to believe that ancient peoples could have had the skill to create a ley circle nearly 9.6 kilometres (6 miles) in radius. By then, at least, I knew that I was not chasing a mirage. I had hard evidence to support my theory.

Over the next few weekends, I visited each site in turn, photographing the churches. Ancient stones could sometimes be seen at ground level in the foundations of the churches hinting at the possibility of the re-use of a much older site. I meticulously noted the details of my visits, including any subjective 'atmosphere' I felt at the sites. This was palpable in some places. Full descriptions of the circle sites are given in Appendix 1.

The rolling chalk uplands of the Marlborough Downs, dotted here and there with small clumps of trees on tumulus sites, are impressive. The past seems to seep from the landscape, giving one the sense that something deep and ancient lies sleeping in these hills. And as I travelled around the area, I became impressed by the sheer size of the undertaking that building such a circle would have entailed.

My greatest disappointment came when I visited the centre of the circle which I calculated to lie in the village of Ogbourne St Andrew. The actual centre is located in a little field, a short distance from the back gardens of some houses, close to an abandoned railway embankment. There is no obvious archaeological evidence in the vicinity, although I found a tumulus in the churchyard about 500 metres (1640 feet) to the west of the point I had calculated. I have pored over old archaeological maps of the area, but I have been unable to discover whether any megalithic site or stone marked this position. Probably because this area was so close to the railway embankment, any surface features would have been removed. Earth from a burial mound or tumulus would have been a welcome source of material for those building the railway.

The Marlborough Downs plateau rises to 272 metres (892 feet) at its highest point, making it impossible to see across the entire circle. The best vantage point is from a steep ridge about a mile to the east of the centre. This happens to coincide with a trackway which was once a Roman road. From here, both the centre of the circle and the tree-backed hump of the East Kennett long barrow, 9.6 kilometres (6 miles) away, can be seen clearly, but no other circumference points are visible.

What was still a complete mystery to me was how these individual sites could have been set out on the circumference of a vast circle. I would have to look further afield, at other researches, to discover the level of skill needed to carry out this sort of surveying work. Then I was reminded about the work of Professor Alexander Thom.

The stone circle builders

In the late 1950s and early 1960s Professor Alexander Thom, a retired Scottish engineer, surveyed more than 300 stone circle sites in the British Isles. In 1967 he published his findings in *Megalithic Sites in Britain*. His book set the academic world on its heels with the suggestion that our ancient forbears had a sophisticated knowledge of geometry, astronomy, surveying and engineering techniques. Already, archaeologists at that time could not deny the incredible construction feats of places like Stonehenge, Avebury and Silbury Hill. But these were seen as an anomaly as the ancient peoples of the time were known to have led very basic lives. As Euan MacKie said in his book *The Megalith Builders*:

> *His [Thom's] conclusion that there was a highly skilled class of profes-*
> *sional astronomer priests and wise men in existence when the stand-*
> *ing stones were being built simply does not fit with the picture of late*
> *Neolithic Britain which has been built up over many decades by*
> *many hands and from a great variety of archaeological evidence. This*
> *was a picture of a relatively simple society, barbarian and rural, prob-*
> *ably with chiefs and a ruling hierarchy of some kind but with no sign*
> *of the sophisticated, semi-civilized priesthood that Thom's work*
> *should imply.*

Many stone circles exist throughout the British Isles. Although a good many more have sadly been lost with the passage of time, new ones are still being discovered. The majority of these circles were regarded, before Thom's surveys, as very crude structures. Many were not even circular, which seemed to attest to the ignorance of the builders. Thom showed that, far from being inexact circles, their dimensions revealed the use of sophisticated geometric principles which incorporated ovals and ellipses. Invariably, their layout was based on Pythagorean triangles. These are right-angled triangles where the base, height and hypotenuse are whole numbers – the most famous employs the proportions 3:4:5.

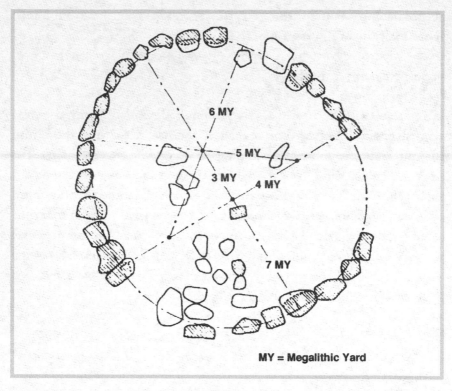

6 MY

5 MY

3 MY 4 MY

7 MY

MY = Megalithic Yard

Fig. 8. Druidtemple stone circle near Inverness (according to Thom)

An example of this design can be found in the Druidtemple stone circle near Inverness, Scotland (Fig. 8). Thom suggested that once the 3:4:5 triangle had been established and set out on the ground, an egg-shaped circle could be created, using arcs drawn from the three points of the triangle. This could easily be done using pegs and set lengths of rope or twine. Thom believed that the builders were trying to produce whole number ratios between the circumference and the radius by using this method. He discovered many examples throughout Britain of egg-shaped circles, as well as flattened circles such as Castle Rigg in Cumbria (see Fig. 72). And, on occasions, he discovered more complex designs such as the one found at the Avebury henge.

Thom also showed that the orientation of these circles was often aligned to the rising and setting of sun, moon and star positions at specific times of the year. He was not alone in this belief. In an article published in the prestigious scientific magazine *Nature* in October 1963, Professor Gerald Hawkins used computer calculations to establish that Stonehenge incorporated many more significant sun and moon positions than the famous rising of the midsummer sun over the Heel Stone.

The earliest phase of building at Stonehenge was established by radio-carbon dating in 1996 to have been started around 2950BC. This involved the construction of a circular bank and ditch, and setting up four unremarkable stones in a rectangle, which is now known by the rather unprepossessing name of the Station Stone Rectangle (see **photograph 10**). This is no ordinary rectangle. It was carefully planned out, indicating by the different alignments of the stones the midsummer sunrise and the midwinter sunset, as well as the sunrises and sunsets on the February and May quarter days. In addition – and just as significantly – it also depicts the extreme positions of moonrise and moonset in the 18.61 year lunar cycle.

The moon, unlike the sun, does not appear to move on a steady path through the heavens as observed from the Earth. Its rising and setting positions change throughout the seasons and over a cycle of 18.61 years. This lunar cycle throws up the extreme positions of the moon's rise and setting positions and it was these that are indicated by the Station Stone Rectangle.

Let us pause for a moment to consider these four seemingly insignificant stones which are set out in a very neat rectangle, hardly warranting a second glance among the other megaliths at Stonehenge. It just so happens that it is only at the exact latitude of Stonehenge that the four marker stones depicting these important sun and moon positions form a precise rectangle. Move north or south by a distance of a few miles, and the rectangle turns into a parallelogram with the precise right-angled symmetry of its four corners lost. Moreover, the rectangle is based upon another Pythagorean triangle with a ratio of sides of 5:12:13, a significant point brought up by Robin Heath in his book *A Key to Stonehenge*.

So here we have four small stones, set up at the beginning of the cultural shift that started 5000 years ago, that tell us a lot about the builders of the first phase of the Stonehenge complex. They show that the people who erected them:

1) understood the principles of geometry, as they were able to set out a rectangle on the ground using whole number ratios for the sides and the diagonal;

2) had made a careful study of several 18.61 year cycles of the moon, implying that they had the ability to pass on information from generation to generation;

3) had made a careful study of the sunrise and sunset positions at the solstices;

4) were capable of combining the information obtained from 2) and 3) to work out where they would need to be so that the criteria needed for 1) could be met.

The place they arrived at became the site for Stonehenge, which also falls on the alignment from the Clearbury Ring hillfort that passes through Salisbury Cathedral and Old Sarum (see Fig. 2). These facts imply a

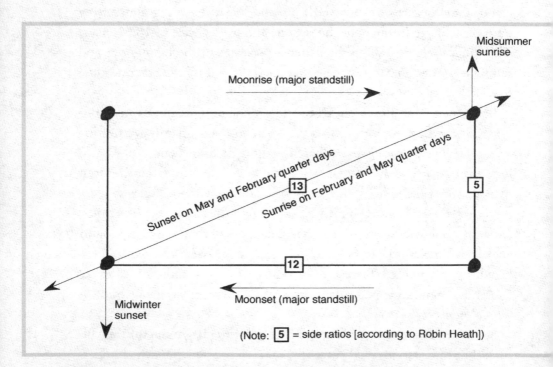

Fig. 9. Station Stone Rectangle at Stonehenge showing solar and lunar alignments (according to Hawkins)

profound knowledge and highly developed mathematical astronomical and surveying skills – not the hallmarks that one would associate with an unsophisticated culture.

The evidence from Stonehenge supports Thom's assertion that the megalithic peoples possessed considerable geometric and astronomical knowledge. And there is good evidence from many parts of the country that one of the functions of stone circles was observation of the heavens.

The Megalithic Yard

The other startling idea postulated by Thom was the existence of a standard unit of measurement which he called the Megalithic Yard, calculated to be 2.72 feet or 0.829 metres. In terms of the human, this length is approximately the distance between the centre of the chest and the base of the fingers when the arm and hand are stretched out to the side. So it could have arisen in a natural way, although there is powerful evidence to show that it is based on an exact proportion of the Earth's equatorial circumference.

While accepting Thom's rigorous methodology, some archaeologists have challenged his findings. If correct, they would have meant that the megalithic peoples of the British Isles maintained a high level of social order. Thom's findings would have required a continuity of culture, allowing both ideas as well as fixed measurements to have been disseminated from Cornwall in the south, to Ireland in the west, and to Orkney and Shetland in the north. Coherent concepts and information would have to have been handed down from generation to generation, so that they could be both added to as well as refined. The way that this has usually been achieved is through writing, which is the hallmark of all known sophisticated societies. Yet there is no evidence of writing in this period.

At the very least, this continuity could only have been achieved if there was a relatively peaceful and stable populace. But this is at odds with the archaeological evidence. Meticulous excavation and research conducted over many years has built up a picture of a sometimes violent and unstable semi-barbaric existence.

However, the evidence from Alexander Thom's study of stone circles and Gerald Hawkins' computer analysis of Stonehenge is in keeping with my discovery of the circular landscape pattern. It is clear that the circle, as a geometric form, was an intrinsic part of the culture that was established in Britain around 3000BC. The sophistication of Stonehenge suggests a people with advanced concepts in astronomy, engineering and geometry. Could these same people have exhibited the same ingenuity that would be needed to survey and set out the Marlborough Downs pattern?

To put all these concepts into context, we need to examine what is known about the inhabitants of these islands in the late Neolithic and early Bronze Age periods, and their relationship with other cultures in different parts of the world.

3

THE STAMP OF THE PAST

*The date 3100BC is also significant in at least two other parts of
the world*

Since the mid-1960s, two pictures of Britain's late Neolithic past have
emerged. On the one hand there is a meticulous work of archaeologists
which has revealed a fairly primitive society not unlike that of Native
Americans prior to the arrival of Europeans. From the flint arrowheads
discovered with many Neolithic skeletons, it is clear that life was far from
peaceful. These may not have been isolated instances. 'Warfare may have
been known amongst these people,' according to archaeologist Aubrey
Burl. Even so, woven into their lives was a religious perspective which
invested considerable energy into erecting megalithic monuments and
studying the movement of the sun, moon and stars. Set against this picture is the work of Watkins, Hawkins, Thom and myself. This suggests a
much more sophisticated level of knowledge of surveying, geometry,
astronomy and engineering than would have normally been found in such
a primitive society.

What we do know is that the era of stone circle building lasted for more
than 2000 years. The final phase of Stonehenge, for example, was not completed until around 1100BC. So, Thom's Megalithic Yard, if used throughout the British Isles, was maintained as the standard for two millennia.

The two pictures of megalithic culture rest uneasily side by side. The
evidence from orthodox archaeologists suggests an illiterate, barbaric

culture, where people were living very basic lives and appear unlikely to have been able to maintain the levels of continuity demanded by Hawkins and Thom's discoveries. However, Hawkins and Thom give us a picture of a society with an advanced astronomical awareness, which could only have occurred if ideas and observations could be passed on from one generation to another.

In answer to this apparent contradiction, Euan MacKie, in his book *The Megalith Builders*, suggests:

> *A quite different kind of stratified Neolithic society can be postulated, similar to that of the ancient Mayan people of Central America, in which a small élite class of professional priests, wise men and rulers was supported with tribute and taxes by a predominantly rural peasant population. Such a society could have achieved all that Thom has suggested it did because the members of the élite would have been free from the need to obtain their own food and building their own dwellings and could have devoted their entire time to religious, scientific or other intellectual pursuits.*

To grasp this new picture we need to examine what is known about the forbears of the British people and how it relates to other contemporary cultures.

Neolithic Britain

There has been evidence of human activity in what is now the British Isles for a very long time – at least 500,000 years. However, it is not until Britain was free of ice in the beginning of the post-glacial epoch, 8–10,000 years ago, that any clear cultural development can be discerned. From then on, there is a continuity in the artefacts left behind. These show that the earliest peoples of the Neolithic period were hunter-gatherers who made their homes in woodland clearings. Farming eventually developed and, by about 3600BC, the upland areas of the Marlborough Downs had been cleared and were under cultivation.

The earliest megalithic burial structures first appeared in Europe, in the Iberian peninsular, around 4700BC. Temple structures also appeared on

Malta and Gozo. In Britain, the first passage graves date from about 3700BC. These eventually developed into the 'long barrows' found extensively in the southern part of Britain.

Long barrows are tapering rectilinear mounds, up to 100 metres (300 feet) in length, 20 metres (60 feet) in width and from 2–3 metres (6–10 feet) in height. At one end there is usually a small burial chamber taking up no more than one seventh of the mound's length. The rest of the structure appears to have served no practical purpose concerned with burial and must have had a symbolic or religious significance, or served another, as yet unknown, function.

Although farming had replaced hunting, life was still short and, often brutish. According to Aubrey Burl's *Prehistoric Avebury*:

 From the burials of these early farmers emerges a stark picture of their health. Arm fractures and wounds were not uncommon amongst men. Spina bifida was known amongst the women. Most adults suffered from arthritis . . . Amongst the children the defective diet and malnutrition led to rickets and often to death. Some people suffered from polio, sinusitis, tetanus, tuberculosis; and to this dreadful list must almost certainly be added plague and malaria.

Death came early. Many men were dead by thirty-six, women by thirty, and although some endured in life to the great age of seventy perhaps as many as half the children died before they were three years of age.

Near Avebury, at Windmill Hill, there are the remains of one of the largest known settlements of that time. It covered more than 8 hectares (20 acres) and had extensive fortifications around its perimeter. As well as being a trading centre – pottery from Cornwall was found there – it was a religious complex used for ritual and magical purposes, suggested by phallic figurines unearthed at the site. The area was plainly a focus for much activity in Neolithic Britain, around 5500 years ago.

Somewhere around 3200 to 3100BC a dramatic change occurred within a very short space of time all over the British Isles. People stopped building long barrows. Instead they erected henges, stone circles and round barrows. Rectilinear structures gave way to an open circular form. The first phase of Stonehenge was started at this time.

In Ireland, one of the most impressive of these newer megalithic monuments was erected at Newgrange, Co. Meath (see **photograph 15**). This magnificent structure was faced with white quartz stone, making it shine in sunlight. Its inner chamber is precisely aligned to the rising of the midwinter sun. It is illuminated by the first rays of the solstice sun as they come flooding across the horizon. Those who have witnessed this attest to the power of the experience. It seems like a river of gold flows into the chamber, irradiating the back stone wall which glows with light for several minutes after the initial moment of sunrise.

Newgrange, built around 3200BC, shows another new development: rock art. Circles, spirals, cup and ring markings were carved into stones. No one has been able to interpret what they may mean, yet. However, Professor Thom analysed these markings, which are also found extensively throughout Ireland, Scotland, Cumbria and Yorkshire. He suggested that they, too, were based on a precise unit of measurement, which he calculated to being exactly 1/40 of a Megalithic Yard. It is likely that they express religious ideas, almost certainly indicating the movement of the sun, moon and stars. These markings are the only tangible evidence of a sort of 'writing', where concepts could be conveyed, in a form of pictograms, from generation to generation.

Soon after the completion of Newgrange, Stonehenge, Silbury Hill and Avebury were begun. Within a few hundred years, a vast number of stone circles, henge monuments and burial chambers sprang up across the British Isles.

The reason for this sudden architectural innovation is unknown. The most likely explanation, though, is the arrival of a new people with a new culture. The dating and distribution of the monuments, surprisingly, suggests they came across the sea from the west, not via the short channel crossing to the south-east of Britain.

The Tuatha de Danann

Irish mythology speaks of a number of invasions of ancient Ireland. One of the most colourful of these fabled invaders was that of the Tuatha de

Fig. 10. Spiral motifs on the entrance stone at Newgrange, Co. Meath, Ireland

Danann or 'the children of the goddess Dana'. They are said to have brought with them many magical gifts, including a cauldron which could restore the dead to life. Some see this as a prototype for the Holy Grail myths that developed when Christianity came to Britain. The Tuatha people were defeated by another invading group and were said to have retreated into the barrows and tumuli. Like King Arthur, it is said that they are set to re-emerge at some future date. Although it is impossible to identify these people with a new culture that came from the west, this myth does provide a flavour of the tradition of repeated invasion handed down through time.

Astronomer-priesthood

Euan MacKie's concept of an independent astronomer-priesthood quoted above, supported by a local peasant populace, which provided the sophistication of the megalithic culture, is not so far-fetched. After all, in the more recent Celtic times, from around 850BC, the Druids fulfilled a similar role.

No direct written evidence has come to us on specific Druidic beliefs. Their knowledge was passed on through an oral Bardic tradition, woven into song and story – a tradition that could well have pre-dated the

Celtic invasions. The Druids, who undoubtedly wielded great power and influence, were perhaps the mystical descendants of those who inspired the great megalithic monuments. This idea at least goes some way to reconciling the orthodox view of a barbarian culture, with that of sophisticated concepts found from the researchers of Thom, Watkins and myself.

The Aubrey Holes, Stonehenge

Alongside the Station Stone Rectangle, another early feature at Stonehenge is a series of 56 small circular holes about one metre (3 feet) across and half a metre (1.5 feet) deep, evenly spaced out around an 87-metre (285-feet) diameter circle. Named after the seventeenth-century antiquarian John Aubrey, these holes remained an enigma until the 1960s. Gerald Hawkins, writing in *Nature* (June 1964), and Professor Fred Hoyle, *Nature* (July 1966), showed how they could have been used to predict the eclipses of the sun and moon. Their idea was that two markers, representing the sun and the moon, were placed in these holes, then moved on a precise cyclical pattern around the circle. When the two markers arrived in any one hole at the same time, this would indicate an eclipse date. The best way to imagine this is to think of the two hands of a clock, each moving at different rates yet coinciding at one position – at twelve o'clock, say – every twelve hours. Different ways of moving these markers have been suggested, but the principle remains the same.

Such a system could only have originated from careful observations made over a long period of time. It should be remembered that most individuals in this period would be dead before their fortieth birthday, so the information acquired would have to be handed down to subsequent generations.

Through the Station Stone Rectangle, Stonehenge also displays knowledge of the 5:12:13 ratio Pythagorean triangle. Thom's research on other stone circles shows the use, not only of the more famous 3:4:5 triangle, but also, surprisingly, the 12:35:37 triangle. All this suggests a sophisticated knowledge of geometry and of Pythagorean triangles thousands of years before Pythagoras is believed to have 'discovered' them.

European megaliths

The development of stone circles and henge monuments in the third millennium BC is a peculiarly British affair. However, of comparable antiquity
are the stone rows at Carnac, north-west France. Passage grave structures
had been built in many areas of western Europe for several hundred years
prior to 3000BC. A number of examples can be found in the Carnac area.
But the three groupings of the Carnac stone rows are unlike any other type
of megalithic structure in Europe. The Menec alignment, for example,
consists of eleven parallel rows of stones running for more than 1000
metres (3280 feet) and, at each end, there is evidence of a stone circle, like
those found in Britain. Professor Thom carefully measured the alignments
and deduced that they were built using a basic measurement he labelled
the Megalithic Rod, which he claimed was two and a half times his
Megalithic Yard.

The Grand Menhir of Brise is also found in the Carnac area. It was the
largest known standing stone ever erected – 20 metres (65 feet) high and
weighing over 340 tons. Thom suggested it was probably used as a moonrise siting point, working on the 18.61 year lunar cycle. Unfortunately
this stone fell down in the nineteenth century and is now broken into four
pieces, so it is difficult to confirm Thom's conjecture.

There are a few examples of stone circles in this part of France. Yet
those there are do not possess the grandeur of the British monuments.
This has led to some speculation that there was little cultural connection
between western France and southern Britain at that time. However, artefacts found in tombs indicate that trade was carried out across the
Channel.

Circles on the ground: circles in the sky

We know that a people existed in the Wessex area of southern Britain
around 3000BC who were capable of producing monuments such as
Stonehenge, Avebury and Silbury Hill. Conceptually, my discovery of the
landscape circle of the Marlborough Downs fits into this general ethos.
On one level, it could be viewed as a stone circle, but on a much larger
scale. The use of the circular form could be seen as a natural expression of

a people engaged in astronomical observation and study. Both the sun and moon are visibly circular and the Great Bear, for example, travels in a circle around the Pole Star. Whether such people had the expertise to survey and lay out a circle in the landscape of some 19.3 kilometres (12 miles) in diameter I had yet to discover. But given the level of skill and ingenuity they displayed in building their megalithic monuments, it was not beyond the bounds of possibility.

What orthodoxy accepts is that in the 100 years between 3200 and 3100BC a major change took place in Neolithic Britain which saw the beginning of the construction of some of the most significant megalithic structures in the British Isles. Monuments such as Newgrange in Ireland; Stonehenge, Silbury Hill and Avebury in southern England; Callanish in the Western Isles of Scotland; Maes Howe and the Ring of Brogar on the Orkney Islands; Castle Rigg in Cumbria were all begun within a few hundred years of this date. The central question is, was this change a sudden spontaneous development within British culture? Or was it inspired by some outside influence? Certainly the date 3100BC is also significant in at least two other parts of the world.

Dynastic Egypt

In the fertile Nile valley there is evidence of human activity over a very long period. Around 4000BC, a culture, known as Badarian, produced linen garments, pottery and small ornaments. There were minor developments until around 3200 to 3100BC when Egypt was united under one king, called Narmer Menes.

At that point, fully developed hieroglyphic writing appeared. Rapidly, ancient Egyptian civilisation took a giant leap forward. Art, architecture, medicine, and social order all reached a high level within a very short period. In religion, human beings were placed within a divine hierarchy, which was headed by a supreme deity known as Atum-Ra, symbolised by the sun, and Heliopolis, now a suburb of modern Cairo, became the centre of the new priesthood.

The first of the stone pyramids – the Step Pyramid at Sakkara – was built for King Zoser by his vizier, the sage Imhotep, around 2640BC. The monument at Avebury was started at around this same date and completed in about 2400BC. Between 2575 and 2565BC the vast pyramids on the Giza plateau were constructed, reaching a hitherto undreamt of pinnacle of engineering and technological skill (see **photograph 16**). The Egyptians polished and shaped their stones in a way that was never attempted in the British monuments, with the possible exception of Stonehenge. There is a distinct quality in these Old Kingdom structures which is unlike anything else found in later Egyptian dynasties. So, as in Britain, Egypt experienced a cultural acceleration somewhere between 3200 and 3100BC.

The speed of development of Egyptian culture cannot easily be explained in terms of a steady homogenous development. This had forced some authorities to conclude that an outside influence must have been involved. One suggested origin is the Summerian civilisation from the Euphrates river valley, because of similarities between their mythologies, building techniques and architectural styles. However, as Professor Walter Emery states in his book *Archaic Egypt*:

The impression we get is of an indirect connection, and perhaps the existence of a third party, whose influence spread to both the Euphrates and the Nile . . . Modern scholars have tended to ignore the possibility of immigration to both regions from some hypothetical and as yet undiscovered area. [However] a third party whose cultural achievements were passed on independently to Egypt and Mesopotamia would best explain the common features and fundamental differences between the two civilisations.

If the rapid development of ancient Egyptian science, mythology, writing, architecture, art and culture cannot be explained by 'steady development' theories, from where did this impulse originate? Who was the third party Professor Emery alludes to?

The Roman historian Diodorus Siculus, writing in the first century AD and drawing, most probably, from local tradition informs us:

The Egyptians were strangers, who, in remote times, settled on the banks of the Nile, bringing with them the civilisation of their mother country, the art of drawing and a polished language. They had come from the direction of the setting sun and were the most ancient of men.

Professor Emery's theory of a dynastic race who entered Egypt at that time and laid the foundations for its rapid cultural development has not been generally accepted by Egyptologists. But neither has it been disproved. There is evidence of some cultural influence from contemporary civilisations in the Middle East, but not sufficient to easily explain the rapid growth of Egyptian culture. The most recent excavations being carried out at Abydos by a German archaeological team may hold the answers.

Yet if Professor Emery is correct and Egypt was seeded from outside, where could these people have come from and could there be a link with the changes that took place in Britain during this period? After all, another mysterious development in this same time span can be found in a very different part of the world – on the other side of the Atlantic.

The Mayan calendar

In Central America, significant events in the development of the civilisation there also occurred towards the end of the fourth millennium. The Mayan calendar commenced its present cycle, in terms of our calendar, on 12 August 3114BC. The Maya were an extraordinary people who developed a dating system which is more accurate than the Gregorian calendar we use today.

Unfortunately for all calendar makers, the Earth does not revolve around the sun in an exact number of days. As most schoolchildren know, there are 365 days in a year. But not quite. To be more accurate, it is closer to 365.25 days, which is why we add an extra day every fourth year. This was the basis of the original Julian calendar used in western Europe until the end of the sixteenth century. Yet this, too, is not quite exact enough.

A year is actually eleven minutes and a few seconds less than 365.25 days. So, over time, a discrepancy grew between the calendar and the seasons. In 1582, to bring the calendar back into line with the solar cycle, Pope Gregory XIII published a bull, effectively annulling ten days. He also instituted a refinement into the Julian calendar where the years that close a century – that is, years that end with 00 – and are not divisible by 400 were to be ordinary years and not leap years. In this Gregorian system, the years 1600 and 2000 (being divisible by 400) are leap years, while 1700, 1800 and 1900 were not. This is the system we use today.

The Mayan calendar system is complex. It is based on a 260 day cycle, known as a *tzolkin*, a vague year of 365 days and a 'calendar round' of 52 years. There is not enough space here to describe the methods they used to reconcile the solar cycle to their calendar dates. Like other cultures, their system was based on the movements of the sun, but they refined their calculations using the cyclical revolutions of the planet Venus. The result was a system that involved cycles of days that became part of larger cycles. For example, a *Baktun* was a cycle of 144,000 days. Thirteen Baktun completed a full epoch cycle. The current one will complete on 22 December AD2012. The calendar which the Maya produced is more accurate over a 5000 year span than its Gregorian equivalent.

Although the Maya did not emerge as a recognised culture until about AD100, they started their calendar at the obscure date of 3114BC. The Maya flourished for a brief Golden Age between AD600 and 800, then abandoned their cities and disappeared as mysteriously as they had emerged. Like the ancient Egyptians, the Maya built pyramids, produced great sculptures and developed a complete writing system. Yet the civilisation of ancient Egypt had long since ceased to exist before the Maya reached the height of their development.

Nevertheless, the starting date for the Mayan calendar is curious for, like our modern calendar, it is usual to begin from some significant event in the past. What was so special to the Maya about 12 August 3114BC?

We may never know for certain. The Spanish *conquistadors* in their enthusiasm to convert the Aztec and other Indian peoples to Christianity, destroyed most of their writings. As the Bishop of Yucatan, Diego de Landa, said: 'We found great numbers of books written in these characters, but as they contained nothing that did not savour of superstition and lies, we burnt them all.'

Fortunately, some writings survived, largely the carvings on their monuments, and have been translated, which is how we now know about the Mayan calendar, their counting systems and something of their myths and history.

While the Maya have been credited with the invention of their calendar, there is some evidence that it stemmed from an early Meso-American culture known as the Olmecs. Little is known about these people, but the earliest possible date of the beginning of their civilisation is around

1500BC – still a long way short of the 3114BC starting date of the calendar. Further archaeological research may eventually produce the answers. However, what is curious about the Olmecs is their statues (see **photograph 19**). They show two clearly distinct racial groups, one Negroid, the other Caucasian. This suggests that the origins of these people lay not in the Americas, but on the other side of the Atlantic.

The idea of cultural links between Eurasia and the Americas, pre-dating Columbus, is not new. There are similarities in ideas, language and architecture between the continents. Thor Heyerdahl's *Ra II* expeditions in the 1970s demonstrated that the ancient Egyptians could have crossed the Atlantic in reed boats which, in their style and construction, are remarkably similar to those found around Lake Titicaca in Peru. Others have suggested the Phoenicians, renowned sailors and navigators, crossed the Atlantic.

3100BC – a crucial date

So, in the history of human civilisation, this date, 3100BC, is crucial. It marks:

- ▲ the beginning of dynastic Egypt;
- ▲ the shift to open architectural stone circles in the megalithic developments of the British Isles;
- ▲ the inception of the Mayan calendar.

On the surface, this may appear to be a quirky coincidence. However, there is compelling evidence that shows a close connection between at least two of these three seemingly unrelated events and, probably, all three.

Comparative chronology chart

Date	British Isles	Age	Egypt	Egypt Period	Meso-America	Other	Climate	Climate Period
4000 BC	Hunter-gathers	NEOLITHIC AGE	Tasian	PRE-DYNASTIC			Equable stable climate northern hemisphere	ATLANTIC
3500 BC	Forest clearance and agricultural developments		Badarian		Archaic Period	Mesopotamian civilisations; Maltese temples	Temperature 1° - 3° warmer than Sub-Boreal period in Europe and North America	
3000 BC	Windmill Hill; West Kennett long barrow		Gerzean					
2500 BC	Newgrange (Ireland); Stenness (Orkney); Sanctuary 1; Silbury Hill; Avebury		Dynastic (start) Narmer Menes; Step Pyramid - Zoser; Great Pyramid; Chephren Pyramid; Mycerinus Pyramid	OLD KINGDOM	Start date of Maya calender pottery	Growth of Indus Valley civilisation; Carnac alignments France	Piora Oscillation; Elm decline in Ireland; Sahara becomes desert	SUB-BOREAL
2000 BC	Stonehenge 2	BRONZE AGE	Pyramid Texts; Amenemhet 1	MIDDLE K.				
1500 BC	Stonehenge 3		Hyksos invasion; Amenophis 1; Tutmosis 1 & 2; Hatshepsut; Tutmosis 3; Amenophis 3; Akhenaten; Tutankhamun; Ramses 2	NEW KING.	Olmec civilisation	Shang Dynasty China; Santorini eruption destroying Minoan civilisation in Aegean	Cooler phase glacial advance	
1000 BC	Celtic invasions	IRON AGE						SUB-ATLANTIC
500 BC			Persian invasion; Alexander's invasion	PTOLEM.				
0 AD	Roman invasion		Cleopatra	ROMAN	Mayan civilisation (start)			
500 AD	Dark Ages; King Arthur?			ARABIC	Mayan civilisation (collapse)			
1000 AD	Norman Conquest							
1500 AD					Spanish conquest of Aztec and Inca empires			

4

THE MYSTERY DEEPENS

*Was it possible that here, in the landscape of England, was a
geometric link to the most famous monument of the ancient world?*

A circle has exact geometric properties. Once the length of the radius or
diameter is known it is possible to calculate its circumference and its area.
Having established these for the Marlborough Downs circle it was then
possible to check the distances against known ancient measures such as
the Megalithic Yard. At the time, this seemed the most fruitful avenue for
research.

Livio Stecchini, Professor of Ancient History at William Paterson
College in New Jersey, in the appendix of the book *The Secret of the Great
Pyramid* by Peter Tompkins, provides compelling evidence that ancient
peoples were aware of the size of the Earth and based their measurements
upon it. According to his research, they principally used proportions
related to lengths of the lines of latitude in the region where they lived.
This is quite a startling concept, but in principle it is no different from the
metric system. Originally, the French fixed the metre as precisely one ten
millionth part the distance from the pole to the equator along the meridian that ran through Paris. Stecchini's researches were primarily based on
the measurements found in use in ancient Egypt, Babylonia and the classical worlds of Greece and Rome.

I was intrigued by Professor Stecchini's idea that peoples in the ancient
and classical worlds were aware of the size of our planet and based their

measurements on it. I reasoned that if I could show that the Marlborough circle was related to the size of the Earth that would link it to other ancient measures and, by implication, other cultures. It would lend substantial weight that the circle was a deliberate creation rather than a statistical fluke. That would imply that the creators of the circle possessed advanced mathematical knowledge, which would make it more likely that they would have the necessary surveying skills to create such a pattern in the landscape.

Stecchini's research suggested that many ancient measurements were based on the distances between degrees of latitude. These could be calculated using shadow lines and the movement of the sun through the seasons. What I had forgotten, or rather initially overlooked, is that the Earth is round at the equator but flattened at the poles. This means that distances between lines of longitude are always equal at any set latitude, while distances between lines of latitude vary as one travels from the equator to the pole.

Missing this salient point I first chose to determine whether there might be any relationship between the length of the equatorial circumference of the Earth and the circumference of the Marlborough circle. What emerged from this oversight was something curious.

There are a number of authorities which give the equatorial circumference, all of which fall within a few hundred metres of each other. *The World Almanac*, for example, determines the size as 40,074.06 kilometres (24,901.55 miles) which was about the average of the others and the one I chose to use. The calculated circumference of the Marlborough circle is 60.243 kilometres (37.433 miles) and dividing this into the global circumference (40,074.06 ÷ 60.243 = 665.21), a figure of just over 665.

The most recent satellite survey from the International Union of Geodesy and Geophysics gives the radius of the Earth as 6,378,136 ± 1 metres. Taking this figure and dividing it by the radius of the Marlborough circle (6,378,136 ÷ 9588 = 665.22), which confirms the original calculation.

At first glance this did not seem significant until I thought about that enigmatic number 666 found in the *Book of Revelation*. It was a long shot, but just suppose, that 666 was the intended ratio. What effect would it have on the size of the circle?

A quick calculation showed that by reducing the circle's radius by a little over 11 metres from 9588 metres to 9576.78 metres gave an exact fit. This was close to my built-in margin of error of ten metres and still fitted the sites. But was this intentional or just another coincidence? Anyway, what was so special about the number 666?

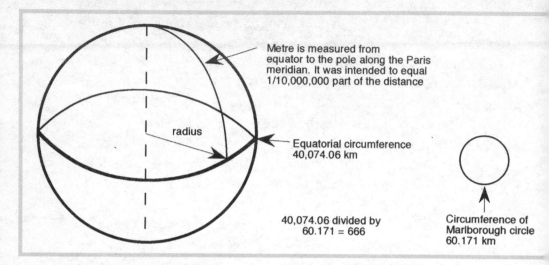

Fig. 11. The relationship of the Marlborough circle to the Earth

The number 666

The *Book of Revelation* says:

 Here is wisdom. Let him that hath understanding count the number of the beast: for it is the number of man; and his number is six hundred, three score and six.
(13:18)

Many people have associated 'the beast' with the anti-Christ and interpreted this quotation to mean that 666 is the Devil's number. But the *Book of Revelation* is full of enigmatic numbers. For example, it talks of the measurement of the New Jerusalem:

 And he that talked with me had a golden reed to measure the city, and the gates thereof, and the wall thereof. And the city lieth foursquare,

*and the length is as large as the breadth: and he measured the city
with the reed, twelve thousand furlongs. The length and breadth and
height of it are equal.*
(21:15–16)

A cubed city of twelve thousand furlongs would be of immense size particularly as it would reach 1500 miles into the air – the stuff of science fiction. St John might have glimpsed a distant technological future of planet Earth, but it is much more likely that the verse has symbolic rather than factual meaning. Number symbolism, found extensively throughout the Bible, is very significant in Judaic belief. Indeed, as I was to discover, the first mention of the number 666 is not in *Revelation* at all, but in the *Book of Kings* which says:

 Now the weight of gold that came to Solomon in one year was six hundred, three score and six, talents of gold.
(10.14)

The name Solomon is derived from the Hebrew word *shalom*, meaning peace, but has been translated in the King James version as an alchemical amalgam of *sol* (sun), and *omon* (moon).

Alchemy, as it emerged in the Middle Ages, had its origins in the Hermetic sciences that stemmed from the esoteric wisdom of ancient Egypt. The ancient Egyptian name for their land was *Kemet*, from which we get the words chemistry and alchemy. The esoteric Judaic tradition seen in the Kabbalah is also thought to have derived some of its concepts from Egyptian beliefs. Running in parallel with orthodox religious beliefs of Judaism, Christianity and Islam, there has been an esoteric element which carried concepts that were deliberately hidden from the regular believers. These hidden systems known as the 'mystery traditions' regularly used numbers to express philosophical concepts. Again, this is an idea which almost certainly stemmed from ancient Egypt.

A.T. Mann explains how this worked in his book *Sacred Architecture*, where he says:

 *Symbolic mathematics was at the core of the ancient mystery schools
and determined the sacred principles which regulated people's beliefs*

and lives. While the nature of each god and its planetary equivalent could be represented by a number, the science of gematria attributed each letter to an equivalent value. The system was integral to Hebrew and Greek alphabets . . .

By using gematria, the dimensions of temples and monuments, the verses in poetry, the musical rites and other attributes could be correlated to the gods and their powers. It is possible to decipher any name or word and determine its deeper, symbolic qualities. Platonists, Hermeticists, Rosicrucians, Christian Gnostics, alchemists, masons, members of chivalric orders and many others utilized this sacred secret language.

In alchemy, the sun and the moon expressed two archetypal principles which, when united, symbolised the harmonious relationship between the masculine and feminine elements. Writing in 1650, alchemist Thomas Vaughan said:

 The sun and moon are two Magicall Principles, the one active the other passive, this Masculine, that Feminine. As they move so move the wheels of Corruption and Generation: they mutually dissolve and compound.

Gold, in alchemy, represents the purified spirit and is also traditionally associated with the sun. The year, of course, relates to the solar cycle, so there is a suggestion in the Biblical quote from *Kings* of a link between the number 666 and the sun.

There is another mention of the number 666 in *Ezra*, referring to the peoples who returned to Judah from Babylon:

 The children of Adonikam six hundred, sixty and six.
(2:3)

The word Adonikam means: 'In praise of the Lord.'

It is possible that the biblical references to 666 have no other meaning than what is presented on the surface. Yet St John, in using the number 666, was connecting into a Judaic mysticism which used number symbolism allegorically. He was conveying a message that could be understood by those initiated in the tradition, although precisely what he meant is now obscure.

Coincidentally, the first six Roman numerals written in their correct descending order (DCLXVI) represent 666:

$$D = 500$$
$$C = 100$$
$$L = 50$$
$$X = 10$$
$$V = 5$$
$$I = 1$$
$$666$$

So it is possible that the allusion to 666, being the number of the beast, could have been a sideways swipe at the Roman authorities, who were responsible for the crucifixion.

During the early development of Christianity in the British Isles, the number 666 found its way into the building of the famous Glastonbury Abbey, founded by St Dunstan in AD 946. This was revealed in Bligh Bond's survey in 1920. He discovered that the Abbey was based on a nine

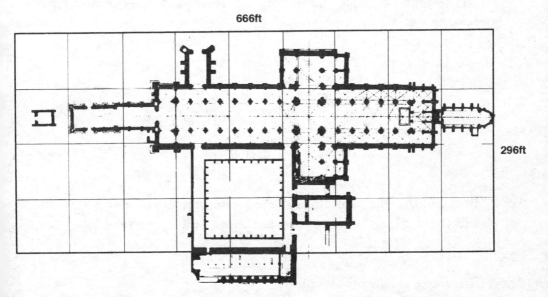

666ft

296ft

Fig. 12. Ground plan of Glastonbury Abbey, based on Bligh Bond's survey, 1920

by four square grid with each side 74 feet. Seventy-four feet, incidentally, equals 888 inches. So the ground plan was 666 feet long by 296 feet wide. It seems that the architects of the Abbey thought this number of sufficient importance to incorporate it in their design and were not deterred by St John's reference to 'the beast'.

Magic squares

The number 666 also emerged in another context – through the number symbolism of magic squares. Magic squares, which entered Europe via Italy in the fifteenth century, were initially only a curiosity to mathematicians. But medieval alchemists, seeking symbolic clues in all things, adopted magic squares as a form of mandala or talisman and invested them with magical properties.

Magic squares occur when consecutive numbers, starting from one, are laid out in a square grid, where the numbers in each row and column add up to the same total. Seven principal magic squares were discovered. Each was associated with one of the seven known heavenly bodies – the sun, moon, Mercury, Mars, Venus, Jupiter and Saturn.

The simplest magic square uses the numbers 1 to 9, laid out as follows:

2	7	6
9	5	1
4	3	8

In this square, the numbers in all the columns, rows and long diagonals add up to 15. According to the alchemists, it was associated with the sacred planet Saturn.

The magic square of the sun

The magic square of the sun contains all the numbers from 1 to 36 and is laid out as follows:

6	32	3	34	35	1
7	11	27	28	8	30
19	14	16	15	23	24
18	20	22	21	17	13
25	29	10	9	26	12
36	5	33	4	2	31

Total number of figure = 36
Sum of each row and long diagonals = 111
Sum of numbers of perimeter = 370

The magic square of the sun has the curious property that if all the numbers between 1 and 36 are added together the total is 666. That this number should again have been associated with the sun — as in the *Kings* quotation mentioned earlier — may indicate some fragmentary knowledge or tradition from the distant past. Symbolic associations were undoubtedly important to ancient peoples. Yet it is also likely that originally there was some valid practical thinking behind their number symbolism. We do not know what this can be, so we can only surmise.

To continue our investigation of 666, let's take a close look at the number itself. The factors of 666 are $2 \times 3 \times 3 \times 37$ or 18×37. The number 37 has the unusual properties that many of its multiples have repeated digits:

$$1 \times 37 = 37$$
$$2 \times 37 = 74$$
$$3 \times 37 = 111$$
$$6 \times 37 = 222$$
$$9 \times 37 = 333$$
$$10 \times 37 = 370$$
$$12 \times 37 = 444$$
$$15 \times 37 = 555$$
$$18 \times 37 = 666$$
$$21 \times 37 = 777$$
$$24 \times 37 = 888$$

Although a prime number, 37 strikes a subliminal chord within the human psyche, as psychological research into people's preferences has shown. Offered the opportunity to select at random any number between 11 and 50 with two non-repeating digits – not 22, 33 or 44 – people are most likely, statistically, to select 37. This has recently been highlighted by the British National Lottery. The reason why this should be so is not known, but it is a fact nonetheless.

Of its factors, the numbers 111 and 370 are woven into the magic square of the sun and the number 18 ($18 \times 37 = 666$) may also have been seen as significant because this number is the sum of 6+6+6.

My research into 666 was tantalising but inconclusive. Nevertheless, if ancient measurements are related to the size of the Earth and the number 666 has some ancient symbolic significance, it seemed appropriate at the time to adjust my original calculations so that the circumference of the circle was exactly 1/666 of the Earth's circumference at the equator. This meant reducing the radius I had calculated from the map radius by just 11 metres to 9576.78 metres, which in turn gave a circumference of 60,171.27 metres (37.3897 miles). Although this seems like cooking the books, I soon found evidence to support this decision.

But before then, I made another dramatic discovery, which was to set me off on a completely new tack. Instead of there being just one circle laid out in the landscape of the Marlborough Downs, I found a second overlapping circle *of identical size*. This discovery started me on a journey which was to lead to a complete re-assessment of one of the oldest mysteries from the ancient world. Clearly the Marlborough Downs had many secrets to reveal.

A second circle?

I had discovered the first circular pattern on the landscape of the Marlborough Downs simply by drawing a circle on a piece of tracing paper and placing it on a map. Having discovered one, I suspected there may be others, although I thought it unlikely that they would be in the Avebury area. I had also been lucky that all of the first circle lay on just one map. Imagine if a circle overlapped on to two, three or four adjoining maps, it would be very difficult – if not impossible – to spot. So, for a while, I put off any attempt to look for more.

But intuition had served me well the first time and something kept niggling at me to check if another circle existed in the same area. Eventually I listened to this inner prompting. I dug out the original tracing of the first circle and set about looking to see if another might exist.

At the time I was working on the old 1″ to the mile maps which covered a greater land area than the present 1:50000 scale maps. This proved to be fortuitous. I initially reasoned that if another circle existed it would probably form a true *vesica pisces* with the first and so moving the tracing paper across the map with its centre set to the circumference of the first circle, I carefully looked for another circle. But to no avail; nothing fitted. I sat back somewhat disconsolate, it seemed too improbable that I might discover another circle and I nearly gave up the search. Yet something inside kept prompting me to look further.

This time disregarding any reference to the first circle I moved the tracing paper over the map setting both the centre and circumference on different key points. Then suddenly like a camera coming into focus there it was. To my amazement and disbelief another circle jumped out at me, close enough to the first to overlap.

Lying a little to the west, this circle ran through fourteen possible sites, one fewer than my original discovery. Its centre fell inside the circumference of the first circle, and lay on an approximate bearing of 242°W. This in itself would prove significant.

In later years when translating these findings on to the 1:50000 scale maps it can be seen that both circles fall on two maps – OS sheets 173 and 174. It is a sobering thought that I would probably never have made these discoveries if I had been working with these modern maps. Luckily, it just so happened that both circles were contained on the old 1 inch to the mile map – OS sheet 157.

It seemed too good to be true that I should have found another circle so easily. And the discovery of a second circle of exactly the same radius leant further weight against the argument that the circles had occurred accidentally. In a state of mounting excitement, I returned to the Ordnance Survey offices in Southampton to check out the exact grid references.

This time, when I carried out the same mathematical analysis I had employed on the first circle, the second showed a mean radius of 9570 metres (31,390 feet), just under seven metres short of the 9576.78 metres, which I had calculated as 1/666 of the Earth's radius at the equator. In addition, I found that the church at Bishops Cannings was aligned to the two centres (Fig. 14).

Visiting the centre also proved more fruitful. Located in a field about 300 metres (1000 feet) east of the ancient Ridgeway track nothing today marks the spot. Yet within 20 metres (65 feet) of the position is a small clump of trees in the corner of which I found seven or eight large Sarsen stones. These had clearly been removed and placed there from the adjoining field. I have been unable to discover whether they marked the

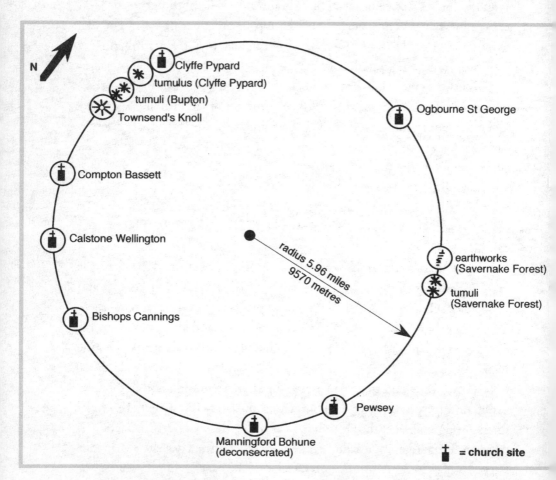

Fig. 13. Plan of western circle

precise point of the centre, the farmer could have just moved individual stones scattered over the field, but their proximity to the position of the centre at least indicated that this was possible.

The pattern that had started to emerge made it even more convincing that these two interlocking circles had been made deliberately. But, spaced as they were, they presented me with a fresh puzzle.

Interlocking circles were used extensively as a foundation pattern in sacred medieval art and architecture, but they conformed to a traditional design, known as a *vesica pisces*. This simple pattern, which underpins much 'sacred geometry', is produced by drawing two circles, of equal size, so that the centre of each lies on the circumference of the other (Fig. 15).

Site	OS grid ref.	Distance from centre in metres	Variance from circumference	Type of site and remarks
Centre of circle	1220 6868	–	9570	–
Bishops Cannings	0376 6418	9565	–5m	church
Calstone Wellington	0271 6816	9504	–66m	church
Compton Bassett	0309 7160	9567	–3m	church
Townsend's Knoll	1013 7490	9641	+71m	earthwork
Bupton	0629 7615	9525	–45m	tumulus
Bupton	0632 7624	9577	+7m	tumulus
Clyffe Pypard	0680 7662	9602	+32m	tumulus
Clyffe Pypard	0746 7698	9558	–12m	church
Ogbourne St. George	1956 7469	9502	–68m	church
Savernake Forest	2180 6818	9613	+43m	earthwork
Savernake Forest	2155 6624	9663	+93m	tumulus
Savernake Forest	2144 6591	9646	+76m	tumulus
Pewsey	1638 6012	9526	–44m	church
Manningford Bohune	1235 5919	9491	–79m	church

Mean of measured radii from postulated centre	9570 metres
Variance (N Weighting)	3216
Standard deviation (N – 1 Weighting)	56.71
Error on Mean (Standard deviation)	7.53 metres

Table 2. Statistical analysis of Western Circle

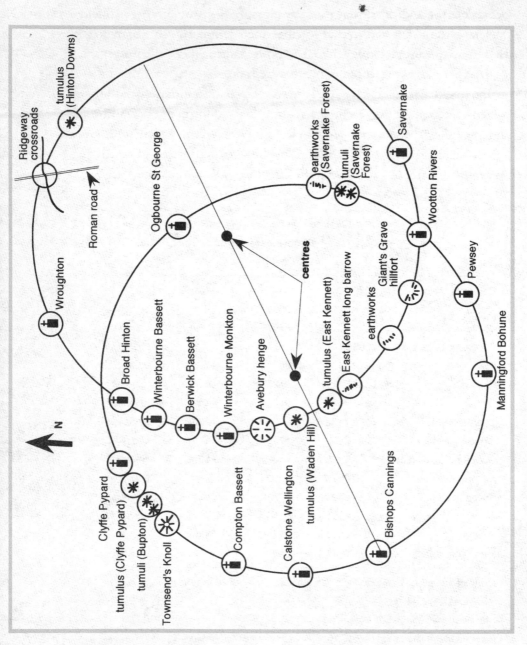

Fig. 14. The twin circles of the Marlborough Downs

The *vesica* became central to Christian mysticism in the middle ages and found its way into both religious painting and the design of the great Gothic cathedrals of Europe (see **photograph 13**). But although it held a special place in Christian art, origins of the *vesica pisces* are more ancient. It was used by both the classical Greeks and the ancient Egyptians.

Much as I wished otherwise, the twin circles did not fit this ancient pattern and I puzzled long and hard on what significance their strange geometric relationship might have. But then I made another startling discovery.

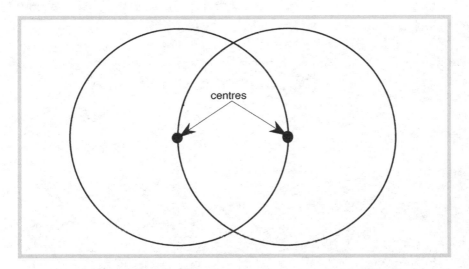

centres

Fig. 15. *Vesica pisces* design

Long distance alignments – the St Michael ley

When Alfred Watkins published his book on leys in the 1920s, the examples he gave showed maximum distances of up to 40 kilometres (25 miles). It seemed feasible that ancient peoples, using simple sighting techniques could maintain relatively good accuracy over such a distance. Longer alignments seemed much less feasible. Watkins also believed that leys essentially highlighted trackways connecting ancient settlements rather like an early version of the Roman road.

However, John Michell, in his book *View Over Atlantis*, gives an example of a long distance alignment which has since become famous, at least among the ley hunting and New Age fraternity. Michell suggests this alignment starts at St Michael's Mount near Marazion in Cornwall. Travelling eastwards, it passes through a well known stone circle on Bodmin Moor called the Hurlers. Then it runs on to Glastonbury Tor, passing through a number of churches dedicated to St Michael on the way. From Glastonbury, it heads eastwards to the Avebury henge, then on to the abbey church of Bury St Edmunds (Fig. 16). This alignment runs a distance of nearly 500 kilometres (310 miles). Others, such as Hamish Miller and Paul Broadhurst in their book *The Sun and the Serpent*, have subsequently suggested that this alignment marks a primary energy meridian of the planet which encircles the globe.

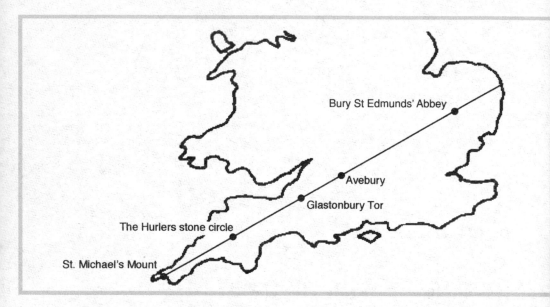

Fig. 16. Principal sites on the St Michael ley (as proposed by John Michell)

Long distance alignments are a controversial subject, even among ley hunters. If they exist, they would require a much higher level of surveying skill. Indeed, as subsequent researchers were to prove, Michell's alignment is not actually straight. Slight deviations can be shown in the line, particularly at its western end.

As the henge monument at Avebury was both a key site on my eastern circle and prominent on Michell's St Michael ley, as it has come to be

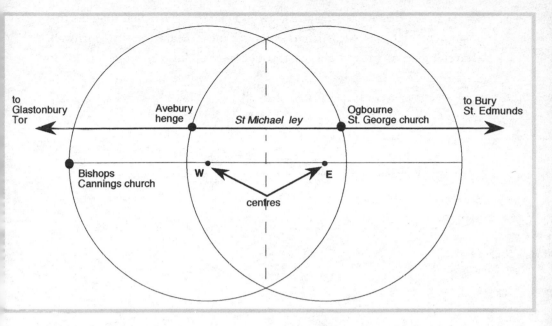

Fig. 17. St Michael ley parallel to line joining the two centres

known, it seemed a good idea to plot the ley on my map. When I did, it immediately became obvious that the ley ran parallel, although slightly to the north, to the line that ran through the two centres of the two circles and through the church at Bishops Cannings.

Again, this was surely more than a coincidence. It suggested some geometric link between the two forms of landscape patterning. If I could establish that link, the case for both the St Michael ley and my circles would be greatly strengthened.

The answer took a long time coming. I spent many frustrating hours hunched over my drawing board pondering this puzzle. I do not remember what it was that prompted me to think of equilateral triangles. Perhaps, it was the triangular ley pattern between Grovely Castle, Old Sarum hillfort and Stonehenge mentioned in Chapter 1. Anyway, one day in the spring of 1976 I drew an equilateral triangle on my map, with two of its points at the centres of the two circles and the third – the apex – lying to the north-west (Fig. 18). I then connected the apex to the two places where the alignment of the two centres crossed the circumferences of the two circles. This produced a new triangle which immediately

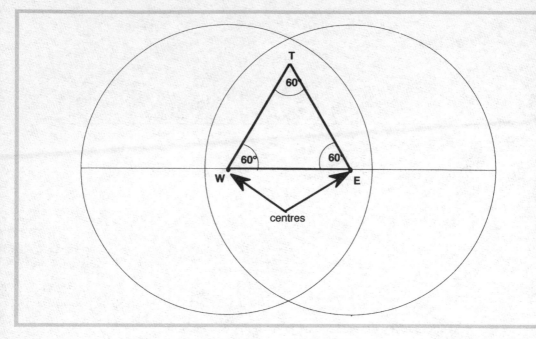

Fig. 18. Step 1. Create an equilateral triangle WET

looked familiar to me. I checked its base angles with my protractor and found that it was very nearly 52°.

This was an angle that I instantly recognised from my studies of ancient Egypt. *It is the slope of the Great Pyramid of Khufu* (Fig. 19).

I was euphoric, but I still had to carry out rigorous mathematical calculations to back this analysis. First, I had to calculate the grid-co-ordinates for these three new positions, then work out the internal angles of this new triangle. But when I had done all that, I was not disappointed.

The base angle turned out to be 51.94°. The angle of slope for the Great Pyramid is usually given as 51°–51′ or 51.85°. So the angle I had discovered hidden in the landscape patterns of the Marlborough Downs was within 0.09° or 5 minutes of arc of that of slope of the Great Pyramid. Was it possible that here, in the landscape of England, was a strong geometric link to the most famous monument of the ancient world?

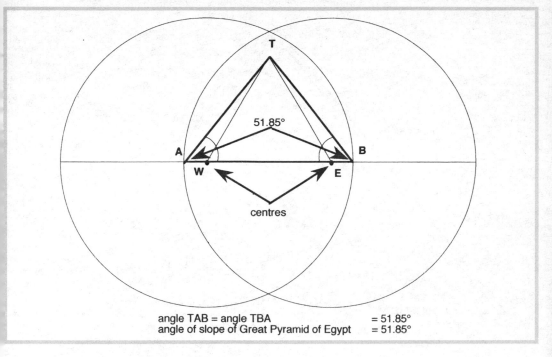

angle TAB = angle TBA = 51.85°
angle of slope of Great Pyramid of Egypt = 51.85°

Fig. 19. Step 2. Create a triangle ATB

The Great Pyramid

Standing on the Giza plateau near modern-day Cairo, the Great Pyramid is the only surviving monument of the Seven Wonders of the Ancient world (see **photograph** 17). It is a colossal structure composed of about 230,000 blocks of stone, each averaging in weight about 2.5 tonnes, and covering more than thirteen acres. It has inspired people down the centuries. More books have been written about this structure than any other ancient monument, and it still holds many mysteries. It is practically unique among the pyramids of Egypt – there are over eighty. Almost all the others are solid structures, built over burial chambers which lie under or on the ground. But in the Great Pyramid of Khufu the principal inner chambers lie within the body of the pyramid itself (Fig. 20).

I quickly reproduced a cross-section of the pyramid to the same scale as the triangle on my map and I found to my amazement that the position

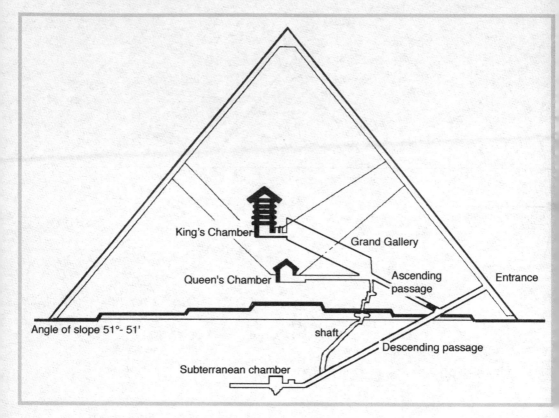

Fig. 20. Cross-section of the Great Pyramid of Giza

of the King's Chamber fell exactly on the St Michael ley at a place known as Temple Farm. Just as significantly, the line of the ascending passage and the Grand Gallery ran between the centre of the eastern circle and the point where the St Michael ley crossed the line joining the two points where the landscape circles intersected (Fig. 21). The odds against this happening by chance must be astronomic.

Within 150 metres (492 feet) of the crossing point of the St Michael ley and the dividing axis of the two circles, there lies a Neolithic long barrow, excavated in the nineteenth century. It has been completely destroyed since then. No evidence of it remains and the intersection point is now marked by a clump of beech trees.

I was no longer in any doubt that the motivation and inspiration behind the construction of the Great Pyramid was also behind the circular

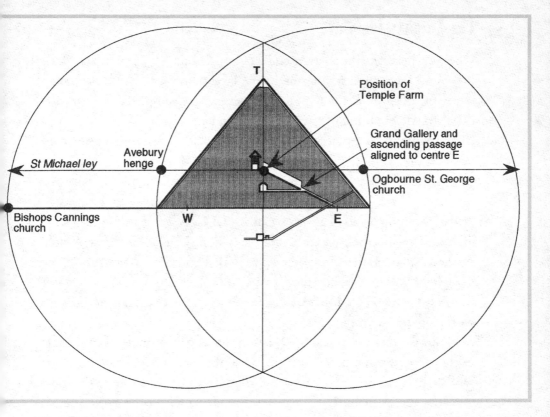

Fig. 21. Superimposition of a rescaled cross-section of the Great Pyramid onto the Marlborough circles showing the St Michael alignment or ley passing through the King's Chamber position and the alignment of the Grand Gallery to centre E

ley patterns of the Marlborough Downs. Here I saw, depicted clearly in the landscape of Wiltshire, a geometric blueprint of the Great Pyramid of Giza. However, believing something to be the case is a long way from proving it.

Each discovery I had made so far raised more questions than answers. Why did the creators of this blueprint put so much effort into something that, by its very nature, lies hidden? What was so significant about this part of the British landscape that a group of people in the distant past would choose it to set out and design a vast temple landscape? What were the links between the Marlborough Downs and ancient Egypt? These questions and more raced through my mind.

The Knights Templar

One link between the eastern end of the Mediterranean and the Marlborough Downs was staring me in the face. The very place on the map where the position of the King's Chamber lay was Temple Farm. It immediately made me think of the Knights Templar.

The Knights Templar were a mysterious chivalric order founded in AD1119 and who are known to have owned land in this area. The order was founded by ten French knights, inspired by St Bernard of Clairvaux, founder of the Cistercians. In that year, these knights, led by Hugues de Payns (meaning 'of the Pagans') went to the Holy Land where they were given quarters in the palace of King Baldwin in Jerusalem. This was close to the church of the Holy Sepulchre and was built on the site of the Temple of Solomon. They took a vow to protect pilgrims journeying to the Holy City, and pledged chastity, poverty and obedience, in accordance with monastic tradition.

However, there is much speculation about what these knights were really after and what they discovered in Jerusalem. Whatever it was, these ten knights founded a military order that was to become one of the most powerful forces in Europe, owing direct allegiance to the Pope and no other sovereign. Many flocked to join the Templars and they were given substantial grants of land. Because of their international connections the Templars became the first bankers, developing a system of bonds that could be exchanged for goods in different parts of the Christian world. This further increased their wealth.

They maintained close ties with the Sufis and shared their esoteric knowledge of alchemy and the Kabbalah. Stories began to circulate about their secret rituals and mystical pursuits. Eventually, their wealth provoked the envy of King Philip IV of France, known as Philip the Fair. In a coup, on Friday 13 October 1307, 189 years after the foundation of the Order, Philip's men seized the Grand Master, Jean Jacques de Molay and 140 of his knights, charging them with heresy, blasphemy and witchcraft. The Order was then persecuted throughout Christendom. Many of its adherents were tortured by the Inquisition to extract confessions of their idolatrous practices.

In 1312, Pope Clement V officially abolished the Order, transferring their estates to the Knights Hospitaler. Before he died at the stake, the Grand Master, protesting his innocence, summoned Philip IV and Clement V to appear before the judgement seat of God to answer for their crimes against the Templars. Philip was given a year; Clement a month. Both the king and the pope died in agony within the time allotted: Philip was thrown from his horse and Clement died from cancer.

At the time, it was believed that the Order had been dissolved completely, but it is now thought that remnants of the Templar tradition were incorporated into Freemasonry, which now embodies some of the Templars' rituals.

The shroud of secrecy has made it difficult to uncover the beliefs and initiation ceremonies of Templars. The confessions of Templars extracted under torture provide no real guide. However, there has been speculation that the knights who founded the Order made an important find while in Jerusalem, perhaps discovering the location of the Ark of the Covenant. It is also said that they knew about hidden powers within the landscape, invoking these energies in their rituals, and that their esoteric knowledge was incorporated into the hidden geometry found within the proportions of Gothic cathedrals.

The Templars amassed their wealth through gifts from the many aspiring knights who wished to join the Order. They gained ownership of the area of the Marlborough Downs I was investigating in 1155, when they were given a hide of land by John Marshall, an ancestor of the Earls of Pembroke. Records are scarce and it is thought that only a farm existed with a number of tenants. No church building has yet been found, so this is not known as a major Templar site. Its association with the Templar tradition, who gave their name to the place, is another intriguing connection. To find out more, I would have to travel eastwards to Egypt and study the pyramids of the Giza plateau.

5
THE PYRAMIDS OF EGYPT

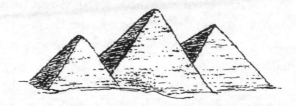

The Giza complex was based on a coherent design intended to portray a spiritual theme

Since I was first given a history book on ancient Egypt when I was twelve, this extraordinary civilisation has held an enduring fascination for me and I have visited Egypt often. Many times I have stood in awe in front of the three great mountains of stone that make up the pyramids on the Giza plateau (see **photograph 16**). I have also been fortunate enough to visit the magnificent temples of Upper Egypt. On some occasions I have taken groups to explore these sites, where many feel that they connect to something that is irrational, intangible yet so immensely powerful that it touches the core of one's being.

From their many religious texts, such as the Pyramid Texts and the Book of the Dead, we know that the ancient Egyptians believed in the power of magic and we can infer that they understood and worked with forces beyond the realm of the physical world. The use of signs such as the ankh, amulets such as the scarab and the reciting of magical spells were an intrinsic part of their culture. They found extensive expression in their burial tombs. I am also sure, from my own feelings in these places, that they were in touch with their gods and goddesses in a way that was not just an intellectual exercise. The presence of their deities was felt and experienced directly. This hidden dimension is, for me, as much a part of Egypt as its ancient monuments.

Yet in thinking of Egypt, most people's minds immediately turn to the pyramids and particularly the most famous of them all, the Great Pyramid of Khufu (or Cheops as he was known to the Greeks). Erected around 2500BC, in the early days of this fabulous civilisation which lasted for just over 3000 years, it is this pyramid that links to the pattern on the Marlborough Downs. I needed to examine its origins, its geometry and its relationships with other pyramids in the hope of uncovering its mysterious links with ancient Britain.

The pyramid of Khufu – the Great Pyramid

The pyramid of Khufu, or the Great Pyramid as it is known, stands with eight other pyramids on the Giza plateau at the centre of the delta made by the River Nile, close to the 30° latitude (see **photograph 17**). It marks a high-point in Egyptian constructional achievement. However, little is known about how it was built or the pharaoh who is supposed to have been responsible for its erection.

The ancient Egyptians, of all the peoples in ancient times, kept the most extensive records. Yet on the Giza pyramids, they are strangely silent. No hieroglyphs adorn their passageways, nor do any records show the methods used in their construction. The earliest account we have is by the Greek historian Herodotus. It was written in the fourth century BC, some 2000 years after the Great Pyramid was completed. He says the pyramid was built in honour of the pharaoh Khufu and took 100,000 men twenty years to complete. Herodotus's sources were the Egyptian priests, who passed on their knowledge of that distant time.

Khufu was one of the kings of the 4th Dynasty, which began about 2613BC and ended around 2465BC. It would seem that the Great Pyramid was completed by about 2494BC. In *The Orion Mystery*, authors Robert Bauval and Adrian Gilbert suggest a slightly later date of 2450BC. The northern shaft from the King's Chamber is aligned to the star Draconis. According to Bauval this sets the date for the construction of the pyramid. Of Khufu, there is little mention. A diminutive 7.6 cm (3 inch) ivory sculpture is the only representation that has been found of this great king. Herodotus tells us that he was a tyrant who coerced his people to complete his monument under enormous duress. Even his own daughter had to sacrifice herself to his ends, by working as a prostitute to earn money for the building. But for all we know, this may have been a fable fed to a gullible historian by a roguish priest.

The Giza group

I have often walked on the Giza plateau and admired the work of these early Egyptian kings. But even standing at the foot of the Great Pyramid and looking up at its huge blocks of limestone, it is difficult to appreciate its immense size. Then in 1987, I met an Egyptian guide and Egyptologist, Ahmed Fayed, who has since become a good friend. He comes from a long line of archaeologists who have worked on the Giza plateau and he now owns a house directly in front of the Sphinx. It is three storeys high and has a flat roof. Looking towards the pyramids from this clear vantage point their vast size becomes apparent. They are without doubt a stupendous undertaking, which show a high level of skill and ingenuity.

Seen from Ahmed Fayed's house, three main pyramids dominate this horizon. Alongside the Great Pyramid, in the middle of the group, is a slightly smaller pyramid. It is attributed to Khafre who, according to Herodotus, was Khufu's brother. Because it stands on slightly higher ground, its height appears to equal that of its larger neighbour. The third pyramid, ascribed to Menkaure, is approximately one quarter the size of Khafre's pyramid. Nevertheless, it is still a major construction and would have risen to some 65.22 metres (214 feet) when it was completed.

Although there is a saying that 'all men fear time, but time fears the pyramids', these monuments have not fared well during the last 2000 years. The pyramids of Khufu and Khafre were originally covered with smooth white Tura limestone. Only the upper courses of the pyramid of Menkaure were faced with limestone, the lower ones were faced with red granite.

Much of this outer casing has now gone, stripped off by the Arabs who used it to build their mosques in Cairo. Only one small section remains on the northern face of the Great Pyramid, and some upper courses of Khafre's pyramid still give a glimpse of how magnificent they must have appeared when they were first erected.

Excavation work, using dynamite, in the last few hundred years has left deep scars on Menkaure's pyramid. The blasting was carried out in the search for ancient treasures. But both archaeologists and treasure hunters have been disappointed. Nothing of note has been found within these pyramids.

This has posed a problem. Conventional wisdom suggests that the pyramids were erected as tombs for dead kings. It is true that granite sarcophagi have been found in each of the three pyramids, but there was never any evidence of burial. It is assumed that the pyramids were looted soon after their occupants were interred. But, again, there is practically no evidence to support this.

When the Caliph Al-Ma'mum and his workmen first broke into the inner chambers of the Great Pyramid in the ninth century AD, they found absolutely nothing. To gain access they had first to bore past three enormous plugs of granite, which they had discovered accidentally. These clearly had not been disturbed since the pyramid was sealed up.

Later, another way into the two upper rooms, which the Arabs had named the King's Chamber and the Queen's Chamber, was discovered. This was a well shaft which ran from the descending corridor up to the start of the Grand Gallery. Egyptologists have suggested that this was the exit route for all the treasures that had been buried with the mummified pharaoh. But this shaft, which descends nearly 50 metres (160 feet), twists and turns. At its widest, it is only 0.9 metres (3 feet) in diameter. But if one considers the amount of treasure amassed for just one minor pharaoh, Tutankhamun, imagine the amount Khufu, the builder of this giant edifice, might have possessed. It would surely have been impossible to remove all traces of such a vast cache of treasure from those upper chambers via such a tortuous route. The only conclusion is that Khufu and his queen were never interred there. Yet why go to such great effort, to create these chambers, only to seal them up empty when they were completed?

Stellar alignment

In *The Orion Mystery*, published in 1994, Bauval and Gilbert suggested that the pyramids on the Giza plateau were established as a group, to depict the three stars in the belt of the constellation of Orion. This is a captivating theory as it suggests that a unified plan links the positioning of the three main pyramids.

The ancient Egyptians laid great stress on this star pattern, known as Sahu, which they believed represented the god Osiris. Their most important star however, was Sirius or Sothis, which was associated with the goddess Isis and is visually aligned to the belt of Orion. It was the helical rising of this star, in midsummer, which heralded the flooding of the Nile inundation that brought fertility to the land of Egypt.

In 1993, I had the opportunity to visit the pyramids with a small party of people interested in healing and esoteric studies. It is possible for private groups to hire the Great Pyramid for special evening ceremonies of healing and dedication. The opportunity of being with a group of like-minded individuals within the stillness of those inner chambers is priceless. On a busy day the pyramid can be packed with tourists, making the air hot and stifling. The chattering voices and the continual procession of people marching through the King's Chamber destroys any hint of an atmosphere. Visiting it when it is closed to tourists is a totally different experience, especially with a group who feel a sense of awe and sanctity for this place.

The sensation of a power within the chambers of the Great Pyramid is very potent on such occasions and we were all aware of some profound mystery held within this hallowed space. After our little ceremony of inner dedication and attunement to world peace, we descended the Grand Gallery to make our way out. We emerged at the foot of the pyramid which now loomed up black against a cloudy night sky. Gazing back at its huge bulk, someone asked 'Where's Sirius?'

We searched in vain for the light of any stars flickering through the cloudy black sky. Then in a momentary gap in the clouds, we saw Orion, with the slope of his belt pointing towards the flattened summit of the pyramid. The clouds closed in, but we waited, hoping that the sky would clear again. At last, as though in answer to our prayers, the clouds parted and, sparkling bright in the dark velvet sky, was Sirius, positioned precisely at the apex of the pyramid.

We were at the exact spot on the plateau at the north side of the pyramid at the exact time in the star's nightly journey on the particular night of the year that put Sirius, like a starlit beacon, on the summit of the Great

A = Waden Hill
B = West Kennett long barrow
C = Silbury Hill

1) An aerial view of Avebury henge, Wiltshire, looking south. Silbury Hill can be seen in the top right-hand corner and the back of Waden Hill to the left.

2) *Top:* Avebury henge showing a section of the huge circular earth bank and ditch with the outer ring of stones.

3) A massive 70 tonne stone at the eastern entrance to the Avebury henge.

4) *Top:* Silbury Hill, Avebury, Wiltshire, looking north. One expert has estimated that it would have taken 250 people 20 years to build, but for what purpose? See Chapter 12.

5) View from the top of Silbury Hill looking east. The back of Waden Hill **(A)** can be seen in the foreground and beyond that the Marlborough Downs **(B)**. The positions of two tumuli **(C & D)** can be clearly seen, marked by clumps of trees.

6) *Top:* East Kennett long barrow, Avebury, Wiltshire. Built as a surveying platform rather than a burial chamber? See Chapter 12.

7) The Sanctuary stone circle, Avebury. Was this intended to act as a sundial, calendar *and* abacus? See Chapter 13.

Pyramid. We could only stand in stunned amazement at the synchronicity that had produced such a powerful moment that touched us all. I also became very aware that, on a practical level, this same plateau area could have been used as a precise astronomical computer for calculating the angles and declinations of the different stars and constellations. For both reasons, this was a moment to savour as we made our way back to the Mena House Hotel on the Giza plateau. From that time on, I could not doubt that Sirius and the constellation of Orion were somehow connected to the mystery of the pyramids.

However, my own researches have taken a different line from Bauval and Gilbert's main thesis that the placement of the three Giza pyramids mirrored the star positions of Orion's belt. I do not doubt that their discovery has highlighted one of the reasons for the curious alignment of these three pyramids, but the geometric patterns on the Marlborough Downs hinted that there is more than one way that the Giza group could be viewed as a whole.

Of gods and goddesses

We do know that, in their religion, the ancient Egyptians held special reverence for trinities – made up of a god, his consort and their son. This 'triune' concept is almost certainly the inspiration behind the origin of the Christian Trinity, of Father, Son and Holy Ghost. In the pyramid age, the religious centre of Egypt resided at Heliopolis, now part of modern Cairo. The priests there worshipped three main gods: Osiris, Isis and their son Horus. The myths surrounding these three gods were the central pivot of the Egyptian belief system which held sway for nearly 3000 years. It is a tale worth recounting.

The myth of Isis and Osiris

Before time began, the supreme creator god Ra-Atum was born from Nun, the waters of chaos. He in turn brought into being the god Shu (wind) and the goddess Tefnut (moisture), who produced two children, Geb, the male earth and Nut the female sky. From their union, four gods were created Osiris, Isis, Seth and Nepthys as well as all creatures that resided on Earth. Osiris, being the eldest of the gods, became king. He was a wise and beneficent ruler who governed the land of Egypt with his sister and consort, Isis. He brought the benefits of civilisation and agriculture to his people, and everyone living in his domain prospered.

Osiris decided that this knowledge should be made available to the rest of humanity, so he set off to do this. While he was away his brother, Seth, was left in charge. Seth enjoyed the power and decided that he was not giving up the kingship when his brother came back.

When Seth heard of Osiris' imminent return to Egypt, he hatched a plot to kill his brother. He had a sarcophagus made the exact size of Osiris. At a magnificent banquet in Osiris' honour, Seth produced the sarcophagus and said he would give it to whoever it fitted exactly. One by one the courtiers tried it for size, without success. Then Osiris was persuaded to lie down in the coffin. Seth quickly sealed the lid and threw the sarcophagus in the Nile. Isis was distraught and went in search of her husband's body. She found it but, before she could bring him back to life, Seth caught up with the couple. He cut the body of Osiris into fourteen pieces and scattered them throughout Egypt.

Isis searched for her husband's body parts, using her magical arts. She found them all except his penis, which had been eaten by a Nile crab. She reassembled him and breathed life back into the corpse. Then she fashioned a new penis, impregnated herself and eventually gave birth to a son, called Horus. Osiris was, understandably, fed up with ruling on Earth and so he returned to the spiritual realm, leaving his son Horus, the falcon-headed god, to fight Seth.

The ancient Egyptians believed that after death the souls of all human beings were brought before Osiris to be judged on whether they had been 'true of heart' while on Earth. If they passed this test they were allowed into the heavenly realms, but if they failed they would be devoured by the crocodile. This judgement scene was painted frequently in the tombs and is known as the 'weighing of the heart' ceremony.

The Osiris myth can be interpreted on many levels. Some scholars have suggested that Osiris and Isis may have been real people. On a symbolic level, it shows the split between the materialistic side of our nature, in the person of Seth, and our spiritual side, symbolised by Osiris.

In dynastic Egypt, the pharaoh was seen as the incarnation of Horus, wrestling with the forces of disorder and chaos. One of the earliest known plaques – the palette of Narmer, dating from the unification of Upper and Lower Egypt in the 1st Dynasty – shows Horus hovering above the king.

The pyramid 'trinity'

Sitting one evening on the flat roof of Ahmed Fayed's house watching the sunset behind the pyramids, I was suddenly struck by the symbolism of the size of these monuments. When viewed against the brilliant backdrop of an evening sun, the silhouette shows the bulk of each of the three pyramids distinctly. Two are large, appearing of nearly identical size, while the third is, in comparison, quite small. I was suddenly struck by the thought that the three pyramids might have been erected to represent the three gods of the Heliopolitan cosmology: Osiris, Isis and Horus; father, mother and child.

A powerful feeling came over me as I watched the sun dipping below the horizon. To my right, from where I sat, it seemed as though Osiris was smiling at me from his seat within the great Pyramid. To my left, there hovered the falcon-headed god Horus above the small pyramid of Menkaure, while in the centre stood Isis, stretching out her divine wings over the pyramid of Khafre, the link between husband and son.

All right, so there is no factual information to support this notion. There are no records that tell us of a dedication ceremony. If accounts ever existed, they would have been burnt in fires that destroyed the famous libraries at Alexandria. But absence of evidence is not evidence of absence. The link between Osiris, Isis and Horus and the pyramids of Giza is a theme that I shall return to towards the end of this chapter.

Size and construction of the pyramids

There is so much mystery surrounding the pyramids of Giza. As yet, no fully satisfactory explanation has yet been given for how the Great Pyramid was built. Its construction entailed moving blocks of stone weighing 2.5 tonnes to the top of a monument more than 146 metres (480 feet) high. A number of different theories have been proposed. Scientists favour ramps and levers. Psychics have dreamt up bizarre methods of levitating the blocks through sonics or some other mysterious force. These work fine, on paper.

But even the prosaic method of using ramps, which is front-runner in the field, is beset with practical problems. Sir Flinders Petrie, one of the early investigators and an authority on the pyramids in the mid-1880s, estimated that to build a ramp to carry blocks to the top would have required as much material as the pyramid itself. To give some idea of how much that is, Napoleon once calculated that there was enough stone in the three pyramids of Giza to build a wall around the whole of France, 3.7 metres (12 feet) high and 0.3 metres (1 foot) thick. So, if a ramp was used, what has happened to all the material used to make it? It has never been found.

But leaving aside what we do not know, we do know the precise proportions of the pyramids – particularly the Great Pyramid. It is the most surveyed of all the monuments of the ancient world.

Measurements of the Great Pyramid

The Great Pyramid is almost exactly square, with its sides orientated to the four cardinal points of the compass – north, south, east and west. The maximum deviation in just 0.058° or 3.5 minutes of arc. One of the most accurate surveys was carried out by J.H. Cole in 1925. He gave the following ground plan measurements:

South side = 230.454 metres (±6 millimetres)
North side = 230.251 metres (±10 millimetres)
West side = 230.357 metres
East side = 230.391 metres

Adding together the lengths of all four sides gives a total of 921.453 metres (3023.14 feet). It so happens that one degree latitude at the equator covers 110,573 metres (362,679 feet), making each minute of arc 1842.88 metres (6045 feet). This is almost exactly twice the perimeter of the Great Pyramid (921.453 × 2 = 1842.906 metres). So the sum of the four sides is equal to half a minute of equatorial latitude. The error is only thirteen millimetres. With such accuracy, the implication must be that this relationship was deliberate.

The pyramid would have risen to a height of 146.59 metres (480.94 feet) when completed. Its upper courses are now missing, so it is now nearly 9.5 metres (31 feet) shorter. But when it was built, the Great

Pyramid had a height to base ratio of 7:11. This ratio has some important geometric properties. Implicit in it are both the formula for pi (π) and that for the golden mean proportion, usually depicted by the Greek letter phi (φ) (see Figs. 22 and 23).

Phi and pi

The golden mean proportion is a geometric construction that was used extensively in Greek architecture. It is also a natural ratio, embodied in a famous progression of numbers called the Fibonacci series, named after an Italian mathematician. This series runs 1, 1, 2, 3, 5, 8, 13, 23, 34, 55, 89, 144 ... and so on, where each number is the sum of the two preceding numbers. (For example, 1+1 = 2; 2+1 = 3; 3 + 2 = 5 and so on.) In the natural world, this series manifests in, among other things, the spiral seed patterns of the sunflower and the fir-cone. When counted, these will always add up to two consecutive numbers in the Fibonacci series. It also appears in the growth stages of a nautilus shell.

The golden mean, or phi (φ), is given by dividing a number in the Fibonacci series by the number that precedes it. As you move up the series to higher and higher numbers, this gives phi a higher and higher accuracy. For example, 144 by 89 gives 1.6179775 ... which, like pi, produces a string of decimal places that stretches to infinity with no apparent repetition. However, phi is usually stated numerically as 1.618. The simplest way to geometrically construct this ratio is by using the diagonal of a two by one rectangle (see Fig. 35).

The number pi (π) is used for calculating the various properties of a circle. In ancient Egypt it was expressed by the ratio $^{22}\!/_{7}$. Today, it is given the value of 3.1416 to four decimal places.

The Great Pyramid embodies both phi and pi in a simple way. Firstly, the sum of the distance of the pyramid's four sides equals the circumferences of a circle whose radius equals its height (Fig. 23). This can be demonstrated using the 7:11 height to base ratio. The formula for calculating the circumference of a circle is $2\pi r$, where r is the radius. Here the radius is 7 units, and we are taking π to be $^{22}\!/_{7}$.

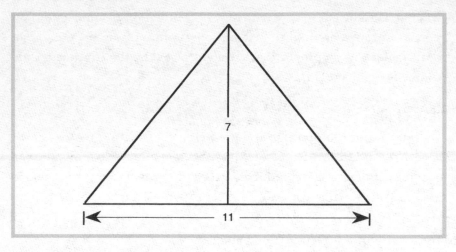

Fig. 22. Ratio of height to base of the Great Pyramid

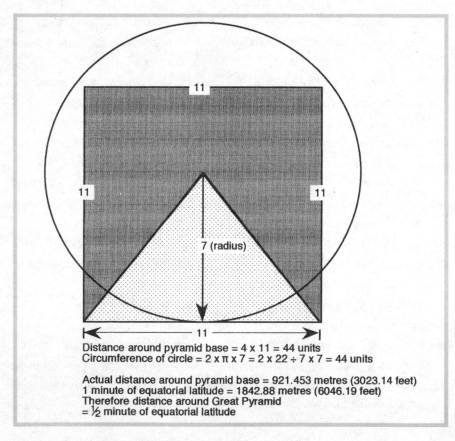

Distance around pyramid base = 4 x 11 = 44 units
Circumference of circle = 2 x π x 7 = 2 x 22 ÷ 7 x 7 = 44 units

Actual distance around pyramid base = 921.453 metres (3023.14 feet)
1 minute of equatorial latitude = 1842.88 metres (6046.19 feet)
Therefore distance around Great Pyramid
= ½ minute of equatorial latitude

Fig. 23. The pi ratio of the Great Pyramid

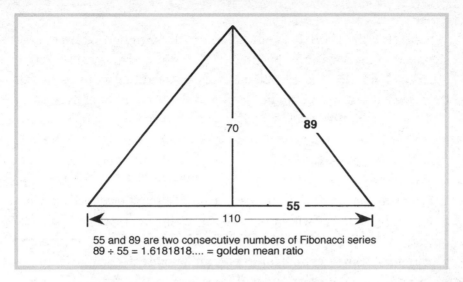

55 and 89 are two consecutive numbers of Fibonacci series
89 ÷ 55 = 1.6181818.... = golden mean ratio

Fig. 24. The golden mean relationship to the Great Pyramid

$2 \times (22 \div 7) \times 7 = 44$ units

So, if each side is 11 units, then the sum of all four sides is:

$11 + 11 + 11 + 11 = 11 \times 4$

which is 44 units again.

The golden mean proportion, phi, can be found in the ratio of the pyramid's base and the length of the pyramid's apothem or slope (see Fig. 24). Pythagoras' theorem says that the square on the hypotenuse – in this case the slope – is equal to the sum of the squares on the other two sides, in other words the height and half the base. So, the length of the hypotenuse, or slope, is the square root of $7^2 + 5.5^2$ or 8.9022. If we scale up both 5.5 and 8.9022 by 10 we get 55 and 89.022 and, by disregarding the digits after the decimal point, we have two consecutive numbers – 55 and 89 – in the Fibonacci series. So, half the base length and the apothem are in golden mean proportion.

Of course, these relationships could have entirely escaped the ancient Egyptians. The Great Pyramid's height to base ratio, 7:11, could have been chosen for entirely different reasons. But the precision and sophistication of the design of the pyramid mean that the architects would have appreciated that these ratios were implicit in what they were building.

Inner chambers

What makes the Great Pyramid unique is the inclusion of large inner chambers in the body of the pyramid itself. In the case of practically every other pyramid, the inner chambers were excavated underground first or they were constructed at ground level and the pyramid built over them. Only in the North Pyramid at Dahshur is there any chamber above ground level. In this case, it is a small chamber within the body of the pyramid, which is accessed, via a short passage, from one of its ground level chambers.

Although the Great Pyramid has an underground chamber, its main rooms and galleries lie within the bulk of the pyramid (see Fig. 20). The positioning of these rooms and other architectural features, such as the provision of what were thought to be ventilation shafts, has given rise to speculation that the Great Pyramid must have had some function other than the burial place of a dead pharaoh. My researches on the Marlborough Downs indicate that there were also important geometric reasons why these features were positioned as they are.

But before examining the relationship between the Great Pyramid and the patterns on the Marlborough Downs in more detail, I thought I should explore whether the two other main pyramids on the Giza plateau could help me further with the investigation of my circles.

Measurements of the pyramid of Khafre

The pyramid of Khafre is the middle pyramid of the group and is inferior in many ways to its neighbours. It lies to the south-west of the Great Pyramid and originally rose to a height of 143.51 metres (471 feet). At the base, its sides average 215.26 metres (706.21 feet). Like the Great Pyramid, it is orientated to the cardinal points of the compass, but with not quite the same level of accuracy as its maximum deviation is over 6 minutes of arc. Its stonework also lacks the superior finish of the Great Pyramid. Nevertheless it is still an impressive monument. Standing on slightly higher ground, it appears to be very nearly the equal of its more illustrious neighbour.

It has an angle of slope of 53.13° which shows that it too is built on a simple height to base ratio – in this case 2:3. This ratio means that the elevation embodies the famous Pythagorean 3:4:5 triangle. Some authorities have suggested that the ancient Egyptians were not aware of the 3:4:5 right-angled triangle as it does not appear in any of their mathematical texts. Yet here it is in Khafre's pyramid (see Fig. 26).

There is also a simple numeric ratio between the base size of the Khafre and Khufu pyramids. Dividing the average lengths of the sides into each other ($230.36 \div 215.72 = 1.068$) gives a ratio between the two that is almost exactly 16:15 (1.067). This suggests that the Giza pyramids were intentionally related to each other and laid out to a coherent plan.

The entrances to all pyramids lie on their northern sides. In the case of Khafre's pyramid, there are two separate passageways. One was excavated in the bedrock; the other, just over 15 metres (49 feet) directly above it, is in the side of the pyramid. The upper passageway descends at an angle of just under 26° before levelling off. It finishes in a chamber 14.173 metres (46.5 feet) long by 5.029 metres (16.5 feet) wide.

On the eastern side of the pyramid, there is a causeway that leads down from the mortuary temple, to the valley temple, with its surviving columns and walls. Close by this Valley Temple lies the famous statue of the Sphinx, which was originally thought to be a representation of Khafre (see **photograph 18**). But its facial proportions indicate that the Sphinx could well have been modelled on another pharaoh. Indeed, there is great controversy on the dating of this monument.

Some authorities suggest that the Sphinx was carved as long ago as 5000BC or earlier. Weathering patterns in the surrounding rock indicate it was caused by rain, rather than wind erosion blasting sand against it. So it could only have occurred at a time when Egypt experienced a much higher rainfall.

Egypt's present climate stabilised around 3100BC. Prior to that, the whole of the Sahara region, including Egypt, was much wetter. The erosion patterns suggest that the Sphinx was created during this earlier wetter phase. Weathering of the outer casings of the three pyramids that remain do not show any signs of this water erosion. This is further evidence that the pyramids were built at a later date, *circa* 2500BC. So, if the Sphinx was there first, it would have been used as the primary surveying point when the rest of the site was laid out.

Measurements of the pyramid of Menkaure

The smallest of the three major pyramids lies to the south-west of the other two and is a fraction over one quarter the size of Khafre's pyramid (Fig. 25). Originally rising to a height of 66.4 metres (217.86 feet), its base sides average 108.66 metres (356.5 feet) giving an angle of slope of 50.71°. Here, too, another simple height to base ratio, 11:18, has been used in the construction (Fig. 26).

Although much less imposing than its two neighbours, Menkaure's pyramid has a number of unique features. While its upper tiers were covered in Tura limestone, its 16 lower courses were covered with red granite, quarried 800 kilometres (500 miles) to the south, at Aswan. These courses have not been dressed which suggests, or as some suspect, the pyramid was never properly completed.

As in Khafre's pyramid, the main chamber lies below the structure, in the bedrock. But the chamber follows the design of the Great Pyramid,

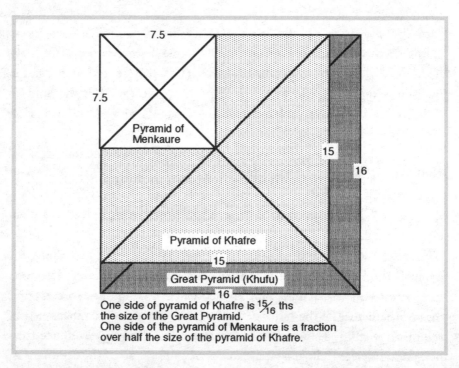

One side of pyramid of Khafre is $^{15}/_{16}$ ths the size of the Great Pyramid.
One side of the pyramid of Menkaure is a fraction over half the size of the pyramid of Khafre.

Fig. 25. Ratio of sizes between the pyramids of Khufu, Khafre and Menkaure

with the walls, floor and ceiling being faced with granite. In his book, *Fingerprints of the Gods*, Graham Hancock points out one of the enigmas attached to the Menkaure pyramid. The roof of this chamber, which measures some 3.657 metres (12 feet) by 2.438 metres (8 feet) is composed of 18 huge blocks of granite, each weighing many tons, shaped into a perfect barrel vault. These blocks are fitted together with great precision to create a gable roof. Yet, because this is underground and set in the solid bedrock, these blocks had to have been raised from within the small chamber. This room could, at best, hold only a few people at a time. How they managed to raise these huge blocks in so small a space remains a complete mystery.

This and much other evidence has led Egyptologists to believe that the ancient Egyptians must have had some mechanical method for moving and raising the stones which has since been lost.

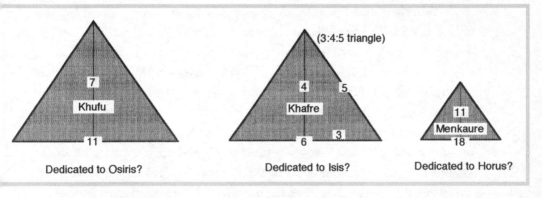

Fig. 26. The ratios of the three main Giza pyramids (approximate scale)

Number symbolism

Whenever I have wandered across the Giza plateau examining both the pyramids and mortuary temples, I have been struck by the way in which specific numbers are woven into the design of these monuments. In the case of Menkaure's pyramid, the 18 blocks of stone that form the roof of the inner chamber echo the height to base ratio 11:18 embodied in the pyramid itself.

This inner chamber is approached from a descending corridor which opens out into two ante-chambers. Carved into the walls of the first of these ante-chambers is a series of 22 rectangular stepped niches, 11 on each side (Fig. 27). This picks up another of the ratios of this pyramid.

The emphasis on the number 11 can be found again in the magnificent funerary temple of Queen Hatshepsut from the 18th Dynasty, which was built around 1450BC, more than a thousand years after the pyramids. This temple, at Deir El Bahari on the west bank of the Nile opposite Luxor, rises in three tiers with a sloping central causeway running to its upper level. Each tier has a visible facade of 22 columns, 11 on each side of the causeway. The three tiers making a total of 66 columns. But what is so special about the number 11?

The tradition of numerals that has been handed down from ancient Egypt via Pythagoras suggests that the number 11 symbolises initiation into the inner mysteries, while 7 is the number of spirituality and mysticism.

Within the Great Pyramid, the King's Chamber is approached by way of the famous Grand Gallery. Here, too, a clearly visible numeric design feature has been built into its structure. The walls of the Grand Gallery taper towards the ceiling in a series of 7 corbelled steps. Why build in such a feature unless it carried special meaning? Again, the height to base ratio of the Great Pyramid is 7:11.

Discovered under the floor of Khafre's mortuary temple is a famous statue of the pharaoh, showing the power and majesty that he commanded. Within this temple there are placements for 22 other statues, 11 on each side. The repetition of the number 11 here again shows that certainly this, and other, numbers held special significance for the ancient Egyptians.

The eminent authority on the pyramids, Dr I.E.S. Edwards, says in his book *The Pyramids of Egypt*:

 Opposite each of the openings in the cloister [of Khafre's mortuary temple] was a deep niche that may have contained a statue of the king. The significance of the five statues – a number which does not vary in any of the subsequent mortuary temples – may be that each bore one of the five official names assumed by the king on his accession. It is, however, equally possible that the number was dictated by the need to represent the king in association with five different cult-symbols.

This quote, about yet another number, again draws attention to the significance the ancient Egyptians placed on numeric repetition. In these cases, the numbers expressed are explicit in that the number of statues, niches, columns or whatever can be counted. But in the proportions of a pyramid, they are implicit, or hidden. Once the pyramid had been erected, these numbers could only be rediscovered by those capable of re-measuring the structure and working out the ratios.

It is worth re-stating the proportions of the three main pyramids on the Giza plateau. Remember that these are ratios of the units of measure that were used in the construction and not the units themselves. The height to base ratio of each pyramid and the angles they generate can be shown thus (Fig. 26):

Khufu pyramid   = 7:11   = 51°–51′
Khafre pyramid   = 4:6   = 53°–8′
Menkaure pyramid   = 11:18   = 50°–43′

For Khafre's pyramid I have shown a ratio of 4:6 and not 2:3 because the former implies the 3:4:5 triangle. The number 5 is contained implicitly in the length of the angle of slope of the pyramid.

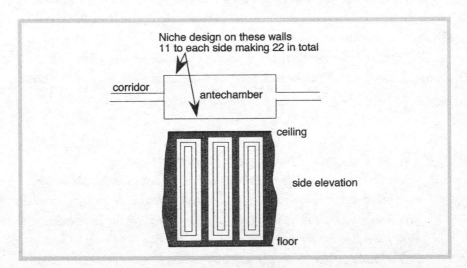

Fig. 27. Niche design in the antechamber of Menkaure pyramid (not to scale)

Mathematics and the pharaohs

I had arrived at these ratios before discovering that this was precisely the system used by the ancient Egyptians. Egyptologists know something about the ancient Egyptians' systems of calculation and measurements from the discovery of a few mathematical papyri. These take the form of posing problems which the scribes then have to work out. One of the most famous is the Rhind Mathematical Papyrus which now resides in the British Museum. Going through these problems, Egyptologists discovered how the ancient Egyptians dealt with the different quantities that arose from their calculation of weights, measure and volume, which often involved the use of fractions. It also showed how they handled angles.

In today's world, to measure an angle, we use a protractor which divides a circle into 360°. Each degree is then divided into 60 minutes, which are then sub-divided into 60 seconds. The ancient Egyptians, on the other hand, used a very different method for calculating angles. It was a system based on the ratio of the height to the base of a right-angled triangle. Effectively, they expressed any angle in terms of the gradient. A similar system could still be seen, until recent times, in British road signs indicating a steep hill ahead. These signs gave the gradient of a hill as a numeric ratio, such as 1 in 6. This meant that six units along the horizontal gave a climb of one unit vertically.

Similarly, in ancient Egypt, the gradient of slope was expressed as a whole number ratio known as the *seked* of the angle (Fig. 28). In his book *Mathematics in the Time of the Pharoahs*, Richard Gillings explains:

 The seked *of a right pyramid is the inclination of any one of the four triangular faces to the horizontal plane of the base, and is measured as so many horizontal units per one vertical unit rise. It is thus a measure equivalent to our modern cotangent of the angle of slope. In general, the* seked *of a pyramid is a kind of fraction, given in so many palms [units of measure] horizontally for each cubit of vertical rise, where 7 palms equals one cubit. The Egyptian word* seked *is thus related to our modern word 'gradient'.*

It transpired that understanding this simple system was crucial to working out the surveying techniques of the ancient Britons on the Marlborough Downs.

By understanding the method the ancient Egyptians used, it became clear why 'strange' angles of slope, such as the 51°–51′ of the Great Pyramid, occur. It is derived from a simple numeric ratio between the height and the base of the pyramid, which in the case of the Great Pyramid is 7:11. This is true for all the pyramids, a simple fact which I have never found mentioned in all the books that I have read on this subject. The numeric key to the pyramids must lie in the ratio of their height to their base.

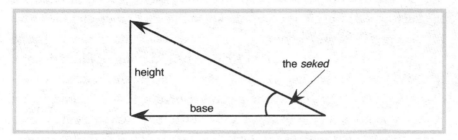

Fig. 28. The *seked* of an angle is the ratio of the base to the height of a right-angled triangle

In practical terms – and the ancient Egyptians were certainly a practical people – this method is the easiest way to create the templates that would have been necessary to continually check that the correct angle of slope was being maintained while the pyramid was being constructed.

But the questions that now needed to be asked were why, in the Giza group, did the ancient Egyptians choose to use different angles of slope for each of the pyramids? What was significant about the different ratios? Would it not have been more practical to build all of the pyramids to the same ratio as the Great Pyramid, once the formula had been set?

Egyptologists would have us believe that each pharaoh wished to express his individuality and this gave rise to the differences. But there could be another reason. Perhaps they wished to incorporate different symbolic associations implicit in the different ratios that were used.

There is at least one other pyramid based on the 7:11 ratio. It is at

Meidum, more than 160 kilometres (100 miles) south of Giza, and is attributed to Senefru who was Khufu's father. Another pyramid, at Abusir, attributed to Sahure, one of the kings of the 5th Dynasty, has an angle of slope calculated at 51°–42′. This is within a fraction of the Great Pyramid's angle and it is likely it used the same 7:11 ratio. The problem with Sahure's pyramid, like many others in Egypt, is that the removal of the outer casing has made it very difficult to accurately assess its true angle.

The angle of slope of Khafre's pyramid is the same as that of the pyramid of Pepi II, one of the kings of the 6th Dynasty who reigned from 2278 to 2184BC. This pyramid is now in ruins, but the angle of slope has been deduced from what remains of the outer casings. The construction of the later Egyptian pyramids was inferior to the Giza group and they have suffered greatly through the passage of time. Many have now collapsed into heaps of rubble. However, in Khafre's case, the angle of his pyramid, (based on the 3:4:5 triangle) is highlighted in three of the problems (numbers 57, 58 and 59) posed on pyramids in the Rhind Mathematical Papyrus. So it was a ratio that was well known to the ancient Egyptians.

In fairness to those Egyptologists who maintain that the ancient Egyptians did not know about the 3:4:5 triangle, the length of the hypotenuse – 5 – is never given. But mathematical problems, and those involving the pyramids, are always calculated in terms of the *seked* of the angle, the ratio of height to base. In the case of the 3:4:5 triangle, the *seked* is the ratio of 3 to 4. But as no mention was ever made of the length of the hypotenuse, it was inferred that the Egyptians had never worked out the length of the third side.

Are we really supposed to believe that a people who could design and build a monument to the precision shown in the Great Pyramid, or the pyramid of Khafre, involving exact measurements over considerable distances, would never have measured or worked out the lengths of the hypotenuses of the triangles they were using? Surely, any people seeking precision of measurement would check all lengths as a matter of course as part of their general exploration of number, form and geometry. It would be an essential part of their working methods. So, I would maintain that simply by using the ratio 3:4 in their building plans, they implicitly knew the length of the third side.

The height to base ratios used in the pyramids of Giza were certainly known to the ancient Egyptians. They appear in examples given in the various mathematical texts. It is, of course, possible that the ratio for each of the pyramids was chosen arbitrarily. But this flies in the face of the importance of number symbolism found in all aspects of Egyptian artistic expression. It is highly probable that these ratios had a significant meaning expressing specific religious concepts. In other words, the whole of the Giza complex was based on a coherent design intended to portray a spiritual theme. This would explain why the pyramid designers chose different angles of slope for the three pyramids.

In *The Orion Mystery*, Bauval and Gilbert have presented compelling evidence for linking the Giza pyramids to the constellation of Orion, and in particular with the stars in Orion's belt. This constellation is also woven into the myth of Isis and Osiris and, as I have already suggested, a case could be made for viewing each pyramid as a representation of the three principal deities of this group; Osiris, Isis and Horus.

Games with numbers

Number symbolism was important to ancient peoples. This tradition was eventually enshrined in the teachings of Pythagoras, who, it is thought, derived many of his ideas from ancient Egypt. He maintained that odd numbers expressed a masculine principle while even numbers were feminine.

Earlier, I made the association between the pyramids and the three deities – Khufu pyramid with Osiris, Khafre pyramid with Isis and Menkaure pyramid with Horus. The height to base ratio of the Great Pyramid of Khufu contains two odd numbers, 7 and 11. This fits the masculine Osiris. The ratio of Khafre's pyramid, 4:6, could be reduced further to 2:3, giving one odd and one even number, expressing both the masculine as well as feminine principle. However, if this reduction is made, the inherent Pythagorean 3:4:5 symmetry would be destroyed as the length of the hypotenuse would cease to be a whole number. The use of whole numbers, rather than fractions, was an intrinsic part of the tradition. So, I maintain that the primary ratio of the Khafre pyramid should be 4:6 which, both being even numbers, expresses a feminine principle – Isis.

The third pyramid, of Menkaure, has both a masculine number, 11, over a feminine number, 18. But 18 could be expressed as 6+6+6, another manifestation of 666. The third god of the Osiris trinity is the masculine Horus, which I maintain is associated with the Menkaure pyramid, who waged a perpetual war against his evil uncle Seth in the myths. Could he be the beast referred to by St John in *Revelation*?

The ancient Egyptians recognised their pharaohs as incarnations of the god Horus, whose task on Earth was to strive continually to create order out of chaos. Symbolically, the pharaoh could also be seen to represent our spiritual self striving to overcome the baser aspects of our human nature.

The colour associated with the god Seth was red, and it is just possible that the two-tone design of the Menkaure pyramid – its upper courses of white Tura limestone and lower courses of undressed red granite – was intended to represent the tussle between Horus and Seth; of order over chaos; of our spiritual nature fighting for control over our material self.

Ancient Egypt was known as the 'Two Lands' – Upper and Lower Egypt. The colour white was symbolic of Upper, while Lower Egypt was symbolised by red. The inclusion of these two colours, in Menkaure's pyramid, could also symbolically relate to the 'Two Lands'. This point was noted by George Hart in his book *Pharaohs and Pyramids*, where he says:

 Thus, although Menkaure's monument did not dominate the Giza plateau in terms of size, it would have presented an attractive appearance with the contrasting colour of the white limestone and red granite. One is struck once again ... by the pervading dualism of Egyptian symbols. For in Menkaure's pyramid more than any other, the line of the colour change would be higher and more emphatic, stressing his role as 'Lord of the Two Lands' by the very casing blocks of his funerary monument.

On the other hand the inclusion of the two numbers 11 and 18 within Menkaure's pyramid could also express the need to balance both masculine and feminine elements in the psyche.

Numerological tradition takes one further step by adding together the individual digits in any number to reduce that number to its primary form. This would normally be any number between 1 and 9. For example, the number 18 could be reduced to the number 9 by adding together the two digits: $1 + 8 = 9$. There were some exceptions to this system. Ancient peoples placed great store on numbers with repeating digits, such as 11, 22, 33, 44 and so on, and these numbers would have had special significance. So, 11 ($1 + 1$) would not, generally, have been reduced to 2.

Such a concept has no place in modern science and is regarded as superstitious nonsense. However, the ancient Egyptians set great store by their canon of measures and proportions which has given rise to their very distinctive art forms. According to Plato, maintaining this harmonious system of proportions was the primary reason why the Egyptian civilisation flourished for so many thousand years. We can infer from the teachings of Pythagoras, who was initiated into the Egyptian priesthood, that the numerological principle of reducing numbers to their primary form was a method adopted by priests. It is therefore a principle we need to understand if we are going to access their mind-set and unravel some of the concepts embedded in the design of the pyramids.

Applying this principle to the three pyramids gives the following ratios:

Khufu (7:11) $7 + 11 = 18$; $1 + 8 = 9$

Khafre (4:6) $4 + 6 = 10$

Menkaure (11:18) $11 + 18 = 29$; $2 + 9 = 11$

From this it is clear that patterns of numbers, particularly 11 and 18, can be found woven into the design. The rhythm of 9, 10 and 11 reflecting the construction sequence of the pyramids (Khufu, Khafre and Menkaure) adds up to 30 ($9 + 10 + 11$), which can be expressed as 3×10. In Gematria, the Judaic system of relating numbers to the letters of the alphabet, the number ten is ascribed to the equivalent Hebrew letter 'h'. In Judaism, ten is the number of God and the letter 'h' terminates all words, such as Jehovah, which are thought to reflect the deity. Through this tradition and number symbolism, we have an oblique connection of the three pyramids to the divine. (The traditional meaning of these different numbers can be found in Appendix 2.)

The ratios woven into the pyramids of the Giza plateau throw additional light on the hidden associations within these monuments. They can also be seen to express symbolically the eternal truths, found in the myths and religious beliefs of the ancient Egyptians. The Giza pyramids may have little more to do with the personal aggrandisement or providing an after-life resting place of three pharaohs, than the great cathedrals of medieval Europe do with the glorification of individual kings of Christendom who built and often lie buried in them. Medieval kings may have provided funds for these great churches and used them as their last resting place, but this was not their main purpose. In the same way, attributing names of the pharaohs who built them to the pyramids may well obscure their true religious purpose.

All this is, of course, only conjecture and is a radical departure from what orthodox Egyptologists would have us believe. But it implies a coherence in the design of the Giza complex which only became accepted with Bauval and Gilbert's work linking the site to the three stars of Orion's belt and it gives a new way to examine the significance of the pyramids.

However, while numbers were very important to these early cultures, they were not the primary source of mathematical wisdom. Plato maintained that all eternal truths could be obtained from the compass and the straight edge. In other words, pure geometry lay at the heart of all things. Pure geometry can be defined as patterns derived by using only a compass and a straight edge, without reference to number or measure. The next key to the puzzle lies in the geometric basis of the site plan at Giza. But to understand the significance of the pattern that overlies the Marlborough Downs and its relationship to the Great Pyramid of Egypt, we need to explore the concepts of sacred geometry.

6

SACRED GEOMETRY AND
THE GIZA PYRAMIDS

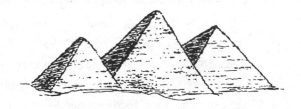

*The alignment of the pyramid's Grand Gallery pointed to the
centre of one of the circles*

Above the entrance to Plato's Academy at Athens was the legend 'Let none
ignorant of geometry enter here'. To the ancient Greeks, pure geometry
lay at the heart of all things. It was the way of reconciling the world of the
divine with the form of the world we see. The golden mean proportion,
for example, can be depicted in terms of geometry but not number. It can
be drawn, but the number that represents it cannot be written down as it
runs to an infinite number of decimal places. Geometry can be seen as a
way of defining what is otherwise indefinable.

Our knowledge of the use of pure geometry in ancient Egypt is more
tenuous. We do not have any papyri which give the geometrical equivalent
of the equations of Plato, Thales and Euclid, epitomising ancient Greek
thought. However, Plato considered that Egypt possessed a profound
canon of knowledge based on harmony and proportion. We can infer that
the ancient Egyptians were as adept with the compass and the rule as their
Greek counterparts. This knowledge would have influenced their art and
architecture. Unravelling how the Egyptians might have selected the
proportions they used is a way of reaching back into the roots of their
civilisation.

The patterns on the Marlborough Downs also appeared to be based on pure geometry. Our next step, therefore, must be to draw together these disparate parts of the puzzle and discover the underlying geometry that unites them.

Sacred geometry

The term 'sacred geometry' can be misleading as the fundamentals of geometric proportion are found extensively throughout the natural world as well as in art and architecture. Why are some elements sacred and not others? There is no easy answer to this question. Nevertheless, a tradition has grown up which has placed a special emphasis on certain geometric relationships and proportions found most commonly in the design of buildings used for religious purposes. To the general observer, these proportions are simply pleasing. Artistically, this is analogous to music. Using different groupings of notes and internals, harmonious or discordant sounds can be created. Some music, such as Gregorian chants, can put us more in touch with spiritual feelings. Other music puts us directly in touch with our emotions. Indeed, one of the great philosophers, Pythagoras, demonstrated the links between music, sound, number and form.

Three basic geometric shapes are central to religious tradition: the circle, the triangle and the square (Fig. 29). These were taken to represent three levels of our being: spirit, mind and body. Like systems of counting, no one knows who first used a compass. It was probably just a piece of

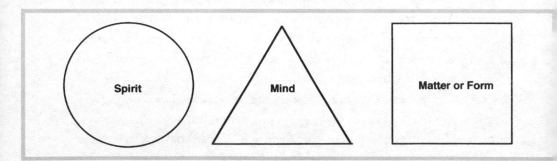

Fig. 29. The three basic shapes in geometry

string and two pegs, but this development paved the way for a symbolic exploration into the realm of ideas and forms. All regular geometric shapes can be derived using a compass. God, who has sometimes been called the 'Great Geometer', is often depicted wielding a pair.

Linked to geometry was the study of numbers. Whole numbers were considered the ideal. A completeness was perceived in them; while fractions represented numbers in the stage of becoming. In this sense, they were sometimes considered as the dynamic power of the divine moving through creation. Whole numbers were knowable, but ratios such as pi (π) could only be approximations and therefore unknowable. This was the unfathomable hand of God that permeates all things.

But while individual numbers are either rational (whole numbers) or irrational (fractional numbers), geometry can bridge this divide. The circle can both represent a rational whole number principle in its diameter as well as an irrational function along its circumference. A square and its diagonal also produce a similar phenomenon. For example, a square with sides of one unit has a diagonal which is the square root of 2 (√2) in length (Fig. 30). The term root, as in 'square root', is of ancient origin and implies a concept drawn from nature. The root of a plant is hidden yet generates and feels what lies above the surface.

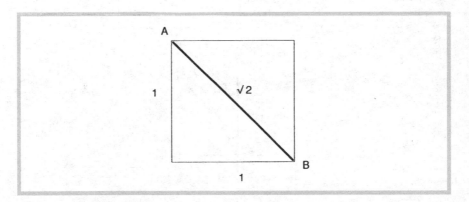

Fig. 30. Root √2 from a square

In the same way, square roots of numbers are hidden, yet are also implicit in them. For example, the square root of 16 is 4 (4 × 4 = 16). But the square root of 15 is an irrational number and not so easily calculated.

Seeking to uncover the square roots of numbers was a central theme for the ancient mathematicians. But if the square root of a number could not be resolved numerically, it could always be generated geometrically. Hence the power of geometry in the ancient mind.

Geometry was seen as a gateway into the higher aspects of human consciousness, which is why its fundamentals became woven into sacred art and architecture. Working backwards from the proportions in sacred art and architecture, we derive the concept of sacred geometry, which could perhaps best be defined as the hidden geometry found in religious building and sacred forms.

The circle, triangle and the square

The easiest geometric form to create is the circle. All you need is a pair of compasses or a string, peg and marker. Two interlocking circles can be produced by moving the compass point to the circumference of the first circle and drawing another of equal size. From this *vesica* design the three most important 'roots' (√2, √3 and √5) can be derived (Fig. 31).

Taking the radius of the circles as 1, the square root of two (√2) can be obtained from the diagonal of the square generated by the line between the

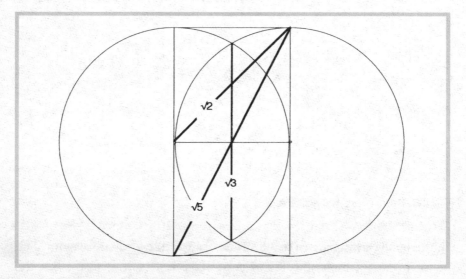

Fig. 31. Three root proportions derived from *vesica*

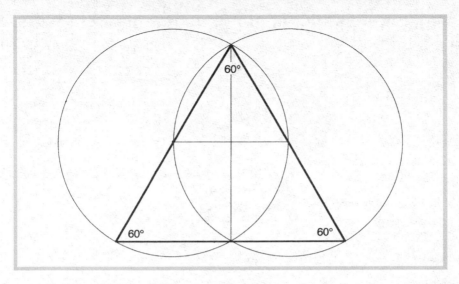

Fig. 32. Equilateral triangle derived from vesica

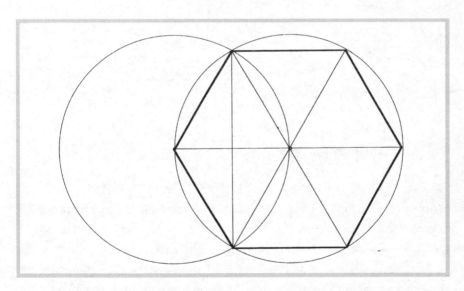

Fig. 33. Hexagon derived from vesica

two centres and two radii at right angles to it. The square root of three (√3) is given by the bisecting line that cuts the two points where the *vesica* circles intersect. The square root of five (√5) is found on the diagonal of the 2 by 1 rectangle. This rectangle also can be used to discover the 'golden mean'

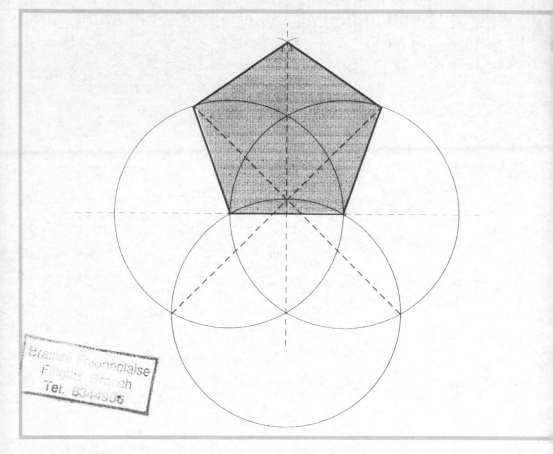

Fig. 34. Pentagon derived from vesica

proportion (see Fig. 35; Figs. 36, 37 and 38 show alternative methods for deriving the 'golden mean'). As we shall see later, the *vesica* and the 2 by 1 rectangle were central to the derivation of ancient measures.

The triangle was seen as a transitional form between the square and the circle. Eventually it came to represent a triad of gods and goddesses, usually, as in Egypt, a father, mother and son. This concept formed a central pivot of many religious belief systems and manifests itself in Christianity as the Father, Son and Holy Ghost. The triangle's most perfect form was considered to be equilateral, where the sides and the angles are all equal. Another triangle that was widely used was the one attributed to Pythagoras, although it certainly predated him by a very long time. Its

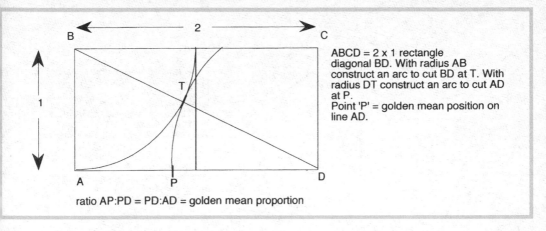

ABCD = 2 x 1 rectangle
diagonal BD. With radius AB
construct an arc to cut BD at T. With
radius DT construct an arc to cut AD
at P.
Point 'P' = golden mean position on
line AD.

ratio AP:PD = PD:AD = golden mean proportion

Fig. 35. Construction of golden mean from 2 × 1 rectangle

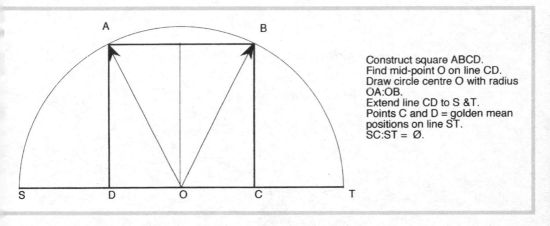

Construct square ABCD.
Find mid-point O on line CD.
Draw circle centre O with radius
OA:OB.
Extend line CD to S &T.
Points C and D = golden mean
positions on line ST.
SC:ST = Ø.

Fig. 36. Construction of golden mean from a square and a circle

sides are in the whole number ratio 3:4:5. This triangle produces the simplest version of a right-angled (90°) triangle with sides that can be expressed as whole numbers. Because of the simple numeric ratios employed, it was used in surveying as well as in art and sculpture. The pyramid of Khafre is based on it.

The circle, triangle, square and rectangle form the basis of all sacred architecture. They were, by tradition, related to each other by specific proportions. These proportions attempted to portray the inherent harmony of the cosmos. One such proportion was the 'gnomon' which was defined

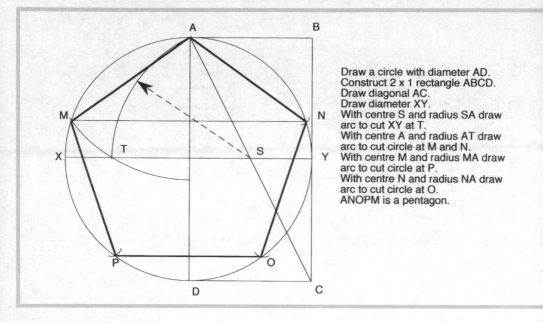

Draw a circle with diameter AD.
Construct 2 x 1 rectangle ABCD.
Draw diagonal AC.
Draw diameter XY.
With centre S and radius SA draw
arc to cut XY at T.
With centre A and radius AT draw
arc to cut circle at M and N.
With centre M and radius MA draw
arc to cut circle at P.
With centre N and radius NA draw
arc to cut circle at O.
ANOPM is a pentagon.

Fig. 37. The construction of a pentagon

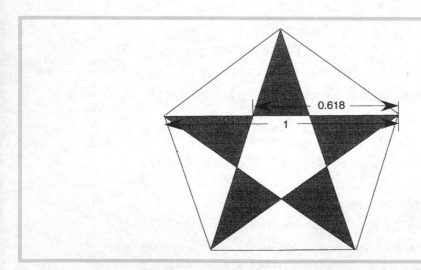

**Fig. 38. The golden mean proportion within a pentagram. It can be derived
from the pentagram and pentagon as shown**

by Aristotle as: 'Any figure which, when added to an original figure, leaves the resultant figure similar to the original.' In other words, the ratios between each additional step are always maintained. An example of this is the 'golden mean' proportion which can be expressed through the numbers 1, 1, 2, 3, 5, 8, 13, 23, and so on, where the ratios between any two adjoining numbers rapidly converge as you move up the series. The Fibonacci series is the most well known example of a gnomic ratio, but others exist.

Robert Lawlor, in his book *Sacred Geometry*, gives examples of 'gnomonic' spirals such as the one based on the Fibonacci series, which is derived from the ratio of 1:2. These expanding patterns are sometimes called 'whirling squares', giving rise to spirals which are frequently found in the natural world (Fig. 39).

Examining 'gnomons' of different ratios, I made a significant discovery. One of the 'gnomons' based on the ratio 1:3 is directly relevant to the Giza

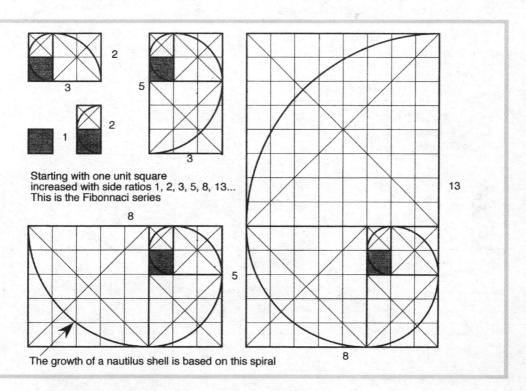

Starting with one unit square
increased with side ratios 1, 2, 3, 5, 8, 13...
This is the Fibonnaci series

The growth of a nautilus shell is based on this spiral

Fig. 39. Gnomonic spirals from square ratios 2:1

pyramids. It so happens that from this one ratio the basic proportions of Khufu's, Khafre's and Menkaure's pyramids can all be derived (Fig. 40). The development starts by drawing three abutting squares in line, to create a 3 by 1 rectangle. A square is then drawn on the longer side at each stage of its development.

The first square creates a rectangle with a ratio of 3:4. Doubling it reveals the ratio of Khafre's pyramid, 6:4. Adding two more squares, in turn, to the 3:4 rectangle gives the ratio of Khufu's pyramid, 7:11.

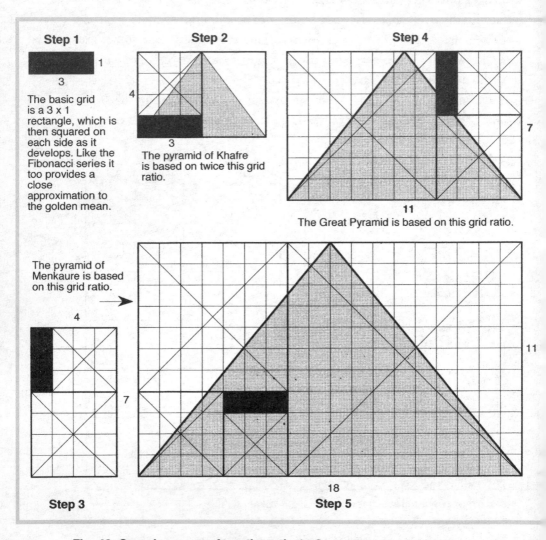

Step 1

1

3

The basic grid is a 3 x 1 rectangle, which is then squared on each side as it develops. Like the Fibonacci series it too provides a close approximation to the golden mean.

Step 2

4

3

The pyramid of Khafre is based on twice this grid ratio.

Step 4

7

11

The Great Pyramid is based on this grid ratio.

The pyramid of Menkaure is based on this grid ratio. →

4

7

Step 3

11

18

Step 5

Fig. 40. Gnomic squares from the ratio 1 : 3

Another square gives the proportions of the pyramid of Menkaure, 11:18. This device of adding squares, starting with a 3 by 1 rectangle, dramatically reveals that the pyramids reflect a natural mathematical progression in their height to base ratios. Whether through chance or choice they are linked by a harmonious geometric series.

What could have been so significant about a 3:1 ratio? Perhaps it reflected the symbolism of the Egyptian trinity of Osiris, Isis and Horus. We will probably never know for sure, but this pattern gives a valuable insight into Egyptian methods.

This discovery is also in accordance with what is known about Egyptian design methods which always seem to have been derived from squared grid patterns. There are numerous examples existing in Egyptian art, showing painters and sculptors first drawing a grid on the wall that is to be painted or carved so that fixed proportions could be maintained. The simple numeric ratios of these grids lie at the heart of all the great artistic achievements of the Egyptians.

This method was also used by many of the great Renaissance artists, such as Leonardo da Vinci. In ancient Egypt, this is exemplified in the Great Pyramid and establishes a further link with the pattern on the Marlborough Downs.

With compass and grid

Laid out over the Marlborough Downs are two interlocking circles each of 19.3 kilometres (12 miles) diameter. In this case, the circles do not form a true *vesica* pattern and so do not obviously relate to a known geometrical form.

As I was eventually to discover, the placement of these circles was not arbitrary, but conformed to a specific ratio found in the proportions of the Great Pyramid of Khufu. By superimposing a cross-section of the Great Pyramid on to the map (Fig. 21), a geometric explanation was revealed for the alignment of the galleries, passages and chambers of the pyramid. In particular, the alignment of the pyramid's Grand Gallery pointed to the centre of one of the circles.

This indicated that it would be possible to account for the position and size of all the internal chambers and galleries of the Great Pyramid in terms of pure geometry. It was an exciting prospect. To unravel this mystery, we need to discover how the Egyptians might have arrived at the design of the Great Pyramid using pure geometry before making the adjustment to fit a 7:11 grid.

It was an equilateral triangle which gave the clue in the Marlborough Downs pattern. Using this triangle as the basis, the inherent geometry of Khufu's pyramid can be revealed through Figs. 41 to 46. This simple step-by-step design sequence fixes the positions of all the chambers and passageways of the Great Pyramid.

But pure geometry creates irrational proportions. Having established the basic pattern, the next step was to convert this into a form that could be expressed in rational or whole numbers. This is the great value of the grid. When overlaid on the geometry, measures can be read off to great accuracy. We can infer that this is how the Great Pyramid was designed, as the pure geometry would create an angle of slope a fraction less than occurs in what we find in practice.

By establishing a grid with the exact proportional ratio of 7:11, everything slots neatly into position and a perfect compromise is made between pure geometry and its harmonious expression into the world of form.

Superimposing a 7:11 grid on to the pyramid shows that the King's Chamber is positioned two squares up ($\frac{2}{7}$ of the way up) from ground level, while the Queen's Chamber is one square up from ground level, or $\frac{1}{7}$ the height of the pyramid (Fig. 47). The entrance to the pyramid was, I believe, calculated from the bisecting quadrant of the first square where it cuts the side of the pyramid.

The ascending and descending passageways have angles of slope of 26°–31′–23″. At first sight, this seems very strange, but it is actually a simple gradient formed by the ratio 2:1. In other words, the passage climbs one square for every two squares it moves horizontally, forming the diagonal of a 2 by 1 rectangle. This would have been very easy to set out and construct, and it was no doubt used because of this rectangle's position in sacred geometry, in particular in the creation of the golden mean.

Using these methods all the internal passageways and chambers can be shown to be based on simple geometric proportions, although the

Figs. 41 to 46. Showing geometric development steps of the Great Pyramid

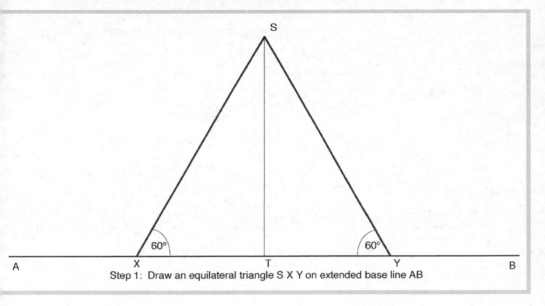

Step 1: Draw an equilateral triangle S X Y on extended base line AB

Fig. 41

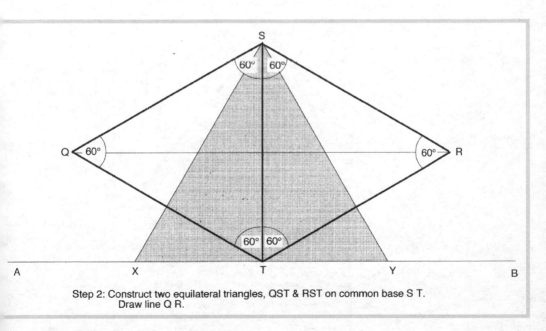

Step 2: Construct two equilateral triangles, QST & RST on common base S T.
Draw line Q R.

Fig. 42

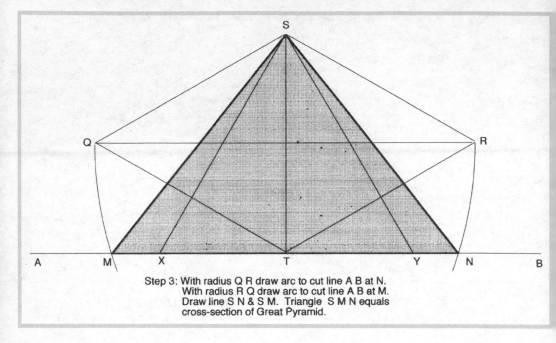

Step 3: With radius Q R draw arc to cut line A B at N.
With radius R Q draw arc to cut line A B at M.
Draw line S N & S M. Triangle S M N equals
cross-section of Great Pyramid.

Fig. 43

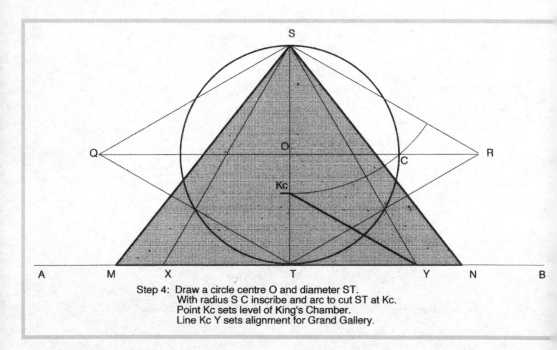

Step 4: Draw a circle centre O and diameter ST.
With radius S C inscribe and arc to cut ST at Kc.
Point Kc sets level of King's Chamber.
Line Kc Y sets alignment for Grand Gallery.

Fig. 44

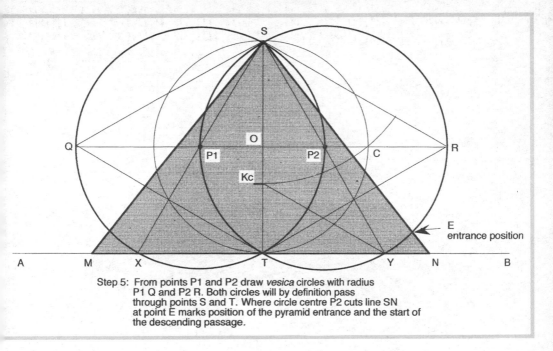

Step 5: From points P1 and P2 draw *vesica* circles with radius
P1 Q and P2 R. Both circles will by definition pass
through points S and T. Where circle centre P2 cuts line SN
at point E marks position of the pyramid entrance and the start of
the descending passage.

Fig. 45

so-called ventilation shafts do not fit to this pattern quite so neatly. This
suggests that they were probably established as part of the pyramid's astronomical alignments, as Bauval and Gilbert suggested in *The Orion
Mystery*.

Once the primary grid ratios had been established, it would then be a
simple exercise to set up angular templates which, when used with a vertical plumb, would ensure that the gradients of the various passageways
could be maintained with great accuracy.

The Giza site

Egyptologists have always maintained there is no coherent design, or
overall plan, to the layout of the pyramids on the Giza plateau. I do not
understand how they could have arrived at this conclusion. The simple
application of the known principles of ancient Egyptian measurement to
the Giza plateau clearly shows an underlying pattern. The grid pattern was

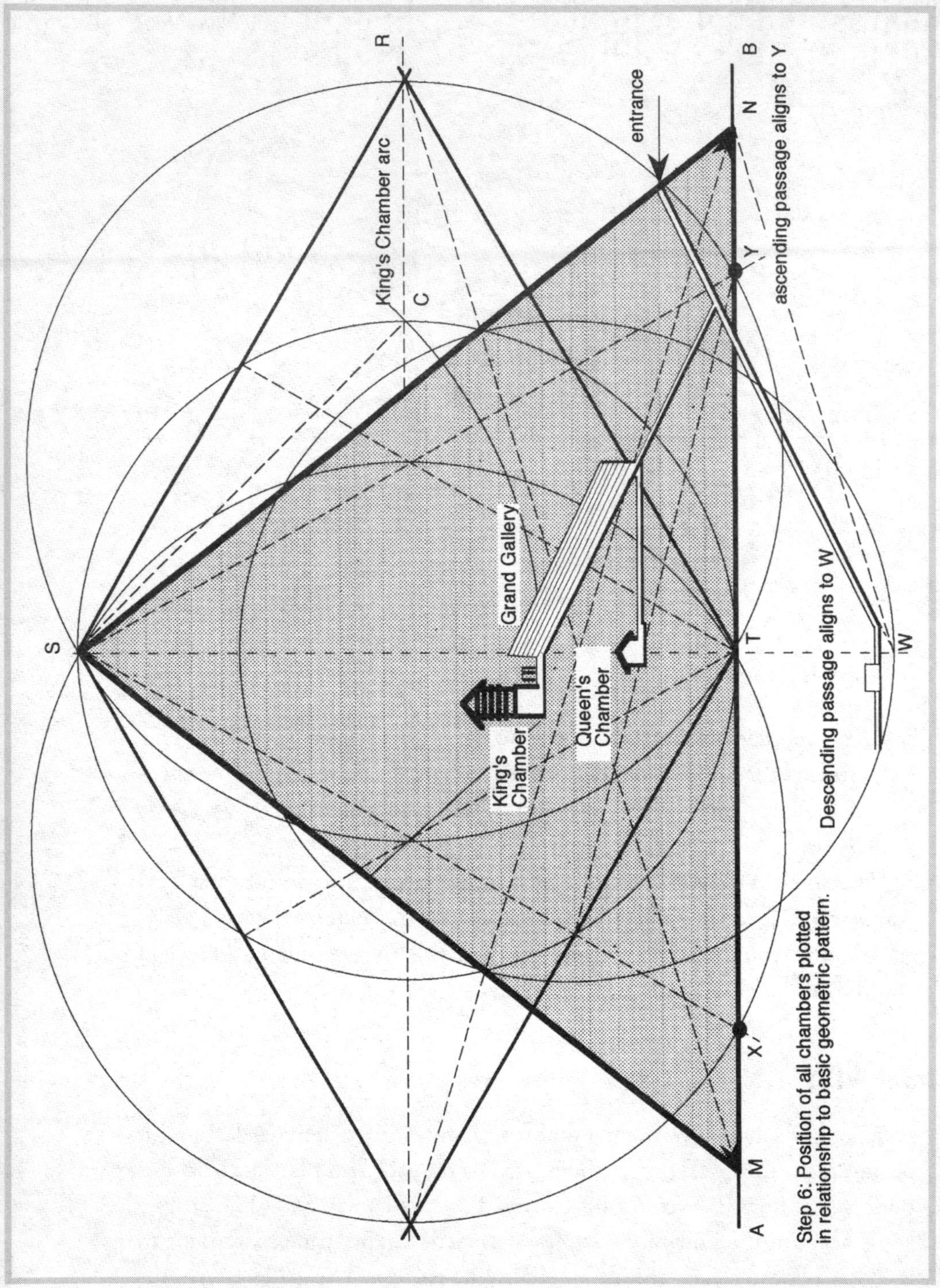

R
C
King's Chamber arc
entrance
B
N
Y
ascending passage aligns to Y
S
Grand Gallery
King's Chamber
Queen's Chamber
T
W
Descending passage aligns to W
X
M
A
Step 6: Position of all chambers plotted
in relationship to basic geometric pattern.

Fig. 46. The underlying geometry of the Great Pyramid

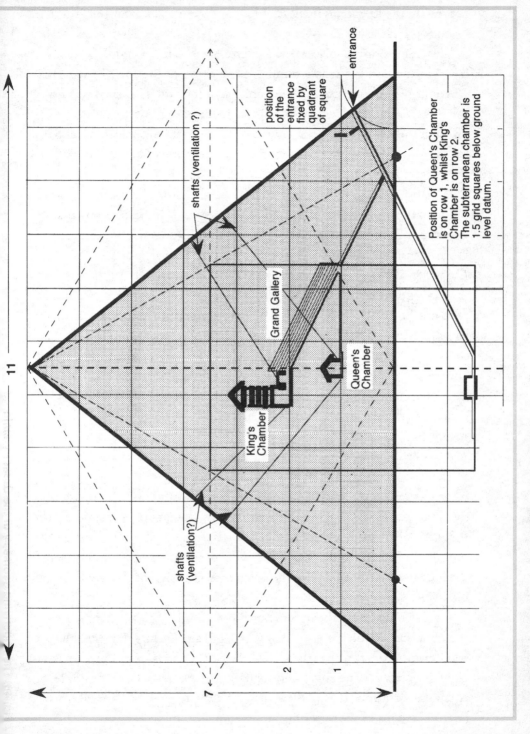

entrance

position
of the
entrance
fixed by
quadrant
of square

shafts (ventilation ?)

Grand Gallery

King's
Chamber

Queen's
Chamber

shafts
(ventilation?)

Position of Queen's Chamber
is on row 1, whilst King's
Chamber is on row 2.
The subterranean chamber is
1.5 grid squares below ground
level datum.

11

7

2

1

Fig. 47. Design of Great Pyramid based on a 7:11 grid

the system the Egyptians used. All I had to do was to look for the grid that best fits the Giza site.

The clue lies in the placement and size of the Great Pyramid which we have already said is a whole-number proportion of the size of the Earth. The unit of measure used in the construction of the Great Pyramid was the Royal Cubit. Each side is 440 Royal Cubits long. A grid pattern composed of squares of 220 Royal Cubits – half the pyramid side – overlaid on to the Giza plateau immediately fixes the positions of the pyramids of Khafre and Menkaure, as well as the Sphinx (Fig. 48).

It is a simple design, which maintains the powerful numeric ratios found in the proportions of each of the pyramids. It indicates immediately why the pyramid of Khafre is off line in its diagonal relationship to the Great Pyramid, a point heavily emphasised by Bauval and Gilbert in *The Orion Mystery* as evidence for the link with Orion's belt.

It can now be shown that the southern and eastern edges of Khafre's pyramid fit neatly on the grid. The displacement of the diagonal arises simply because it has been built with a slightly smaller ground plan than the Great Pyramid. Khafre's pyramid is 412.5 cubits square making it almost exactly $\frac{15}{16}$ the size of the Great Pyramid. Moreover, the two grid lines that determine the position of Khafre's pyramid are in golden mean proportion to the larger square grid that encompasses all three pyramids.

The chest and face of the Sphinx are positioned exactly two squares east of the eastern edge of the Great Pyramid and its chest and front right-hand paw fall on the golden mean arc from the north-eastern corner of the pyramid (see Fig. 48). The northern edge of Menkaure's pyramid fits to the grid, while its east-west position is determined by being centred on one of the north-south grid lines. The position of these monuments demonstrates, without doubt, the coherence in design of the whole of the Giza site.

I was also struck by the number of Royal Cubits – 220 – that makes up the basic squares of the grid. Being brought up on imperial measures, I was drawn to the fact that there are 220 yards in a furlong. There are also eight furlongs in one mile, and eight grid squares to half a minute of equatorial latitude. It was then that I began to wonder whether these ancient systems of measure and proportion were linked.

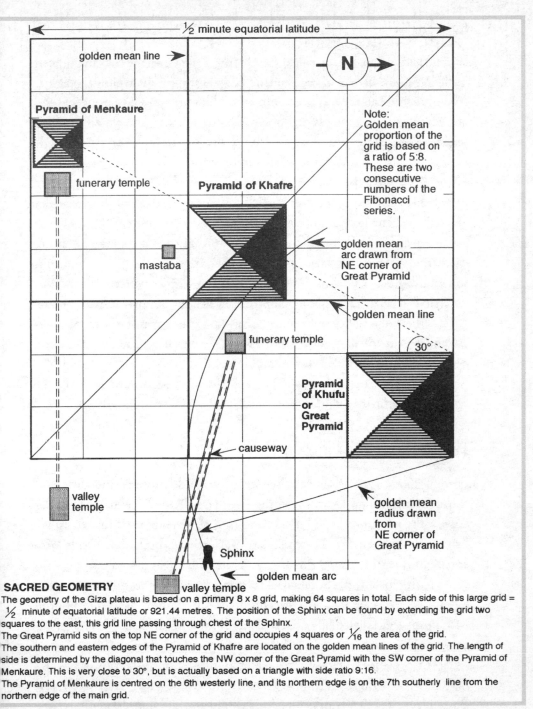

SACRED GEOMETRY

The geometry of the Giza plateau is based on a primary 8 x 8 grid, making 64 squares in total. Each side of this large grid = ½ minute of equatorial latitude or 921.44 metres. The position of the Sphinx can be found by extending the grid two squares to the east, this grid line passing through chest of the Sphinx.

The Great Pyramid sits on the top NE corner of the grid and occupies 4 squares or ¹⁄₁₆ the area of the grid.

The southern and eastern edges of the Pyramid of Khafre are located on the golden mean lines of the grid. The length of side is determined by the diagonal that touches the NW corner of the Great Pyramid with the SW corner of the Pyramid of Menkaure. This is very close to 30°, but is actually based on a triangle with side ratio 9:16.

The Pyramid of Menkaure is centred on the 6th westerly line, and its northern edge is on the 7th southerly line from the northern edge of the main grid.

Fig. 48. Geometry of the Giza Plateau

Giza revisited

In February 1996 I returned to Egypt to put my grid pattern hypothesis to the test. Site visits, I have found, are always important as they reveal features that you cannot easily see on maps. The south-east corner of the grid is a key position in the placing of Khafre's pyramid. I discovered that it is positioned on a plateau of land with good views to both the pyramids of Khafre and Menkaure, although a direct view of the eastern edge of the Great Pyramid is blocked by a knoll of ground. This would not have posed an insurmountable problem. Sighting poles could easily have been erected to overcome this difficulty.

The inspiration for analysing the structure of the Giza pyramids using mathematics and geometry came from the landscape patterns I found in the Marlborough Downs. The idea of using a grid pattern came from ancient Egyptian artists and sculptors. It fits the known measurements within the Giza site, would have been simple to set up and there is no cogent reason to suppose that it was not the architectural and planning method adopted by the pyramid architects.

Now it was time to see whether anything I had learned from Egypt would throw further light on the Marlborough Downs pattern.

The Marlborough Downs grid

Finding that a 7:11 grid fitted the Great Pyramid, I applied the same grid to the Marlborough Downs. In other words, I divided the distance of the base of the pyramid shape I had found into eleven and used that to establish a grid pattern for the whole site. It turned out that each side of a square of the grid created this way measured just over one kilometre.

As I anticipated, the St Michael ley ran two squares to the north of the baseline. However, with the exception of the church at Winterbourne Monkton, the cross-roads on the Ridgeway and the Giant's Grave, no other site on the eastern circle falls exactly on the grid (Fig. 49).

At first glance, the western circle appeared more promising. The churches of Bishops Cannings, Calstone Wellington and Compton Bassett, plus the earthworks on Morgan Hill and the tumuli on Cleavancy Hill all fall on the grid – a total of five sites out of thirteen. Despite these

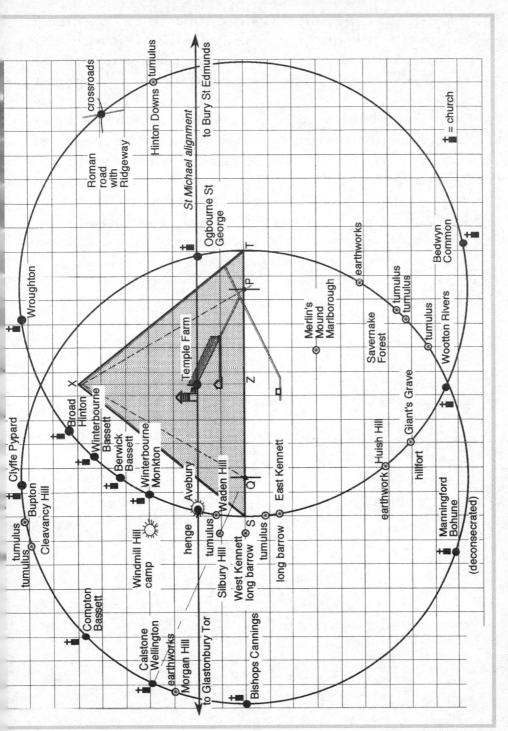

Fig. 49. Grid overlaid on Marlborough Downs

coincidences, if a grid pattern had been used it could not have been the only method employed. Not enough sites conformed to it. Some other surveying method had to have been used, based, not on grid patterns, but on pure geometry. I began looking for another way this could have been achieved.

The answer, I felt sure, lay in the relationship, in terms of geometry, I had demonstrated between the pattern on the Marlborough Downs and the Great Pyramid of Egypt. But how were these creations linked practically? Had members of the Egyptian ruling elite visited Britain to lay out and establish the landscape pattern? Or, even more bizarrely, had the Neolithic inhabitants of Britain gone to Egypt to lend a hand to the Egyptian architects who were building the pyramids? My next step was to look for illusive links between the two cultures.

7
THE ATLANTEAN CONNECTION

The links between Britain and Egypt can also be explained by a
derivation from a single cultural origin

We can be reasonably sure, from the radiocarbon dating of monuments
such as Avebury, Silbury Hill and the Sanctuary (a stone and wood circle
at the end of one of the Avebury avenues) that the twin circle pattern of
the Marlborough Downs was conceived somewhere around 3000BC.
Silbury Hill has been dated to 2750BC, while the Sanctuary is a little
earlier at around 2900BC. Allowing time for the conception of the project
to come to fruition, 3000BC is a reasonable assessment for the beginning
of the initial survey work.

This coincides with the cultural shift at the start of the third millennium BC which saw the first stages of construction of some of the most
significant megalithic sites in Britain, from the Stenness Stones of the
Orkney Islands to Stonehenge on the plains of Wiltshire – the two sites
are 840 kilometres (520 miles) apart – to Newgrange Co. Meath, Ireland
and to Castle Rigg in Cumbria. All the evidence indicates that the landscape surveying and planning in the Marlborough Downs was part of this
same cultural movement. We now need to consider whether this was a
spontaneous evolution of ideas from the native stock of the British Isles,
or whether the impulse came from elsewhere.

Climatic changes

Before considering the evidence for the origin of the landscape circle builders, something needs to be said about a dramatic climatic shift that occurred within 100 years of 3000BC. This sudden change seriously affected Europe and was probably a world-wide phenomenon.

The study of the Earth's climate over the past 100,000 years is a fascinating subject. It draws from many diverse scientific disciplines. Clearly, no meteorological charts are available from the ancient past, so it is impossible to be certain about weather in any one place on a particular day. However, it is possible to discover the shifts from one climatic period to another. The picture is built up like a jigsaw from archaeology, radiocarbon dating, geology, pollen analysis, tree-ring dating, ocean sediments, lake sediments, ice cores, isotope measurements, fossilised insects and so on.

We are now living in a relatively warm period following the end of the last Ice Age which finished around 15,000BC. This date is approximate as the retreat of the glaciers did not happen overnight. There were certainly minor variations during the following few thousand years, with the most rapid warming taking place between 8000 to 5000BC. By 5000BC the climate had settled down into what is known as the 'Atlantic' period when, in Europe and North America, the climate was from 1°–3°C warmer than today.

Writing in the *Journal of Quarternary Research* in 1974, W. Wendland and R. Bryson pointed out, from extensive analysis, that five major post-glacial epochs of environmental change, coincided with five major epochs of cultural change. There is clearly a link between these two phenomena. Around 3000BC there was a sudden climatic shift which coincided with the founding of dynastic Egypt and the beginnings of the open circle stone monuments in Britain. Prior to that date Egypt and North Africa experienced a much wetter climate than today. For example, in the millennium before 3000BC, the level of lake Chad in the Sahara desert was 30 to 40 metres (98 to 131 feet) higher than it is today, indicating that annual rainfall for the whole area was much higher at that time.

As we have already seen, the erosion effects of rain during this period suggests that the Sphinx must have been completed during this earlier wetter phase. Since 3000BC there has not been sufficient precipitation to account for the extensive water erosion found in the excavated area surrounding the

Sphinx. This is still a controversial subject for Egyptologists as they are reluctant to accept that the Sphinx could have been carved before the start of dynastic Egypt. Conversely, the limestone outer casings of the pyramids, such as remain, do not show any significant water erosion, which generally supports the orthodox dating of these monuments.

The climatic change around 3000BC was marked, in the Alps, by an advance of the glaciers. This became known as the Piora Oscillation after Val Piora where the first evidence was discovered. Pollen analysis there indicated a cold fluctuation. As Professor H.H. Lamb says in his book *Climate, History and the Modern World*:

> The duration of this colder episode seems to have been quite short, at most four centuries, but traces of it or of parallel vegetation changes extend to Alaska and the upper forest limit in the Colombian Andes and on the mountains of Kenya. There was evidently some disturbance of the global regime. Moreover it marked the end of the most stable warm climate of post-glacial times ... referred to ... as the 'Atlantic' climate period.

There is evidence from as far away as Australia that dramatic climatic upheavals occurred around the same time, supporting the concept of a major world-wide shift in climate. This wobble lasted for a few hundred years before settling down to what is known as the 'sub-boreal' epoch which lasted until about 1000BC.

This perturbation was picked up in the analysis of bristle-cone pine tree-rings made famous for their re-calibration of radiocarbon dates. Summing up the climate of this period, Professor Lamb says:

> Various peoples at various time have had legends of a Golden Age in some earlier time. The notion occurs in the literature of classical Greece and Rome and other peoples. Often it refers to an idealised state of society but occasionally there are references to a lost landscape, the best known being the Biblical tale of the Garden of Eden. It may be that some of these myths enshrine some of the changes with which this book is concerned. The times of highest civilization and their decline were, of course, not generally synchronous in different regions.

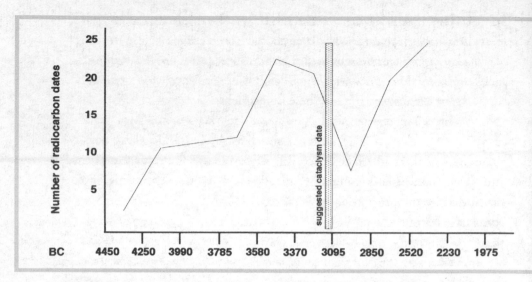

Fig. 50. Graph showing the fall in radiocarbon dates (after Burl: *Prehistoric Avebury*)

> *But there does seem to have been a very wide-ranging reduction of occupation of the north African and Arabian desert lands around 3000BC.*

Lamb may have added that Britain witnessed something similar around that period. As well as coinciding with new developments in the British megalithic structures, this period saw important changes in agriculture. Up to the end of the fourth millennium BC the upland areas of the chalk downs had been cleared of trees and the land cultivated, but this process suddenly reversed and the natural vegetation started to return. From 3200 to 2970BC, there was a marked decline in human activity, as shown in a dramatic decline in artefacts radiocarbon-dated to that period. This suggests that some calamity had overtaken the people around that time. There is also evidence of a move away from crop growing to animal husbandry. As Aubrey Burl, author of *Prehistoric Avebury*, says:

 The years between about 3250 and 2650BC constitute a 'Dark Age' in the prehistory of southern Britain, an obscure time from which little has survived . . . The evidence obtained from articles that can be

securely dated by the Carbon-14 process graphically illustrates this decline ... the evidence of steadily growing activity in southern and eastern England from the earliest Neolithic onwards, around 4450BC, suddenly and dramatically declines between 3100 and 2850BC, before recovering its steady rise as population and output began once again to increase.

The cause of this sudden change is uncertain, although it is most probably the same climatic cooling seen in the Alps and elsewhere. But, paradoxically, despite the drop in population this phase coincides with the beginning of some of the most impressive Neolithic monument buildings in the whole of Europe. So what is the connection?

From the early part of the twentieth century until relatively recently, it was thought that the developmental impulse which had fathered the cultural changes in Britain arose from the diffusion of ideas from the Middle East and Mediterranean. But a re-calibration of radiocarbon dates, which arose when tree-ring analysis pushed back the chronology, shows that the British Neolithic monuments were built in a period before the equivalent developments in Crete and elsewhere in the Mediterranean basin. As no obvious source for these new ideas could be found, the diffusionist concept was abandoned and they are now considered part of an indigenous development within Britain.

The challenge of the Marlborough circles

The existence of the Marlborough Downs landscape circles poses a serious challenge to any suggestion of an evolutionary development within Britain itself. The monuments in Wiltshire all started within a relatively short period of each other and suggest a clarity of concept unlike anything that had gone before. Nor was Wiltshire alone in this. Sites as far apart as Newgrange in Ireland and Maes Howe on the Orkney Islands carry the same cultural imprint. The skill displayed in building techniques of these monuments, aligned as they are to the midwinter sunrise and sunset, is of a very high order that does not have any obvious precedents. They are also among the oldest circular sites within the British Isles.

I have not studied these other localities in enough depth yet to ascertain whether these monuments are also part of larger landscape patterns. But I am aware of at least one other landscape circle of identical size to the two on the Marlborough Downs. It can be found in the Cotswold area in England and contains on its circumference, among other sites, the Rollright stone circle. I have not chosen to include information here on this circle because I believe it is important to establish the validity of the Marlborough Downs pattern in its own right. I am also all too aware of how easy it is to see patterns where they do not exist, at least as consciously created forms. Yet I am also sure that, given time and further study, other landscape circles will emerge.

An analysis of the location of circular monuments – stone circles, henges and round barrows – shows them heavily weighted in the western half of the country, declining drastically in number as one moves towards the east. The one exception is Aberdeenshire, on the eastern coast of Scotland, which originally held one of the most extensive concentrations of stone circles in the whole of the British Isles.

Access to island sites such as Callanish in the Outer Hebrides could only have been from the sea. There would also have had to be a seaborne link from the north of Scotland to Ireland and to the western seaboard of France and the Iberian peninsular where other similar sites are found. However improbable, the only logical conclusion is that there was an influx of people around 3000BC that came not from the east but across the sea from the west, probably landing initially in Ireland before spreading into the western half of the British Isles. But where did these people come from?

This same timeframe also saw the start of dynastic Egypt with its sudden flowering of a sophisticated cosmology, a written language and refined artistic skills. As with the development of the British monuments, some authorities have suggested that this was an indigenous development, while others believed that it was spawned by influences from the Indus and Euphrates. The third alternative, raised by Professor Emery, was that this impulse came from another as yet undiscovered area.

Despite some objections, there is good circumstantial evidence to support the following ideas:

▲ Both Britain and Egypt experienced a cultural acceleration around 3100BC which could have stemmed from the infiltration of a new group of people with more sophisticated concepts;

▲ This date coincided with a hemispheric climatic disruption of sufficient intensity to cause the decline in numbers of the indigenous peoples in both Britain and North Africa;

▲ The design of the Great Pyramid and the geometry of the Marlborough Downs landscape pattern somehow connects the ancient cultures of Britain and Egypt.

If the answer is that this new sophistication was brought by the influx of a new people, we have a new problem. They have no obvious cultural home. This has been one of the main stumbling blocks for Egyptologists when it comes to accepting Professor Emery's ideas.

The Atlantean realm

The evidence from the British Isles shows, from an analysis of radiocarbon dates, that the cultural shifts moved from west to east. In France, the magnificent monuments of Carnac on the Atlantic seaboard have no developmental cousins inland to the east. The evidence in Spain and Portugal, which again border the Atlantic Ocean, suggests that the peoples who put up these monuments came by sea. Egypt is, of course, an exception. It does not lie close to the Atlantic Ocean, although it is very likely that the cultural impulse that led to the building of the pyramids entered Egypt by way of the Nile delta. And Egypt lends the most important clue to the origin of these people.

Since it was first mentioned by Plato in the *Timaeus*, the concept of Atlantis has been the inspiration of writers and the bane of academics. Sceptics see Plato's account as nothing more than an allegorical tale, while believers claim that he was speaking from factual information. So what did Plato actually say? The following is the account he gave which I have taken from Murry Hope's book *Atlantis – Myth or Reality?* In the style of the time it is written as a dialogue between Socrates and his pupil Critias. In the account, Critias is reporting information he has received from a Greek poet called Solon, who had in turn gained the information from the Egyptian priests at Sais in the Nile delta. The account goes on:

 At the head of the Egyptian delta, where the river Nile divides, there is a certain district which is called the district of Sais, and the great city of the district is also called Sais, and is the city from which Amasis the king was sprung . . . Now, the citizens of this city are great lovers of the Athenians, and say that they are in some ways related to them. Thither came Solon, who was received by them with great honour; and he asked the priests who were most skilful in such matters as about antiquity, and he made the discovery that neither he nor any other Hellene knew anything worth mentioning about the times of old. On one occasion, when he was drawing them to speak of antiquity, he began to tell them about the most ancient things in our part of the world . . . Thereupon, one of the priests, who was of great age said, 'O Solon, Solon, you Hellenes are but children, and there is never an old man who is a Hellene.' Solon hearing this, said 'What do you mean?' 'I mean to say,' he replied, 'that in mind you are all young; there is no old opinion handed down among you by ancient tradition, nor any science which is hoary with age. And I will tell you the reasons for this: there have been, and will be again, many destructions of mankind arising out of many causes. There is a story which even you have preserved, that once upon a time Phaëthon, the son of Helios [the sun], having yoked the steeds in his father's chariot, burnt up all that was upon the earth, because he was not able to control them and was himself destroyed by a thunderbolt. Now, this has the form of a myth, but really signifies . . . a great conflagration of things upon the earth . . . Our histories tell of a mighty power which was aggressing wantonly against the whole of Europe and Asia to which your city put an end. This power came forth out of the Atlantic Ocean, for in those days the Atlantic was navigable and there was an island situated in front of the straits that you call the Pillars of Hercules [Straits of Gibraltar]. This island was larger than Libya and Asia put together, and was the way to other islands, and from the islands you might pass through the whole of the opposite continent which surrounded the true ocean . . . Now, in the island of Atlantis there was a great and

wonderful empire, which ruled over the whole island and several others, as well as over parts of the continent; and besides these, they subjected the parts of Libya . . . as far as Egypt . . . But afterwards there occurred violent earthquakes and floods and in a single day and night of rain . . . the island of Atlantis . . . was sunk beneath the sea.'

Plato, in the dialogue, then goes on to describe the achievements of Atlantis portraying it, at the height of its power, as an ideal state. Its destruction he placed 9000 years before the time of Solon which would have been around 9600BC.

Like ancient Egypt the story of Atlantis has held a perennial fascination for me. I once jokingly said in my early twenties that I had two ambitions in my life. One was to see Atlantis rise from its watery grave, the other to go for a trip in a flying saucer. This probably speaks volumes about the balance of my mind at the time, yet I have continued to follow the Atlantis story closely as it has emerged over the years.

With so many books devoted to exploring the Atlantis story, I could not hope to do justice in one short chapter to all the evidence that has been presented by the writers, each with their own theories on whether it existed, its location and the date of its destruction. I can only summarise some of the salient points.

The legend of a universal flood is found scattered widely through many mythologies and legends on both sides of the Atlantic. It is best known, of course, as the biblical story of Noah's ark. But the diversity of these flood stories suggests that they have been founded on a real event, most probably occurring at the very edge of chronological history. The *Encyclopaedia of World Mythology* says:

 The traditions of many widely separated peoples include legends of a great flood which, at some time in the remote past, overwhelmed vast tracts of land and flourishing cities, and drowned all or nearly all the inhabitants, men and beasts alike. One man only, with his family and, usually, a number of animals, manages to escape, being supernaturally warned of the coming disaster . . . Eventually, after a period varying in different traditions from a few days to several months, the anger of the gods is appeased, the floods recede and dry land reappears.

Before accepting any new concept, science requires hard and repeated evidence to support ideas that are not already part of the perceived wisdom. This is both its strength and weakness. However, in the last decade the idea that the Earth was once hit by a comet or asteroid has gained credence. Scientists now accept that such a collision probably caused the extinction of the dinosaurs around 65 million years ago. There is now speculation about when, not if, another cataclysmic collision will occur. So the concept of a global catastrophe has now been accepted.

Paul Dunbavin, in his thoroughly researched and detailed book *The Atlantis Researches*, published in 1992, presents powerful evidence to show that the impact of a large comet or asteroid could cause the Earth to tilt by only one or two degrees on its axis. This would be sufficient to cause a huge displacement of the seas which, due to the rotation of the Earth, bulges out around the equator. The displacement of this bulge would create a vast tidal surge, sufficient to swamp many land masses until geophysical forces re-adjusted themselves. The resulting wobble would also cause a climatic disturbance lasting several hundred years. Such a climatic upheaval occurred around 3000BC which, according to Dunbavin, is when Atlantis was destroyed.

I found it interesting that I had arrived at exactly the same conclusion independently, before reading Dunbavin's book. It is the most authoritative work that I have come across in presenting scientific evidence in support of a global catastrophe of sufficient intensity to cause the destruction of a large landmass.

The Maltese temples

The Maltese archipelago, composed of the main islands of Malta, Gozo and Comino and the two small islets of Cominotto and Filfla, lies about 80 kilometres (50 miles) south of Sicily. Small as they are, Malta and Gozo between them contain one of the highest densities of prehistoric temple sites in the world. They are also some of the oldest. There are 43 temples on Malta and nine on Gozo, which principally date from a period between around 3500 to 3000BC, although some temples are as early as 4500BC and cave sanctuaries have been dated to around 5000BC. A few of these temples were excavated in the nineteenth century, but it was not until Professor Zammit became Director of the Malta Museum, around 1909, that a systematic study was undertaken.

One of the most famous of these temples is Hagar Qim on the southern coast of Malta (see **photograph 21**). Curiously shaped, it looks like the cross-section of a skull and is dated to the end of the fourth millennium BC. It contains some massive stones weighing as much as thirty tonnes. From the discovery of statues and statuettes in this and other Maltese temples, it is thought that they were dedicated to the worship of a 'goddess'. This was also expressed in the architecture through curved semi-circular and elliptical chambers which in some temples, like Ggantija on Gozo, were linked together in a 'trefoil' pattern.

Despite its long history, temple building came to an abrupt halt around 3000BC and the entire population disappeared from the islands which were not re-inhabited for 500 years. As Marija Gimbutas says in her book *The Civiliation of the Goddess*:

 With the great temple of Tarxien, the temple building period of Malta came to an end. It is not known what happened to the temple builders, but perhaps they abandoned the islands because of deforestation or crop failure, followed by famine, plague or crop failures.

Archaeologist Joseph Ellul has his own ideas on what caused Malta to be abandoned. In his book, *Malta's Prediluvian Culture*, he plots the history of the famous temple sites to their destruction about 5000 years ago. Examining the temple site of Hagar Qim, archaeologists found some of the huge stone blocks of the temple had been thrown down on one side as though hit by some huge force travelling from west to east. Ellul also mentions:

 The people of Hagar Qim used mortar to cover up unwanted holes or crevices. Some of this mortar or cement has joined some of the fallen blocks and petrified itself into hard stone. The fact reveals that when the temple crumbled it was under water for some time, so that the mortar had time to dissolve, settle down under water, and then, when dry again became hard and subsequently petrified. Had the mortar

*not fallen under water it would have crumbled into dust and
remained so, without sticking to anything.*

Joseph Ellul is convinced that what is today the Straits of Gibraltar was
originally blocked off from the Atlantic Ocean. At some point around
3000BC, the sea broke through this barrier sending a huge tidal wave surg-
ing through the Mediterranean. In the process, it inundated the temples
of Malta depositing a layer of silt and sand a metre deep over the entire
island. In the same book he mentions the town of Xari Suste, in
Mesopotamia, which was buried under sand to a depth of three metres,
leaving tables set ready for meals and skeletons in sleeping positions, suggesting that it had suddenly been overwhelmed by a catastrophe.

Further evidence of this destruction, which also appears in Summerian
mythology and legend, was unearthed in 1929, when Sir Leonard
Woolley excavated Ur, which lies near the city of An Nasiriya in modern
Iraq. The *Encyclopaedia of World Mythology* says:

*The deluge is also mentioned in the Summerian king lists wherein are
enumerated their rulers from the countries' first beginnings. After
some early kings have been listed it is stated: 'Then came the Flood.
And after the Flood, kingship again descended from heaven.'
Archaeologists of the twentieth century have proved that the historians
of the far-off days were right in supposing that their land had once
been devastated by a catastrophic flood. In 1929, during his excavations at Ur, Sir Leonard Woolley found clear evidence of a wide-
spread inundation, greater in extent and magnitude than anything
subsequently known in the region, which had occurred about 3000BC.*

Further evidence was to show that this flood had been vast enough to
cover practically the whole of Lower Mesopotamia and drown most of its
inhabitants.

French sea levels

Significant changes also occurred in other parts of Europe at that time. In
an article by C.J. Carre ('Late Neolithic and Bronze Age in Western

France', *Proceedings of the Prehistoric Society*, 1982), he considered the effect of sea level changes on late Neolithic and Bronze Age settlements in the marshlands of the Marais poitevin and noted that 'the sea level was not regular, but that there was a peak around 3000BC, followed by a trough, and then a gradual rise towards the present levels during the last two millennia'.

These findings reflect the same pattern of significant climatic changes at or slightly before 3000BC.

There is not space here to list all the corroborative evidence in support of a serious global disturbance sufficient to cause dramatic sea level changes and climatic perturbations around 5000 years ago. In addition to those already mentioned, others include:

1) a sulphate concentration in the Greenland ice cores. Causes for this are unknown but possibly volcanic or comet impact;
2) the Dead Sea levels suddenly rising 1000 metres (300 feet);
3) an acid peak in the Greenland Dye 3 isotope ratio;
4) heavy flooding in the Navajo country of the American Southwest, based on the studies from eight sites;
5) a rise in sea level in the Nile delta;
6) massive climatic perturbation discovered from alluvial lake deposits in a box canyon in south-east Utah, USA.

The Atlantean cataclysm

There may well have been cataclysms in earlier times, such as that indicated by Graham Hancock in his book *Fingerprints of the Gods*, which he dates to around 10,500BC. But if, as many exponents of Atlantis claim, the Atlantean diaspora sent the seeds of civilisation to Egypt, one would have expected to see those same seeds germinating within a short time of their arrival, not lie dormant for 8000 years. This, I believe, is the great flaw with any earlier datings for an Atlantean cataclysm.

Important cultural shifts can be seen clearly in Europe and Egypt, but what of the Americas? Here the evidence is more tenuous. There is little direct archaeological evidence that points to an Atlantean origin. There is plenty of circumstantial evidence though. The mythologies of many of the

Native American tribes speak of global destruction by floods. One description of this destruction can be found in the *Popul Vuh*, one of the sacred books still preserved from Central America. This account is taken from Ignatius Donnelly's book *Atlantis*:

 Then the waters were agitated by the will of the Heart of Heaven, and a great inundation came upon the heads of these creatures . . . They were engulfed, and a resinous thickness descended from heaven . . . the face of the earth was obscured, and a heavy darkening rain commenced – rain by day rain by night . . . Water and fire contributed to the universal ruin at the time of the last great cataclysm which preceded the fourth creation.

The book-burning Bishop of Yucatan, Diego de Landa, believed that the early peoples of Central America had come from across the sea to the east. He reported home:

 Some of the old people of Yucatan say they heard from their ancestors that this land was occupied by a race of people who came from the east and whom God had delivered by opening twelve paths through the sea.

When the Spanish first arrived in Mexico, they were told by the Aztecs that their race originated on a large island called Aztlan which lay in the ocean to the east. H.H. Bancroft, in his book *Native Races of the Pacific States* published in 1874, said:

 The original home of the . . . [ancestors of the Aztecs] . . . was Aztlan, the location of which is subject to much discussion. The causes that led to their exodus from that country can only be conjectured; but they may have supposed to have been driven out by enemies, for Aztlan is described as a land too fair and beautiful to be left willingly in the mere hope of finding better.

The geographic location of Aztlan, which means the 'place of the cranes', has been much debated by modern scholars. Some say that it is in the north, near the Pacific coast in the west; others that it is on the Isla de los Idolos in Tamiahua lagoon, on the Gulf of Mexico in north Veracruz. The Aztecs believed that Aztlan was in the middle of the Atlantic Ocean.

Add to that the Mayan calendar, which starts at 12 August 3114BC on our calendar. The Maya believed the start of their calendar marked the destruction of the previous race of men. The evidence now confirms that this was a time of climatic disturbance which could have been commensurate with a cataclysm and inundation affecting the sea levels detected by Carre. The Maya placed their homeland somewhere in 'the region of the rising sun' – to the east – which we could infer was in the Atlantic Ocean.

Plate tectonics

In the early part of the twentieth century, the German meteorologist A.L. Wegener postulated the concept of 'continental drift' to explain the link between geological and fossil records on either side of the Atlantic. His ideas eventually evolved into the theory of 'plate tectonics' which explains how the continents move. It can easily be seen that the west coast of Africa and the east coast of South America fit together like a jigsaw. They were once joined and have slowly drifted apart. The fit between the two sides of the north Atlantic is not so precise. If they were pushed back together again there would be a 'hole' which occurs near the islands of the Azores. Could this hole be where Atlantis belonged? If lands can rise to create mountains, surely they could also fall, particularly in volcanically sensitive areas?

In his book *The Secrets of Atlantis*, Otto Muck studied the impact that the removal of a large landmass in mid-Atlantic would have had upon the direction of the ocean currents, particularly the Gulf Stream. We now know that all currents have a great influence upon climate and any change in the direction of the Gulf Stream would have undoubtedly created great climatic upheaval until adjustments had been made to the changes. This could be another explanation for the Piora climatic anomaly, around 3000BC.

There is no room here to examine all the different theories on the causes of the destruction of Atlantis, but there is much circumstantial evidence that it did happen. It is true to say that 'facts' can easily be adjusted to fit pet theories, but the arrival of the same sophisticated geometric, astronomical and mathematical knowledge in dynastic Egypt and the circular megalithic culture in Britain at the same time is consistent with the destruction of an Atlantean civilisation around 3000BC.

It is possible, of course, that after the cataclysm, dispersed groups of survivors tried to maintain a level of contact with each other. In his book *Isis and Nepthys in Wiltshire*, published in 1938, J.R. Harris suggested that certain British place-names like 'Tot' are of Egyptian origin and postulated that the British Isles were visited in dynastic times. Thor Heyerdahl's *Ra II* expedition demonstrated that it was possible for the ancient Egyptians to have crossed the Atlantic on rafts in the pharaonic era. We know that the Egyptians visited and traded with other lands. Egyptian faience beads have been discovered in some Bronze Age burial mounds in Britain. This does not prove that the Egyptians themselves visited Britain, as the beads could have changed hands many times on the way. However, tied into this discovery, research is going on in Egypt as to whether the ancient Egyptians had the technical sailing ability to make a sea connection. It is possible that their adventurous spirit could have brought them to Britain, a belief firmly held by some scholars in the nineteenth century. This case was argued more recently by John Ivimy in his book *The Sphinx and the Megaliths*, published in 1974. He says:

> ... in 1913, the Australian anthropologist Sir Grafton Elliot Smith wrote a paper in which he ascribed the origin of the megalithic people's chambered tombs to the mastabas built in Egypt in the early part of the third millennium BC. Referring to this paper in his book on prehistoric Wales, Sir Mortimer Wheeler said 'the general analogy between mastabas and many types of chambered tomb is too close to be accidental'.
>
> If the similarity was not accidental, it could only have come about as a result of a movement of people from Egypt to England about the time ... of the Third and Fourth dynasties when the civilisation of Egypt was at its height.

The discovery of the Marlborough Downs pattern lends weight to a link between ancient Egypt and Britain. There is a chronological synchronicity between building developments in both lands during the first 500 years of the third millennium BC. The links between Britain and Egypt can also be explained from a derivation from a single cultural origin at the end of the fourth millennium BC.

In music, language, myth and art, there is evidence that widely disparate groups had some common origin. The musician Bob Quinn has discovered clear links between the distinct sean-nos singing of Connemara in Ireland with the Berber music of North Africa. In his book *Atlantean*, he also describes a visit he made to a stone-circled tumulus at M'Zora, Morocco. After much searching, he came across the mound near the small town of Sidi Yemani. He describes his visit like this:

 It took another two miles of squelching through mud to reach the site. It was set in the middle of a cluster of houses and gardens. The last time I saw an identical stone was at Punchestown, in Naas, Co Kildare (Ireland). Coming nearer we could see the circle of stones, some of them trespassing on gardens. It was the remains of the tumulus. Most of the central part had been gouged out, probably for the stones and gravel, just as similar tombs had been in Ireland. There were 167 stones in the circle according to our count. A pillar dominated the landscape. Newgrange once boasted such a stone. It was last seen in 1770.

Despite the apparent architectural link in the style of this mound with those in Britain, Quinn could find no academic support for a cultural connection. It was suggested that, although this mound was seemingly related to its British cousins, it was the result of an independent expression at some stage of the distant past. But if one accepts the idea of Atlantis and its destruction, the connection becomes readily understandable.

What is missing to fully cement the link between Neolithic Britain and dynastic Egypt is the hieroglyphic inscriptions found on Egyptian monuments. Their absence on the British monuments of the same era cannot be easily explained away if, as I am postulating, both cultures stemmed from a common source. Nor was there any attempt to fashion and dress the stones in the British monuments, except at Stonehenge, although specific shapes of natural stones were often selected. This can be seen more clearly with the lozenge stones of the West Kennett Avenue.

It is possible that the survivors from Atlantis did not arrive in sufficient numbers to dominate the lands where they made landfall. Perhaps all they could do was adapt and modify the culture already instigated by the indigenous people. In Egypt, this led to the development of pictorial writing, while in Britain the ideas were symbolically represented in rock art carvings. Perhaps, the enigmatic spirals, lozenges, wavy lines and cup and ring markings found at Newgrange in Ireland and elsewhere along the Atlantic seaboard – the Gavrinis mound in Brittany and on standing stones at Carapito in Portugal – are pictograms that could be interpreted only by those who knew the key. It is interesting to note that the symbols of certain Egyptian hieroglyphs, such as the 'n' sound, depicted as a horizontal zigzag line, are found carved on to monuments such as Newgrange in Ireland.

Many monuments from this period, such as Stonehenge, are aligned to significant solar positions indicating the importance of the sun within these cultures. The solar cult was also the most powerful part of the Egyptian belief system.

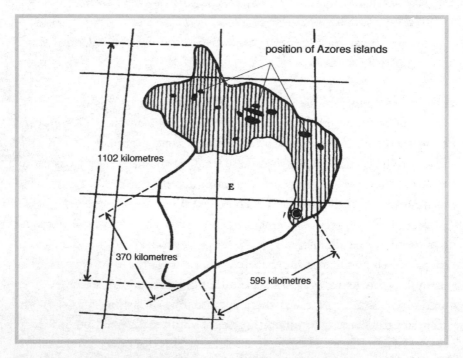

Fig. 51. Detailed map of Atlantis as suggested by Otto Muck

There are undoubtedly many unanswered questions, yet in both cultures there is evidence of swift progress to a high level of attainment followed by a gradual decline. Nothing resembling the magnificence of the pyramids and the Old Kingdom monuments was ever achieved again in Egypt while the monuments at Newgrange, Silbury Hill, Maes Howe, Stonehenge and Avebury were not matched until the building of the cathedrals in the Middle Ages, more than 4000 years later.

The latitude of Atlantis

There is one other piece of circumstantial evidence from ancient measurements that could help us fix the position of Atlantis. The Earth is not a perfect sphere. Because of its rotation, the Earth bulges slightly at the equator and is flattened at the poles. This means that the length of each degree of latitude increases as one travels away from the equator. For example, there are 110,573 metres (362,679 feet) in one degree latitude at the equator. At the pole, this increases to 111,697 metres (366,366 feet). The latitude where the number of metres shifts from the 110,000 range to 111,000 is just under 39°.

However, there are a group of ancient measures which make this shift between latitudes 32° and 33°. This group includes the Brasse and Remen, two measures derived from ancient Egypt. The Egyptians counted a minute of arc as being a 1000 Brasse, while the Remen was related to the cubit. The Brasse, for example, moves from 59,999 Brasse per degree on 32° latitude to 60,008 at 33° latitude, while the Remen shifts from 299,995 to 300,041 in the same way. Both the Brasse and the Remen are products of a system based on an 11.55 metre (38 feet) measurement. There are precisely 9600 of these units between 32° and 33° latitude. With factors of 8 and 12 (12 × 8 = 96), this number could have been chosen deliberately because it embodied important numeric symbolism. This suggests that, if Atlantis was the motherland of ancient measures, then its most likely position would be between latitudes 32° and 33°.

These parallels run to the north of Egypt, and miss most of the north coast of Africa. They cut through the Atlas mountains in Morocco before crossing Madeira, sometimes thought of as a possible site of Atlantis.

Morocco is the home of the Berber peoples whose language and songs can be understood by the Gaelic-speaking Irish. From his research into Atlantis, Otto Muck fixes the position of Atlantis between latitudes 32° and 40°. This would fit with the idea of the 32° parallel being pivotal to the fixing of ancient measures.

In fairness, it should be pointed out that the 32° parallel also runs through Mesopotamia, the homeland of the Babylonian civilisation, which is another contender for the origin of these ancient measures.

The continent of Atlantis

In Plato's dialogue, the size of Atlantis is given as larger than 'Libya and Asia put together'. This is surely an exaggeration. Even plate tectonics and theories of continental drift make it difficult for scientists to believe that such a large landmass existed in the middle of the Atlantic Ocean. But if we can discount Plato's date for the destruction of Atlantis, why not its size too? After all, a large continent is not necessary for the development of an advanced culture.

Crete is an island of just 8,614 square kilometres (3326 square miles), about twice the size of the county of Hampshire in England. But it boasted the sophisticated Minoan culture and has been identified, by some, as Atlantis. Egypt itself, although geographically a large area, is in practice restricted to the very narrow habitable corridor of the Nile valley and the area around the Delta. A total area of this habitable area is only 28,490 square kilometres (11,000 square miles), about one third of the size of Ireland.

For comparison, the total area of the nine volcanic islands of the Azores is around 2380 square kilometres (919 square miles) less than a third the size of Crete. However, these islands, stretching across 640 kilometres (400 miles) of ocean, cover an area of more than 259,000 square kilometres (100,000 square miles), larger than that of Great Britain. Were these islands joined together as one landmass they would certainly be an Atlantean contender. However, the depth of the ocean around the Azores means that the sea-level rises caused by the pole shift suggested by Paul Dunbavin could not in itself be sufficient to explain the complete submergence of a landmass in this area unless affected by some other catastrophic event. Geological studies on and around the Azores have shown this to be unlikely. A more tenable area would be further to the north somewhere along the North Atlantic ridge which is the most recent geologically. It is not beyond the bounds of possibility for volcanic activity in conjunction with a pole shift to have caused the complete destruction of a landmass or island in this area of the Atlantic.

In this context we should not forget the sulphate concentration obtained from the Greenland ice-core samples which have been dated to around 3100BC. This could have been caused by either volcanic activity or comet impact and perhaps both.

The Atlantis legend will probably never be put to rest until the whole of the Atlantic's ocean floor is explored and mapped to the same level of precision available to terrestrial cartographers. With the submersible and ultrasonic techniques being developed today, that time cannot be far away. Indeed, reports surface from time to time suggesting cyclopean structures discovered deep on the floor of the Atlantic sea-bed. When photographs are produced, with the same clarity as those of the wreck of the *Titanic*, we will then know one way or another whether Atlantis is myth or reality. Until such time, we can only wait and speculate.

There is not the space here to put forward more arguments both for or against the existence of Atlantis, only to suggest that it is the most likely explanation for the cultural impulse that entered both Egypt and Britain around 3100BC. The date of this destruction is much later than most Atlantologists would accept but it is the one that, to my mind, best fits the facts.

Perhaps the last word on the final days of Atlantis should come from a booklet called *Atlantis Past and to Come*. It reproduces the report of a medium 'channelling', who said that they had obtained a message from a discarnate being who claimed to have had an incarnation on Atlantis. Channelling is gaining a following, particularly in America. It is based on the idea of a medium creating a sympathetic rapport with a discarnate being and then relaying whatever messages are being conveyed to them. I appreciate that such an idea might stretch the credulity of readers. Nevertheless, it does describe the sort of destruction that might have taken place and hints at pre-diluvian Atlantean influences on Egypt and elsewhere:

The days and cycles passed and strange signs began to appear in the skies, signs that meant little to the 'evil' practitioners but much to the high priests of truth. There were also earthquakes where they had never before been experienced. Volcanoes occurred and the seasons became less and less defined ... Soon it became apparent that something was wrong. The planet Lucifer that shone so brightly in the heavens no longer smiled on mankind from his customary seat in space but now appeared nearer to Earth, growing steadily larger and brighter every month ... Fear spread its icy cloak around a strangely tense land. But the spirits of the great ones did not desert their charges in the hour of need. 'You must leave your homes and familiar cities and villages, leave the good land which has been so much part of you for so long and journey forth into the dark unknown ...' In small bands they set forth from the shores of their native land, eastward, westward, to the north and the south. Only a few of the true high priests remained like the captains who stay as their ship goes down, for they felt their path lay with their homeland.

Before the last dark day began, the reigning Chief High Priest, called together all the spiritual powers that were used by the priests of light on the Atlantean vibration. By the use of a certain ritual he concealed and sealed these energies so that none could call on them until the time came when there would be people incarnate on Earth who would possess the right knowledge and wisdom to unseal them. The key to this seal he placed in a certain country of the world, the land you call England. Its symbol is the Sword of the Archangel Michael – or the Excalibur of Arthur – and its withdrawal will signify the birth of a new Atlantean race.

Many Atlanteans who had left their land some years previously had already begun to build thriving communities. In Khemu [Egypt] they met with success laying the corner stone for dynastic Egypt, as also in parts of Central and South America, Europe and Greece. For many years the Atlanteans were able to maintain their way of life but, as time went on, the ways of the natural inhabitants predominated increasingly. Stories of the deeds and teachings of these tall fair strangers have come down to you in legend form although much distorted by the physical surroundings of those times.

Then came the cataclysm. Great particles of matter were hurled through space; burning meteorites streamed down followed by black rain that swamped the people it settled upon. The bowels of the Earth heaved in protest and the mountains spat back. The great land of Atlantis and those upon it sank beneath the waves.

This was written in the 1960s, before current ideas of comets or asteroids hitting the Earth became the vogue.

8

BY ROD AND CUBIT

*An encoded message from the past waiting to be deciphered by those
in a future generation*

In Europe we have adopted the metric system as the basis of our measures. This system was instituted as one of Napoleon's reforms to sort out the mess of the pre-Revolutionary French measures which had become hopelessly confused and debased. A commission of enquiry was set up, which eventually decided to base a new measurement on the distance between the North Pole and the equator along the line of the Paris meridian. In 1801, the length of this measure, to be known as the metre, was fixed as one ten millionth part of the quadrant of that meridian.

This was a significant step, linking a system of measures to the dimensions of the planet Earth. But the circles on the Marlborough Downs suggest that this was not the first time this link was made. It has been shown here that an ancient people had calculated the equatorial circumference. I can also show that they calculated the polar meridian. Through my studies of the circles on the Marlborough Downs, I can demonstrate links between many, if not all, of the ancient measures that emerged in the western world and the proportions of the planet. This may seem like an extravagant claim but my researches bear it out.

Unified measures

Many students of the ancient world have intuitively felt that there had to be an underlying basis unifying ancient measurements and that there might also have been a common source of origin. In *The Secrets of the Great Pyramid*, Livio Stecchini says: 'All the measures of length, volume, and weight of the ancient world, including those of China and India, constituted a rational and organic system, which can be reconstructed from a fundamental unit of length.'

In the latter half of the nineteenth century, Friedrich Hultsch, an eminent authority on this subject, believed all ancient measures could be derived from the Egyptian foot of 300 millimetres (11.8 inches) and the cubit of 450 millimetres (17.7 inches). From his studies on the relationship between the Egyptian and Roman foot, Stecchini himself came to the conclusion that the true basis was the Geographic or Greek foot of 307.7957 millimetres (12.1 inches).

The quest for the source of both ancient and modern measures has taxed many minds. Naturally, I wondered whether the answers to the riddle could be found in the proportions of the twin circles on the Marlborough Downs. The task of unravelling the mystery was to take many years. My first step was to see if there was any connection between the various ancient measures and the radius and circumference of the circles.

Earth measures

Fortunately, Livio Stecchini had already worked out the nominal metric value of a number of important measurements from ancient Egypt and the classical world. He listed them as follows:

Egyptian foot	0.300 metres	(11.8 inches)
Geographic or Greek foot	0.308 metres	(12.1 inches)
Remen	0.3696 metres	(14.5 inches)
Geographic Cubit	0.462 metres	(18.1 inches)
Royal Cubit	0.525 metres	(20.7 inches)
Pyk Belady	0.5775 metres	(22.7 inches)
Fathom	1.848 metres	(72.7 inches)

Alongside these measures, I also decided to consider two imperial measures, the foot (0.3048 metres) and the furlong (201.168 metres), which are known to be of ancient origin, and the Megalithic Yard (0.829 metres) discovered by Professor Thom.

When I converted the dimensions of the circles into these ancient measures it became plain that I had to adjust the nominal radius of the Marlborough Downs circles down again, very slightly, from 9576.78 metres to 9574.95 metres. This still falls within the original margin of error. The circumference was calculated from the ancient Egyptian nominal value of pi being $^{22}/_7$, giving the dimensions of the circles in the various measures as:

Measure	Radius (units)	Circumference (units)
Metre	9574.95	60,184.4
Egyptian foot	31,916.5	200,618
Geographic or Greek foot	31,087.5	195,407.14
Remen	25,906.25	162,839.29
Geographic Cubit	20,725	130,271.43
Royal Cubit	18,238	114,638.86
Pyk Belady	16,580	104,217.14
Fathom	5181.25	32,567.86
Foot	31,413.88	197,458.66
Furlong	47.6	299.18
Megalithic Yard	11,550	72,600

The Megalithic Yard

There seemed to be a number of interesting possibilities from the list but I was particularly struck by the number of Megalithic Yards in the radius (11,550) and circumference (72,600) because both were whole numbers, divisible by ten. This seemed unusual and warranted further attention.

The significance of numbers in these circumstances can best be assessed by reducing individual numbers to their primary factors. This is a process learned at school and involves dividing a number by its smallest divisible factor. The process is repeated until all the whole number factors are revealed. For example, the number twelve can be divided by two to produce six. Six can then be further sub-divided by two to produce three and three divided by three to produce one. The factors of twelve are then 2 × 2 × 3 × 1. The number one is generally disregarded as all numbers can be divided by one.

To make this process clearer, I will go through the process step by step and examine the conclusions we can draw. The number of Megalithic Yards in the radius and circumference can be factorised as follows:

Radius (11,550)	Circumference (72,600)
11,550 ÷ 2 = 5775	72,600 ÷ 2 = 36,300
5775 ÷ 3 = 1925	36,300 ÷ 2 = 18,150
1925 ÷ 3 = 385	18,150 ÷ 2 = 9075
385 ÷ 5 = 77	9075 ÷ 3 = 3025
77 ÷ 7 = 11	3025 ÷ 5 = 605
11 ÷ 11 = 1	605 ÷ 5 = 121
	121 ÷ 11 = 11
	11 ÷ 11 = 1

This process gives the factors of radius as: 2 × 3 × 5 × 5 × 7 × 11. The circumference's factors are: 2 × 2 × 2 × 3 × 5 × 5 × 11 × 11. If we divide both the radius and the circumference by the number of the other common factors, 2 × 3 × 5 × 5 × 11 (or 1650) we get:

Radius	Circumference
11,550 ÷ 1650 = 7	72,600 ÷ 1650 = 44 (2 × 22)

This ratio 7:11 springs inevitably from the fact that I have chosen to adopt a value for pi (π) as $^{22}/_7$, the value used in ancient Egypt. The formula used to work out the circumference of a circle from its radius is $2\pi r$, where r is the length of the radius. In the case of a circle with a radius of seven units, we get $2 \times \frac{22}{7} \times 7$. The 7s cancel each other out leaving the circumference to equal $2 \times 22 = 44$ units. These units could be millimetres, miles or kilometres, it does not matter. The principle is always the same. Any circle with a radius of 7 units will produce a circumference of 44 units if the value of pi is taken as $\frac{22}{7}$.

As we have already seen, ancient peoples liked to produce whole number ratios in their monuments and structures. Here they used Megalithic Yards, picking a whole number radius that is divisible by 7, so that the circumference is also a whole number.

For practical surveying purposes, a basic measurement coming somewhere between half to one metre, capable of further sub-division, is ideal. The imperial yard, the Royal Cubit and Professor Thom's Megalithic Yard all fall into this category. As we know, the Marlborough circles are in a whole number proportion to the dimensions of the Earth and the Megalithic Yard is in a whole number proportion to the circles, therefore the Megalithic Yard is in whole number proportion to the size of the Earth. It is the only measure of comparable size that meets these criteria.

Thom obtained his measure from a statistical analysis of some 300 stone circles throughout Britain. In his book *Megalithic Sites in Britain*, he gave 1 Megalithic Yard $= 2.720 \pm 0.003$ feet. In terms of millimetres, this is 829.04 ± 0.91438 mm. The implications of what Thom revealed were earthshattering enough. His discovery suggested that they all incorporated the same system of measurement; there was a coherence in the design and construction of the stone circles throughout the country and over a thousand-year period, an idea which archaeologists are still reluctant to accept.

To this picture is added my own findings, that the Megalithic Yard is in a whole number relationship with both the radius and the circumference of the Marlborough Downs circles (see Fig. 52) and, consequently, to the Earth. It was this very whole number relationship to both the radius and circumference that Thom considered the ancient Britons were seeking when they set out stone monuments that were elliptical or oval.

Because of the Megalithic Yard's relationship to the radius and circumference of the Earth it is now clear that the builders of Avebury, Stonehenge and other stone circle monuments had accurately defined the proportions of the Earth and, with considerable precision, based their unit of measure upon it.

The use of the Megalithic Yard in the construction of the Marlborough Downs circles ties them into the stone circle culture that emerged in Britain around 3100BC. This was a good beginning, but more was to follow.

To be systematic in my investigation of the different ancient measures, I needed to analyse each in turn in their relationships to the radius and circumference of the Marlborough Circles. Only then could a complete picture be seen.

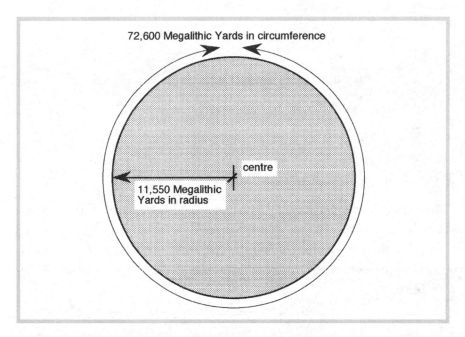

72,600 Megalithic Yards in circumference

centre

11,550 Megalithic Yards in radius

Fig. 52. Relationship of Megalithic Yard to radius and circumference of Marlborough Downs circle

Radius

At a quick glance, there did not appear to be any special relationship between the other ancient units of measure and the Marlborough circles, so I was not very excited when I started to break them down into their individual factors. But what emerged set me off on another trail of enquiry which was to prove one of the most fascinating of my entire quest. It took a number of years to bear fruit, not, to be honest, because of its complexity, but because of my inability to see what was staring me in the face.

In my own defence, I would say that my researches into the Marlborough circles were dispersed over many years. Bits of information were scattered throughout different files. It was only when I put them together in different ways, like bits of a jigsaw, that the full picture began to emerge.

I began by factorising the 16,580 Pyk Beladys:

$$16,580 \div 2 = 8290$$
$$8290 \div 2 = 4145$$
$$4145 \div 5 = 829$$

Its factors then are $2 \times 2 \times 5 \times 829$.

The factors of 18,238 Royal Cubits are:

$$18,238 \div 2 = 9119$$
$$9119 \div 11 = 829$$

Its factors are $2 \times 11 \times 829$.

Note that the ratio between the Pyk Belady and the Royal Cubit from this table is 10:11. This will become significant later on.

Incredibly, it eventually emerged that 829 was a common factor in most of these measures for the radius of the Marlborough circles:

$= 829 \times 6.25$	Fathoms
$= 829 \times 20$	Pyk Belady
$= 829 \times 22$	Royal Cubits
$= 829 \times 25$	Geographic Cubits
$= 829 \times 31.25$	Remens
$= 829 \times 37.5$	Geographic feet
$= 829 \times 38.5$	Egyptian feet

This dramatically supports Stecchini's contention that a unifying measurement links together these ancient measures, not as he thought they would be linked by a smaller unit but by a larger one. Dividing the radius of the circles in metres by 829 gives 11.55 metres. It is true to say that a sufficiently high common denominator would link all measures together, but not one as low as 11.55 metres.

But what was so special about this distance? It was not a measure that produced a whole number for either the circumference of the Marlborough Downs circle or the polar meridian. It was, of course, related to the equatorial radius of the Earth (829 × 666 × 11.55) but this was not very helpful.

I wondered whether it was related to the measure of time and the rotation of the Earth. Stecchini's work had suggested that peoples in the past were aware of the speed and rotation of the globe, hence the distance a point on the Earth's surface turned in one second or one minute of time. I tried working with these distances, but nothing quite fitted.

For a long time, I wrestled with the prime number 829. It seemed to have no significant meaning except that it united these ancient measures. I tried every method of mathematical analysis that I knew, without success. Then, one day, in one of those curious moments of illumination, I was suddenly struck by the fact that the Megalithic Yard was some 0.829 metres. For some reason it had completely eluded me. In my mind, perhaps I disregarded the significance of the metre because it is a modern measure.

At first, I dismissed this relationship, thinking that somehow I had created a circular argument. It just seemed too improbable that they were

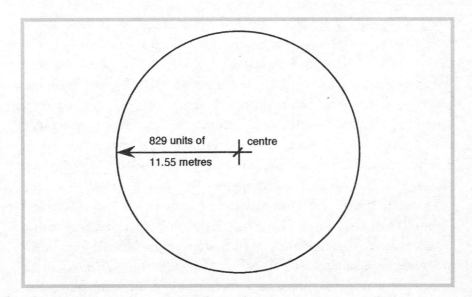

829 units of
11.55 metres

centre

Fig. 53. Relationship of 11.55 to radius of circle

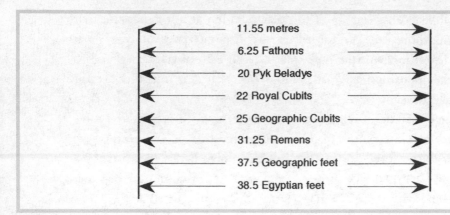

Fig. 54. The proportional relationship of ancient measures with 11.55 metres

linked. In the end, I was forced to the conclusion that there had to be a relationship between all these measures – Professor Thom's Megalithic Yard, the classical and ancient Egyptian measures already given and the modern metre.

The French metre

Stecchini thought that ancient measures were related to latitudinal distances. Because of polar flattening, the fixed distance between degrees of latitude varies. Differences of the length of such set measures as the Egyptian and Roman foot are thought to have arisen through differences in latitude between the centres of these different cultures. In Egypt, for example, between parallels 29° and 30°, which includes the majority of pyramid sites, the distance is 110,835 metres (363,539 feet). Twelve degrees further north, the approximate latitude of Rome, one degree of latitude is 111,063 metres (364,287 feet), a difference of 228 metres (748 feet).

However, I have demonstrated that Fathoms, Pyk Beladys, Royal Cubits, Geographic Cubits, Remens, Geographic feet and Egyptian feet are all related to the set distance of 11.55 metres (37.88 feet). The French metre was one ten millionth part of the distance between the pole and the equator. So how could these ancient measures and the metre be related? The answer, when it came, was deceptively simple.

It was while calculating the various ratios within an equilateral triangle that I hit upon the solution. I found that if each side of an equilateral triangle is 11.55 units, then the distance from any one angle to the midpoint on the opposite side equals 10 units.

In simple surveying terms, if a line was pegged out on the ground 10 metres long – that is, exactly one millionth of the distance between the pole and the equator – and an equilateral triangle set out so that this line bisected it, then the length of each side of the triangle would be 11.55 metres (see Fig. 55).

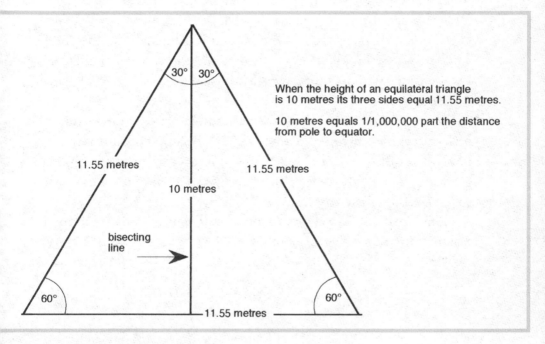

When the height of an equilateral triangle is 10 metres its three sides equal 11.55 metres.

10 metres equals 1/1,000,000 part the distance from pole to equator.

Fig. 55. Equilateral triangle base for ancient measures

So Stecchini was right in claiming that ancient measures are derived from the distance between the pole and the equator, but not directly as he supposed. The secret tradition that found its way into these ancient measures was not to use the direct and obvious distance, which we use today in the metric system – the distance between the pole and the equator – but a ratio based upon it: formed from the equilateral triangle.

We can only wonder at the esoteric reason for this. It suggests that an equilateral triangle carried some powerful symbolic significance. It is the same triangle that led to my discovery of the pyramid pattern over the Marlborough Downs and can be found incorporated in the geometry of the design stages of the Great Pyramid. It is now evident that this same triangle provides the cornerstone for a whole series of ancient measures.

It also powerfully demonstrates the French were not the first people to come up with the metre. Somewhere in the distant past, a civilisation had accurately calculated the distance between the pole and the equator and established a set basic measurement of ten metres – one millionth part of this distance. The ancient Egyptian and classical Greek measurements were all derived from it. Although the Megalithic Yard established by Thom was related to the equatorial circumference, I was eventually to discover a way that it can be reconciled to the polar meridian too.

Having cracked the code for the relationship between the metre and such ancient measures as the Remen and Pyk Belady, it became very clear how each of these measures were derived from 11.55 metres using pure geometry. (The word geometry, incidentally, means 'measure of the earth', so it is an appropriate term.)

Further analysis showed that another factor, though not a whole number, united most of these measures. It was 2.5:

6.25	Fathoms	$= \underline{2.5} \times 2.5$
20	Pyk Belady	$= \underline{2.5} \times 8$
22	Royal Cubits	$= \underline{2.5} \times 8.8$
25	Geographic Cubits	$= \underline{2.5} \times 10$
31.25	Remens	$= \underline{2.5} \times 12.5$
37.5	Geographic feet	$= \underline{2.5} \times 15$

The ratio of 2.5 is derived from the division of a circle using the *vesica pisces* design. For example, Fig. 53 shows how the Pyk Belady can be accurately defined using simple geometric methods, once the fixed distance of 10 metres has been established. In practical terms, this was probably done by using two pegs and a length of string to form a compass. By adopting this system and by simple division, the different ancient measures can be discovered.

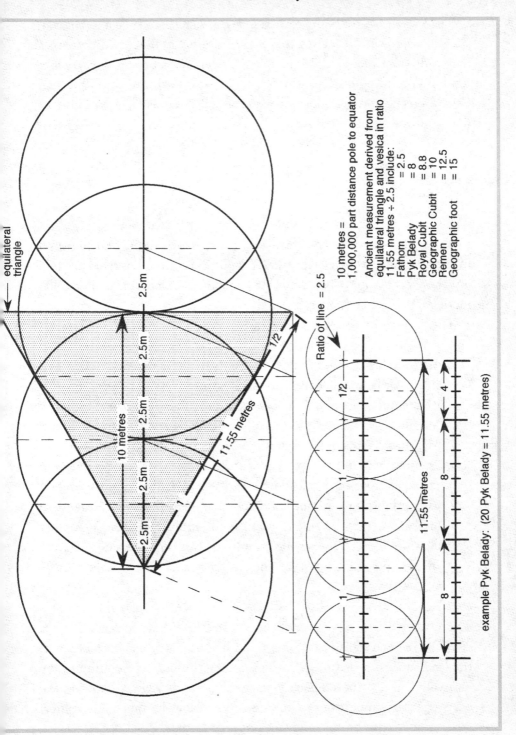

equilateral
triangle

2.5m

10 metres =
1,000,000 part distance pole to equator

Ancient measurement derived from
equilateral triangle and vesica in ratio
11.55 metres ÷ 2.5 include:

Fathom   = 2.5
Pyk Belady   = 8
Royal Cubit   = 8.8
Geographic Cubit = 10
Remen   = 12.5
Geographic foot = 15

2.5m

2.5m

10 metres

2.5m

11.55 metres

2.5m

1

1/2

Ratio of line = 2.5

1/2

1

1

11.55 metres

4

8

8

8

1

example Pyk Belady: (20 Pyk Belady = 11.55 metres)

Fig. 56. Ancient measures derived from 10 metres

The Megalithic Yard can be fitted into this same pattern in another way, yet still based on 10 metres (see Fig. 56). This produces a line with a length of 8.29 metres (27.2 feet) which can then be sub-divided into tenths to produce the Megalithic Yard. Not only does the Megalithic Yard have a precise relationship to equatorial measurements, it can also be derived from the polar meridian.

The canon of measures

The facts that have emerged so far give support to the notion that there was an advanced people in ancient times, capable of setting out measures in harmony that were related to the proportions of the Earth. This could only have been achieved by the Earth's equatorial circumference and polar meridian being accurately calculated.

The findings can be summarised as:

▲ the Megalithic Yard of 0.829 metres is the only measure of comparable size that precisely fits, in whole number ratio, both the equatorial circumference and radius of the Earth. There are $666 \times 1650 \times 7$ Megalithic Yards in the radius of the Earth and $666 \times 1650 \times 22 \times 2$ Megalithic Yards in its circumference.

▲ At some time in the distant past the distance between the pole and the equator was accurately measured and sub-divided into a million parts producing a distance of exactly ten metres. Using this standard measure as the bisecting division in an equilateral triangle another distance of 11.55 metres was established from any one side of the triangle. From this length, the ancient Egyptian and classical measures were derived.

The evidence was now overwhelming that the Marlborough Downs circles were not a statistical anomaly, but had been deliberately laid out in the landscape. But before attempting to determine how a culture in the past could have achieved such a staggering feat as well as knowing the exact size and proportions of the Earth, we can take this mathematical analysis of systems of measurement one step further.

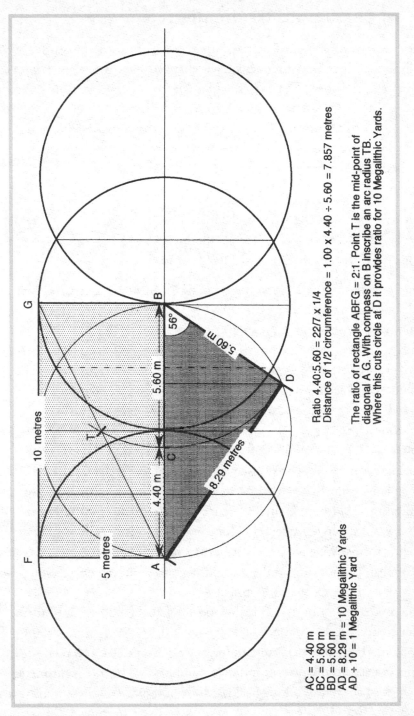

Ratio 4.40:5.60 = 22/7 x 1/4
Distance of 1/2 circumference = 1.00 x 4.40 ÷ 5.60 = 7.857 metres

The ratio of rectangle ABFG = 2:1. Point T is the mid-point of diagonal A G. With compass on B inscribe an arc radius TB. Where this cuts circle at D it provides ratio for 10 Megalithic Yards.

AC = 4.40 m
BC = 5.60 m
BD = 5.60 m
AD = 8.29 m = 10 Megalithic Yards
AD ÷ 10 = 1 Megalithic Yard

Fig. 57. Proposed geometric calculation for Megalithic Yard (Thom) based on ten metres

Imperial measures and the circumference

So far we have not looked at the imperial measures of the yard, foot and furlong. These measurements have changed over the years as measurements have varied. The present standard for the yard was only fixed in 1824. In Tudor times, it was a fraction shorter – 35.963 modern inches or 2.99692 modern feet. So the Tudor foot was 11.988 modern inches. In Roman Britain, where British measure is thought to have originated, the foot was as little as 11.65 modern inches. For comparison then:

Imperial foot (est. 1824)	= 12 inches
Henry VII's foot	= 11.988 inches
Romano British foot	= 11.65 inches

When considering the Marlborough circles in imperial measures, I was struck by the fact that there are 299.12 furlongs in the circumference which is very close to the number 300.

Today, we are accustomed to divide a circle into 360 degrees, a system derived from ancient Mesopotamia. Each degree is then sub-divided into 60 minutes and each minute into seconds, showing a correlation between time and angular measure, a practice which originated in astronomical observation.

360 is 6 × 60. The number 300, on the other hand, is 5 × 60. The six-based angular measure we use today has considerable general value in calculating angles but there could be an argument for a five-based measure, produced by dividing the circumference of a circle into 300 rather than 360°. It would help considerably if one was looking to create pentagonal geometric forms. We have already seen that the pentagon incorporates the golden mean proportion, so there could have been an esoteric reason for the division of a circle into 300 units.

The modern furlong is a fraction too long to fit 300 times into the circumference of the Marlborough circles. 60,171.27 metres ÷ 300 = 200.571 metres, while the standard furlong measures 201.168 metres.

For a precise fit, the present furlong would have to be 59.7 centimetres (23.5 inches) shorter. Working backwards from there, if all the same ratios of inches to feet (12), feet to yards (3) and yards to furlongs (220) were maintained then the yard would need to be reduced to 2.991 feet or the foot to 11.964 inches.

This would make the foot 0.024 inches, or about 1/42nd of an inch shorter than that established by Henry VII. This distance is barely discernible and would only become evident when multiplied up into larger units of measure.

For ease of reference, I will call this new measure, 1/300th of the circumference of the Marlborough circles, a short furlong (SF). Correspondingly, we have the short yard (SY) and the short foot (SFt) (Fig. 58).

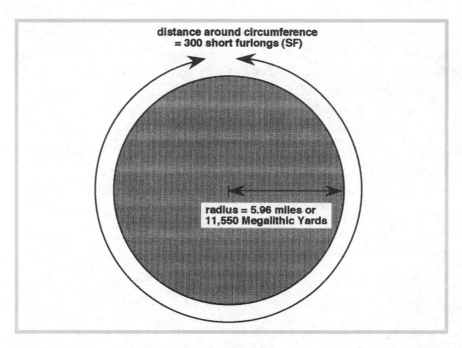

Fig. 58. Number of short furlongs in circumference of Marlborough Downs circles

Furlongs

The word furlong is of Saxon origin and means 'furrow-long' as it was a measure used for assessing the length of ploughed strips of land. According to R.D. Connor in his book *The Weights and Measures of*

England, it is derived from the 'rod', a unit of measure of 5.5 yards. Forty rods is one furlong. Other authorities suggest different origins for the furlong measure, but it is generally accepted that it was established because of its pragmatic use in agriculture and land area assessment as it is directly related to the acre (1 furlong × 4 rods = 1 acre). There is also a link with the Roman Stade in that eight Stades made one Roman mile and 8 furlongs equal 1 imperial mile. Yet the short furlong, at just over 658 feet does not quite fit with the Stade, which is only 600 feet.

Rods

The rod, which R.D. Connor believed was one of the basic units of British measure, is derived from the Saxon word 'gyrd'. Accurate assessment of ancient measurements is very difficult because of slight local variations. As we have seen, even the official sizes of imperial measures have varied over the past 500 years, which is noticeable when making accurate measurements of old buildings. There are thought to be two origins of the rod, one the continental Drusian foot of 0.333 metres and the other the Natural foot of 9.9 inches or 0.2515 metres.

Assuming the short furlong is the original correct measure, this would make the short rod 5.014 metres (200.5709 ÷ 40 = 5.014 metres). If the accepted lengths of the Drusian and Natural foot are accurate, then when divided into the short rod, we get:

1 Rod ÷ 1 Drusian foot = 15.06 (5.014 ÷ 0.333 = 15.06).
1 Rod ÷ 1 Natural foot = 19.976 (5.014 ÷ 0.251 = 19.976).

These ratios are both close to whole numbers. To correct these measures so that the rod equals exactly 15 Drusian feet and 20 Natural feet, the Drusian foot would have to be increased by one millimetre to 0.334 metres and the Natural foot reduced by 0.8mm to 0.2507 metres. This is well within a tolerated margin of error for these two measures. In fact, these slightly adjusted Drusian and Natural feet, make a much better fit with the short rod, than the unadjusted measures do with the present Imperial standard rod. This tends to support the use of the short furlong. In other words, because of the variations that have occurred in the precise values of the British Imperial standards, it seems eminently reasonable to postulate a measure which was based upon the exact division of the Marlborough Downs circle into 300 units – a measure which we have called a short furlong.

The Megalithic Yard and the short furlong

In establishing the length of the short furlong as 200.5709 metres, one three-hundredth of the circumference of the Marlborough circles, a significant relationship to the Megalithic Yard becomes obvious. There are 72,600 Megalithic Yards in the circumference (72,600 ÷ 300 = 242). In other words:

1 short furlong (SF) = 242 Megalithic Yards.
This is significant because the factors of 242 are 11 × 22 or 11 × 11 × 2. There are 220 imperial yards in a modern furlong. 220 has factors of 10 × 22 or 11 × 10 × 2.

So there is an exact 10:11 ratio between the Megalithic Yard and the short imperial yard. This ratio is precisely the same as that found between two

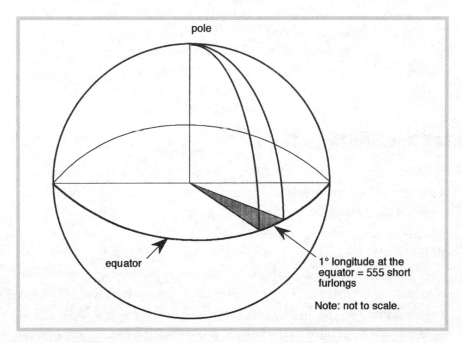

pole

equator

1° longitude at the equator = 555 short furlongs

Note: not to scale.

Fig. 59. Number of short furlongs in 1° equatorial longitude

Egyptian measures already mentioned, the Pyk Belady and the Royal Cubit.

10:11 is an important ratio for calculating and reconciling areas and volumes. And, according to Stecchini, measures with a similar ratio are found extensively throughout the ancient world. So it is quite probable that two versions of the yard were used in ancient times – Professor Thom's Megalithic Yard and a short imperial yard which current British measures have been derived from. These measurements are reconciled as both the short furlong and the Megalithic Yard are in whole-number proportion to the Earth's equatorial circumference.

The short furlong and the equatorial circumference

Something curious also happens when we use the short furlong to measure the equatorial circumference of the Earth. Each degree of longitude at the equator equals 69.170971 miles (24,901.55 ÷ 360 = 69.170971). Dividing that by the short furlong goes precisely 555 times. Put another way: 1 degree equatorial longitude = 555 short furlongs.

The factors of 555 are 37 × 15 and in this we have an echo with the number 666 which has factors of 37 × 18. The ratio, then, between these two is 15 to 18 or 5:6. This ratio (5:6) was to become significant when I started to uncover the systems of surveying used by the megalith builders.

Latitude and longitude

Because of the shape of the Earth, the length of each degree of longitude at the equator is greater than the length of each degree of latitude. But the length of a degree of latitude increases as one moves away from the equator towards the poles. The length of one degree of latitude and one degree of longitude is equal at latitude 55°, the approximate position of Hadrian's Wall in England. There, one degree of latitude and one degree of longitude are exactly 555 short furlongs. Could it just be coincidence that the point on the Earth where the lengths of degrees of latitude and longitude are reconciled – the fifty-fifth parallel (55°) – should also be divisible by the symbolically associated number 555? I think not.

All of these correlations support Stecchini's contention that:

 On the basis of my research into ancient geography, I am now convinced that there existed on this planet a people with an advanced mathematical and astronomical science several millennia before classic Greece.

My own research lends weight to this proposition. Is it conceivable that all the facts that have emerged from the study of the twin circles on the Marlborough Downs could have been the result of chance? Surely they had to have been deliberately created. To discover how and why was my next challenge.

By choosing a distance of a fraction under 9.6 kilometres (6 miles) for the radius of each of the twin circles on the Marlborough Downs the creators of this pattern established a harmonious relationship between the Megalithic Yard and other ancient measures, linking them to the Earth's radius, equatorial circumference and the polar meridian. It is a feat of stunning achievement and indicates a clear grasp of the Earth's dimensions.

These two circles contain enough information to tell us that its creators must have had a deep mathematical knowledge. It is like an encoded message from the past waiting to be deciphered by those in a future generation with sufficient skills to unravel the mysteries it holds. The discoveries that flowed from my decision to assume that the intended size of each circle was exactly 1/666th part of the circumference of the Earth have, in my opinion, more than justified this choice.

Despite the exciting findings I had already made, I was still faced with a number of immense problems. I was sure that the twin circles of the Marlborough Downs had been deliberately created, but I still had to discover how this was done. There is some evidence of gold artefacts being created around 2800BC, but bronze was not to make its appearance for several hundred years at around 2500BC. So the surveyors of these megalithic circles had no metal instruments. They had to create these landscape patterns using only the most basic of equipment, such as the 'sighting staff'. The next stage of my quest had to be an exploration into the surveying techniques of those early British surveyors.

9

THE ANCIENT SURVEYORS

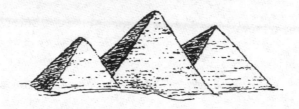

*This ingenious method is similar to the system used in ancient
Egypt, strengthening the likelihood of a cultural link*

Surveying the landscape

Despite my background in town planning and architecture, I could not
conceive how the early peoples of the British Isles could have surveyed the
landscape in the way that the evidence from the Marlborough Downs
landscape patterns seemed to suggest. Surveying today is a highly sophisticated occupation, which uses laser technology and satellite communication systems. The Global Positioning System (GPS) was originally
developed by the American military using space technology. It will give the
exact latitude and longitude of any position on Earth down to the nearest
metre. Using a hand-held GPS device, you can tell immediately where you
are on the planet. As a system, it is of primary importance to sailors but it
is also now an important part of modern mapping techniques.

Generally, surveying involves three basic operations:

▲ measuring and setting out angles;
▲ measuring distances;
▲ setting out positions to a pre-determined plan.

Before GPS, surveying was carried out using high precision theodolites.
These instruments are used to make very accurate measurement of angles

between siting points. By use of triangulation, from one measured reference line, any site can be surveyed this way. For example, if I wished to set out an equilateral triangle in the landscape with each side 100 metres (328 feet) long, I would need to first accurately measure one side of the triangle. By placing my theodolite over the two end points in turn and setting it to 60°, I could lay out the other two sides. Where the two 60° lines intersected would be the third point of the triangle. The key to the process is the establishment of an accurate base line and the ability to measure the required angles.

As we journey back in time the accuracy of the instrumentation decreases, but the process remains the same. Roman surveying equipment was unsophisticated, but it played an important part in the planning of their road network. Nevertheless, to lay out a circle of 9.6 kilometres (6 miles) radius with any degree of accuracy is no small undertaking. It would challenge the best of modern surveyors, at least until the advent of GPS. Despite the evidence of these circles on the ground, it did not seem feasible to me that they could be produced with the equipment available in the late Neolithic era. The challenge that I now faced was uncovering how this might have been done.

Setting out alignments is quite feasible for a culture restricted to the use of simple equipment. It requires no more than a few straight staves. The measurement of angles, when I first thought about it, seemed to be a much more difficult undertaking. Yet to create the Marlborough Downs pattern, ancient surveyors would have to do this to a high degree of accuracy.

The modern theodolite is a sophisticated piece of equipment. Even the Roman version, basically a metal sighting device on a circular calibrated ring, is quite elaborate. Nothing like it has ever been discovered in all the archaeological excavations of Neolithic times. So there had to be some other solution.

To unravel this mystery I would have first to work out the angular relationships between a large number of sites. While it is not complicated mathematically, this task is an incredibly tedious business without the aid of a computer. I bought a new one in the autumn of 1991. This new machine packed enough punch to make good in-roads into the project. But my researches at the time had taken me away from the Marlborough

Downs, back to the area of my earliest discoveries in the Cotswolds and, in particular, the sites around Bredon Hill.

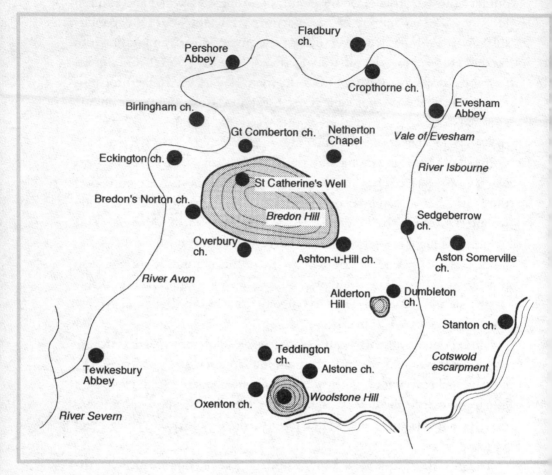

Fig. 60. Arrangement of Bredon Hill sites

Bredon Hill and the surrounding area

The area under study is approximately 17.7 kilometres (11 miles) east-west by 14.5 kilometres (9 miles) north-south. This region is part Cotswold, part Vale of Evesham and part Severn Valley. It is bounded on the north and western sides by the gently meandering Avon, one of the most picturesque rivers in Britain, linking the great abbeys of Evesham, Pershore and Tewkesbury. To the east and south lies the Cotswold escarpment, which rises steeply from the flood plain of the River Isbourne. Set in the middle, like the back of a sleeping turtle, lies Bredon Hill. A prominent outlier from the limestone escarpment, it is some 6.4 kilometres (4 miles) long by 3.2 kilometres (2 miles) wide. At nearly 300 metres (1000 feet), its summit provides spectacular views in all directions. Limestone from Bredon Hill and the nearby Cotswolds has provided the building material for much of the area which is reflected in the distinctive architecture of the Cotswolds. Buildings along the edge of the Avon, with is water meadows and reed beds, use the more traditional materials of brick, timber and thatch.

It is not an area particularly rich in archaeological remains, at least when compared with the Marlborough Downs. The earliest finds date from late Neolithic times, around 2600BC, although long barrows nearby on the Cotswold escarpment suggest the area was inhabited before 3200BC. There is an Iron Age hillfort on Bredon Hill where fifty bodies were excavated. Caught up in some skirmish, the men there were hacked to death as they tried to defend their camp. There is a similar small fort on Woolstone Hill to the south, but with the exception of a few marker or standing stones there is little else of antiquity.

Christianity came to the area around the middle of the seventh century and soon after a bishopric was established in nearby Worcester. The famous Abbey of Evesham was founded in 701. Legend has it that a swineherd called Eoves was tending his pigs when one wandered off into the nearby forest. Suspecting that she had just given birth to some piglets, he followed her only to be confronted by a vision of the Virgin Mary with two angels singing hymns. He reported his experience to Egwin, the Bishop of Worcester, who returned to the spot and saw the same thing. He was told to found an Abbey there. He did and named it Eoves Holme after the good swineherd Eoves. It grew to become one of the most powerful in the country and a centre of pilgrimage from all over Europe.

In 1265, Evesham was the site of the bloody defeat of Simon de Montfort, known as the Father of Parliament. Chroniclers reported that when he died 'the sky grew black, as the sound of thunder and huge bolts of lightning shook the earth'. Such was the veneration the church held him in that his mutilated body was buried under the high altar. It spawned a number of miraculous cures, and lent further weight to the Abbey's prominence in Britain. The Abbey was destroyed in Henry VIII's Dissolution of the Monasteries, which enriched the king's exchequer rather than the Pope in Rome, and all that remains of note today is the bell tower.

Pershore Abbey fared a little better. Early Christian settlements of the time were constantly at the prey of the marauding Danes and many monastic cells were overrun and destroyed. Practically nothing of the early church remains. The revival of the Abbey began in 983 when Odda, the grandson of a local chieftain, purchased the bones of the revered St Eadburga and buried them in the Abbey. Eadburga was the grand-daughter of Alfred the Great. She entered a convent at Winchester and died there in 960 after, no doubt, a blameless existence.

As at Evesham, several miracles were reported at her shrine, which became a minor centre of pilgrimage. But all that remains now from this extensive Abbey is the choir, the tower and the south transept of the church, and the almonry nearby. The dedication of the Abbey was to St Eadburga and St Mary.

The Abbey Church of Tewkesbury still stands, saved from Cromwell's henchmen by the local townsfolk who purchased the building for the princely sum of £453. It now boasts the second largest parish church in Britain. Its huge Norman columns are the largest in Europe. It was founded in the seventh century by a monk named Theoc, who built a cell there. The Benedictines established a monastery in 715 but this was destroyed by the Danes. The present Abbey dates from Norman times and is dedicated, like Evesham and Pershore, to the Blessed Virgin Mary.

There is a high proportion of female dedications among the other church sites, which range in date from the eleventh and twelfth centuries. Other churches dedicated to Mary include those at Sedgeberrow and Aston Somerville. The church at Overbury is dedicated to St Faith, that at Ashton-under-Hill to St Barbara, and Netherton Chapel and St Catherine's Well to – who else? – St Catherine. Male dedications bring up the rear with the churches at Cropthorne, Stanton and Gt Comberton dedicated to St Michael, and Fladbury and Beckford to John the Baptist. Other churches include St Peter's (Dumbleton), St Nicholas (Teddington), Holy Trinity (Eckington) and St Giles (Bredon's Norton).

Not all churches in the study area are included here. The most notable exceptions are those at Little Comberton, Bricklehampton, Elmley Castle, Hinton on the Green, Bredon, Kemerton and Alderton. They were omitted from my computer study because they did not form part of my original research into the area. I also chose to leave out the fort on Bredon Hill, not because it does not fit into any pattern – it does. But the site is so large that it could take in a number of alignments and still appear to fit (see Fig. 60).

The pattern emerges

In *The Old Straight Track* Watkins says:

> ⊚ *Make a rule to work on siting points, and not, tempting as it is to take a bit of road or track as evidence [for a ley] . . . If supported by three or four points, it becomes corroborative evidence. Three points alone do not prove a ley, four being the minimum.*

Watkins leys were generally considered to run for up to 32 kilometres (20 miles). Applying these criteria to the sites surrounding Bredon Hill did not yield promising results. There is a four point alignment between Stanton, Sedgeberrow, Netherton Chapel and Pershore, but that is all. There are a number of three point alignments such as Tewkesbury, Overbury and Evesham, and Oxenton, Dumbleton and Aston Somerville. Yet they are hardly adequate to be designated as a ley. It is only when I analysed the angular relationships that any significant pattern emerged.

The process was simple. I keyed into my computer the names and grid co-ordinates for the different sites and, with the aid of a simple mathematical program, worked out the angular relationships between lines running between them. The computer could calculate this to many decimal points, but this level of refinement seemed unnecessary. In a distance of one kilometre, the variance produced by an angle of one degree is only 17.455 metres (57 feet). So the maximum error in such a small area, for one degree, would only be about 300 metres (984 feet). To make things easier, I decided to round each calculation up, or down, to the nearest degree.

In theory, a random distribution of sites should give an even spread of angular relationships. If some pre-determined plan existed, I reasoned that obvious angles such as 60° and 90° should be part of it. So I set up my computer to pick out these angles. I initially analysed ten sites which produced over 800 different angles. I was later to go on and analyse the angular relationship between many of the churches in the area – there are more than 50. Each calculation in that study produced more than 2800 angles.

Although there were many examples of 60° and 90° angles, in my initial survey, one church site stood out from the rest. Table 3 shows the angular relationships between Dumbleton Church and nine other sites. It was this site in particular that provided an important clue which helped me unravel the underlying geometry of the area. To interpret the table, look at the site on the left hand column and read it against the sites mentioned along the top. For example, the angle between Tewkesbury, Dumbleton and Pershore is 70°, while the angle between Gt Comberton, Dumbleton and Overbury is 30°.

It so happens that in this selective table all the angles are multiples of 10° which is unusual. A multiple of 10° will be found in the series 1° to 180°, 18 times which is 10 per cent of cases. There are 36 possible angles between the nine sites, so, in any random sequence of sites, we would expect 10 per cent of them (36 ÷ 10 = 3.6) to have an angular relationship which is a multiple of 10. Instead, we have all 36 divisible by 10, nine times what we would expect by chance.

The odds on this happening in a random pattern of similar size are about one in eleven million, but in this case the sites are not totally random because they have been selected out from the rest. Nevertheless, it still seemed an impressive array:

10° × 2	30° × 2	40° × 3	50° × 3
60° × 4	70° × 1	80° × 2	90° × 5
110° × 1	120° × 3	130° × 1	150° × 4

The high incidence of 60° and 90° angles would be expected if conscious planning had been carried out. I assumed that this would have been based upon a system of pure geometry, for it is very easy to create a right angle

Dumbleton	Tewkesbury	Pershore	Evesham	Overbury	Gt. Comber	Sedgeb.	Woolstone	Netherton	Stanton
Tewkesbury Abbey	0	70	120	30	60	120	150	80	150
Pershore Abbey	70	0	50	40	10	50	100	10	140
Evesham Abbey	120	50	0	90	60	0	150	40	90
Overbury Ch.	30	40	90	0	30	90	60	50	0
Gt. Comberton Ch.	60	10	60	30	0	60	90	20	150
Sedgeberrow Ch.	120	50	0	90	60	0	150	40	90
Woolstone Hill	30	80	150	60	90	150	0	110	120
Netherton Chapel	80	10	40	50	20	40	110	0	130
Stanton Ch.	150	140	90	0	150	90	120	130	0

Table 3. Angular relationships between Dumbleton church and nine other church, abbey and hillfort sites near Bredon Hill, Worcestershire

(90° angle) using a few pegs and some lengths of twine. By halving the angle, using similar methods, additional angles of 45°, 22½° and so on can be established. In a similar way, it is possible to set out angles of 60° which in this case only requires three pieces of equal length rope. Angles of 50° and 40° pose another problem for they cannot easily be established by geometric methods. Each occurs on three separate occasions in Table 3, so there had to be some way of generating these angles.

The answer, when it came, showed both the extreme simplicity of the system, as well as the mathematical genius in its comprehension.

The solution at last

It was while I was analysing the properties of a right-angled triangle with angles of 40° and 50° that I hit upon the solution. I discovered that a triangle with these angles has base and perpendicular sides of five and six units respectively. In other words, there is a simple whole number ratio (5:6) between two non-hypotenuse sides. At first, I thought that this was a lucky coincidence. It had been selected because it fulfilled the criteria of having a degree base divisible by 10, with angles of 40°, 50° and 90°. But I quickly came to realise that it might be possible to generate a large number of angles using very simple numeric ratios. Once a right-angled triangle has been set out on the ground, by adjusting the side ratios, precise angles can be easily established. All I now had to do was discover the ratios for generating the different angles.

This was, coincidentally, exactly the same system used by the ancient Egyptians to establish the slope of their pyramids, already discussed using the *seked* of the angle. The difference was that the Egyptians used the ratio to establish gradients while the ancient Britons appear to have used it to set out angles on a horizontal plane. By knowing which ratios to use, a whole range of angles could be easily created without complicated geometry or instrumentation. Now it was clear why no archaeological theodolites had been found. Such angles could be created using simple and commonly available materials.

All that is required to set out an angle on a piece of level land is a thin rope, a few pegs and a measuring device to fix the ratios. A straight piece of sapling one to two metres in length would be ideal. The trick is to know the ratios of the angle required, then the angle can be marked out easily on the ground.

The system is simplicity itself. All that is demanded is the knowledge of which ratios will produce the required angles. For example, in the triangle already described, all the ancient surveyors would need to remember is the 6:5 ratio. The exact angles this ratio produces are 39.81° and 50.19°, which are a very close approximation to 40° and 50° (Fig. 61).

The margin of error using this method and these particular ratios would be less than 3.5 metres (11.5 feet) in a distance of 1 kilometre (0.62 miles). Some ratios have a much greater level of accuracy. In the case of a 6° angle, which is produced by a 19:2 ratio, the accuracy is 1 in 4000. That accuracy is the equivalent of travelling from London to New York and being less than a mile off course at your destination.

A somewhat similar system is used today in trigonometry which has established specific ratios for the calculation of angles. These are known as sines, secants and tangents, and their reciprocals are known as cosine, cosecants and cotangents. Sines and cosines can be used for calculating angles where the length of the hypotenuse is known, while tangents relate to the relationship between the base and perpendicular sides of a right-angled triangle. Computers or calculators work these figures out in fractions of a second, but when I was at school we used to have to look them up in a series of tables.

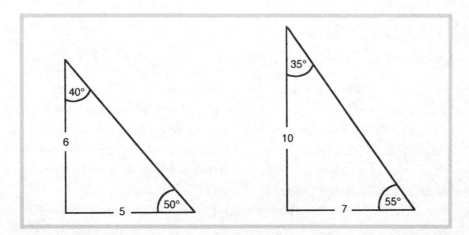

Fig. 61. Tangent ratios to set angles

The Bredon Hill pattern

With this easy system of creating angles, it is possible to lay out patterns in the landscape in a simple yet precise way. The most commonly used ratios that I found in the Bredon Hill location were:

40° and 50° = 6:5 ratio
35° and 55° = 7:10 ratio
70° and 20° = 11:4 ratio

I assumed, at the time, that angles of 30°, 60°, 45° and 90° had been obtained through geometric construction, although later, as we shall see, I was to revise this view.

I suspected that another geometric pattern must link together sites in this area. The 30°, 60° and 90° angles I had found, I was certain, indicated some form of deliberate planning. I felt confident that I was about to discover another pattern, like that already found on the Marlborough Downs. This would strengthen the case that such patterns were a widely distributed phenomenon. I initially looked for circles but none were obvious. However, wherever I looked there were more triangles that could have been produced by significant ratios.

My previous researches indicated that an equilateral triangle would figure somewhere in the design, and I set about trying to discover it. When I found it, it proved to be pivotal in setting out a triangulated matrix of primarily church sites.

Geometry of Bredon Hill sites

The primary triangle is formed by Dumbleton Church, Woolstone Hill and Overbury Church. Woolstone Hill has a commanding view over much of the area, while Dumbleton Church nestles at the foot of Alderton Hill which blocks the line of sight to either Overbury Church or Woolstone Hill. Overbury Church stands on the southern slopes of Bredon Hill. Today its view to Woolstone Hill is blocked by houses, but there would certainly have been a clear line of sight in past times, providing any trees were removed. The distance between these three sites is 6250 metres (3.88 miles).

8) *Top:* St Nicholas church, Berwick Bassett, Wiltshire, is one of the churches on the circumference of the circle to the north of the Avebury henge. Sarsen stones were used as grave markers here. Could it have been built on a much older sacred site?

9) The alignment from the top of Old Sarum, Wiltshire, looking south (see Chapter 14). The top of the spire of Salisbury Cathedral, in the middle distance, can be seen between the trees and beyond that in the far distance the clump of trees on the Clearbury Ring hillfort.

10) An aerial view of Stonehenge, Wiltshire. The four marker positions of the Station Stone rectangle (see page 29) are indicated.

11) *Top:* Stonehenge, Wiltshire. Is this an astronomical temple with many additional hidden messages in its design and proportions?

12) Castle Rigg stone circle, Keswick, Lake District National Park, Cumbria. One of the oldest circles in this area, it has many intriguing aspects in its siting, astronomical alignments and sacred geometry.

13) *Top:* The *vesica pisces* design on the lid of Chalice Well, Glastonbury, Somerset. The *vesica* was first used by Classical Greeks and Ancient Egyptians (see Chapter 4).

14) The area surrounding the Neolithic site of King Arthur's Hall and Rough Tor (in background) on Bodmin Moor, Cornwall, is steeped in a powerful spiritual energy (see Chapter 10).

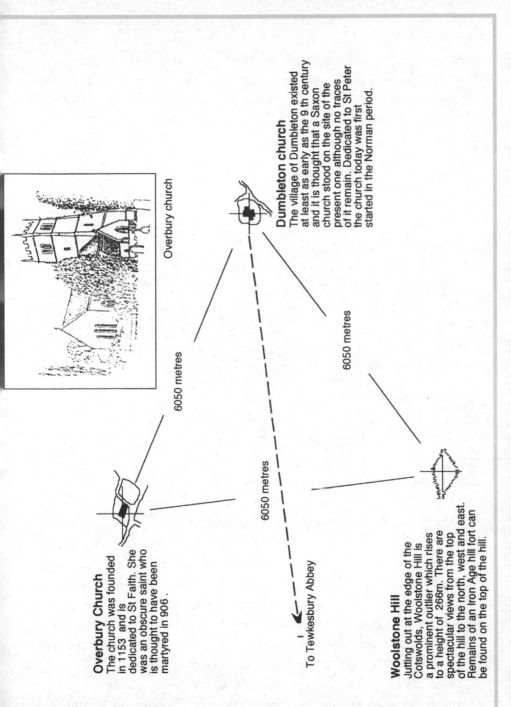

Overbury Church
The church was founded in 1153 and is dedicated to St Faith. She was an obscure saint who is thought to have been martyred in 906.

Overbury church

Dumbleton church
The village of Dumbleton existed at least as early as the 9th century and it is thought that a Saxon church stood on the site of the present one although no traces of it remain. Dedicated to St Peter the church today was first started in the Norman period.

6050 metres

6050 metres

6050 metres

To Tewkesbury Abbey

Woolstone Hill
Jutting out at the edge of the Cotswolds, Woolstone Hill is a prominent outlier which rises to a height of 266m. There are spectacular views from the top of the hill to the north, west and east. Remains of an Iron Age hill fort can be found on the top of the hill.

Fig. 62. Site relationship between Dumbleton, Overbury and Woolstone Hill (not to scale)

Figure 63 shows the relationship of the three principle sites of Overbury Church, Dumbleton Church and Woolstone Hill, which have been marked ABC respectively. It can be seen that angle ABE, the alignment to Tewkesbury Abbey, is 30° as is the angle CBE. The line CB therefore bisects AC at point S. Extending the line AB to point T, with the distance of BT equal in length to BS locates the position of Stanton Church.

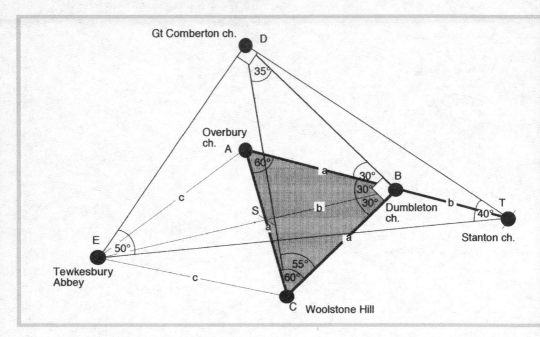

Fig. 63. Geometry of Bredon Hill churches – primary triangle

Having established the initial triangle, the next logical step was to investigate how the position of Gt Comberton Church fitted into the pattern. My computer analysis of the area indicated that this church was positioned at 90° from a line running from Woolstone Hill to Dumbleton Church. Closing the triangle with a line from Woolstone Hill to Gt Comberton Church produced an angle of 55° at Woolstone Hill and one of 35° at Comberton Church. Fig. 61 shows that a right-angled triangle with angles of 55° and 35° can be produced by a 7:10 ratio.

The 7:10 ratio used in ancient Egypt was used in the calculation of land areas. A simple approximation can be made for the doubling of any area of land by using the 7 to 10 ratio, as $7^2 = 49$ while $10^2 = 100$.

Once the position of Gt Comberton Church had been established, it would then be possible to fix the position of Tewkesbury Abbey by creating another right-angle triangle. By connecting DT (Gt Comberton and Stanton) and constructing a right angle at point D, the point E, the position of Tewkesbury Abbey, then falls where that line crosses the line BS, the line that bisects the apex of the original equilateral triangle (see Fig. 64).

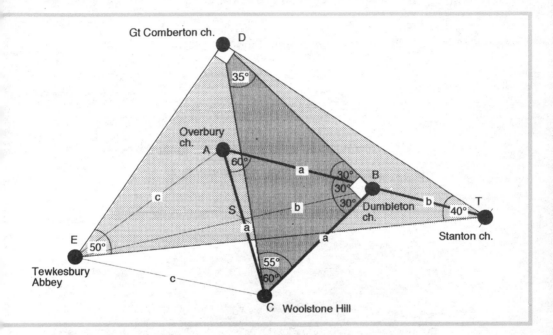

Fig. 64. Geometry of Bredon Hill churches – secondary triangle

The pattern of triangles within triangles continues as the Tewkesbury Abbey–Stanton line forms one side of another important triangle. If an angle of 60° is constructed at Tewkesbury, where the intersection of this line meets the extended Woolstone Hill–Gt Comberton line it locates Pershore Abbey. The placing of Evesham Abbey can be found in a similar way by constructing a right angle at Dumbleton Church from the Dumbleton–Overbury Church line and extending it until it meets the Tewkesbury–Overbury line. The intersection locates Evesham Abbey.

The position of Sedgeberrow Church can be obtained from the intersection of the Dumbleton to Evesham alignment with the Stanton to Pershore alignment. Once these locations have been fixed then the positions of all the remaining churches can be found through simple triangulation techniques.

The main triangles used in this pattern are:

50°, 60°, 70° (Stanton, Tewkesbury, Pershore);
40°, 50°, 90° (Stanton, Tewkesbury, Gt Comberton);
100°, 50°, 30° (Pershore, Evesham, Tewkesbury);
60°, 60°, 60° (Dumbleton, Woolstone, Overbury);
55°, 35°, 90° (Woolstone, Gt Comberton, Dumbleton).

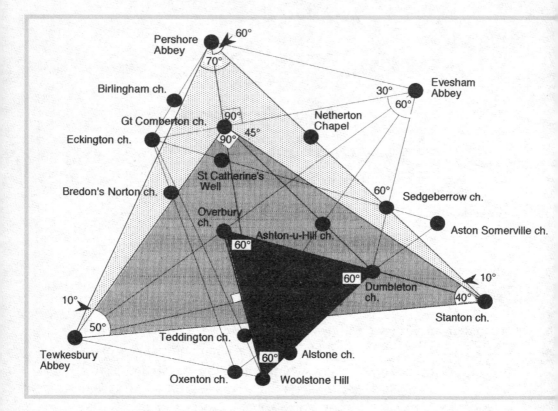

Fig. 65. Triangulation of mainly church sites on Bredon Hill and environs

The keys of the ancient surveyors

What had emerged from my researches into the Bredon Hill area was the realisation that precise angles could be laid out in the landscape using simple numeric ratios. Such a system of triangulating sites would have been well within the capabilities of ancient surveyors using basic equipment, providing they understood the principles involved. This ingenious method is similar to the system used in ancient Egypt, strengthening the likelihood of a cultural link.

However, the flaw in trying to demonstrate a conscious system of planning stemming from Neolithic times with my Bredon Hill survey was the fact that I was using, largely, the sites of medieval churches. Despite a few notable exceptions, there is only anecdotal evidence to connect the majority of medieval churches to known pagan sacred sites. One of the greatest criticisms levelled against Watkins by archaeologists is the concept of the continuity of usage.

But my study of the Bredon Hill area had achieved one thing though. It had revealed a system that could have been used for setting out sites within the landscape. But in order to verify that this system dated from Neolithic times, I needed an area to study with sites which clearly dated from the beginning of the third millennium BC. After careful consideration, I turned my attention to the south-west, to the area of Bodmin Moor in north Cornwall where there are some 15 stone circles within a 7.5 kilometre (4.65 mile) radius.

10

THE WHISPERING STONES

Similar patterns of site relationship can be shown to exist between
prehistoric sites and medieval churches

In the summer of 1975 I stayed with my family in a cottage in the village of Cardinham on the edge of Bodmin Moor. This gave me an opportunity to explore some of the impressive archaeological sites on the moor, and visit many of its fifteen stone circles. Although these monuments were probably erected over a period of several hundred years, the continuity of cultural ideas is evident. Since my original visit, the moor has frequently drawn me back. It is a haunting place and its sacred sites touch something very deep within my psyche. Over the years I have had many powerful psychic experiences within the stone circles, which have given me insights into the way they were used.

If the positioning of these circles could be shown to conform to the patterning of the Bredon Hill area of the Marlborough Downs, then the case for this type of landscape planning would be sealed. This area also served my purposes because it had already been thoroughly studied, and detailed surveys of the different monuments were available.

Bodmin Moor

Bodmin Moor, a large granite moorland, has been relatively undisturbed since prehistoric times, a rarity in the British landscape. To the north, the

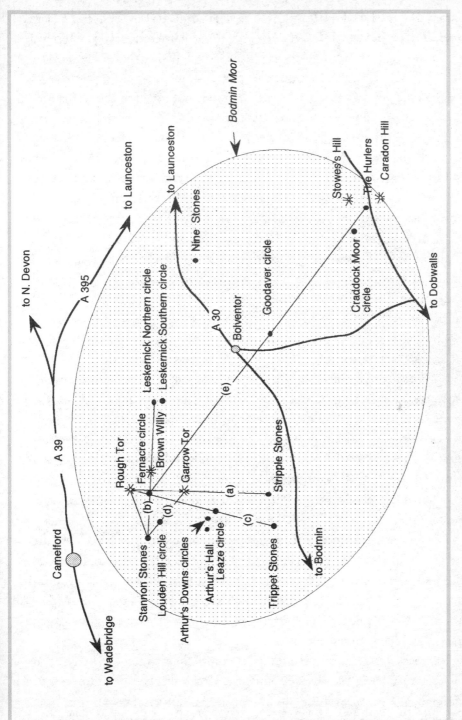

Fig. 66. Bodmin Moor area and its stone circles

pyramid-shaped peak of Rough Tor rises to some 400 metres (1312 feet) (see **photograph** 14). It is clearly visible from many miles away. Close by is the rounded hump of Brown Willy. Although slightly higher, at 414 metres (1358 feet), it is not quite such a prominent sighting point as its neighbour. Most of the stone circles in this area lie north of the A30 trunk road, a primary dividing feature of the moor. But south of this road are a major triple circle, called the Hurlers, plus the smaller circles of Craddock Moor, Goodaver and the Nine Stones of Altarnum (see Fig. 66).

Just off the moor, but still in the area, there is the intriguing stone circle at Duloe. It is small in diameter, just 10 metres (32 feet), but its stones are pure white quartz, ranging in height from 1.49–2.65 metres (4.89–8.69 feet), making them the tallest stones of all those found in the Cornish circles. There are two other historic sites in the locality, which could be linked to the moor circles. These are the henge monuments of Castilly and Castlewich. Castilly lies to the south-west, close to the junction of the A30 with the A391. Castlewich is in the south-east near the town of Callington.

In the distant past, this area had been extensively forested. But, like many upland areas, the moor was cleared in Neolithic times and is now, as then, used for grazing. It is a place of rugged beauty which endures the extremes of the British climate. The granite uplands take the full force of the westerly gales which, in the depths of winter, make it a desolate inhospitable place. Then the open moorland can be very boggy, but the dry summer months give easy access to the megalithic sites that remain.

The circles here do not have the same grandeur as those in Wiltshire. Sometimes they are barely discernible until one is almost on top of them. In many cases, the stones have fallen down or have been removed, as in the Louden Hill circle which has only recently been rediscovered. There are also a lot of hut circles (foundations of ancient dwellings), probably contemporary with the stone circles, which show that the moor was widely populated. The presence of so many stones makes the spotting of larger, partially hidden circles very difficult.

In most circles, the stones average no more than a metre in height and in some cases even less. Despite this, the circles display many impressive features. Their astronomical alignment to key sunrise positions has been noted by different researchers. The Stannon Circle, for example, picks up the May Day and Lammas sun as it rises between two peaks of Rough Tor. Alignments are made at the equinoxes when the sun rises over Brown Willy. This also coincides with a terrestrial alignment to the Fernacre Circle and the Leskernick Northern Circle.

The diameters of the circles range from the 13 metres (43 feet) of the Nine Stones Circle at Altarnum to more than 45 metres (148 feet) in the Louden Hill Circle. The size of these circles does not obviously reflect the estimated populations of the nearby settlements. Unlike parish churches, which generally stand at the heart of a village, stone circles are placed away from the centres of habitation. This may well be because their positioning was governed by astronomical and geometric considerations, or because the religious practices carried out there required them to be set apart.

In an article in *World Archaeology* (vol. 28(2) 1996), about the monuments on the moor, Christopher Tilley proposed:

 I want to argue that these were stones by which to learn, stones by which to remember, stones by which to orient, and stones by which to think. Learning, remembering, orientation and thinking are all processes requiring education and instruction. And such knowledge was both empowering to the individual, and offered a potential for structures of ritual authority to be effective ... I want to argue that one vitally important part of the ritual knowledge embodied in the stones, to be both conveyed and selectively 'released' by ritual specialists, was knowledge of the landscape and the spirit powers embedded in it.

Some of the circles are 'true circles' having been laid out with a peg and set diameter cord, others are irregular. The Fernacre Circle and the Stannon Circle are flattened circles, which Thom suggested were created by sophisticated geometry. Others have suggested that they were laid out by eye.

The Bodmin Moor patterns

My first step entailed re-checking all the grid co-ordinates contained in John Barnatt's excellent study, *Prehistoric Cornwall*. The main error involved the co-ordinates of the Stannon Stones, which Barnatt gives as

SX 1257 8010. This error also appears in the booklet *The Earth Mysteries Guide to Bodmin and North Cornwall* by Cheryl Straffon. The correct co-ordinates are SX 1257 8000. Being precise is very important. Even small discrepancies can throw out the angular relationships appreciably, particularly when sites are close together. As with the other studies of this book, all calculations are accurate to within 10 metres (32.8 feet).

Initially, I thought of using just the stone circles for the study, but then I decided to include some of the Tors which would have been used for sighting, as well as the henges at Castlewich and Castilly just off the Moor. Support for using the Tors as part of this study is born out by Christopher Tilley in his article cited above:

 That a desire that prominent Tors be visible from the circles played a major role in their precise location is evident from a consideration of a number of specific instances. Had the Leaze circle, positioned on a slope, been located no more than 30 metres or so to the south of its present position the outline of Rough Tor would have been invisible. Locating the Louden Hill circle south and down-slope from its present position would have had a similar effect.

I also included Trethevy Quoit and the earthworks at Arthur's Hall where more than 50 stones are set out in a rectangle within an earth bank. It is thought to have been for ceremonial purposes and is almost certainly contemporary with the circles and henges of the area. Table 4 gives details on all the sites included.

In the nineteenth century, in the *Journal of Royal Anthropological Institute*, A.L. Lewis published information on alignments of circles with each other and to other significant features on the moor. The three he listed which are relevant to this study are:

1. Stripple Stones–Garrow Tor–Fernacre Circle–Rough Tor
2. Stannon Circle–Fernacre Circle–Brown Willy
3. Trippet Stones–Leaze Circle–Rough Tor

Checking these against the computer showed that from the Stripple Stones, in the first alignment, there is a one degree error between the

Site	Grid Ref (sx)	Type	Size	Preservation
Craddock Moor	2486.7183	Stone circle	39m	Poor
Fernacre	1448.7998	Stone circle	46m	Good
Goodaver	2087.7515	Stone circle	33m	Good
Hurlers	2582.7139	Triple circle	43–33m	Fair
King Arthur's Downs (North)	1345.7751	Stone circle	23m	Poor
King Arthur's Downs (South)	1348.7750	Stone circle	23m	Poor
Leaze	1367.7729	Stone circle	25m	Fair
Leskernick (North)	1859.7990	Stone circle	31m	Poor
Leskernick (South)	1881.7961	Stone circle	30m	Poor
Louden Hill	1320.7949	Stone circle	45m	Poor
Nine Stones	2361.7810	Stone circle	15m	Fair
Stannon Stones	1257.8000	Stone circle	43m	Good
Stripple Stones	1437.7521	Henge	46m	Poor
Trippet Stones	1312.7501	Stone circle	33m	Fair
Castlewich	3707.6853	Henge	49m	Fair
Castilly	0310.6274	Henge	49m	Fair
Duloe	2345.5825	Stone circle	12m	Good
King Arthur's Hall	1296.7765	Earthworks and stones	48 × 21m	Fair
Trethevy Quoit	2594.6881	Portal dolmen	–	Good
Rough Tor	1453.8080	Alignment point	–	–
Brown Willy	1575.7975	Alignment point	–	–
Garrow Tor	1448.7850	Alignment point	–	–
The Beacon	1968.7929	Alignment point	–	–

Table 4. Bodmin Moor and area sites

Fernacre Circle and Rough Tor which, over a distance of some 5.5 kilometres (3.41 miles), is about 100 metres (328 feet). The alignment between Stannon Circle, Fernacre Circle and Brown Willy is accurate, but also includes an additional site of the Leskernick Northern Circle. The alignment of the Trippet Stones, the Leaze Circle and Rough Tor is also accurate. John Barnatt gives another alignment between Garrow Tor, the

Louden Circle and the Stannon Circle. Depending upon the position selected on Garrow Tor, this alignment also checks out. The computer gave an additional alignment between the Hurlers, Goodaver Circle and Fernacre Circle which is a distance of just over 14 kilometres (8.69 miles).

This gives five separate alignments in all:

1. Alignment A: Stripple Stones–Garrow Tor–Rough Tor
2. Alignment B: Stannon Circle–Fernacre Circle–Brown Willy–Leskernick (northern) Circle
3. Alignment C: Trippet Stones–Leaze Circle–Rough Tor
4. Alignment D: Stannon Circle–Louden Circle–Garrow Tor
5. Alignment E: The Hurlers Circle–Goodaver Circle–Fernacre Circle

Some of these alignments actually cross. If they do not, they would if extended far enough. The angular relationships between them, in degrees, works out as follows:

	A	B	C	D	E
Alignment A	0	90.44	12.05	51.57	54.22
Alignment B	90.44	0	102.49	38.87	36.22
Alignment C	12.05	102.49	0	63.61	66.27
Alignment D	51.57	38.87	63.61	0	2.66
Alignment E	54.22	36.22	66.27	2.66	0

When originally calculated this list did not look very promising. The only obvious significant angle was that between Alignment A – Stripple Stones to Rough Tor – and Alignment B – Stannon Circle to Leskernick Circle – which is just over 90° and the possibility that the angle produced between Alignment A and Alignment D of 51.57° which could have been related to the angle of slope of the Great Pyramid, 51.84°. However, calculating the angles between the sites themselves proved much more fruitful.

The angle at the Stannon Circle to Rough Tor and the Leaze Circle is 90°, while the angle at Rough Tor to the Stannon Circle and the Leaze Circle is 55°, which makes the angle at the Leaze Circle to the Stannon

Circle and Rough Tor 35°. This is a 35°–55° right-angled triangle, based upon a 7:10 ratio, which is exactly the same as one of the primary triangles that I found at Bredon Hill.

Here was the first clear evidence of a link with the Bredon Hill church sites. Precise angles of 35° and 55° between the two circles and the Tor are unlikely to have occurred by chance. It so happened that this triangle proved to be the primary triangle for the whole area. From it, all other circle sites could be generated. Fig. 67 demonstrates how this is done.

So, the design concepts behind the Bredon Hill sites and the Bodmin Moor sites – and, as I was later to discover, the Marlborough Downs pattern – are similar. The Bodmin Moor sites are Neolithic. The Bredon Hill pattern was primarily based on medieval churches, but included two Iron Age hillforts. And the Marlborough Downs circles spanned all three periods.

The evidence of site continuity, manifested through these geometric relationships, now appeared substantial. This continuity could have arisen through continuous usage over the millennia as Watkins suggested. There is, however, another possibility. If these sites were the home of some form of energy, this would be something that could be 'picked up' whatever the epoch. The resonance that I experienced throughout my body when I visited these sites could be my way of detecting this energy. Similarly, early monks could have been attracted to build their churches at those places which 'felt' right, places where they too experienced a resonance.

In that hot summer of 1975 when I first visited the stone circle sites on Bodmin Moor, my wife Diane joined me in our meditations and attunements at the places we visited. Our two young children would moan frequently: 'Not another stone circle daddy'. They preferred to be down on the beautiful Cornish beaches with a bucket and spade, but would thankfully play quietly among the stones while we tried to still our minds to sense the atmosphere of those sacred places. Many impressions followed that gave insight into how and why the circles were erected and provided us both with sufficient belief in the inherent power of these haunting sites.

But to return to the Bodmin circles. Once the initial triangle had been set out the next step would be to precisely locate a reference point on Garrow Tor. This can be found from a 55° angle from the Leaze Circle

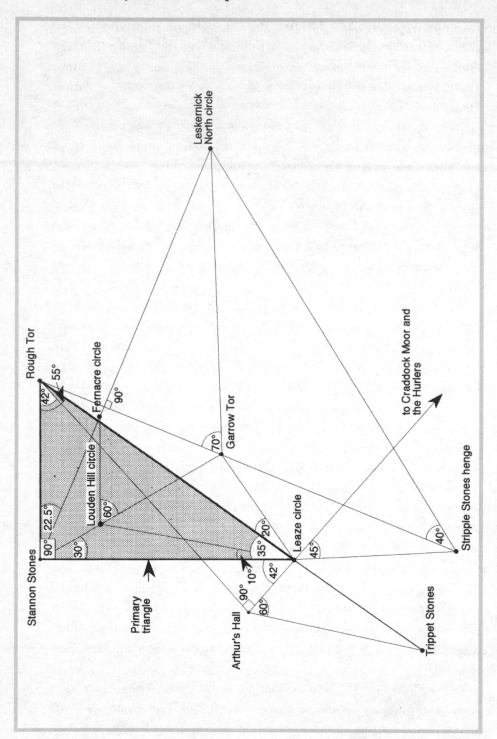

Fig. 67. Site relationships on Bodmin Moor

(Stannon–Leaze–Garrow Tor) and a 30° angle from the Stannon Circle (Leaze–Stannon–Garrow Tor). With the fixing of the Garrow Tor reference point, all other sites can be surveyed from the four sites of Stannon, Leaze, Garrow Tor and Rough Tor using a series of simple triangulations, based on the ratios I had already uncovered.

In practical terms, certain problems are posed by these four sites. Two of them are fixed landscape features, while two are movable. The pinnacle summit of Rough Tor is a very precise spot visible over a great distance. Garrow Tor, on the other hand, has a less well defined summit offering slightly greater flexibility in the exact positioning of a fixed reference point. At first glance, it would seem preferable to establish the alignments between the two Tors before trying to locate the circles, as the Tors are fixed sites. However, it is difficult to set out precise angles from the top of a mountain. While such places make good sighting points, much flatter areas are needed for the sort of landscape surveying we are talking about here.

After extensive trials that necessitated checking and re-checking the angles between all 23 sites, I came to the conclusion that the Stannon Circle was the key starting position. This process is one of gradual elimination, seeking all the time to evaluate whether it is possible to easily generate the position of other circles from the sites already marked. It is rather like following a river back to its source.

I would surmise that the Stannon Circle was probably established both by careful observation and by trial and error as it holds significant solar marking points.

Circle analysis

Having demonstrated again that it was possible to establish a geometric pattern that could link sites together, I began a more detailed appraisal of the site angles (Fig. 68). Initially, I analysed all the angles between the Stannon Circle and the other 22 sites in the survey. On this occasion I decided that as I was dealing with the angles between straight lines, all angles should be recalculated to fall between 0° to 90°. All obtuse angles (angles greater than 90°) would be represented by their acute equivalent. For example, 120° would be represented by 180° minus 120°, or 60°.

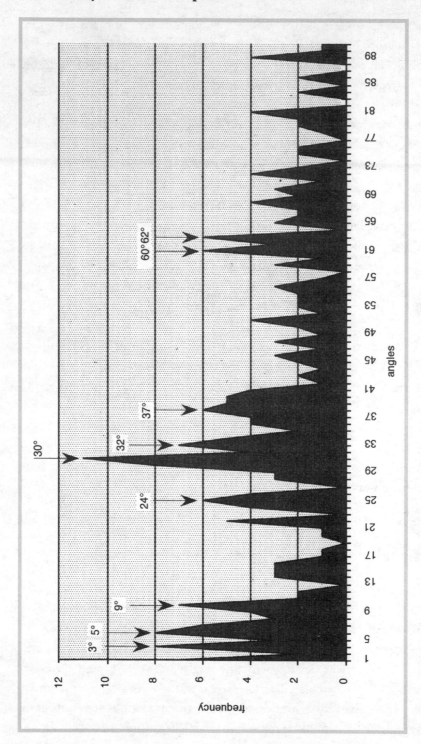

Fig. 68. Histogram of the angles generated from the Stannon Stones circle

I had two reasons for making this change. Firstly, it made the analysis easier. But secondly, in practical terms, setting out obtuse angles in the landscape can only be achieved easily by first creating their acute equivalent. For example, to set out a 125° angle it was easiest to first set out its reciprocal, 55° (180° − 125° = 55°).

The 231 angles generated between the 22 different sites and the Stannon Circle have the following order of frequency:

11 × 30°
8 × 3°, 5° and 29°
7 × 1°, 9° and 32°
6 × 6°, 24°, 37°, 60° and 62°
5 × 21°, 33°, 38° and 39°
4 × 8°, 23°, 25°, 31°, 35°, 36°, 40°, 50°, 67°, 71°, 80° and 88°
3 × 4°, 7°, 14°, 15°, 27°, 28°, 45°, 47°, 55°, 58°, 61°, 64° and 69°

All remaining angles occurred less than three times.

The expected average for a randomly distributed sequence for each angle can be shown as 2.78 occurrences, therefore any repetition in excess of three is above what would be expected. The 30° angle occurs nearly four times more frequently than chance alone would predict. Coupled with this, some of the 29° angles could have been intended to be 30°. For example, the angle from Stannon to Louden Hill and the Stripple Stones, computed as 29°, is based on two sites that are less than 1 kilometre (0.6 miles) apart, which means that one degree is less than the margin of error. Moreover, studies have shown that alignments are often made to the edge of circles and not their centres, which is where I established the grid co-ordinates.

The high incidence of 1° angles might also have been intended to be 0°, or straight lines. Again such variations can occur within the margin of error, particularly where sites are close, such as the Stripple and Leaze circles, and the Stripple Circle and the two circles on King Arthur's Downs.

Of course, you could use this same argument the other way around. What appears as 30° could actually be 29°, and 1° would be 2°, rather than 0°. Accepting that these errors would probably cancel each other out, there is still a high proportion of significant angles from this site.

Some angles that occurred with surprising frequency on Bodmin Moor also appeared in my Bredon Hill studies, but some were new. I wrote a simple computer program to generate all the angles between 0° and 90°, from their simplest ratios. It immediately became apparent that only 45 ratios are actually required. The ratio to produce, say, a 20° angle (11:4) is the same as that required for a 70° angle (4:11).

From this study, it was clear that 75 per cent of all the angles could have been easily constructed using no more than a few pegs, a measuring rod, some sighting poles and some lengths of twine, combined with the knowledge of a few simple ratios.

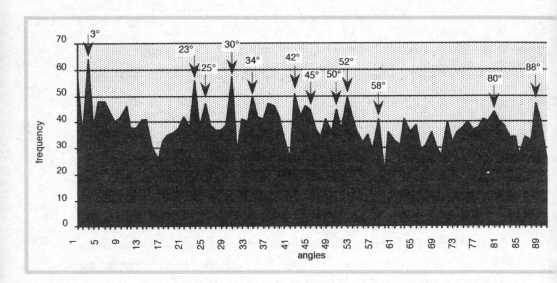

Fig. 69. Histogram of angle frequency between seven Bodmin Moor circles

Setting out the angles

The list of primary ratios given in Appendix 3 shows that in the majority of cases the highest numeral in the ratio falls below 20. Two that do not are 5°, which I have suggested is constructed from a 23:2 ratio, and 2°, which can be created approximately from the ratio 30:1. Many of the angles are in fact based either on a 19 unit ratio (including 19:1, 19:2, 19:3 and 19:11) or a 5 unit ratio and its multiples (including 10:9, 10:7, 5:6, 5:8 and 15:8).

The simple way to incorporate these ratios into a pattern would be to set up a circle with a diameter of 20 units. Following Professor Thom's studies we could assume, for this example, that the standard unit used was the Megalithic Yard and make the diameter 20MY. Using a backsight, the intersection point between the diameter and circumference could be marked off and the diameter line set out. The 19MY point on that line would have to be marked off and a right angle constructed there. This could easily be achieved, using small pegs and lengths of twine to make a standard 3:4:5 triangle.

Marking off this new line in lengths of 1MY, 2MY and 11MY would give the angles of 3°, 6° and 30° set from the backsight. The 30° angle could be checked, if necessary, by creating an equilateral triangle, but in practice the 19:11 ratio is accurate to 4.2 minutes of arc, which in most circumstances would be sufficient. The 6° angle is accurate to within 32 seconds of arc. The precision of this angle from its numeric ratio, I believe, played a fundamental part in ancient mathematics, astronomy and surveying.

Minutes and seconds

We divide the day into hours, minutes and seconds, which is based on a system that stems from ancient Mesopotamia. The Babylonians appreciated, from their astronomical observations, that time and space were related. The time that a star moved through a set arc in the sky was carefully measured using simple water clocks. This is why today both time and angles are measured in 'minutes' and 'seconds'. If a circle is divided into 60, each segment is 6°. By using a 19:2 ratio, a circle can easily be divided into 60 equal segments. Subdividing each segment into two will accurately give a 3° angle and, for most practical purposes, individual degrees could be fixed by dividing a straight line drawn across any 3° segment into three equal parts. Additional subdivisions could also be used to obtain very close approximations for minutes and seconds of arc.

To mark out those degrees which are based on the ratios of five or ten, it would only be necessary to mark off 10MY on the diameter of the original circle, construct a right angle there, then mark off the new line.

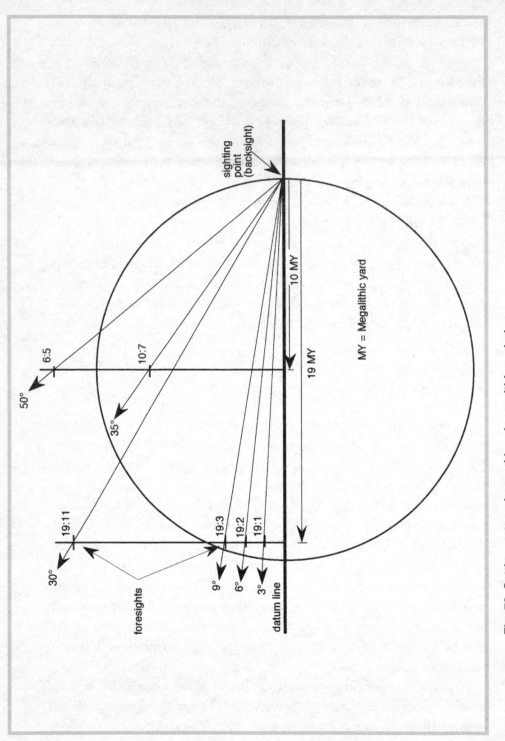

Fig. 70. Setting out angles and bearings within a circle

For example, setting the marker at 7MY gives an angle of 35°; while 12MY gives 50° (12:10 is the same as 6:5).

Although Professor Thom suggested that the Megalithic Yard was the standard unit for circle surveying, in practice, aligning sites is not dependent upon any fixed measures. Once the position of any site had been determined its relationship to its neighbour could be established by triangulation using any number of different units. I believe that there is a very good case to be made for the Megalithic Yard being used in the Marlborough Downs circles, but I am less convinced that it was the standard in all other cases.

All that would have been necessary to create these angles was one fixed measure. This could have been provided by using two straight equal staves 1–2 metres (3.28–6.56 feet) in length. The first would be laid on the ground. The second would be butted to it, end to end. If you then picked up the first and laid it at the other end of the second, repeating the process until you had counted off the required number of units, lengths could be measured off to a high degree of accuracy. For maximum precision, the line would need to be cleared of any obstacles or irregularities and laid on level ground. A small dowel peg driven into the earth could be used as a surveyor's pin to mark off the measurements.

As long as a 90° angle was constructed accurately, which is very easy to do, and the proportions measured exactly, angles of great precision could be set out on the ground. These angles could then be projected across the landscape using simple sighting techniques. So, stone circles and other megalithic focal points, such as barrows and menhirs, could have been placed with great accuracy. As we have seen, barrows are often sited on the horizon, which would have made them ideal surveying points.

I finished off my study on Bodmin Moor with a more extensive analysis of nearly 3500 angles between seven main sites in the northern part and discovered a similar patterning. The most frequently occurring angle was 3° with 64 incidents, followed by 30° which came up on 57 occasions. All the other angles that have a high incidence have already been discussed, except one – 52°. This is very close to the precise angle of slope of the Great Pyramid of Egypt, normally given as 51.85°. An angle of 52° is found between the Leaze Circle, Rough Tor and the Leskernick Southern Circle.

The alignment between Leaze and Leskernick crosses Codda Tor, which then forms a 'pyramid' angle with Rough Tor at its apex.

Stone circles and leys

No one is entirely sure why prehistoric man felt the urge to create stone circles. In some cases, such as Avebury or Stonehenge, their construction entailed enormous amounts of physical effort. They clearly had a special function, but how much was religious and how much practical we can never know.

The concept of leys is even more problematic. Despite claims for their existence going back nearly a century, orthodox archaeologists have yet to accept them. I am sure that the concept of angular site relationships will meet similar resistance. But what my Bodmin study demonstrates is the feasibility of landscape planning, not its probability. However, my studies are not the first to throw up this type of patterning. In his thorough research into the circles of the Peak District in Derbyshire, published in *Stone Circles of the Peak* in 1978, John Barnatt says:

 When the alignments between circles were investigated they pointed to a new direction for study, namely geometric relationship between circles. A large number of these have been found, particularly isosceles and right-angled triangles.

Barnatt analysed the alignments between the 20 circle sites and discovered more than 140 separate significant triangles. He concedes that any 20 randomly placed sites would produce a number of seemingly significant relationships, although he insists: 'The number of triangles found would be more than would form by coincidence.'

Fig. 71 shows one of Barnatt's designs, which incorporates the famous henge monument of Arbor Low. Barnatt notes:

 The triangles already examined are all on large scale with sides of between one and fifteen miles in length. They are measured along the horizontal, rather then following the contours of the land, and most of the circles are not intervisible. Obviously prehistoric man did not

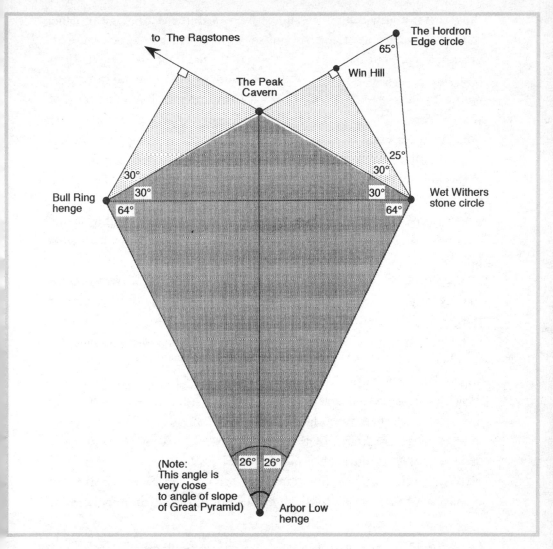

Fig. 71. The 'kite' formation of sites in Derbyshire (discovered by John Barnatt)

conceive or construct these, as it would be beyond his resources to measure the lengths without maps of the same accuracy as the Ordnance Survey maps used for this study.

His conclusion was the suggestion that Neolithic man must have aligned his sites to some invisible energy grid. However, my intention has been to show that not only could men and women, with the technology available to them, have geometrically laid out sites more than 5000 years ago with great precision, but that there is ample circumstantial evidence to suggest that this is precisely what they did, without reference to invisible geopathic forces. Not, I hasten to add, that I am implying that some form of subtle 'energy' is not a part of the picture, only that site relationships are not dependent upon an invisible energy grid.

In a similar vein, Josef Heinsch, in studies carried out in Germany and France during the 1920s and 1930s on the relationship of ancient sacred sites, concluded that they were based on 'fundamental triangulation using angles of 30° and 60° and the diagonals of a square and double square amongst other geometrically significant angles'. (Quoted in *Shamanism and the Mystery Lines* by Paul Devereux.)

The key to achieving this type of patterning is by knowing which ratios to use that give the required angles from a right-angled triangle. Learning these ratios by rote would not have been difficult. At the very most, the ratios of only 45 separate angles would have to be remembered, and this number could well have been reduced by the bisection of even-numbered angles. For example, an 18° angle can be generated from a ratio of 21.5:7. However, it could well have been easier to establish an angle of 36° using a ratio of 11:8, then bisecting it to obtain 18°. Similarly, 7° would probably have been generated by bisecting the 14° created by the simple 4:1 ratio, rather than using the complex ratio of 24.5:3 that generates 7° directly. By this method, the number of ratios that a Neolithic surveyor would have to remember could be reduced by a third at the very least.

Cosmological perspective and psychic overview

It should be remembered that to accurately locate a new site requires only two fixed positions and two precise angles. Once these have been established the rest is relatively easy. On a philosophical level, it becomes understandable that ancient peoples would want to expend time and energy on setting out patterns in the landscape if they looked upon the landscape as an integrated whole. Inclusive cosmologies, such as those found among the Native Americans, see heaven and earth as reflections of each other. Each circle site, whether dedicated to a god or goddess, or to a stellar or solar influence, would then be seen as the means to accessing spiritual influences that would infuse the life of the people. What better way to represent this harmonious concept than by linking together sites in an integrated geometric pattern?

It was while exploring the Bodmin Moor sites that I started to gain a perception of the different qualities of 'energy' that can be infused into the landscape.

I have already mentioned that in my early visits to different sites in the Cotswold area I had experienced what I could only describe as a strong tingling sensation in different parts of my body, but particularly in my back, hands and arms. Through my studies into healing, I had begun to differentiate 'flavours' in this energetic experience. I did this by simply checking out my feelings at the time of the experience. In some cases, the sensation would be vibrant and stimulating, while others were more diffuse and calming. Images also started to flood into my mind. I had similar experiences when dealing with healing cases. But then these images would relate to the client. In the landscape, however, my impressions seemed to connect to events in the distant past.

Each of the circles that I visited on Bodmin Moor had a different quality of feeling related in some way to the wider landscape pattern. They all related to some aspect of healing or spiritual study. Some of the circles appeared to have strong connections to the stars, while others seemed to create powerful links with the psychic matrix of the planet. But at all of them I felt a spiritual presence that I could best describe as the 'guardian' angel of the site.

I was aware that specific circles were used at set times of the year, such as the summer solstice and midwinter solstice, for special ceremonies. Perhaps these called forth spiritual energies which would then feed in, through this inter-linked network, to the matrix of the whole area. It showed me that a powerful spiritual awareness informed the vision that created these sites. It is a concept that I shall return to again.

Stone circle analysis

My research so far had attempted to show that sites were laid out in a specific geometric pattern. However, one other piece of circumstantial

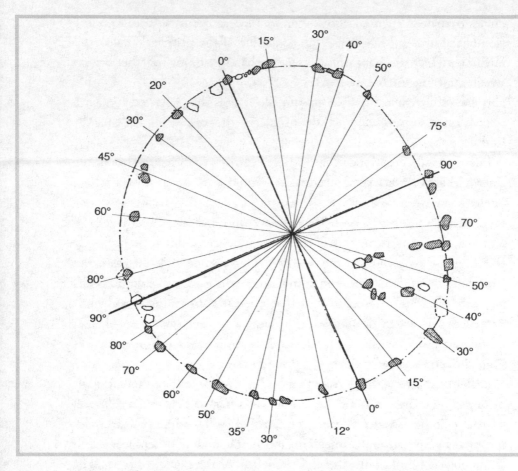

Fig. 72. Castle Rigg stone circle, Cumbria, showing position of stones in degrees from central axis

evidence deserves mention: this is the angular positioning of the individual stones that make a stone circle. The evidence of landscape planning suggests that certain angles were used frequently. If similar angles occurred within the stone circles themselves, then the case for these same angles in the landscape is again strengthened.

Some sites, such as the Rollright Stones of Oxfordshire do not lend themselves to this type of investigation because they contain many small stones placed close together. The ideal sites to study needed to be composed of single isolated stones that can be easily checked for their angular positioning. A problem, particularly on Bodmin Moor, is that many of the circles have been restored. So one cannot be certain that the present position of the stones is where they were placed originally.

Books which describe the different sites sometimes mention stones which mark the cardinal points or some astronomical alignment, but they also mention 'irregularly placed stones'. I had hoped to find research already carried out in this area. It would have made my task much simpler. Of the books that I have read, John Barnatt's *Stone Circles of the Peak* comes closest to this line of thinking, but while geometric forms are suggested for the circles in his study there is no analysis made of the angular relationship between the stones themselves. I have been unable to discover any other detailed analysis on whether the stones are randomly placed or have been laid to a specific geometric plan. I had to set about the job myself.

For my own investigations, I used the survey plans produced by Alexander Thom, Aubrey Burl and John Barnatt. Fortunately, these are generally well presented and, I assume, accurate. This made the task a little easier. To speed up the process of analysis, I scanned the plans into my computer. In sites with large stones and small diameters, such as the Duloe Circle, each stone covered at least a 10° arc, in some cases more. In larger monuments, such as Castle Rigg in Cumbria, each stone covers up to 5°. The ideal sites for assessment should contain about a dozen stones and have a diameter of at least 15 metres (49.2 feet). In all, I have analysed ten different sites within the British Isles which meet this criterion.

The first step in the analysis is to find a reference line which the angles of the stones can be related to. In sites that are pure circles, I took the north-south axis as the reference line. Where one of Professor Thom's oval or flattened circle shapes appears, I took the reference line from the axis of the design. One example of this was the Barbrook circle in Derbyshire, which contains eleven upright stones and which Thom defines as a flattened type. The reference line runs through the widest part of the circle, passing through the centre of one of the stones and lies at 55° from true north (Fig. 73). To make analysis easier, all angles are adjusted to fall within the 0° to 90° range. To determine the angles of each stone, you start from a 0° axis then work around the circle in either a clockwise or anti-clockwise direction (see Figs. 72–74).

In the Barbrook circle the 0° line passes through one of the stones. Moving in a clockwise direction from this stone the 30° angle passes close

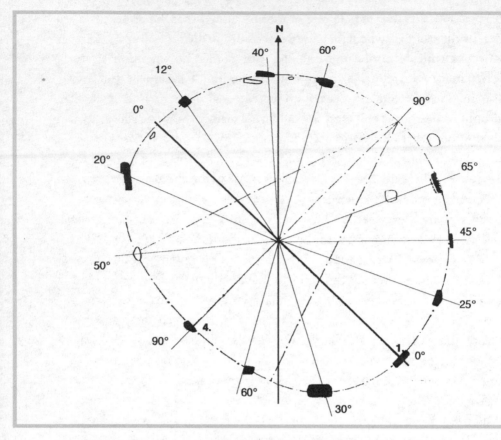

Fig. 73. Barbrook circle, Derbyshire, showing position of stones in degrees from central axis

to the centre of the next stone which sits within an arc of 25° to 35°. The 60° angle touches the edge of the next stone and the 90° angle passes through the centre of the third stone. In Thom's survey a fallen stone resides in the next placing which picks up the 50° angle, while the last stone in this half of the circle sits on the 20° line. Thom also shows an outlier stone which is positioned on a 30° angle. There is no stone marking the 180° position.

Continuing in a clockwise direction and starting again from 0° the next stone is set on the 12° angle, the next picks up the 40° angle which passes through the centre of the stone and another stone exactly marks the position of the 60° angle. The 90° position is not marked, but the

65° position is picked up. The next stone marks the 45° angle and the last stone is at 25°. In these three latter cases the angle line runs very close to the centre of the stones.

The Barbrook circle is typical of the others that I have studied, two more of which are at Castle Rigg in Cumbria, and the Trippet Stones on Bodmin Moor. The frequency of specific angles from these three sites is as follows:

Angle		Frequency
60°	×	6
30°	×	5
45°	×	4
90°	×	4
20°	×	4
0°	×	3
40°	×	3
50°	×	3
65°	×	3
80°	×	3
12°	×	2
15°	×	2
35°	×	2
70°	×	2
25°	×	1
32°	×	1
75°	×	1

In each of these cases, one stone would appear to highlight either 12° as in the case of Barbrook and Castle Rigg, or 32° as in the case of the Trippet Stones. This seems somewhat curious. There is no obvious explanation except that, by combining the angular position of these stones with one of the nearby stones, a 52° angle is created, at least in the Castle Rigg and Trippet Stone circles, which is almost the same as the angle of slope of the Great Pyramid.

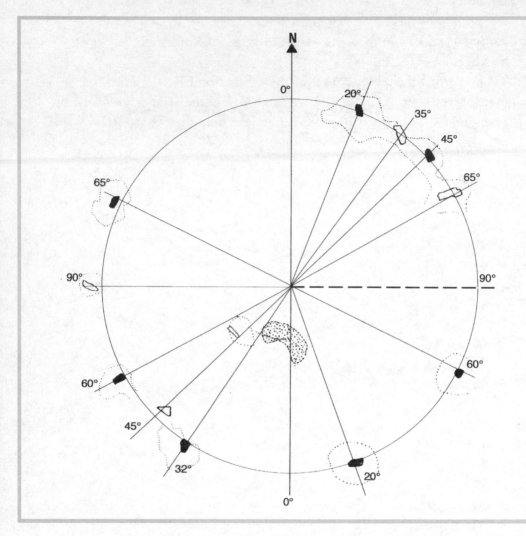

Fig. 74. Trippet stone circle, Bodmin Moor, showing position of stones in degrees from central axis

In all these cases the position of the stones has been indicated from angles radiating out from the central axis point. The repetition of these angles suggests conscious positioning rather than a random design. However, in any one quadrant of the circle there does not appear to be any obvious conformity to that sequence. For example, in the four quadrants of the Barbrook Circle the angles run:

South	West	North	East
0°	–	–	0°
30°	20°	12°	25°
60°	50°	40°	45°
90°	90°	60°	65°

There is a sense of a rhythm about these relationships for in the southern sector of this circle each stone highlights a 30° step (0°, 30°, 60°, 90°). The western sector has a 2, 3, 4 step ratio generated from the spaces between the stones that can be shown thus: 0° (+20°) 20° (+30°) 50° (+40°) 90°, where the figures in brackets are the number of degrees between the stones. Similarly the spacings between the stones in the eastern sector are 25°, 20°, 20°, 25°. The placing of the stones at these intervals might have held some coded significance known to the builders.

Other circles display similar diverse patterning. It is possible that these placements pick up landmark features indicating significant sun, moon and stellar risings. Thom was very careful in looking for these in his research and, although some stones are positioned this way, by no means all of them are.

The repetition of specific angles within these circles suggests that the Neolithic peoples were able to generate simple angles with some ease and precision. My studies on Bodmin Moor and Bredon Hill have shown that this same type of thinking was applied to site relationships. It is just possible that both areas are statistical quirks but the odds against this are enormous. In this context, the high incidence of 30° angles is precisely what one would expect if the sites were planned consciously.

What the Bodmin Moor and Bredon Hill studies confirm is the concept that similar patterns of site relationship can be shown to exist between prehistoric sites and medieval churches. The continuity of consciousness that held certain places sacred could well have travelled down through time. Yet this is a bridge that orthodox archaeologists find very difficult to cross as it does not seem feasible that such a folk memory could have endured for so long. However, if a beacon of 'spiritual' energy was

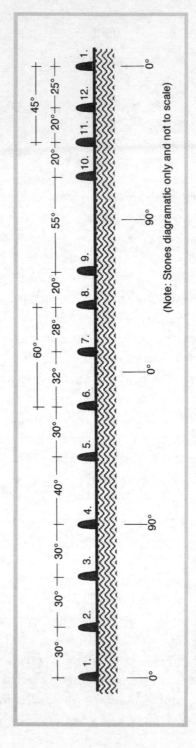

Fig. 75. Angular relationship of stones of the Barbrook circle

established at each site that, like its radioactive equivalent, endured over a long period of time, then we might have a way of crossing this divide.

The power that I experienced at the different Bodmin Moor sites is still very potent despite the 4–5000 years that have elapsed between the creation of the circles and the present day. The energy generated this way could endure through time, being available to those in future generations who were intuitively guided to these sources of spiritual nourishment. The wandering monks of St Augustine might well have sought out the 'holy places' of tradition, but they could equally well have sensed that some places were energetically 'special', suiting their religious needs.

From the circles there is evidence that some peoples, at least, in Neolithic times understood the basics of geometry and could set out angles with precision. It next became necessary to explore how they could have projected these angles across the countryside and the different surveying methods that might have been used.

11

SURVEYING THE LANDSCAPE

*Either the peoples who lived on these shores found time to work out
some fundamentals of geometry, or the knowledge was brought in
from elsewhere*

Since discovering the pattern of the Marlborough Downs and its links
with the geometry of the Great Pyramid of Egypt I had, for many years,
been puzzled as to how the ancient peoples of Britain could have had
sufficient technical expertise to set out the circles. The breakthrough
occurred when I discovered the simple system based on whole number
ratios for setting out angles. This system was similar to that found in
ancient Egypt based on right angle triangles with numerically related
sides, one example being a triangle with sides of ratio 7:10 which produces
angles of 55° and 35°. It was this important key that helped me understand how ancient peoples could have established the angular relationships which my discoveries demanded. The next crucial step involved
testing out this hypothesis in practice and determining the methods that
might have been adopted for generating specific alignments and geometric patterns across the landscape. There are two fundamental parts to
this process:

1) the techniques used for setting out a basic triangle on the ground;
2) the methods used for projecting alignments across the countryside,
   in some cases over considerable distances.

Linked to both these elements is the level of accuracy that might be obtainable. If, for example, it transpired that the tools of prehistoric man would only allow him to produce approximations to specific angles, then the whole concept would fall down. One can never be sure in any of these areas until the process is tried out in practice.

Site triangulation

I reasoned initially that the first step would be to find a level site and, secondly, a place which provided good views in most directions, such as the top of a hill. In practice, few stone circles are placed on the summits of hills, although a hill was sometimes close by. As John Barnatt says in *Stone Circles of the Peak*:

 Circles are rarely placed on the top of hills where the maximum number of accurate celestial alignments can be achieved. They are placed on gentle slopes so that there is a combination of distant and close horizons.

It is clear that setting out angles would require a level site or at worst a gently sloping one so that all distortions are minimised. In this context, hill top positions are not the ideal, which could explain why stone circles rarely appear on the summits of hills. The Bodmin circles confirm this as Christopher Tilley explains:

 A special relationship exists between the circles and individual Tors. All the circles are situated at a short distance, two kilometres or considerably less, from the nearest Tor. Some, such as the Hurlers, Fernacre, Leskernick Hill North and the Stripple Stones circles, are actually situated on the lower slopes of land immediately rising up to the Tor.

Sites which were intended to play key roles in the geometry, such as the Stannon Stones, or Dumbleton Church would need to have been carefully selected. Other sites could be determined by their relationships to those already established. Yet the flexibility of using a selection of different angles would allow a wide variety of potential positions to be examined before a final selection was made.

Once the decision had been taken to erect a new stone circle it would next be necessary to locate it in relation to those that had already been set up. There are two approaches that might have been adopted. The first could entail a local group of people deciding that they wished to put up a circle and then applying to the equivalent of the 'Town Planning Department' for its best placing. The second would depend upon an overall envisioned plan for an entire area that was then systematically created.

The first case scenario would result in circles or sites, having a geometric relationship, but not necessarily forming a coherent design. The second would show up as an overall pattern. My researches to date suggest that the second approach was adopted, at least in respect of the Marlborough Downs and the Bredon Hill sites. However, I have not so far been able to detect the same level of continuity or overall plan between the Bodmin Moor circles. This does not necessarily imply that one does not exist, only that it is not yet obvious.

The problem with the concept of an overall design is the length of time that would be necessary to create the pattern. From the archaeological evidence, it is known that circle building continued over many hundreds of years. This is certainly true of the sites on the Marlborough Downs. It implies that the design either evolved as it went along with different groups adding their piece to the tapestry or that the key sites were initially marked out in some way that allowed subsequent generations to build monuments upon them. Recent archaeological discoveries from Stonehenge have revealed large circular pits with evidence that they held large posts. As the English Heritage archaeologist Dr Wainwright said in an article in the *Daily Mail* in 1996:

 The logical explanation is that the pits held poles similar to those of the north-west Pacific Coast of America or Canada. They were erected at Stonehenge . . . probably as a mark of respect for gods or dead chiefs.

This evidence shows that sites such as Stonehenge could have been marked out at a very early stage, rather like the initial site pegging in a building project. Later, each pegged position could have been turned into a more permanent monument by the erection of a standing stone, burial mound or suchlike. Whether the monuments were set up on a pre-determined plan or the pattern evolved over a period, the first step had to be the marking out of the primary reference line of the site.

Let us travel back in time to the period when the Neolithic peoples had already established themselves on Bodmin Moor and created their first circles at the Stannon Stones and the Leaze, which had been linked geo-metrically to both Rough Tor and Garrow Tor. Using our imagination we could observe the planning stages for the erection of two new circles, one on Louden Hill (Louden Hill Circle) on the Stannon Circle to Garrow Tor alignment; the other at the foot of Rough Tor (Fernacre Circle) on the Stannon to Brown Willy alignment (see Fig. 76).

We do not know why the builders would have wished to place two new circles in these particular places but clearly they did it deliberately, whether their reason was pragmatic or spiritual.

The Louden Hill Circle also falls on a bearing of 45° from the Leaze Stone Circle angled to Garrow Tor. To fix this alignment precisely, the builders would first need to mark out on the ground at the Leaze Circle the alignment to Garrow Tor. Then, from this fixed reference line, they would have to have established a 45° bearing, projecting this back towards the Stannon to Garrow Tor alignment. Where the two lines intersected would mark the position of the new circle. Siting rods, suitably placed, would readily indicate the correct spot. Then would come the process of gathering the stones, and laying out the circle to whatever design was thought appropriate.

This new circle would now contain two reference lines, either of which could be used for future projections to additional sites. It so happens that the Fernacre Circle is set at a 60° angle from the line between Louden Hill Circle and Garrow Tor. The alignment from the Stannon Circle which passes through the Fernacre site, nestling at the foot of Rough Tor, marks the equinox sunrise. Once again, by plotting the two alignments, one from Louden and the other from Stannon, the intersection point of the two lines would mark the position for the new circle. In this way, a com-pletely interlinked matrix of sites could be established.

In time, other features would have been added. Perhaps a local chieftain wishing to feel linked into the spiritual energies of this place would build

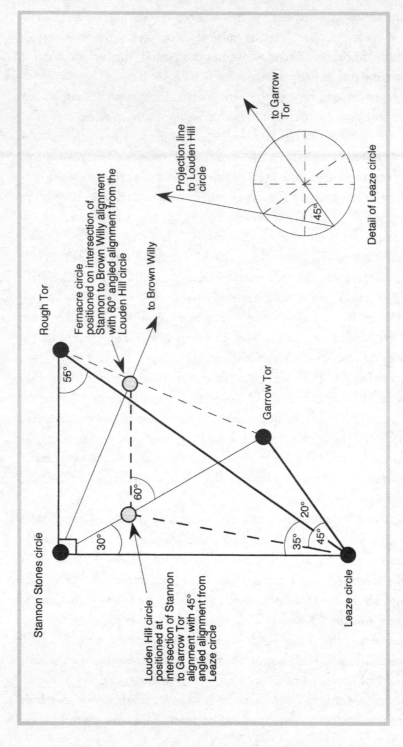

Rough Tor

55°

Stannon Stones circle

30°

60°

Fernacre circle positioned on intersection of Stannon to Brown Willy alignment with 60° angled alignment from the Louden Hill circle

to Brown Wily

Garrow Tor

Louden Hill circle positioned at intersection of Stannon to Garrow Tor alignment with 45° angled alignment from Leaze circle

35°

45°

20°

Leaze circle

Projection line to Louden Hill circle

to Garrow Tor

45°

Detail of Leaze circle

Fig. 76. Proposed siting method of new circles at Louden Hill and Fernacre

a tomb on an alignment. Or, maybe, a family would have an important member buried at a place that was linked into the invisible web of the area. Other features such as standing stones and trackways could have been built into the system. Ritual processional ways linking site to site, spiritual centre to spiritual centre, would also have been an integral part of the life of the communities who resided in these areas.

Establishing the angles

The theoretic process of interlinking sites is not complex, but there is a necessary subtlety and depth of knowledge in the processes involved. Two alternatives are possible. Either the peoples who lived on these shores found time to work out some fundamentals of geometry, or the knowledge was brought in from elsewhere.

There is no reason to suppose that the peoples of those times did not have their equivalent of Einstein. The great sage Imhotep, who lived in Egypt around 2800BC, was regarded as a god after his death such were the advancements he introduced in medicine, philosophy and architecture. The genetic stock of the British Isles could easily have produced similarly inspired individuals. But for genius to flourish, time must be set aside for reflection and study. If the daily life of every individual was taken up with the basics of living – the search for or cultivation of food, the making of clothes, shelter and the preparation of food – developing abstract knowledge would be well nigh impossible. A necessary prerequisite would be that some individuals were given exalted status and supported by the local populace, allowing them time for their observations and studies. This is the same sort of position enjoyed by the Druidic priests many centuries later who, by Roman times, had become an elite group. At some stage, either through their own studies or through ideas coming from another culture, the realisation of how angles could be created from simple ratios would have been discovered.

Ancient surveying techniques

In the previous chapter, I set out the way that angles could be generated on the ground. Having pegged out the required angle, the next step entailed projecting the alignment across the countryside. This would necessitate placing an initial sighting rod, which for accuracy should be positioned at least 100MY from the backsight.

The simple way to achieve this would be by using a weighted plumb-bob suspended by a thread from a cross-beam, positioned over the marker pegs. Ideally the backsight thread needs to be as thin as possible – a horse hair or similar would do. The foresight thread could be slightly thicker to make it visible, say 8 millimetres (0.2 inches). The two alignment threads would then be set just over 19MY apart. By sighting between these two positioning threads a ranging pole could be accurately located by another individual on the precise bearing over 100 metres (328 feet) distance.

I have carried out experimental work using this method and estimate that, with care, an accuracy of less than 2 minutes of arc could be achieved. In practical surveying terms, this would mean an error of only 48 metres (157 feet) in 19 kilometres (11.8 miles).

An alternative method using slightly thicker twine or rope plumbed over the angle pegs could be adopted. In this case the sighting pole is placed when visually the two threads merge together as one. The advantage of this method is that one person could both set up the angles as well as position the ranging poles. Thom proposed that 75-millimetre (3-inch)

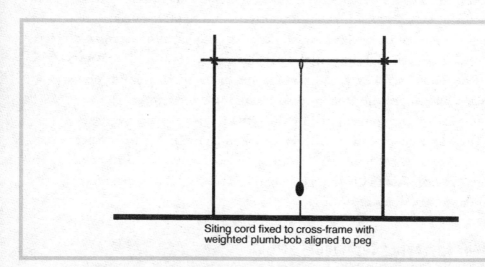

Siting cord fixed to cross-frame with
weighted plumb-bob aligned to peg

Fig. 77. Simple adjustable backsight or foresight marker that could have been used to set out angles

poles set 300 metres (984 feet) apart would give accuracies down to 1 minute of arc. In an article in the *Ley Hunter* magazine 1981, archaeologist R.J.C. Atkinson confirmed from his own fieldwork that sighting rods set out in this way would have an expected error of only 1 metre (3.28 feet) in 50 kilometres (31 miles).

Setting the alignment

Alfred Watkins gave some clues on how alignments might be achieved. He suggested, logically enough, that ley alignments started from the tops of hills. But circles, and indeed churches, are rarely found on the top of a hill. In the Bredon Hill area almost all churches sit at the bottom of the escarpment not at the top. And, as we have seen, a flat level area is a prerequisite for the laying out of angles, but not so suitable for their projection across the landscape. Somehow there had to be a way of linking these pieces together. Finally, I hit upon a solution.

The method, that I now believe was used, was based on a system of transits. This sounds complicated but in practice is simple. The first step involves setting up a backsight alignment from the surveying site, ranging up the side of the hill to the summit. This could be marked out by posts, cairns or other prominent markers. Clearly defined marker posts can be seen from a good distance and when two posts appear to be in vertical alignment, you know that you are on the correct bearing. Precise alignments can be generated using this system of so-called transits.

I discovered the value of transits from my hobby of scuba diving. In the middle of open water it is possible to locate a known wreck site to within a few metres. The system involves sighting on two objects which are some distance from each other. When they come into alignment you know that you are on the correct bearing. The crossing of two transit lines will give a precisely fixed position. I have used transits over 8 kilometres (5 miles) away with pinpoint accuracy. This system, using navigational lights, was adopted to guide ships into port on specific bearings. The further apart the two fixed positions the more accurate the transit, but as a directional method it still works when the distances are relatively small.

As soon as two ranging rods are set, say 100 metres (328 feet) apart, a very precise alignment can be plotted between them. You might like to test this out for yourself using lamp-posts or telegraph poles. Once any two are in line, a movement of your head of only a few inches to either side is easily detectable.

But over normal terrain, ground level alignments are easily obscured by trees and other objects. Ideal sighting positions, as with Ordnance Survey trig. points, are on the tops of hills. These can be seen from miles around.

Fixed object transits

Transits could be fixed with rock cairns, tumuli or siting posts. Rock cairns would be simple to set up but, except when they were on the skyline, they would not be easily visible against the background hill. Any skyline point would be more effective as it could be seen from great distances. Tumuli could also be used as a much more permanent landmark. Indeed, many have endured to this day. In his book *Prehistoric Avebury*, Aubrey Burl notes:

 Over the years that bridged the end of the Late Neolithic Period and the beginning of the Early Bronze Age it became more and more common to heap a round barrow over the grave, a circular mound twenty metres or more across, the height of two men but with no passage or entrance to the burial. Often these barrows stand on the skyline because the builders set them not on the summit of the hills and ridges but slightly down the slope where they would be visible from below. William Stukeley that remarkable field archaeologist, was the first to realise this. 'I observe the barrows of Hakpen Hill and others are set with great art not upon the very highest part of the hills but upon so much of the declivity or edge, as that they make appearance as above those in the valley.'

It is often thought that all round barrows were used for burials, but this was far from the case. In a survey of more than 350 excavated barrows in Wiltshire, 35 per cent of them housed no skeletons, cremated remains or artefacts. Moreover, Burl himself concedes that the Beckhampton long barrow, thought to have been built around 3000BC, on an alignment between Silbury Hill and Compton Bassett in the Marlborough Downs complex, was not a burial site. Like Silbury Hill, the reasons for its erection are unknown.

The placing of barrows in conspicuous positions would make ideal surveying points, which could be used repeatedly by future generations. But again, if they were located below the brow, they would not then be clearly visible against the hill from a distance.

In *Lines on the Landscape*, authors Nigel Pennick and Paul Devereux point out the extensive evidence of careful siting of barrows as part of landscape planning. The archaeologists of the Royal Commission for Historic Monuments have noted that some barrows in Dorset 'appear to be deliberately sited so that a complex system of intervisibility is created . . .' Pennick and Devereux also mention the work of archaeologist David Fraser in the Orkney Islands. As with the Dorset barrows, he found an extensive arrangement of cairns, carefully sited so that they could be seen between and across islands at distances up to 18 kilometres (11 miles).

In an article in the *Proceedings of the Prehistoric Society* in 1996, A.B. Woodward and P.J. Woodward state:

Another recent trend in barrow research has reflected an interest in the landscape setting of barrows. This has been touched on in a physical sense by the work of Tamlin and a more metaphysical sense by Lynch (1993) in her discussion of the selective intervisibility of the 'Brenig' barrows [in Powys] and by Pierpoint for the Yorkshire sites. Pierpoint's work seems to represent the earliest example of an application of 'view-shed' concept of Bronze Age barrow distribution and he provides an interesting analysis of other barrows sited in visible relation to other barrows and major monuments such as the Rudston monolith.

The use of sighting posts from saplings with newly stripped bark would work well provided the trunk was thick enough to be visible over reasonable distances. The light colour of the wood would show up particularly well against the dark background of a hill. It is possible that a white pigment could have been used to make the poles more prominent.

A post on top of a hill would stand out better if the bark was left on, as dark colours show up more clearly on a sky-line. There is evidence that there was such a post on Crickley Hill, Gloucestershire, at the end of

100-metre (328-foot) mound with a shrine at its opposite end. Sighting poles would have to be dug well into the ground, otherwise they would have been damaged by storms. Postholes have been discovered at many megalithic sites, but they have generally been seen as part of a building

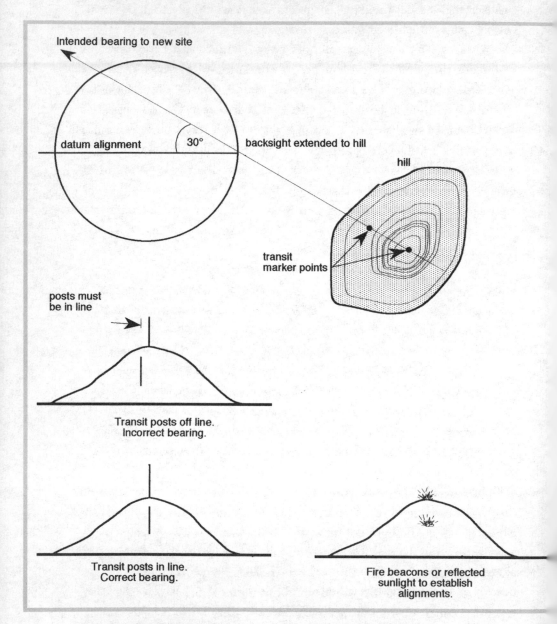

Fig. 78. Proposed methods for setting up angular alignments

structure. Not many postholes have been found on the tops of hills, but maybe this is because no one was looking for them. Professor Thom mentions only a few cases where holes have been discovered at obvious sighting points.

However, recent excavations on round barrows have revealed a number of post holes on the top of, or closely associated with, the barrow. Examples have been found at Buckskin barrow, near Basingstoke, Hants, the Four Crosses round barrows in Powys and the round barrows at Trelyston in Powys.

In areas where light-coloured rocks are found, such as on the chalk downs, cutting through the turf to reveal the chalk would make a highly visible marker. Similarly, a cairn of quartz stones in the Cornwall area would be readily visible, glistening in the sunlight, particularly if splashed with water. The facade of Newgrange in Ireland is totally made up of quartz stones, as is the Duloe Stone Circle.

Light transits

During Queen Elizabeth II's 1977 Silver Jubilee celebrations, the 1988 Armada celebrations and the 1995 VE day commemorations, fires were lit in the evening on top of traditional 'beacon' hills across Britain. The fires were clearly visible over great distances.

To create a fire transit, two fires would have to be established, one at the summit and one further down the hill on the desired bearing. Those watching to place their marker posts would need to be in approximate position before nightfall, of course. Then they would move into a position where the two fires were vertically aligned. This beacon method would fix a bearing with great accuracy.

Reflected sunlight could also be used as a light transit. I once lived in the Malvern area and often used to stroll along the ridge of the hills. The Malverns are aligned approximately on north–south axis. The afternoon sun would catch the windows of the houses around Malvern. As I strolled along, there would be a flash of dazzling light, which diminished again quickly as I took a few more steps. This is something that you can easily test for yourself. I have checked out this method of fixing a bearing and, over a distance of several miles, it is accurate to within a few feet.

To work accurately though, the reflective surface needs to be absolutely flat. If the mirrored surface was either slightly concave or convex the light beams would be diffused and spread over an area. But what would a reflective surface be made out of? Gold is the most likely candidate and gold artefacts have been discovered in Britain dated to around 2800BC, although it is not thought gold was available before then. A lozenge shaped gold plate was discovered in the nineteenth century in a Bronze Age burial mound near Wilsford, in the vicinity of Stonehenge. This plate is 17.8 centimetres (7 inches) long by nearly 15.2 centimetres (6 inches) wide and would appear to be based on angles of 40° × 50°, a 6:5 ratio. Around its edges is an incised chevron design which has nine segments to each side making a total of 36 segments in all. At the centre is a 3 × 3 diamond pattern (see Fig. 79). Its mirrored surface would have been quite capable of reflecting sunlight over considerable distances.

In an article in *Antiquity* entitled 'The Bush Barrow Lozenge: A Calendar for Stonehenge', A.S. Thom, J.M.D. Ker and T.R. Burrows argue a strong case for the lozenge's use for setting out alignments, based on the chevron design, to an accuracy 'better than 5 minutes of arc'. They conclude:

 An engineer, surveyor or astronomer provided with the lozenge could have built for a site, in the latitude of Stonehenge, a megalithic sun calendar and corrected it to the 'ideal' by trial and error in a far shorter time than he would have required if he had to do the work with nothing more than oral tradition.

Whether the lozenge was also used in the reflective way that I have suggested, the proposition put forward by Thom, Ker and Burrows supports the use of surveying techniques being applied to the prehistoric landscape.

On a trip to Newgrange in Ireland, the site guides told me that the previous year they had spent part of a day signalling with hand mirrors to wardens on the hill of Tara around 16.5 kilometres (10 miles) away. The flashing lights were clearly visible. Not only could messages be signalled, using this method but angles could also be set out.

If only one mirror was used it would need to be directed precisely on to the foresight. In practice, it is difficult to hold a mirror with sufficient

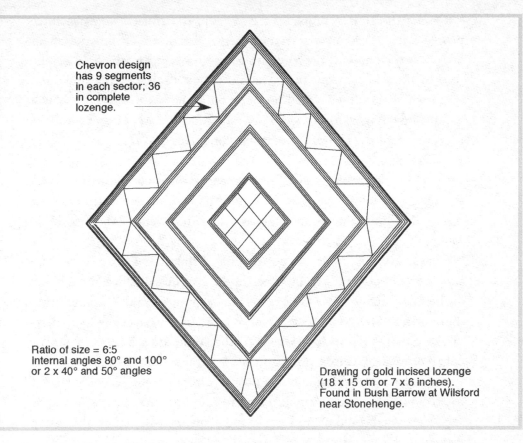

Chevron design
has 9 segments
in each sector; 36
in complete
lozenge.

Ratio of size = 6:5
Internal angles 80° and 100°
or 2 x 40° and 50° angles

Drawing of gold incised lozenge
(18 x 15 cm or 7 x 6 inches).
Found in Bush Barrow at Wilsford
near Stonehenge.

Fig. 79. Gold lozenge – surveying or signalling mirror?

steadiness, adjusting it all the time for the movement of the sun. A two
mirror method would work better. One would be positioned near the
summit of the hill; the other part way down, along the axis of the alignment. The person marking the angle at a distance would then only need
to align the flashing lights to know that they were on the correct bearing.

The symbolic use of fire has been central to the rituals and traditions of
many cultures, as Nicholas Hagger points out in his book *The Fire and the
Stones*. Watkins noted that many place-names associated with leys, such as
Beacon Hill or Golden Hill, had connections with fire, light or gold. The
tradition of beacon hills is well established in Britain and the use of flashing reflected sunlight could well have added to the mystique of the early
surveyors.

One of the greatest problems facing us in the understanding of these people is the lack of written evidence. One of the hallmarks of an advanced civilisation is the ability to write down information that can be used by those in subsequent generations. The Druids, and possibly those who went before them, used an oral tradition where information was handed down by word of mouth. Consigning large amounts of information to memory is not impossible, but requires rigorous training. However, knowledge retained this way is vulnerable. A plague, physical catastrophe or invasion could destroy generations of information at a stroke. All the knowledge that the Druids had accrued died with them at the hands of the Romans on Anglesey. All we have left are the megalithic monuments.

One answer may be in the positioning of stones in a stone circle. The stones do not obviously align to neighbouring circles. For example, none of the stones in the Leaze Circle show any alignment to the neighbouring monuments. This could be taken as an argument against my hypothesis of the interlinking of sites. However, the stones do adhere to a similar coherent angular pattern found in other circles. The evidence suggests that the placing of the stones was precise, although not generally related to astronomical or topographical features. So they may be positioned in such a way that could be read as a code by anyone who had the necessary key.

Astro-alignments

It is well known that Stonehenge is aligned to the midsummer sunrise, Newgrange is aligned to midwinter sunrise, and Maes Howe (Orkney) is aligned to the midwinter sunset. Thom suggested that all circles incorporated astronomical alignments in their design. These also delineate lunar phases, stellar risings, and so on.

From different Bodmin Moor studies, there is evidence that some alignments conform to astrological features, such as the rising or setting of the sun and moon on specific days of the year. My own research reveals another type of relationship dependent not upon the stars or the motion of the sun and the moon, but upon a geometric pattern laid out in the landscape. Both of these aspects could have been incorporated into the alignments, but the difficulty here is discerning which site would be related to which particular heavenly body and the time that it was being observed.

Leys or terrestrial alignments can pass through a number of sites all on the same bearing. However, the topographical features vary considerably around each site. It may be that one site and its alignment act as the key to the whole ley. For example, the alignment depicted in Fig. 1 was claimed by Watkins to show the midsummer sunrise as it climbed over the Malvern Hills, as seen from the Shew Stone, which is about 170 metres (558 feet) from Clutter's Cave. This initial point could have been symbolically seen as firing the energy of the ley which stretches as far as the church of Abbey Dore, many miles distant.

The problem with this is that other points along the alignment would have different times and bearings for their midsummer sunrise. So while astro-alignments might have been incorporated into the design of individual sites, I have not been convinced of its inclusion in

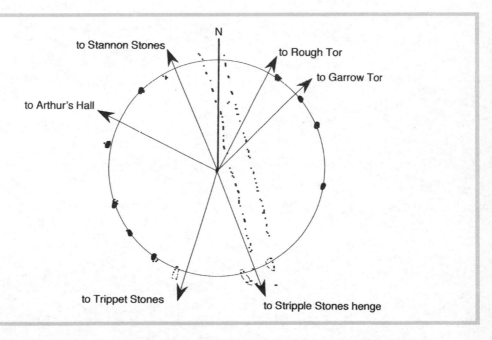

Fig. 80. Leaze circle showing alignment positions to neighbouring circles and tors

the patterns of site relationship, which are more consistent with a geometric design.

I had demonstrated the methods by which megalithic people could have surveyed and laid out sites in the landscape. The next crucial step entailed applying my findings to the Marlborough Downs complex, to understand how the great circular patterns could have been created.

12
THE MYSTERY UNRAVELLED

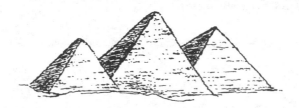

The enigma of Silbury Hill can now be revealed

I had come a long way in understanding the methods that megalithic peoples could have used to set out geometric patterns in the landscape. I was sure that if I and a small group of colleagues were deposited on a desert island, we could lay out a group of geometrically related sites based on what I now knew, using nothing more than the basic materials at our disposal. Yet, at heart, the Marlborough Downs pattern still contained some profound mysteries. I needed to check out, in detail, how this pattern could have been set out in the landscape and in doing so I was to make some further important discoveries. But before exploring the application of these surveying techniques to the Marlborough Downs, let's recap on the facts that have emerged so far.

Laid out over the Marlborough Downs is a vast geometric pattern based on two interlocking circles, each of identical size, 19.3 kilometres (12 miles) diameter, related proportionally to the size of the Earth. Woven into this design is the inherent geometry of the Great Pyramid of Egypt. I was also aware that key sites in this and other patterns held a form of spiritual 'energy' that produced a resonance similar to that which I had experienced in my healing practice. I was not alone in this. Many people have reported similar experiences. To fully uncover the mysteries of the Marlborough Downs, I considered that the following crucial questions still had to be answered:

▲ How, in precise terms, were the circular patterns laid out in the landscape in accordance with set sizes and ratios?

▲ How was it possible to accurately assess the size of the equatorial circumference and the polar meridian of the Earth inherent in the circles?

▲ What was the link between the creators of the Egyptian pyramids and the ley patterns of Britain?

▲ What made the Great Pyramid so special that its design was imprinted into one landscape while its structure was built on another?

▲ What was the relevance of the site energies that I and others have repeatedly experienced at sacred places in the landscape?

The next step had to be the unravelling of the methods used for laying out the Marlborough Downs pattern, though I was mindful of these other questions that still had to be answered.

Laying out a landscape circle

Henge monuments with their banks and ditches could be considered circular. But stone circles are, more accurately, individual stones laid out on a circular plan as the stones in most cases do not run continuously around the circumference.

The circles of Marlborough Downs represent on a grander scale the basic geometry of a stone circle. In other words, they are a series of individual points equidistant from a common centre. They fall on the hypothetical circumference of a circle, rather than form a true circle themselves. This, I believe, is crucial to their construction.

My research into the positioning of sites on Bodmin Moor and in the Bredon Hill area had revealed the use of triangulation, which incorporated fixed angles and distances to establish site relationships. When two sites have been established a third can be located, if one knows either the angles, distances or a combination of the two.

All points on the Marlborough Downs circle are equidistant from a common centre. I needed to consider in landscape surveying terms how this might be achieved. Two basic approaches were possible. Firstly, all measurements could be made from a common centre. Providing that each

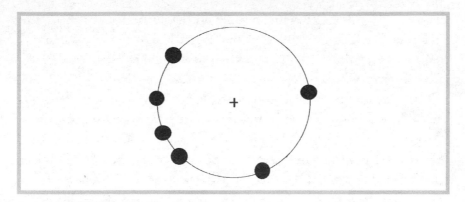

Fig. 81. An imaginary circle drawn through points equidistant from a common centre

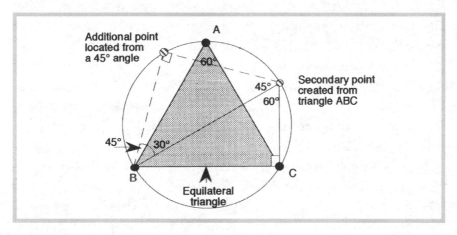

Fig. 82. Points created on the circumference of a circle without reference to its centre

point was the same distance from the centre they would all lie on the circumference of a circle. However, it would be difficult to make such measurements accurately. Secondly, it is possible to establish a series of points that lie on the circumference of a circle without reference to its centre. For example, if an equilateral triangle was laid out in the landscape, its three points would lie on the circumference of a hidden circle – a circle can always be drawn through any three points not in a straight line. Then, if a right angle is constructed at one point of the triangle and another line constructed from a second point so that it bisects the opposite side, where those two lines intersect would also lie on the circumference of a circle. This sounds a little complicated but Fig. 81 shows how this can be achieved. Using this method a series of points could be established on the circumference without reference to its centre.

The evidence from the Marlborough Downs suggests that the length of the radius was important and would therefore have been a starting point. So the centre would have been one of the reference points. At first, I could not conceive how it would have been possible to measure out all fifteen circumference points, a distance of a fraction under 9.6 kilometres (6 miles) from the centre, to the level of accuracy that had been achieved.

Then I realised that a combination of the two methods might have been used. In other words, if the centre and just one point on the circumference was fixed, all other points could be established through triangulation from them, providing the correct internal angles were used. In practice, this would mean that the distance from the centre to the circumference would have to be measured accurately only once, rather than for each of the separate sites. Applying this logic to the Marlborough patterns entailed an analysis of the grid references of the centre and circumference points, and then establishing angular relationships between the places on the circumference.

Initially, I chose to study the eastern circle. I also assumed that the primary reference line coincided with the alignment of the two centres. This proved to be wrong. But I found, by chance, that a whole series of simple angular relationships of 20°, 40°, 50°, 60° and 90° were related instead to the East Kennett long barrow. I was elated. It had taken little effort to make this discovery once all the angular relationships had been worked out.

The starting point of the circle must have been the alignment between the East Kennett long barrow and the centre of the circle. Once these two places had been fixed all the other sites could be calculated and then surveyed out, providing that the correct internal angles were used and the ratios that produced them were known.

The East Kennett long barrow is a huge mound, on the western side of the circle, aligned to its circumference. From it there are clear views through to the escarpment which lies just behind the centre of the eastern 'circle'. Today, it stands on private land, its back covered by many trees which give it a distinct bristly appearance that is clearly visible for several miles. It is thought that it was probably constructed at the same time as its more famous neighbour, the West Kennett long barrow, which has been radiocarbon dated to around 3600BC. However, no radiocarbon dates have been taken from the East Kennett barrow, so one cannot be certain. It is slightly smaller than the West Kennett barrow, being about 90 metres (295 feet) long by 30 metres (98 feet) wide.

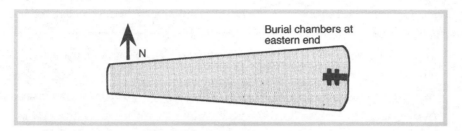

Burial chambers at eastern end

Fig. 83. Diagram of West Kennett long barrow

Long barrows were ostensibly created as burial tombs, but the tomb part of most barrows accounts for no more than an eighth of their total length. No satisfactory explanation has been given for this and the rest of the mound appears to serve no practical purpose. However, as a surveying platform, it could certainly be put to good use. There are puzzling aspects to the burials too. The bones appear to have been stripped of flesh before interment, and some parts were missing. There is also evidence that barrows were used for collective burials over a considerable period of time.

Abruptly, at around 3100BC, all long barrow development ceased. As Aubrey Burl says in his book *Prehistoric Avebury*:

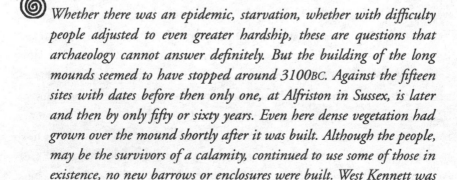

Whether there was an epidemic, starvation, whether with difficulty people adjusted to even greater hardship, these are questions that archaeology cannot answer definitely. But the building of the long mounds seemed to have stopped around 3100BC. Against the fifteen sites with dates before then only one, at Alfriston in Sussex, is later and then by only fifty or sixty years. Even here dense vegetation had grown over the mound shortly after it was built. Although the people, may be the survivors of a calamity, continued to use some of those in existence, no new barrows or enclosures were built. West Kennett was

abandoned. Dry-stone walling tumbled in over the bones and it was not for 'some further interval' that people returned to restore it.

This dating is significant as either the surveyors of the Marlborough Downs circles incorporated an already existing structure into their plan or the layout of the circles was begun at the same time as the building of the mound. The East Kennett barrow was erected on raised ground that gave good sighting lines through to the main points on the western edge of the eastern circle. Table 5 gives the angular relationships between the 'centre' and the East Kennett long barrow to the different sites of the eastern circle.

Most of these angles can be generated from fairly simple ratios and have a maximum error from an exact angle of only three minutes of arc. The angles which are not so easy to reconcile to ratios are 71° (29:10), 44° (29:28), 56° (20:13.5) and 38° (20.5:16). With the tools that were available to the surveyors, the ideal ratios would be those that did not involve large or complicated ratios, particularly ones where both factors were large, such as 29:28. Even if extreme care was taken with the measuring rods, errors would be bound to creep in. Conversely, if only one factor is a high number then errors are minimised. The histogram analysis of the circles on Bodmin Moor shows a high incidence of 88° angles, which I have suggested was generated from a ratio of 30:1 (see Table 4). To be more accurate, this should be 28.5:1 but the difference between these two ratios is only six minutes of arc which is negligible.

The ratios produced from the pattern could have readily been surveyed from both the centre and the East Kennett long barrow using transits. The crossing point of the two alignments from each surveying centre would establish the exact position of the new site. For example, Wroughton church site is on a bearing of 90° from the circle's centre and 45° from the East Kennett long barrow. By constructing these angles at the two sites and projecting the correct alignments across the landscape, their intersection could be established with some accuracy. It so happens in this particular case that there are backsight tumuli for both of these alignments marked on the 1:25,000 scale map. The tumuli on Thorn Hill, about 880 metres (2886 feet) away, would have been clearly visible from the East Kennett long barrow. The tumuli on Poulton Downs are now hidden by a

Site	Angle from centre			Angle from East Kennett long barrow		
	actual	assumed	Ratio	actual	assumed	Ratio
East Kennett tumulus	4°		28.5:2	88°		28.5:1
Waden Hill tumulus	16°		7:2	82°		28:4
Avebury	20°		11:4	80°		17:3
Winterbourne Monkton church	32°		8:5	74°		7:2
Berwick Bassett church	48°		10:9	66°		9:4
Winterbourne Bassett church	51°	(50°)	6:5	64°	(65°)	15:7
Broad Hinton church	60°		19:11	60°		19:11
Wroughton church	90°		1:1	90°		1:1
Crossroads	31°	(30°)	19:11	16°		7:2
Hinton Downs tumulus	16°		7:2	8°		28.5:4
Savernake Forest church	88°		28.5:1	44°		29:28
Wootton Rivers church	56°		40:27	62°		15:8
Giant's Caves earthworks	38°		23:18	71°		29:10
Huish Hill earthworks	22°	(20°)	11:4	79°	(80°)	17:3

Table 5. Angles drawn from the two base lines (East Kennett long barrow and centre of eastern circle) to fourteen sites on the circumference of the circle.

strip of trees which makes siting to the centre impossible at present. But they can still be seen prominently from the opposite escarpments on the main ridge of the Marlborough Downs.

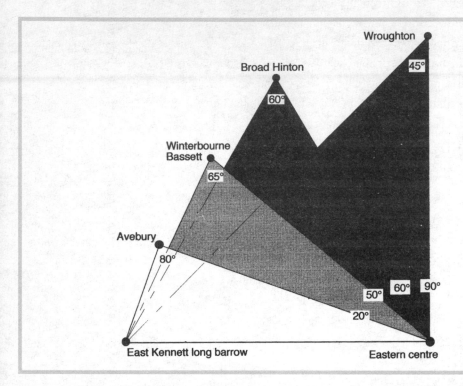

Fig. 84. Angular relationships

From the standpoint of surveying, the centre of the eastern circle is ideally located at the edge of the village of Ogbourne St Andrew. It is in a flat area formed initially by the meandering of the River Og approximately 137 metres (450 feet) above sea level. The valley opens out to the south-west but to the west, north, east and south the steep slopes of the surrounding hills rise up to over 213 metres (700 feet). These slopes make ideal back-sight positions for alignments in all directions. The intersection of the line between the two centres with the circumference of the western circle lies on the side of the escarpment and provides extensive views particularly to the south and west. Even the radio masts on the top of Morgan Hill can be seen nearly 19.3 kilometres (12 miles) away. This is the only place where it is possible to see across the western circle and indicates that this position was chosen with care.

Plotting the alignments on the map from these two bearings from East Kennett to Wroughton church and the centre of the eastern circle to Wroughton church shows several tumuli strategically positioned on the East Kennett to Wroughton line. The alignment from the centre to Wroughton church does not show any additional earthwork features, but this would not necessarily be significant.

Additional significant marker points indicated in other alignments from East Kennett long barrow can be listed as follows:

East Kennett – eastern edge of Avebury henge – Winterbourne Monkton church
East Kennett – stone circle – aligned earthworks – Berwick Bassett church
East Kennett – tumuli – Broad Hinton church
East Kennett – tumuli – Crossroads

There is also a backsight alignment from the western end of West Kennett long barrow through East Kennett long barrow to the Giant's Grave hillfort and earthworks.

Technically, with a small group of helpers, a competent surveyor could have marked out the key sites on the circle in a relatively short time. Naturally, the building of a long barrow would have been a much more

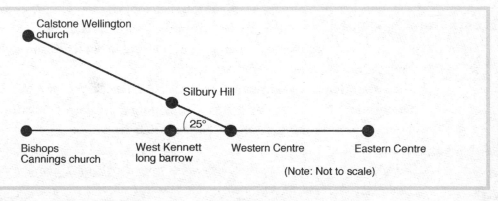

Fig. 85. Diagram of relationship between centres, Silbury Hill and West Kennett long barrow

formidable undertaking and required a considerable amount of collective help. They would, of course, have to have worked to a plan which gave the correct angles between the centre and the circumference. This could have been done using a scale model made of pegs, posts or stones on a level site, like that found at the henge monument of Avebury.

Solving the enigma of Silbury Hill

The layout of the western circle is in principle no more difficult to create than its eastern counterpart, except that the position of its centre would have been determined by geometrical rather than topographical considerations. The alignment of the two centres terminates at the church of Bishops Cannings on the circumference of the western circle, passing through the eastern end of the West Kennett long barrow and some earthworks on the top of the prominent Easton Hill on its way. In the case of the western circle, the two reference points would appear to be the centre and the church at Bishops Cannings. All other sites can be easily fixed from these two positions.

One significant alignment from the western centre passes across the top of Silbury Hill, over a tumulus and on to the church at Calstone Wellington. This is on a bearing of approximately 25° from the reference line.

So here we are back at Silbury Hill, this enigmatic monument, the largest man-made prehistoric hill in Europe which has no known practical function (see **photograph** 4). A conical, flat-topped mound, it rises to a height of about 40 metres (130 feet) from the base and covers an area of over 5.5 acres. It slopes at a precise angle of 30° and its flattened summit is about 30 metres (100 feet) in diameter.

Its composition is also intriguing. It is constructed of layers of organic and inorganic material in a way that gives the mound extreme stability. In his book *Stonehenge and Its Mysteries*, Michael Balfour writes:

 During ... [phase 2] ... chalk was taken from a new ditch, with an internal diameter of 107 metres; this was dug around the existing mound and incorporated into a method of construction also known to the pyramid builders at Giza. A succession of layered chalk block walls

were made, infilled with local rubble and with occasional internal
walls or buttresses directed to the centre; each was of course smaller
than the previous one, and then rose to form a sort of stepped cone.

At this point the builders decided that the mount was not going to be high
enough for their purposes, so the original ditch was carefully filled in to
prevent subsidence and the base extended to its present size. Its construction began around 2750BC and Professor Atkinson has calculated that it
probably took 500 people about fifteen years to build. There is some
doubt that such a large workforce would be available for the erection of a
single monument. The construction could have been spread over up to
150 years, using fewer people.

A number of excavations have been carried out. Tunnels into the centre
of the hill have produced very little in the way of artefacts. There are certainly no sumptuous burial chambers the size of the mound would suggest. To archaeologists, Silbury Hill remains a mystery.

It does not lend itself as a foresight marker for the astronomical observations that Professor Thom considered important. No known sun or
moon positions are indicated from the top of the hill. Yet there it sits,
neither burial marker, nor astronomical observatory. So what was its
function?

From the top of this enigmatic monument, looking through a surveyor's eyes, one function is obvious. The height of Silbury Hill gives
excellent views, to the north, south and west. On the eastern side of
Silbury Hill, about 500 metres (1640 feet) away, there is the long level
high back of Waden Hill. It so happens that, standing on the very top of
Silbury Hill, it is possible to see across the ridge of Waden Hill to the main
uplands of the Marlborough Downs (see **photograph 5**). By coming down
just a few feet the views become blocked.

This surely is the vital clue that explains why the height of this impressive mound was increased. Its builders needed to see beyond the ridge of
Waden Hill through to the distant horizon of the Marlborough Downs
uplands. A few feet lower and this view would be obscured.

Why should it be necessary to see long distances in all directions?
Astronomical observations could be one explanation, but I had already
checked them out and found them not to be significant. Perhaps there was

some religious function but, on a practical level, surveying would be the most important reason for seeing across the top of Waden Hill.

In the summer of 1996, I had the opportunity to test out my theories with surveyor and friend Paul Mills. We had to book the use of a theodolite in advance and prayed that the weather would be kind to us. The day, when it dawned, was slightly cloudy but generally clear. We met in the morning at the Red Lion pub in Avebury and together with my daughter, who was to keep notes, we set out for Silbury Hill.

The climb up to the summit takes a few minutes and we were soon looking at the magnificent views that stretched out in all directions from the top of this amazing monument. The ridge of Waden Hill in the foreground to the east was very clear. Beyond it, we could see the main back of the Marlborough Downs dotted here and there with tumuli topped by towering beech trees making distinct marker points that were visible over a considerable distance.

We first decided to test the visual horizon. By walking only a few paces down the eastern side of Silbury Hill the views to the Marlborough Downs became blocked. This demonstrated what must surely be the primary reason for the builders to increase the size of the hill during its construction: the need to see over Waden Hill to the distant landscape.

We then set our theodolite datum line on the church clock at Avebury and very soon marked out the bearings of a number of prominent ancient sites, like the East and West Kennett long barrows. From this vantage point we could also see a number of church towers and spires including Winterbourne Monkton, Berwick Bassett and Winterbourne Bassett. Our surveying work aroused the curiosity of a few other people who had made the climb.

A modern theodolite, even with the spread of its supporting legs takes up no more than a metre of space. Ancient peoples would have had to have used the whole of the summit of the hill to set out their angles. Yet I am sure that they could have achieved the same level of accuracy in their bearings, using nothing more than staves or suspended string sighting markers. The flat top of this hill with its sloping sides is the ideal site for the simple surveying methods I have described in this book. It is sufficiently large to mark out angles accurately and its views in all directions allow precise bearings to be established from simple numeric ratios. But why here? Why go to all the bother of building a surveying platform at this particular spot? Why did they not establish their surveying point on the top of Waden Hill, which would have entailed considerably less work? There had to be a good reason.

I felt that some clue must lie in Silbury Hill's position on the alignment of the centre of the western circle to the church at Calstone Wellington. A few of the significant angular relationships, from the top of Silbury Hill, include:

Site	Angle	Site
Avebury	60°	Centre (east)
Avebury	80°	Bitham barrow (grid ref. 1373 6742)
Avebury	40°	West Kennett
East Kennett long barrow	50°	Centre (west)
East Kennett long barrow	55°	Stone Circle 1 (grid ref. 0974 6716)
East Kennett long barrow	50°	Tumuli (grid ref. 1811 7020)
Bitham barrow	20°	Centre (west)
Bitham barrow	40°	West Kennett long barrow
Bitham barrow	55°	Stone Circle 2 (grid ref. 1098 6932)
Bitham barrow	15°	Pyramid point (west)
Bitham barrow	40°	Pyramid point (east)
Bitham barrow	90°	Pyramid point (apex)
West Kennett long barrow	80°	Centre (east)
West Kennett long barrow	40°	Bitham barrow
West Kennett long barrow	25°	Pyramid point (west)
West Kennett long barrow	50°	Pyramid point (apex)

The hint of a thunderstorm in mid afternoon eventually drove us off Silbury Hill and back to the pub. We felt we had accomplished sufficient to validate its potential as a surveying point. However, I could not work out why so much effort was put into raising this structure when there was a hill nearby of similar size. The answer would come when I worked out how those ancient peoples calculated distances. But for now, it was plain

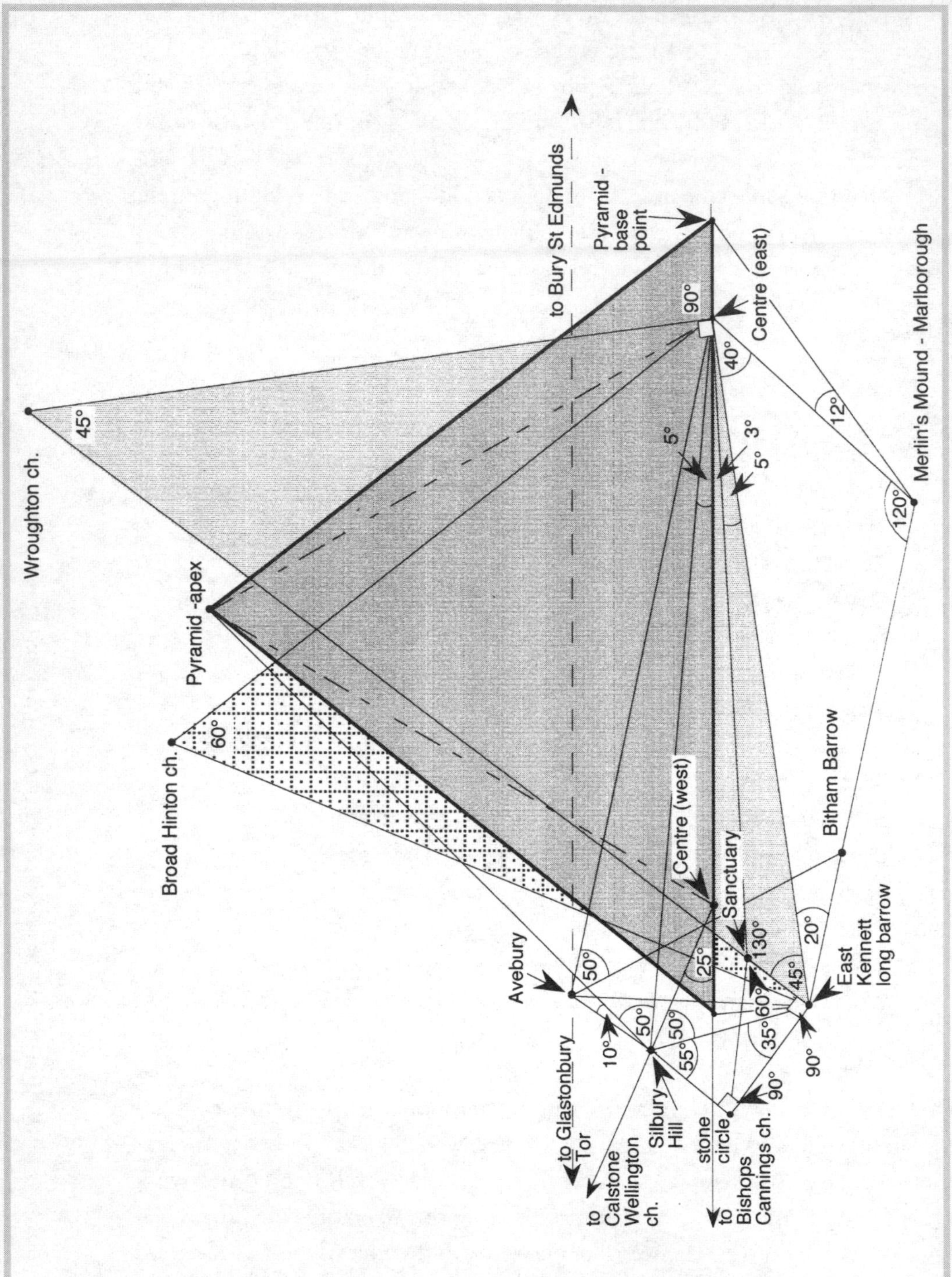
Wroughton ch.
45°
Broad Hinton ch.
60°
Pyramid -apex
to Bury St Edmunds
Pyramid - base point
90°
Centre (east)
40°
12°
5°
3°
5°
120°
Merlin's Mound - Marlborough
Centre (west)
Sanctuary
Bitham Barrow
Avebury
50°
25°
130°
20°
45°
East Kennett long barrow
60°
50°
50°
10°
55°
35°
90°
90°
to Glastonbury Tor
to Calstone Wellington ch.
Silbury Hill
stone circle
to Bishops Cannings ch.

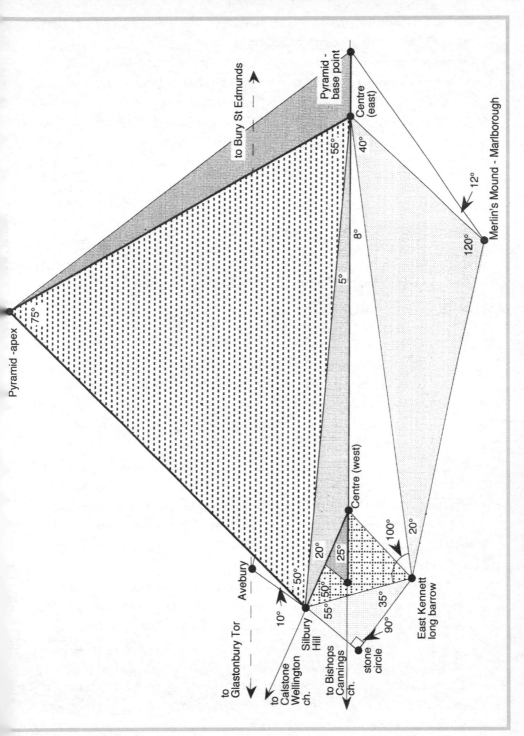

Fig. 87. Key triangulations from Silbury Hill and East Kennett long barrow

that more fieldwork would be required to establish Silbury Hill's credentials as a surveying reference point.

Progress had been made though. When viewed within the context of a culture which laid out its sites geometrically, Silbury Hill's potential as a surveying platform adds considerable weight to the argument that that was its function. It may also have had a symbolic and religious function, but no group would spend so much time and effort on a 'folly'. It must have had prime significance for people to put so much time, effort and care into its construction.

The measured mile

By far the hardest tasks facing the constructors of the Marlborough Downs circles would have been the establishment of the fixed distances. There are three aspects to this:

1) the primary dimensions of the planet, both its meridian and the equatorial circumference, would have to have been worked out;
2) from these measures a calculation would then have been made for the exact ratio to be used;
3) once one centre has been established, another would then have to be fixed at an exact distance from the first.

The ways that the peoples of the past could have accurately calculated the size and proportions of the Earth are covered in Chapter 13. For now, let us assume that the sums had been done and the decision to lay out a circle with a radius of 9.6 kilometres (6 miles) has already been made. How could this distance be fixed?

Short distances can easily be measured using rods of fixed lengths. However, this method becomes less accurate the greater the distance involved. Moreover, in the Marlborough case the radius is measured as the 'crow flies' and the only practical way that this can be achieved is through triangulation. Normal mapping techniques involve taking exact angular measurements between sites. Providing there are two fixed reference points which have been very accurately measured, all other distances can be calculated from the angles generated. It was precisely to achieve this that the modern theodolite, which measures angles down to a few minutes of arc, was invented.

Clearly, megalithic people did not possess instruments capable of measuring angles with such accuracy. Yet we have seen that they could establish bearings with great precision, generated from set ratios. This method would have had to have been used for the calculation and fixing of the centre and circumference of the circle.

The best triangulation angles are those which are close to 45°. If a reference line was set at 100 metres (328 feet) in a right-angled triangle, the difference in length generated by angles of 45° and 46° would be only 3.55 metres (11.64 feet). At the other end of the scale, the difference in length generated by angles of 87° and 88° from that same 100-metre (328-foot) reference line is nearly a kilometre (see Fig. 88).

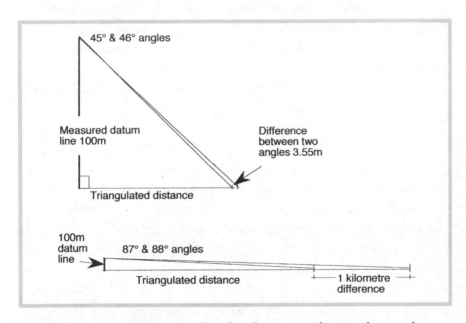

Fig. 88. Triangulated distances showing the greater degree of surveying precision required for angles approaching 90°

On the other hand, it is obvious that a 45° angle is useless when setting out distances, as both the non-hypotenuse sides are of equal length. But an 87° angle gives a ratio of 19:1 between the two non-hypotenuse sides. So, a 100-metre (328-foot) base can be used to establish a 1900-metre

(6232-foot) distance. To achieve reasonable accuracy some compromise would have to be struck between the length of the reference line and the angle or ratio used.

One way to measure out a large distance would be by creating a series of ratioed triangles each producing a reference length greater than its predecessor, until the required distance is finally reached. The problem here is that each step would have an error factor and these errors would accumulate rather than cancel each other out.

An alternative method could use a series of triangulations set up using relatively high ratios such as 19:2. Let us suppose that three such triangulations were created independently. Their intersection points would be unlikely to be at exactly the same positions, but with careful surveying and a bit of luck they might be reasonably close to each other. The three intersection points would then create another triangle from which it would be relatively easy to establish a common centre. The problem with this method would be fixing the initial triangulation points with precision, in correct geometric placement to each other.

The enormous challenge facing the megalithic geometres is clear, yet it was a task they were able to achieve with some considerable level of accuracy – the mean difference between the radii of the two circles is only 18 metres (59 feet). In all likelihood, some considerable time was spent walking the area, getting a feel of the locality and deciding where it was considered appropriate to fix both the centre and some of the sites. For example, the north-western part of the circumference of the western circle runs beautifully around the edge of the chalk escarpment. This was surely no accident but an integral part of the design. We should not forget that surveying the land also means exploring fully the potential that it has to offer.

The first step would have entailed the fixing of a starting point. My initial guess favoured the East Kennett long barrow. I assumed that the barrow was already in existence before the commencement of the surveying operation which probably began somewhere around 3000BC. Records indicate that the East Kennett long barrow is about 90 metres (295 feet) long by 30 metres (98 feet) wide, rising to a height of 4.2 metres (13.8 feet) at its southern end and sloping gradually down to 2.5 metres (8.2 feet) at its northern end. Like the neighbouring West Kennett long barrow it is thought to be chambered, although the chambers might have collapsed. No records remain from the original excavations carried out by the Revd Connor in the middle of the nineteenth century and the barrow is now on private property. It has some Sarsen stones at its southern end, but no radiocarbon dating has been done. The barrow might have been enlarged or modified to suit the surveyor's purposes. Paul Devereux records in his book *Earth Memory* that 'archaeologist Richard Bradley has suggested that some long barrows may have had earth "tails" added to turn them into extra long mounds and cites West Kennett as an example'. Without further excavations, we will never know. It is also just possible that East Kennett long barrow might have been erected when the Marlborough Downs pattern was being planned.

Earlier in this chapter I showed how all the other sites on the circumference could have been positioned once the centre and the position of the East Kennett long barrow had been fixed. Given that the East Kennett long barrow was there already, the most crucial part of the whole operation would be the fixing of the centre of the two circles. Any slight error here would be multiplied up later on. If the East Kennett long barrow was the starting point, the distance to the centre of the east circle had to be precisely 9572 metres (31,396 feet) if it was to be exactly one 666th of the radius of the Earth. Working out how this might have been achieved from the evidence on the ground took me many hours of study.

I assumed that the builders worked in Megalithic Yards and there are 11,550MY between the centre and circumference. Professor Thom suggested that the builders of stone circles also worked in a larger unit which was equivalent to 2.5 Megalithic Yards, which he called a 'Megalithic Fathom'. He suggested that there might be an even larger unit of 10 Megalithic Fathoms which is very close to the Imperial unit of a chain. There are 22 yards in a chain, while Thom's unit is 22⅔ yards. So it seems appropriate to call this distance a Megalithic Chain or MC. It so happens that 11,550MY can be subdivided by 25 (2.5 × 10), so the length of the radius can be given in Megalithic Chains. It is 462MC.

The distance between centres calculated from the grid references can be shown as 392MC. This means that the difference between the length of the radius and the distance between the two centres is 70MC

(462 – 392 = 70). It also so happens that each of these numbers is also divisible by seven giving:

$$462 \div 7 = 66$$
$$392 \div 7 = 56$$
$$70 \div 7 = 10$$

Again a clear pattern emerges here. Neolithic designers would have needed to know these ratios to fix the distances between the centres. And fixing the centres of the two circles was crucial to the laying out of the entire complex.

Linked to the assumption that the East Kennett long barrow was the key reference point, I initially thought that those ancient surveyors would have first located the centre of the eastern circle. I spent many hours checking angles and alignments. Try as I might, I could not work out how the radius could have been established easily and I was forced to look elsewhere. The prime candidate now became the centre of the western circle because its position could be fixed more easily, through triangulation, from the most significant monuments in the area.

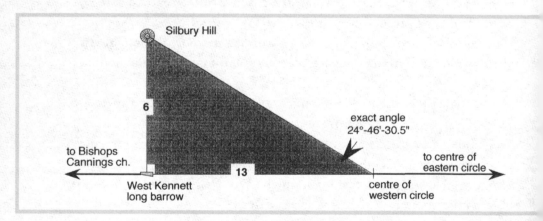

Fig. 89. Primary surveying triangle and side ratios between West Kennett long barrow, Silbury Hill and centre of western circle

When I originally discovered the two circles, I noted that the extended alignment of the two circles passed through the West Kennett long barrow (see Fig. 89). But for many years the significance of this escaped me. The problem with looking for meaningful alignments and triangulations for a monument is knowing where to fix the surveying reference point. The West Kennett long barrow is 104 metres (341 feet) long by 23 metres (75 feet) wide. I assumed that a sighting point was placed on its ridge, which narrows its position down laterally. Yet the reference point could still be anywhere along its 104-metre profile.

For distances to be calculated using set ratios, a right-angled triangle needs to be created. Ideally, one side of this triangle should be aligned with the two centres. As this alignment passes through the West Kennett long barrow I wondered if any right-angled triangles could be formed from this monument. In my original calculations I had initially chosen the eastern end of the West Kennett barrow, where the burials took place, as the reference point. I could find no significant relationships to other sites until I moved the position of the reference point back along the ridge of the barrow to its mid-point. Then Silbury Hill hove into view. A right angled triangle, that key triangle to the surveying concepts suggested here, could now be drawn between Silbury Hill, West Kennett long barrow and the two centres of the western and eastern circles.

Careful calculation showed that the angles between Silbury Hill, the centre of the western circle and the West Kennett long barrow were 65.25° and 24.75°, which as it turns out are produced by a simple ratio of 13:6 (see Fig. 90). This was another of those eureka moments to savour.

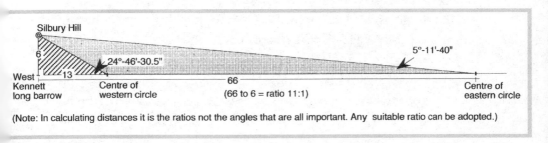

(Note: In calculating distances it is the ratios not the angles that are all important. Any suitable ratio can be adopted.)

Fig. 90. Triangulation to establish position of eastern centre

Everything was now starting to slot neatly into place. It is hard from this perspective to know what came first. Whether it was the alignment between Burrowbridge Mump and Glastonbury Tor which marked the St Michael ley or the position of the West Kennett long barrow. Whatever it was, once the West Kennett long barrow had been chosen and the orientation set then another key surveying point would need to have been established for all surveying needs two points of reference. It would be necessary for this surveying point to be at right angles to the proposed orientation but sufficiently close so that the distance could be accurately measured. Herein lies the genius of the relationship between Silbury Hill and the West Kennett long barrow.

The position of Silbury Hill was carefully chosen because it fitted the necessary criteria. It had to be where it was because this was the best solution for the important simple ratios that were required. The problem was Waden Hill. Only by seeing over the top of Waden Hill could the ratios be easily set out. And so in the summer around 2750BC the first turfs were cut and laid. At one point realising that they were not going to be high enough, the building work stopped and the circumference of the mound was increased for it had to be high enough to see across Waden Hill. One of the greatest enigmas of Neolithic Britain had now been solved, but in so doing raised many more questions about its builders.

Looking east from Silbury Hill can be seen the West Kennett long barrow with its back lying broadly at right angles to the line of site. This simple provision would allow for slight adjustments to be made in the final positioning of the centres of the two circles and the fixing of the western circumference at Bishops Cannings. As my original calculation had shown the eastern end of the West Kennett long barrow did not quite fit, but this extended back of the long barrow would allow for a margin of error in the early stages of the pattern's development.

Figure 91 gives some of the prominent triangulation points of the area. To make this design, I have postulated that there was another survey point just west of the East Kennett long barrow. There is no evidence from the OS maps of any archaeological site at this place but one could, like so many others, have been removed during the course of history. As a point, it is not absolutely crucial but it would certainly ease some of the triangulation steps.

The calculated distance from West Kennett long barrow to Silbury Hill is 1112MY. But Silbury Hill is some 30 metres (98 feet) across at its summit which allows for a considerable margin of error. When 1112MY is translated into other measurements, it does not hold any significance, yet

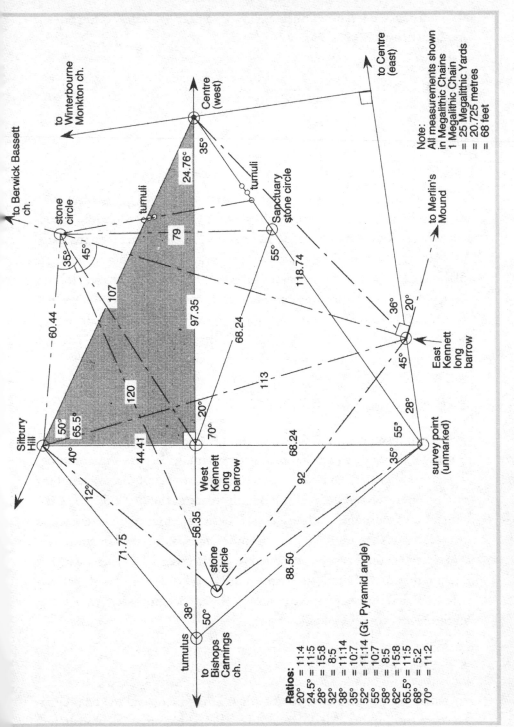

Fig. 91. Details of main survey points around Silbury Hill

if this distance is increased by just 2.77MY or 2.296 metres (7.53 feet) the picture changes. 1114.77MY is:

3080 Egyptian feet
3000 Geographic feet
2500 Remen
2000 Geographic Cubits
1600 Pyk Beladys
498 Fathoms
80 × 11.55 metres

This figure of 11.55 metres, as we have seen before, has a particular significance in the geometry of the ancient world. This is further circumstantial evidence that supports the notion that at least one of the functions of the placing of the various monuments in the Marlborough Downs was for surveying purposes. Despite the enormous efforts required it was quite feasible for the builders of Silbury Hill, Avebury and the other megalithic structures to have surveyed the land and laid out their monuments to a precise pattern that incorporated set dimensions, even at distances of several miles.

Bishops Cannings

So far we have still not established the position of the church site at Bishops Cannings, which lies on the western edge of the western circle. The site is aligned to the West Kennett long barrow and the centres of the circles. But it too can be fixed through reference to Silbury Hill. The computer shows the angle at Silbury Hill to Bishops Cannings to be a fraction over 83°, making the angle at Bishops Cannings a fraction under 7°. These angles could best be generated from bisecting a 14° angle, which is the product of a 4:1 ratio (see Appendix 3). Once again, this shows that Silbury Hill is the primary site in setting out and locating all the key places in the Marlborough Downs complex.

A puzzle solved

Incredible as it would have seemed when I first discovered the twin circular patterns on the Marlborough Downs, I had now demonstrated,

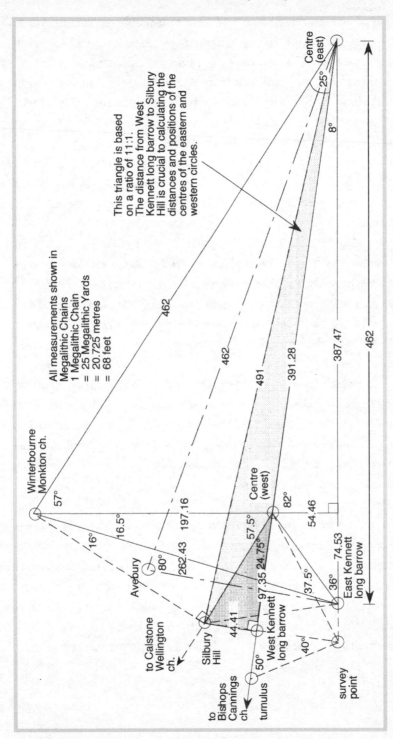

Fig. 92. Primary surveying grid for setting out Marlborough Downs circles and establishing key distances

beyond reasonable doubt, that it was quite possible to lay out this huge design in the landscape using basic surveying techniques. Certainly it needed a sophisticated knowledge of geometry, mathematics and surveying techniques, but the implements used could be found in any woodland thicket. All that was required were a few straight saplings, cut to specific lengths, some rope or twine, and a few pegs. The greatest problem was establishing fixed surveying points. This required huge manpower, particularly in the construction of a site such as Silbury Hill. But nothing seems to have been beyond the capabilities of these ingenious people. The whole area can now be seen as a 'sacred space' as the Woodwards say in their 1996 article in the *Proceedings of the Prehistoric Society*:

A common denominator of all these patterns is that the barrows seem to have formed a major component of a ritual landscape. The barrows were sited at set distances from the monuments and the monuments were placed such that many barrow sites were clearly visible from them. Thus the barrow settings appear to have defined a reserved inner sanctum.

The regular spacing of cemeteries, and the very existence of curvilinear arrangements, suggests that barrow distributions reflect far more than the even spacing of settlements. Rather they may represent concepts of enclosed ritual space, acting as dramatic symbolic boundaries for sacred zones, areas of monumental landscape protected by a cordon sanitaire of the special dead.

The discovery of the crucial function of Silbury Hill as a surveying platform has answered one of the great riddles of the Avebury area. Without it, the twin circle pattern of the Marlborough Downs could not have been created. Many aspects of the mystery of the Marlborough Downs had now been laid bare. I still had to discover how peoples of the past could have calculated the proportions of the Earth. And I was still faced by one further puzzle. Why was this mysterious landscape pattern created?

13

MEASURING THE EARTH

Diverting energy away from the normal pursuits of living into the grandiose scheme envisioned here would only be done if there was a powerful motive

Surprising as it may seem, calculating the dimensions of the Earth is less difficult than working out the distance between London and Edinburgh. In *Mathematics for the Million*, published in 1936, Lancelot Hogben states blandly:

 Fig. 46 is a design ... with which ... you can find the height of your house, your latitude and longitude, the time of the day, and how much the earth appears to tilt on its axis throughout the year (i.e. the inclination of the orbit to the poles, called by astronomers the obliquity of the ecliptic).

He could have gone on to say 'and measure the Earth's polar circumference'. So what was the amazing device shown in his Fig. 46? It is nothing more complicated than a short piece of dowel fixed into a level wooden base (see my Fig. 93). The only difficult part is making sure that the pole is vertical and that its length is known to sufficient accuracy.

Placed in the sun, the dowel casts a shadow which can then be measured at various times throughout the day and at different times of the year. Marking out angles from the top of the dowel allows you to make

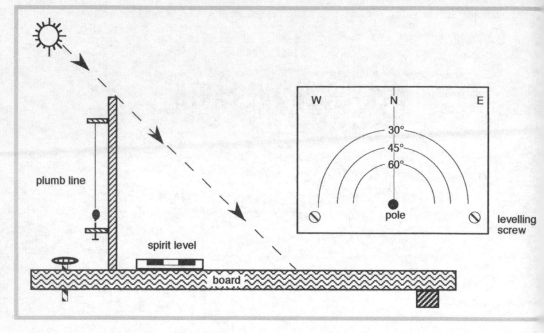

Fig. 93. Design for a home-made shadow pole (From *Mathematics for the Million* by Lancelot Hogben)

exact computations on the solstices (June 21 and December 21) and the equinoxes (March 21 and September 21). For example, at the equinoxes the angle cast by the shadow stick at noon will always equal the latitude. If the shadow cast touches 55.5°, you will know that you are at 55.5° latitude.

This simple idea was used by the ancient Egyptians to establish the length of the polar meridian. The first man known to have calculated the polar circumference was the Greek scholar Eratosthenes, 276–194BC, who lived in Alexandria. He knew that at the summer solstice the sun was directly overhead at Syene, modern Aswan, some 800 kilometres (500 miles) to the south. He measured the angle of the shadow cast by an obelisk in Alexandria at the summer solstice. This angle, 7°, and the estimated distance between Alexandria and Syene allowed him to calculate the length of the polar meridian and the size of the Earth. However, he was almost certainly only repeating what the ancient Egyptians already knew (Fig. 94). As Peter Tompkins says in *The Secret of the Great Pyramid*:

 To compute the polar circumference of the earth the ancients used the sun and the shadows cast by obelisks. To compute the equatorial circumference they observed the passage of stars across such fixed points as obelisks. For the polar circumference they needed merely to measure the distance between two obelisks a few miles apart and the difference in the length of shadows of the obelisks.

There was no need to measure such vast distances as separated Alexandria from Syene. The differences in latitude and hence the fraction of arc separating any two meridian obelisks, can be obtained by the relation of the obelisk's shadow to its height when measured at the moment of the solstice or equinox.

Translate this into the British landscape and you see the Neolithic peoples would only need to put up two vertical poles placed on a north-south meridian, set a few miles apart, to achieve the same result. Providing the angles cast by the shadows were accurately measured and the distance between the two markers known, it is simple to calculate the meridian using simple geometry.

It so happens that in Britain the lengths of a degree of longitude and a degree of latitude are very nearly the same. They are exactly equal on the 55th parallel, close to the line of Hadrian's Wall. The difference between the two in the region of Avebury is only about 88 metres (290 feet). In round terms, if the polar meridian and not the equatorial circumference had been used for the proportions of the Marlborough Downs circles, this would have reduced the radius from 9572 to 9569 metres (31,396 to 31,386 feet), a difference of 3 metres (9.8 feet). So it is possible that those who established the circles based their calculations not on the equatorial circumference but upon the polar meridian which in practice is easier to estimate. However, I believe that they knew both and the equatorial circumference was the model for the circles.

I needed to find some site in the Marlborough Downs area where these studies could have been carried out. Somewhere suitable for observation and calculation of astronomical events; where the necessary geometry of

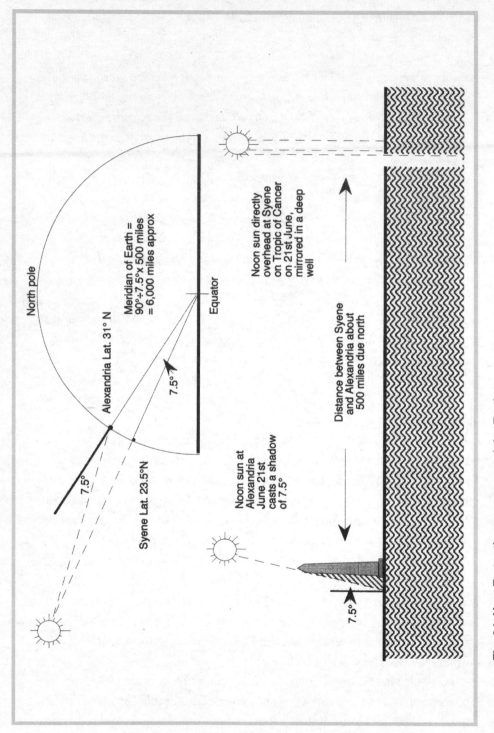

Fig. 94. How Eratosthenes measured the Earth

the twin circles could be set out. Fortunately on this occasion it did not take long to find.

The Sanctuary mystery

The Marlborough Downs area is home to a number of enigmatic megalithic structures. Silbury Hill is one of them. The Sanctuary is another (see **photograph 7**). A circular monument standing on the edge of the A4 road, with good views to Silbury Hill and the long barrows of East and West Kennett, it is made up of a number of concentric rings of postholes and small standing stones. It is thought to have been built in several stages. Construction seems to have started around 2900BC with the erection of posts that are thought to have supported a circular building with a thatched roof. Like other megalithic monuments, the Sanctuary seems to have been dedicated to the study of the sun.

To keep track of the rhythm of the seasons, some system is needed to measure the path of the sun. One way to do this is by recording sunrise and sunset positions as they move across the horizon. Stonehenge records the position of sunrise on midsummer's day. Newgrange marks midwinter sunrise. And Maes Howe picks out midwinter sunset.

If you live in the countryside, you can do this yourself. I used to live on the western side of the Malvern Hills with extensive views out towards the Welsh Hills and, in particular, Hay Bluff near the town of Hay-on-Wye. During the spring and autumn months I could visually mark off the passage of the sun at its sunset positions back and forth along the line of the distant hills. In early October and late February, the sun set in a notch in the hills created by Hay Bluff. I would often look out for this moment. When watching the last rays of the sun dip below the horizon, I was powerfully conscious that recording such an event would be both a religious experience as well as a practical way to keep track of the seasons.

Another way to track the movement of the sun is with a sundial. Providing the sun is shining, the shadow of a vertical post will indicate the approximate time of day. Measuring the length of the sun's shadow at noon will also tell you the season.

The Sanctuary has a posthole right in the middle of the monument which could have held a circular upright post with a pointed end. The

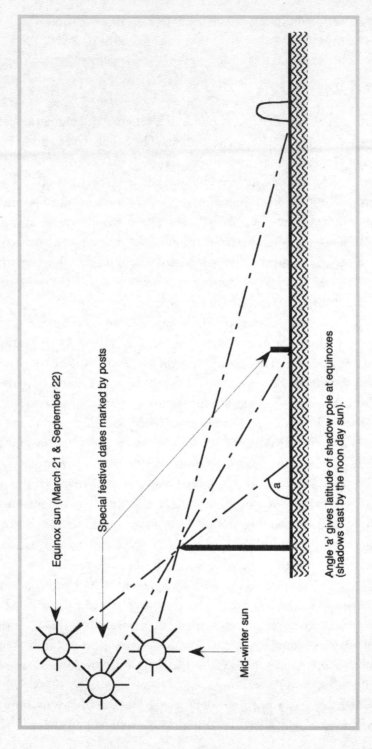

Equinox sun (March 21 & September 22)

Special festival dates marked by posts

Mid-winter sun

Angle 'a' gives latitude of shadow pole at equinoxes (shadows cast by the noon day sun).

Fig. 95. The use of a shadow pole to indicate significant festival days

monument would act like a sundial, indicating the times of day and the seasons of the year, as well as major solar configurations.

Aubrey Burl was no fan of Professor Thom's Megalithic Yard, citing the measurements of concentric rings of the Sanctuary as evidence that megalithic peoples did not use this unit:

 The Sanctuary with its seven concentric rings offers a unique opportunity to examine the validity of this 'yardstick' [Megalithic Yard] because consistency would be expected in the counting and measuring of these closely related rings. Yet, although a counting-base of four is manifest here from the number of posts in each ring, four is never used in the number of Megalithic Yards supposedly making up each diameter. Nor is any diameter an exact multiple of this Yard. Instead of a logical progression of 4 Megalithic Yards, 8, 12, and so on one finds an unconvincing mixture of 4.4 Megalithic Yards, 5.0, 7.1, 11.4, 12.6, 17.2, and 23.8 Megalithic Yards.

These rather odd multiples, I believe, do nothing to undermine the Megalithic Yard. It is simply that the designers of this monument were more interested in marking significant dates of the year as part of their religious calendar.

As the sun travelled through the seasons, the length of the noon shadow would vary. It would be at its longest at the midwinter solstice and at its shortest at the summer solstice. These concentric rings could act as a calendar. Certain dates would be marked by the fact that the sun's noon-day shadow touched a specific ring of the circle. Using the measurements given by Aubrey Burl for the position of the rings I carried out a number of calculations based on the position of the sun's rays for this latitude at different times of the year. But first I needed to fix the length of the shadow pole. Without direct evidence, I could only make a guess – but it could be an informed guess.

At the winter solstice, the noon sun casts a shadow at 15°. At its height in summer, this becomes 62°, while at the equinoxes the shadow is at 39°. I ran through all possible heights for the shadow pole in increments of 0.1 Megalithic Yards and found that the best fit was 3.2MY. A pole of this height erected at the centre of the circle would mark the following dates of the year, based on our calendar, when its shadow touches one of the rings:

Date	Event
20/21 December	Midwinter solstice
30 November	
11 January	21/22 days either side of the solstice
4 February	Imbolc – Celtic festival
5 November	Samhain – Celtic festival
14 February	St Valentine's Day?
27 October	
5 April	Easter?
7 September	
7 May	Beltane – Celtic festival
6 August	Lugnasad – Celtic festival
27 May	
17 July	24/25 days either side of midsummer solstice

Neither the equinoxes nor the summer solstice appear to be indicated, although each of the four main Celtic festivals – Imbolc, Beltane, Lugnasad and Samhain – are marked. If indeed this monument acted as a calendar, as I strongly believe, it supports the idea that Druidic traditions link back to much older pre-Celtic beliefs stemming from Neolithic times.

In order to operate effectively, the priests and priestesses of the Sanctuary would need such a timeplace for establishing a rhythm for the great festivals that undoubtedly took place at Avebury. And if such a pole was erected, the morning light of the sun would cast a shadow across the circle to the great avenue of stones that leads down from the Sanctuary to the Avebury monument. Over the space of just two hours, the shadow line would appear to open the gateway, giving access to this processional path. Through this simple means, the timing of festivals and ceremonies could be judged to perfection.

There are a number of other monuments similar to the Sanctuary, such as the one at Durrington Walls, that comprise concentric rings of wood

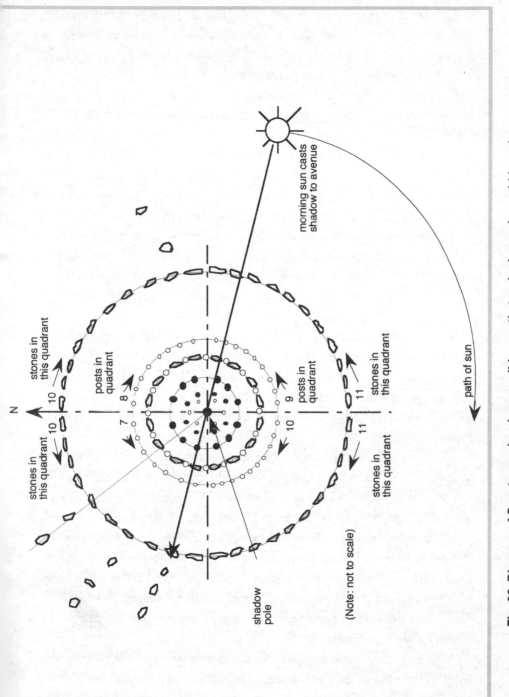

Fig. 96. Diagram of Sanctuary showing possible way that a shadow pole could have been used as a calendar to highlight festival days

stones in this quadrant

posts in quadrant

stones in this quadrant

stones in this quadrant

posts in quadrant

stones in this quadrant

N

morning sun casts shadow to avenue

path of sun

shadow pole

(Note: not to scale)

10 10 8 7 9 10 11 11 11

and stone. However, orthodox archaeologists believe that these buildings were thatched over, in which case their function as a calendar would be greatly reduced – unless of course certain sections remained open to the sky so that specific solar alignments could be observed.

Leaving that aside, a shadow pole erected at the Sanctuary could also be used to calculate the site's latitude, which is the first step in calculating the length of the polar meridian. As we have seen, to do that another pole would have to be erected at another place either directly north or south of the Sanctuary. One contender might be Stonehenge which lies 25.734 kilometres (15.98 miles) due south of the Sanctuary. Shadow poles of 3.2MY placed at each centre would cast shadows with a difference of 17.7 millimetres (0.7 inches) in length at the equinoxes. This translates into a difference of latitude of 13.9 minutes of arc, giving a polar meridian of 9,997.381 kilometres (6208 miles), as opposed to the correct length of 10,001.987 kilometres (6211 miles), an error of only 4.606 kilometres (2.86 miles).

To make this calculation, it would be necessary to measure the distance between Stonehenge and the Sanctuary accurately. In practice, longer shadow poles would be more suitable for the differences in the length of shadow cast would be greater. It is possible that a series of computations might have been taken from different monuments allowing for an average figure to be achieved for the length of the meridian.

Another possible contender for the southern marker to the Sanctuary is Woodborough Hill which is linked geometrically with the other sites in the area. It is only 6.54 kilometres (4.06 miles) south of the Sanctuary. This would make the measurement of the distance between sites less prone to error. However, the measurement of the shadow becomes more critical. If measured from 5.4-metre (17.7-foot) shadow poles, the difference in the lengths of the two shadows would be only 14.196 millimetres (0.45 inches). In practice, it is difficult to measure to more than an accuracy of one millimetre. Even that might have been beyond the capabilities of the Neolithic builders.

A longer shadow pole increases the difference between the two shadow lengths, but this in turn brings other problems. The longer the shadow, the more diffuse it becomes. In fact, the posthole at the centre of the Sanctuary would not have been able to take a very long pole.

Having measured the shadows' lengths the next task was to work out the latitude accurately. The noon shadow of a simple shadow pole at the equinoxes would give the surveyors the approximate latitude. They would know that both sites lie between latitudes 51° and 53°. They could then set about an exact computation for both latitudes using the method outlined in Fig. 97.

A primary triangle would need to be laid out to as large a scale as practical. I have made the base of 540MY, which is approximately 450 metres (1230 feet) and 100 times the length of the shadow pole by the factor of 100. When we come to the lengths of the shadows they too will have to be multiplied up by 100. The perpendicular side is then pegged at 666MY to form a triangle with the angle at s being 51°. If the perpendicular side is then extended to 715.5MY the angle at s is increased to 53°. Pegging out triangle AEC from the figure would allow angles down to one second of arc to be measured off. A triangle of half this size would also work very well and would, incidentally, fit inside the area of the Avebury henge.

The shadow lengths can then be marked off as perpendiculars within the triangle and the exact latitudes of the sites read off. With a little ingenuity, there would be no insuperable problems to establishing the length of the polar meridian and accurately surveying out the landscape. The most important ingredient is the time and patience necessary to accumulate information and establish the surveying points to fix the intended pattern within the landscape.

Physical evidence abounds on the extraordinary efforts made by prehistoric people in excavating and erecting the vast number of monuments within the vicinity of the Marlborough Downs. Diverting energy away from the normal pursuits of living into the grandiose scheme envisioned here would only be done if there was a powerful motive. And this motive must have been passed on from generation to generation. Even the invasion of the Beaker peoples, who arrived around 2500BC, did not diminish the creative vision which survived for at least another 500 years.

Unlike the dynasties of ancient Egypt, we have no written records that can be interpreted that give insight into the minds of those who engineered these amazing accomplishments. All that we have is the mathematical messages hidden in the monuments and the geometric rock carved designs found at such sites as Newgrange.

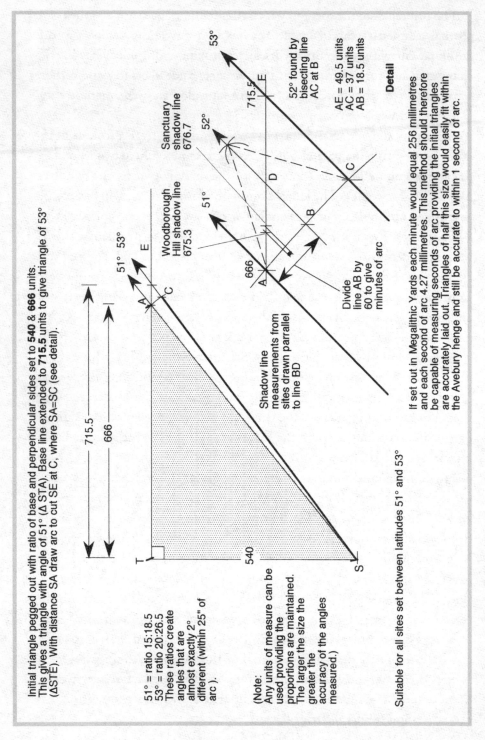

Initial triangle pegged out with ratio of base and perpendicular sides set to **540** & **666** units. This gives a triangle with angle of 51° (ΔSTA). Base line extended to **715.5** units to give triangle of 53° (ΔSTE). With distance SA draw arc to cut SE at C, where SA=SC (see detail).

51° = ratio 15:18.5
53° = ratio 20:26.5
These ratios create angles that are almost exactly 2° different (within 25" of arc.).

(Note:
Any units of measure can be used providing the proportions are maintained. The larger the size the greater the accuracy of the angles measured.)

Suitable for all sites set between latitudes 51° and 53°

If set out in Megalithic Yards each minute would equal 256 millimetres and each second of arc 4.27 millimetres. This method should therefore be capable of measuring seconds of arc providing the initial triangles are accurately laid out. Triangles of half this size would easily fit within the Avebury henge and still be accurate to within 1 second of arc.

715.5
666
540

51° 53°
E
51° 53°
C
A
T
S

53°
E
52° found by bisecting line AC at B

AE = 49.5 units
AC = 37 units
AB = 18.5 units

Detail

715.5
52°
Sanctuary shadow line 676.7
C
D
B
A
666
51°
Woodborough Hill shadow line 675.3

Shadow line measurements from sites drawn parralel to line BD

Divide line AB by 60 to give minutes of arc

Fig. 97. System for determining exact latitude measured to minutes and seconds of arc

The principles of the surveying techniques, the angle ratios and the conceptual geometric patterns could just possibly have been an indigenous development within the British Isles. Yet in line with the other cultural changes that occurred around 3100BC, it seems more likely that these ideas were imported from abroad. All of the surveying techniques used here could have been passed down the generations in the same way that medieval stonemasons and carpenters and their apprentices learnt their trade. The ratios needed to obtain set angles are no more difficult to remember than the multiplication tables learnt at school. There are not more than 45 separate equations that could be broken down further into a few groups. In practice, probably only a small number would have been in regular use.

The ability to set out right angles is, of course, vital. One system used in the past was based upon a rope divided into twelve equal segments by knots. These were then pegged out in the ratio 3:4:5 which is the simplest version of a Pythagorean triangle. Other systems, based on pure geometry, and using pegs and lengths of rope or twine instead of a compass and paper, would be equally simple.

Although we know from the construction of many megalithic monuments that the peoples of the Neolithic and early Bronze Age times possessed great engineering skills, many people find it difficult to accept that they also possessed sophisticated surveying skills. One of the problems here is the archaeological view of the ancient Britons as an unsophisticated society. Burl makes several references to the limited numeracy of these people in his book *Prehistoric Avebury*:

 Modern attempts to transform these peasants into meticulous surveyors are not always based on observation of archaeological facts.

and

 Most primitive societies have had very simple counting bases such as three, four or five. People would count: 1,2,3 3+1, 3+2, 3+3, 3+3+1 and so on, a method easy to learn and not at all inconvenient ... If the Neolithic people around Avebury did have a counting base or radix of three this tells us something about the limited 'scientific' concepts of the builders.

However, both the Romans and the Mayan people had a counting base of five, yet they were still able to accomplish amazing feats of engineering. And Burl concedes that the builders of the Sanctuary over many generations incorporated the number four into its design:

 About six hundred years passed between the first and last rebuilding of the Sanctuary around 2300BC. During all this time the people who built the monuments appear to have counted in fours and this apparently trivial fact is a vital clue to one aspect of their society. That it is a fact seems certain. In phase after phase the number of posts or stones was a multiple or a half of 4:8 and 12 (twice); 8 and 34; 6 and 16; 16 and 42; far too consistent arithmetically for accident.

A Neolithic abacus?

If the Sanctuary was erected as both a calendar and a sundial, as I have suggested, then the base four would have been the obvious choice as it is a simple division of the year. A closer examination of the placing of the stones and posts indicates another sophisticated level of refinement which belies Burl's comments (see Fig. 96).

If the circle is divided (by four) into its quadrants based on a north-south, east-west axis, the postholes of Sanctuary II run in an intriguing sequence. The north-west quadrant has 7 postholes, the north-east has 8, the south-east has 9 and the south-west has 10, making a total of 34 postholes. This neat progression from 7 to 10 was surely no coincidence. The division of the circle into its four quadrants using astronomical observation would be an easy task to the Neolithic observers.

Again the outer ring of stones can be divided into two clearly defined groups of 10 and 11 stones. The two quadrants north of the east-west axis have 10 stones in each, while the quadrants south of the east-west axis have 11 in each making 20 stones in the north and 22 in the south. Dividing the circle down the north-south axis gives 21 stones in each half. The postholes are also symmetrical along the north-south axis, with 17 either side. And we should not forget the 10:11 ratio of the Megalithic Yard to the Short Furlong (SF) and the Royal Cubit to the Pyk Belady.

Going one step further, a number of the key angle ratios are contained within these figures, 7:10 = 55° and 35°; 10:9 = 42° and 48°; 19:11 = 30° and 60°; 11:8 = 36° and 54°; 11:7 = pyramid ratio, and so on. Considered in this way the stone and postholes of the Sanctuary may contain many more secrets than you would see at first glance. They could well have acted as a giant abacus containing all the necessary numeric information to make the surveying angles required to be passed on to future generations. The difficulty, of course, is that 5000 years of history have obscured the reasons people did things and the finer points of their belief systems have been lost.

It is unlikely that explicit evidence for the erection of shadow poles in monuments like the Sanctuary will ever be found. However, if you believe that the Neolithic peoples might have established a calendar measure the way suggested here then the Sanctuary certainly fits the criteria. In folk memory, the traditional Maypole and its celebrations may be an echo from those distant times of an annual ritual of renewing the 'sundial' of the tribe.

The measure of the Earth

It was now clear that the skills needed to calculate the dimensions of the Earth were available in ancient times. Whether they could have arisen independently within the Neolithic culture of Britain is debatable. It is much more likely that these skills, or even that the knowledge of these dimensions, had already been established elsewhere and were imported. From the evidence, it can be demonstrated that all the requirements for the creation of the great circular patterns of the Marlborough Downs were within the capabilities of those who lived in Neolithic times. It is true that such an undertaking could not have been attempted without considerable effort on behalf of the populace. But then the dragging of the 70-tonne Sarsen stones over twelve miles to Stonehenge would have required enormous effort – unless, that is, the Neolithic builders when faced, like their Egyptian counterparts, with moving vast blocks, devised some ingenious system for easing this task.

14

THE PATH OF
THE DRAGON

*If there was a deliberate intention to set out sites in accordance
with a predetermined plan ... their creators were remarkably
successful*

Before tackling the question of why these patterns were laid out in the
British landscape, there is one loose thread that still needs to be tied up. In
Chapter 3 mention was made of a long distance alignment known as the
'St Michael' ley because of the number of church sites dedicated to St
Michael found on it. St Michael and his British counterpart St George are
perhaps best remembered for their tussles with dragons, which are some-
times thought to symbolise the energies within the landscape. In ancient
China, alignments were known as 'Dragon Paths'.

The Michael ley forms a crucial part of the Marlborough Downs pattern. Not only is the bearing between the two centres parallel to it, but it
also highlights the position of the King's Chamber, when a cross-section
of the Great Pyramid of Khufu is superimposed on to the landscape.
Indeed, it could be argued that the Michael ley is crucial to the linking of
the Marlborough Downs pattern to the Great Pyramid of Egypt. So, it is
important to assess the capabilities of the Neolithic people in setting out
long distance alignments, which could generally be taken to mean any
alignment more than 80 kilometres (50 miles).

In my studies I have become aware of the possibility of a more extensive grid network of interlinked sites throughout the country. Long distance alignments would form a part of this picture but there could well be another layer of patterning which computer studies would be able to highlight. The first step was to determine whether alignments of more than 160 kilometres (100 miles) are possible and what evidence can be found for their existence.

Long distance alignments

The idea of long distance leys was first introduced by John Michell in his book *View Over Atlantis*, published in 1969. Michell drew attention to what appeared to be a significant alignment linking the sites of St Michael's Mount in Cornwall with Glastonbury Tor, Avebury henge and the abbey church at Bury St Edmunds (see Fig. 16). It is this alignment which relates to the Marlborough Downs pattern.

If the concept of leys is a problem to archaeologists, the notion of alignments running for several hundred miles is even more outlandish, so they have to be approached with sceptical rigour. When Michell's alignment is drawn on a small scale map of Britain it looks to be accurate at first glance, but detailed analysis has shown this to be far from the case. However, as the Michael ley forms a significant part of the Marlborough Downs pattern I was loath to dismiss it completely. I had shown that all the other skills needed to create the pattern were within the capabilities of Neolithic man and the connection it made to the geometry of the Great Pyramid lends substantial weight to the existence of the Michael ley, in my mind. So I decided to look at another alignment which also fits into the same category. This is the long distance ley that runs through Old Sarum and Stonehenge and appears to run on to the abbey church at Pershore, a distance of just over 134 kilometres (83 miles).

The Stonehenge-Old Sarum alignment

This alignment was first spotted in the last century by Sir Norman Lockyer who pointed out that Stonehenge, Old Sarum hillfort, Salisbury Cathedral and the hillfort of Clearbury Ring were all in a straight line. He could have gone on to mention that this alignment also picks up the hill-fort at Frankenbury, near Fordingbridge. Some researchers have suggested that a northerly extension of this line ends at a tumulus on Alton Downs, but I believe that it ends at the OS trig. point at Charlton Clumps. Fortunately, all these sites can be found on one map – OS chart 184 (1:50,000 Land Ranger Series) – so they are easy to plot.

The alignment does not run through the centre of each site but picks up the western edge of the Frankenbury and Clearbury Ring hillforts, the eastern end of Salisbury Cathedral, the eastern entrance of Old Sarum, the eastern side of Stonehenge and the trig. point itself at Charlton Clumps. Plotting this line on the map shows another possible alignment with the road running out of Salisbury. Watkins suggested that old roads and trackways could be found on leys and included them in his calculations. The exact co-ordinates of the ley position of these sites can be shown as:

Site	NGR
Charlton Clumps	SU 1022.5 : 5455
Stonehenge	1225 : 4217.5
Old Sarum	1380 : 3265
Salisbury Cathedral	1432 : 2950
Salisbury Road	1450 : 2835
Clearbury Ring	1515 : 2440
Frankenbury	1665 : 1152

The distance between Frankenbury hillfort and Charlton Clumps is 39.871 kilometres (24.75 miles), making it a fairly long ley but nothing of the order of that suggested by Michell. Because the line passes through the sites in question, a precise alignment can be shown and we do not need to bother about margins of error. Its bearing is 350.7344° or 350°–44′–4″ from grid north (Fig. 98).

I have carefully evaluated the evidence for the extension of this alignment in both a northerly and southerly direction. To the south, I could find no other significant monuments or sighting positions, except that

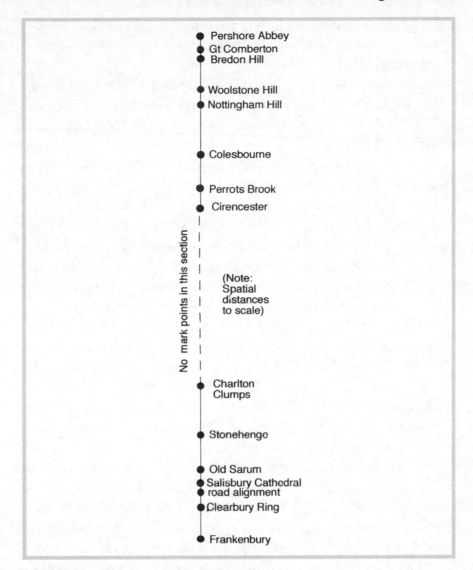

Fig. 98. Frankenbury to Pershore alignment

the OS Tourist Map of the New Forest shows a straight parish boundary coinciding with the ley. It runs for nearly 3.2 kilometres (2 miles). Watkins might have concluded that this followed an ancient trackway. It could only be checked out by walking the ley to see if there were other features not marked on the OS maps. The line crosses Highcliffe Castle on the cliff at the eastern edge of the town of Christchurch. Again, some might see this as significant but I do not consider it sufficient evidence to warrant the extension of the Stonehenge to Old Sarum ley beyond Frankenbury Camp.

To the north, despite passing through the area of the Marlborough Downs circles, the ley picks up no sites of any significance in the immediate vicinity of Charlton Clumps. Looking at a smaller scale map, it would seem that eventually, after a distance of over 40 kilometres (25 miles), this line picks up another alignment: Cirencester Abbey church–Perrots Brook earthworks–Colesbourne church–Nottingham hillfort–Woolstone hillfort–Bredon hillfort–Great Comberton church–Pershore Abbey.

Although this alignment runs very close to the bearing of the Stonehenge ley, it is not exactly on it. Running for more than 44 kilometres (27 miles), it does have a similar accuracy as the Stonehenge alignment. One site, Colesbourne church, is about 50 metres (164 feet) off the line. All the others fit neatly to it. This is because some of the sites are reasonably large targets so the alignment can be adjusted easily to make them fit. Its bearing is 350.2594° from grid north, making it about half a degree (28′–30′) different from the Stonehenge alignment. The two lines very nearly join up, but not quite. The question then is whether these two alignments happen to fall very close to each other by coincidence, or whether they were actually planned as one alignment and any deviation is caused by the inaccuracies of surveying.

The bearing between Charlton Clumps and Cirencester Abbey is 350.52°. The gap between the two sites is around 48 kilometres (30 miles). While there are no substantial mark points, the alignment does pass through the occasional tumulus (with so many on the Marlborough Downs this is hardly surprising and probably not significant) and it would have been technically possible to survey a line between these two sites.

If the whole alignment was intentional, the only explanation of this 48-kilometre (30-mile) gap would be that the two ends were developed independently, but they were symbolically connected through the alignment of their axes. This would suggest that planning was done on a much larger scale than I had previously considered and I should look for much larger groupings of interlinked sites. With that idea in mind, let us now look at the famous St Michael ley.

5) *Top:* The entrance to Newgrange, Co Meath, Ireland, prior to restoration, showing examples of rock art (see Chapter 3).

6) The Giza Pyramids in evening light. The sun is setting behind the small pyramid of Menkaure. To the right are the pyramids of Khafre and Khufu.

17) *Top:* The Pyramid of Khufu, Giza, better known as the Great Pyramid, holds many mysteries in its siting, alignments and geometry.

18) The Giza Sphinx. Was it actually carved as long ago as 5000 BC? See Chapter 5.

19) *Top:* An Olmec head – one of several such statues dating from a Meso-American culture *c* 1500 BC (see Chapter 3).

20) Calendar stone of the Aztecs who came after the Mayan peoples. It indicates both the importance and continuity of astronomical observations, and their relationship to the seasons, carried out by Meso-American cultures.

21) The Neolithic temple of Hagar Qim in southern Malta (see Chapter 7). It was destroyed when a catastrophe overwhelmed Malta *c* 3000 BC. *Below:* a plan of the temple complex looking like a cross-section of a human skull.

The Michael ley

Watkins leys were based on a series of sighted alignments which can be shown to be highly accurate over short distances, normally no more than about a dozen miles. The Michael ley runs nearly 500 kilometres (310 miles) and is riddled with error.

Reputedly starting at the hillfort of Carn Les Boel near Land's End in Cornwall, the alignment then runs through St Michael's Mount near Marazion before picking up the Hurler's stone circle on Bodmin Moor. The next point is Burrowbridge Mump, which has a ruined church on its summit, followed by Glastonbury Tor, which has a church tower on its peak. The line then passes through Avebury henge and the church of Ogbourne St George, before reaching the abbey at Bury St Edmunds. It also passes through a number of minor church sites. Some believe it continues on, beyond Bury St Edmunds, to the coast.

Of all these sites Glastonbury Tor, Burrowbridge Mump and St Michael's Mount are fixed geographical locations. They are hills or, in the latter case, an island off the coast of Cornwall. If we assume that Glastonbury Tor and Burrowbridge Mump, about 17 kilometres (10.5 miles) distant, were the starting points, the intended bearing of the ley would be 62.10°. From this bearing, it is possible to calculate how close the different sites come to true alignment. Running the figures through the computer gives:

Site	Deviation
Carn Les Boel	1112.54 metres south of line
St Michael's Mount	2718.95 metres south of line
Hurlers	717.43 metres south of line
Burrowbridge Mump	true bearing
Glastonbury Tor	true bearing
Avebury henge	98.78 metres south of the line
Ogbourne St George	51.99.21 metres north of line
Bury St Edmunds	1143.73 metres south of line

From these figures, it is clear that the alignment is not straight, although a very small adjustment would bring Burrowbridge Mump, Glastonbury Tor and Avebury into alignment. All the other sites are considerably adrift. However, the bearing between the centres of the two Marlborough Downs circles is 62.11°, which is only 0.01° or 0°–0′–36″ different from the bearing from Burrowbridge Mump to Glastonbury Tor. Furthermore, Ogbourne St George, which lies in the Marlborough Downs pattern, is very closely aligned. The distance between Burrowbridge Mump and Ogbourne St George is 49.5 kilometres (58.68 miles), which certainly puts this ley into the long distance alignment category.

One of the problems of map-making is that the curved surface of the Earth is represented on a flat plan of a map. Inevitably some distortion creeps in. The only way to truly test the accuracy of the Michael ley is through spherical geometry based upon the latitude and longitude of the sites, rather than their OS grid references. Without going into the complex mathematics of how this is done, it can be shown that Bury St Edmunds, Glastonbury Tor and Carn Les Boel are definitely not aligned along one of the great circles of the Earth.

Despite a good alignment from Glastonbury to Avebury and its part in the Marlborough Downs pattern, spherical geometry demonstrates that the rest of the Michael ley is merely wishful thinking. So we are faced with four possible conclusions:

1) The alignment was never intended and is merely the product of a lively imagination;

2) The alignment was intended but the level of skill in surveying techniques left it full of errors;

3) The alignment was intended and deviations were deliberately built in to fit some greater pattern. For example, St Michael's Mount in Cornwall might have been seen as a significant terminal point and the alignment intentionally deviated from, say, Burrowbridge Mump to pick up this feature;

4) The alignment follows some broad band terrestrial magnetic or 'energy' pathway (1 to 2 kilometres wide) which was detected by Neolithic peoples who then erected their monuments upon it.

Perhaps looking at another possible long distance alignment will give us a clue.

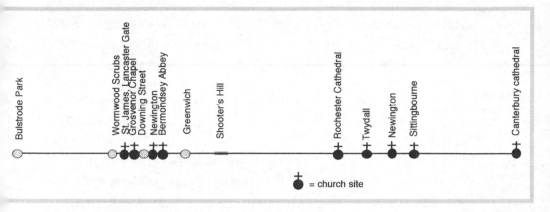

Fig. 99. Canterbury – Bulstrode Park alignment

The Canterbury line

Canterbury Cathedral was built on or close to an ancient Neolithic site. Standing stones still remain in the abbey grounds there. The alignment from Canterbury follows very closely the line of the southeastern extension of Watling Street, one of the primary roads of Roman Britain. In some sections close to London, the alignment coincides with the road, while nearer to Canterbury it runs parallel to it. Taking Canterbury as the starting point, the alignment passes through a number of churches in Sittingbourne, Newington and Twydall, before touching the Cathedral and Castle of Rochester. The next significant place is the Naval College of Greenwich, the site of one of the major palaces of Elizabeth I. After that, the alignment passes through Bermondsey Abbey, London's County Hall and Downing Street, leaving London via the edge of Wormwood Scrubs and Old Oak Common before terminating at Bulstrode Park hillfort. Looking at a map, it very neatly bisects Greater London. The deviation of the major sites from this line is as follows:

Site	Deviation
Rochester Cathedral	36.31 metres north of the line
Greenwich Naval College	37.38 metres north of the line
Bermondsey Abbey	179.13.20 metres north of the line
County Hall	20.44 metres north of the line
Downing Street	24.36 metres north of the line
Bulstrode Park	on bearing

The total distance from Canterbury to Bulstrode Park is just less than 120 kilometres (74.5 miles), again putting this ley into the long distance alignment category. It symbolically links the seat of spiritual power at Canterbury with the seat of temporal power in Downing Street. The use of Downing Street as the official home of the Prime Minister is, however, of recent origin. But Whitehall was the site of one of Henry VIII's palaces. Before that, who knows? If the alignment from Canterbury was fractionally adjusted by a mere 5′–24″ of arc it would run through the Houses of Parliament, which on the alignment given lies 140 metres (460 feet) south of the line. Such an adjustment would only marginally affect the position of the line running through Rochester Cathedral and Greenwich which are in themselves fairly large sites. However, such an adjustment would mean that the alignment would now miss Bulstrode Park hillfort by 200 metres (656 feet) (see Fig. 99).

This ley shows the problems faced when trying to project alignments for long distances. Fractional adjustments at one place on the line produce huge distortions further along it. If there was an intention to maintain a general direction for an alignment, but accepting slight variations to pick up special features, then the present anomalies become understandable. However, we are in danger here of judging the alignments from a twentieth century perspective.

Let us imagine that we had a time machine that could project us back into Neolithic times with all our technological understanding. Using only the tools available at the time, how would we solve the problems of making long distance alignments?

The alignment would need to maintain a constant bearing in relation to the Earth. It would need to follow what is known as a great circle. This is simply the circle whose centre is at the centre of the Earth. The way to achieve this would be to fix an accurate north/south meridian based on the sun's noon day shadow, then set a bearing from it. If the bearing was re-established at each site, this would create a series of lines which would be in broad alignment. Even if this was done using modern surveying techniques, errors would creep in that could only be eliminated by constant re-checking and readjustment. This could be one explanation for the deviations found in the Michael ley.

Technically, then, it is possible to maintain a constant bearing using the angle of the sun's noon day shadow. Similarly the meridian could be set by the Pole star. This would be more difficult technically. Ideally an astrolabe or simple theodolite is needed to check the azimuth of the Pole star, which varies according to the latitude of the observer.

Of all the long distance alignments I have checked out, the Michael ley is the least convincing as a surveyed line. However, it has established itself in the minds of many ley hunters, but the argument that it somehow retains a detectable 'earth current' is the only one that gives it meaning. The Stonehenge and Canterbury alignments all check out with an acceptable degree of accuracy.

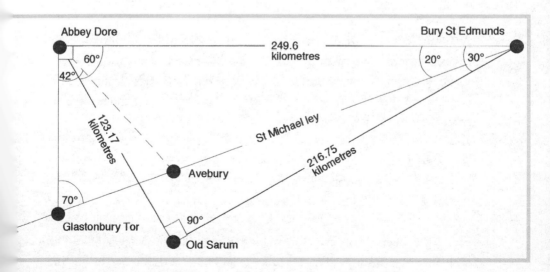

Fig. 100. Landscape geometry linking some major sacred sites

The problem then is the link between the Michael ley and the Marlborough Downs pattern. It is surely not a coincidence that the ley runs parallel to the line of the centres of the twin circles or that it highlights the position of the 'King's Chamber' at Temple Farm.

Large scale geometric patterns

If the idea of long distance alignments was not problem enough, what about the concept of major geometric patterns overlaying the country? Yet, by accident or design, they can be shown to exist. Two are presented here so readers can judge for themselves. Each involves three sites in triangular relationship. The first includes two sites already mentioned: the hillfort of Old Sarum and Bury St Edmunds abbey. The third leg of this triangle is the abbey church at Abbey Dore in Herefordshire with the three sites forming angles of 30°, 60° and 90° (Fig. 100). The distances and exact angular relationships between these three sites are as follows:

Distances		Angles	
Old Sarum to Bury St Edmunds	216.75 kilometres	Old Sarum	90.16°
Old Sarum to Abbey Dore	123.17 kilometres	Abbey Dore	60.23°
Abbey Dore to Bury St Edmunds	249.60 kilometres	Bury St Edmunds	29.58°

A 1° angle at the distances involved covers around 4 kilometres (2.48 miles) so there is plenty of margin for fanciful imagination and I therefore make no claims for the intentional creation of this triangle. If however, the angles were intended to give a 30°:60°:90° triangle, then the error in the site positions would be as follows:

Old Sarum to Bury St Edmunds	605 metres
Old Sarum to Abbey Dore	344 metres
Abbey Dore to Bury St Edmunds	1002 metres

Fig. 100 shows a nominal 90° angle between Glastonbury, Abbey Dore and Bury St Edmunds. The exact angle is 89.97° a difference of less than two minutes of arc.

The second example involves the abbey site at Canterbury, Glastonbury Tor and the Arbor Low henge in the Peak District (see Fig. 101). The distances and angles between these three sites are as follows:

Distances		Angles	
Canterbury to Arbor Low	286.19 kilometres	Canterbury	50.04°
Canterbury to Glastonbury	264.99 kilometres	Glastonbury	69.80°
Glastonbury to Arbor Low	234.05 kilometres	Arbor Low	60.16°

In this case, the internal angles of 50°, 60° and 70° are the same as the triangle of sites between Tewkesbury Abbey, Pershore Abbey and Stanton in the Bredon Hill complex. The errors in distance generated by these angles to the exact positions are:

Canterbury to Arbor Low	200 metres
Canterbury to Glastonbury	185 metres
Glastonbury to Arbor Low	815 metres

Stonehenge falls just off the base line between Canterbury and Glastonbury Tor at an angle of 15° from Arbor Low. If it could ever be demonstrated rigorously that these placements were part of a greater complex, their precise positioning would be crucial. They would each act as a primary reference point in their different areas, giving a continuity of the pattern across the country.

Patterns in the landscape

Considering the mindset of those who created the Marlborough Downs pattern, it is possible that they could have also tried to establish a more extensive grid network of interlinked sites throughout the country. The tools and skills that were available to them would have just about been sufficient. This would have been no easy task and the errors in the alignments could simply be technical failures due to the primitive equipment they were using. After all, they were not living in today's world, where the GPS system can give us the exact longitude and latitude of any place we choose.

If, in Neolithic times there was a deliberate intention to set out sites in the landscape in accordance with a predetermined plan, such as the geometrical linking of 'holy' centres such as Canterbury, Glastonbury and Arbor Low, then their creators were remarkably successful. To be accurate to within a few hundred metres over distances in excess of 200 kilometres (125 miles) is an incredible achievement. But why should they have wanted to do this?

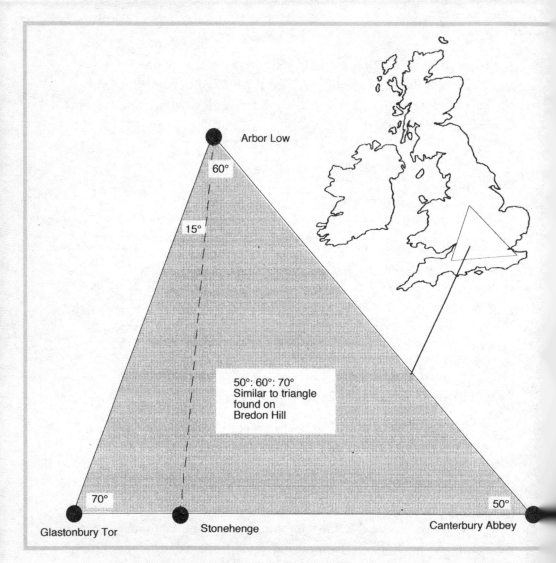

Fig. 101. Geometric relationship of Glastonbury, Arbor Low and Canterbury

15
EXCALIBUR

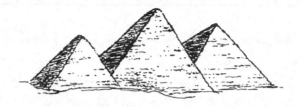

*There is a clear link between ancient Britain and ancient Egypt
... something to do with a way of encapsulating energy*

Of all the questions posed by my discovery of the twin circles of the Marlborough Downs, the hardest to answer is why would anyone set about creating this pattern? To answer it means moving away from the world of hard scientific fact into the realm of science fiction. But then, throughout the course of the twentieth century the speculation thrown up by science fiction has, all too often, turned into scientific fact.

To proceed we must look at some of the current ideas on leys and their possible links with concepts of energy. Then I will need to explain something of my own experiences and the intuitions that I have gleaned from the many visits I have made to those sites which hold, for me, a special presence. I hope then to be able to draw some of the threads together to present at least a cogent explanation for the enormous effort that was made, in physical terms at least, in establishing the matrix of sites that overlays the Marlborough Downs and other places in the British Isles. I believe these concepts have universal implications. They are as relevant to America, France, or any other country of the world as they are to Britain.

Why leys?

As mentioned in Chapter 1, the story of leys really begins with Alfred Watkins, who first drew the general public's attention to this phenomenon in a structured way. Two main themes run through his book, *The Old Straight Track*. The first is that these alignments exist in their hundreds throughout Britain. Secondly, these alignments were used by early peoples for the purposes of travel between different sites. As he said:

In its full development, the old track was no mean achievement in surveying and engineering. Road-making was not part of its scheme, for the attitude seems to have been: 'Mother earth is good enough for you to walk or ride on, and we will pave a way through the streams, soft places and ponds; our chief job is to point out the way.' This the old ley-men did magnificently.

To realize how, imagine a fairy chain stretched from mountain peak to mountain peak, as far as the eye could reach, and paid out until it touched the 'high places' of the earth at a number of ridges, banks and knolls. Then visualize a mound, circular earthwork, or clump of trees, planted on these high points, and in the low points in the valley other mounds ringed around with water to be seen from a distance. Then great standing stones brought to mark the way at intervals, and on banks leading up to a mountain ridge or down to a ford the track cut deep so as to form a guiding notch on the skyline as you come up. In a bwlch, or mountain pass, the road cut deeply at the highest place straight through the ridge to show the notch afar off. Here and there and at two ends of the way, a beacon fire used to lay out the track. With ponds dug on the line, or streams filled up into 'flashes' to form reflecting points on the beacon track so that it might be checked when at least once a year the beacon was fired on the traditional day. All these works exactly on the sighting line. The wayfarer's instructions are still deeply rooted in the peasant mind, when he tells you – quite wrongly now – 'You just keep straight on.'

Watkins' work gained the derision of orthodox archaeologists but set in motion an enormous popular interest in the subject. Shortly after the publication of his book, the Old Straight Track Club was formed. Despite the evidence presented by Watkins that his alignments were trackways, there is little data to support this theory. Aerial photographs which show up, through crop marks, buried features have not indicated any straight trackways of the type envisaged by Watkins. The concept of straight track-ways linking ancient sites has now been discounted by most ley hunters.

Energy lines

The Second World War brought the interest in alignments to a halt and the club was wound up in 1948. Revival came during the 1960s when Egerton Sykes, Jimmy Goodard, Philip Helston and Tony Wedd formed the Ley Hunters Club in November 1962. A wider interest at the time in UFOs and occult subjects raised the idea that leys were lines of various types of terrestrial energy. These energies were seen in many different ways and some associations made with the Chinese concepts of *ch'i* embodied in *feng shui*. This has become quite popular in recent years and generally perceived to involve the relationship of objects and rooms within a building. But *feng shui* also incorporates concepts about the hidden energies within the landscape. To some, leys were lines of magnetic force, while others saw them as more subtle 'thought' lines connecting sites.

In 1977, the Dragon Project was set up to examine ley phenomena from many different perspectives. The idea that leys are related to terrestrial energies is widely accepted these days, except by those who stand at the more 'orthodox' end of ley research.

The problem with the 'energy' theories is determining what type of energy is involved and nobody can assess to the satisfaction of others what is meant by ley energy. Undoubtedly dowsers can detect through their bodies, and their rods, fluctuations in the 'energy' fields to which they are attuned. Yet diviners' fields seem to differ from one another's. I have been with dowsers who have been certain that a ley passed through a specific spot, where I felt no sensation.

The inability of dowsers to produce consistent findings has created a minefield of anomalies and the more serious researchers have steered away from these concepts. Look, for example, at the book *The Sun and The Serpent*, written by two dowsers Hamish Miller and Paul Broadhurst, based on their researches into the Michael ley. Taking John Michell's Michael line (see Fig. 16) as their starting point, the authors produced two more lines that wriggled their way across the countryside like worms in a spasm, picking up almost every site within several miles of the original alignment. To add further confusion, these two lines were called 'Michael and Mary currents'. So for example, in the Avebury area the 'Michael current' snakes its way across Windmill Hill, through Avebury, running from north to south and then following the line of the Avenue up to the site of the Sanctuary. The 'Mary current', on the other hand, comes up from the south, across the top of Windmill Hill, where it crosses the 'Michael current', then on up to the church at Winterbourne Monkton, before heading south through Avebury, back to Silbury Hill, then round to the West Kennett long barrow, before crossing the 'Michael current' at the Sanctuary.

I accept the integrity of both Miller and Broadhurst, but what they have produced has nothing to do with alignments. Linking their ideas with the Michael ley, which at least purports to be straight, only succeeds in muddying the water. From the research presented in this book, I firmly believe that the alignments and patterns created had nothing to do with the detection of 'terrestrial energies' by Neolithic peoples. They surveyed and set up patterned relationships in a similar way that a modern town planner would set out roads and houses to a pre-determined grid. This was a practical task carried out in a practical way using the basic technology available to the people of those times. It was a task carried out with great ingenuity and skill but determined not by 'earth currents' but by something else.

The simple explanation would be to suggest that symbolic relationships were part of the spiritual beliefs of the people who set up these patterns, in the same way that churches are designed so that the cross created by the aisle and the transept is orientated on an approximate east-west axis. Imagine this pattern overlaid on the landscape. One would find a series of churches laid out in a cross-formation stretching over several miles; the macrocosm reflecting the microcosm. To carry a symbolic representation forward on to such a grand-scale, involving vast amounts of labour, would only occur if there was a very powerful incentive.

Great works of such a nature could never be achieved if the people were being coerced into them. There is no evidence that Neolithic society was a slave-state. Nor, despite popular belief, is there any evidence that those who built the pyramids were unwillingly employed. The pyramid builders were more akin to those who built the great cathedrals of the middle ages.

They devoted the whole of their lives to building a monument in praise of the Almighty. Children were apprenticed to their fathers, so that generations of one family would be employed in the same project. Cathedral building, symbolically if not practically, involved the whole populace as it was seen to benefit everyone. It was driven by a religious fervour. Devoting one's life to the Christian ideal in this way was necessary to the salvation of the soul.

The only other motivation which draws such a powerful collective response is warfare and defence. There are structures within Britain, such as Maiden Castle in Dorset, built for this reason, but places such as Avebury and Stonehenge had no military purpose. These monuments were places of worship which linked the deities to the people through to the cycle of the seasons. They also hold an 'energy' which many people have experienced, although here I must be careful in defining my terminology.

The word 'energy' as defined in the dictionary is 'the ability or capacity to produce an effect'. Science restricts the meaning of this word to operations through known physical laws. Yet double-blind experiments conducted in the US involving 'healing' or 'prayer energy' have shown this to be effective, even though it works outside of any known physical laws. Many studies of telepathy, both statistical and anecdotal, support the view that telepathic communication between two people can and does occur. It is not possible to explain this phenomenon within the laws governing the electro-magnetic spectrum. In the case of both healing and telepathy, some form of energy must be involved for the 'effects' have been measured in carefully controlled studies. So a wider application of the word 'energy' is, I believe, necessary to understand these phenomena. This is also relevant to the concept of leys.

Studies have shown that telepathic communication is prevalent amongst primitive societies such as the aborigines or the Native American Indians. For example, Laurens van der Post discovered that the bushmen of the Kalahari knew in advance which of several different pilots would be flying the aircraft that used their landing strip, though there was no direct radio communication. The villagers were also aware when one of their hunters had killed an eland, a very special event, and immediately set preparations for a feast. We could surmise that Neolithic people possessed similar abilities. If the priests or shamans of two neighbouring communities established a telepathic communication between themselves it is possible that this connection might establish a 'straight line' field of telepathic energy that could be detected by a dowser at a later date. Indeed, all human activity of this sort might leave its 'thought' imprints in the psychic web of the planet, which scientist Rupert Sheldrake has called a 'morphogenic field'. Dowsers attuning to these lines of communication at a later stage, rather like turning the radio dial, might pick up hundreds of different stations.

I am not suggesting by these examples that I particularly espouse this line of thinking, only that it could provide an explanation for the diversity of energies that dowsers detect and the possible linking of an energy line between ley sites.

Pyramids and pyramid energies

The concept of 'subtle' energies has also found its way into the folklaw surrounding pyramids and in particular the Great Pyramid of Egypt.

In the mid 1930s, Frenchman Antoine Bovis visited the Great Pyramid and was intrigued to find the bodies of some small animals in it. These animals had obviously wandered in, become lost, and eventually starved to death. What was strange about their bodies was that they showed no signs of serious decomposition. They seemed to have been mummified by just being within the pyramid structure. After he returned to France, Bovis set about building a small-scale model replicating the Great Pyramid's proportions. Aligning this to the four points of the compass, he tested its preservative abilities on a wide variety of food substances, finding to his amazement that some force within this structure appeared to slow down the degeneration process.

Bovis's research came to the attention of a Czechoslovakian radio technician, Karl Drbal, who also started to experiment with scale models of the Great Pyramid. He found that by placing a razor blade, aligned to the north/south axis and positioned at a height equivalent to that of the King's Chamber, the blade stayed sharp far longer than his other razor blades, despite daily use.

In 1949, Drbal presented his 'Pharaoh's Shaving Device' to the Czechoslovak patent board for their consideration. The board rejected his application as a joke, saying that the concept was not scientifically tested. So Drbal spent the next ten years acquiring the necessary scientific validation. He was able to show that the shape of the pyramid interacted with the Earth's magnetic current and produced what he called 'electromagnetic dehydration'. It is the effects of water molecules on the edge of a razor blade that makes them go blunt. Energy marshalled by the pyramid removed these molecules, keeping the blade sharper longer. Eventually Drbal got his patent.

Since that time, much research has taken place in the US and elsewhere, using muscle testing or kinesiology techniques, to assess the effect of pyramid shapes on human beings. There is now a vast amount of anecdotal evidence supporting the view that the energies of the pyramid can interact with human consciousness to produce beneficial healing effects. Some form of subtle or healing 'energy' is involved.

From all of my researches and discoveries there is, I believe, a clear link between ancient Britain and ancient Egypt. We can infer from this and the evidence from the Marlborough Downs and Egypt that the inspiration behind the pyramids arose on Atlantis. This knowledge had something to do with a way of encapsulating energy. In Britain, it was somehow connected into the landscape.

Personal reflections

My own experiences with leys has primarily focused on attuning the 'energies' of the different nodal points on alignments. Many of these are at well known sites such as Avebury, but other less well known places have emerged from my investigations into angular relationships. In some cases I found significant sites within a geometric grid in the middle of a field without any discernible archaeological features.

My initial analysis started when I directed my attention specifically to those sites where I felt a clear sensation through my body. This was manifested primarily as a tingling feeling at the back of my head and in my arms. I made a note of those places where this feeling manifested itself and I disregarded those where this sensation was absent. I know now that such sensations are common to dowsers, but at the time I was not familiar with the experiences of others, so could go only on what I was experiencing myself.

To the sceptic, ideas of listening to one's body in this way will no doubt seem bizarre. I have also wondered whether I might have unconsciously produced this feeling within myself in response to subtle clues that had nothing to do with leys. But I can show that this is not the case.

Recently I was looking for one of London's old 'holy wells', which I knew was not far from Liverpool Street Station. I had discovered this site through research into a particular alignment and had pinpointed the spot by studying ancient maps of the area, then translating the information across onto a modern 1:25,000 scale map of inner London. Then one day, by chance, I found myself in the area and took the opportunity to test my responses.

I had not been prepared for the trip, so I did not have any of my maps with me, but thought I knew the approximate location of the well as somewhere near the junction of Scrutton Street with Holywell Row. I went there, but I felt no inner response. I walked around the area several times only to be disappointed. Eventually I concluded that there was nothing significant about the site and wandered off down Scrutton Street. At the junction with Curtain Road I turned left and was immediately hit by an enormous surge of 'energy' which I could not mistake. I tried to dismiss this experience because I was a long way from the presumed site of the 'holy well'. Nevertheless, the sensation persisted and it was clearly confined to that one particular spot.

When I returned home, I re-checked my maps and discovered that I had made a mistake. The place where I had searched originally was incorrect. The real site of the 'holy well' was exactly where I had experienced the overwhelming sensation. In this case, I knew for certainty that my mind had not produced the sensations in my body. Something deeper had to be at work.

Having satisfied myself that these physical sensations truly came from the sites that I was investigating, I next sought to understand these experiences from other perspectives. This took me into a whole range of inner experiences that are very hard to translate into ordinary terms. Perhaps it is best to consider them journeys into other realms of consciousness. Sometimes I would find myself in conversation with beings who manifested themselves in my mind. Sometimes I would get a sudden insight into what the site was about or, at other times, I would just get a feeling of indescribable bliss.

Fortunately, I was not alone in this. Friends and colleagues had similar experiences. I recognise that it is easy for forms of mass delusion to run through groups, but our researches were carried through with a reasonable degree of detached observation. Moreover, as I have shown, I have experienced strong sensations through my body, even when my conscious mind was trying to override this perception.

Paul Devereux, the author of many books on leys, described such an experience in his book *Earth Memory*. At the time he had been researching the position and significance of Silbury Hill. He said:

> *I knew that the builders of Silbury Hill had to be aware that they were constructing the mound on the line of sight between the already existing West Kennett barrow and Windmill Hill. This was certainly part of the explanation on why the great mound had been placed, in its otherwise inexplicable position, in the lowest part of the Kennett valley.*
>
> *It was becoming clear that Silbury's height must have been tied to some function as a platform. So I began visiting the monument at key solar dates throughout the year to watch sunrises and sets from the summit. Some of these positions linked to skyline features, but not in any definite manner. I knew I was still missing the point. One dawn, I arrived at Silbury to find it in a thick grey mist. I clambered to the top where the sky was clear overhead, but the low mist hung like a shroud over the landscape around. It was like sitting on an island of grass in a cottonwool sea. As I sat, awaiting the sunrise, a clear, bell-like phrase rang out in my mind. It jolted me as much as if someone had spoken in my ear. The 'voice' said, 'In this mystery shall we dwell.' It was definitely something from outside of my conscious mind – it was not the sort of thing one thinks up to pass the time. My immediate sense was that it was somehow Silbury itself communicating, but my rational self saw it as a product of my subconscious being projected into my quiescent, waking mind as a result of being in a strange place at an odd time in rather disorienting circumstances.*

Devereux went on to discover, at a Lammas sunrise, the significant position of the flattened top of Waden Hill to the east which runs exactly parallel to the horizon line; one closely matching the other as two broadly parallel topographical bands. He believed that this was because it allowed the sunrise to be observed twice on the same day: once from the top of Silbury and once just down from the summit on the level area known as the 'terrace'. However, his observation that showed Silbury Hill to be a fraction higher than Waden Hill also fulfils the criterion which makes Silbury Hill such an important surveying point. In these experiences, Devereux felt that he had been in contact with the *genius loci* of the sites he was exploring. Something within the landscape was communicating itself to him. This is very close to my own experiences.

Cosmic connections

Many people enjoy visiting such places as Avebury. Some go because it makes a pleasant day out; others because the presence of the place touches something deep inside them. In the past, it has been fashionable to think of such sites as connecting with terrestrial energies. We could, however, turn and look in the opposite direction; not down but up. The answer might lie not on Earth but in the stars.

It is now generally accepted that the 'air vents' in the Great Pyramid were aligned specifically to certain stars, such as Sirius and the belt in Orion. In *The Orion Mystery*, Bauval and Gilbert argued that this was because the soul of the dead pharaoh needed to journey to these stellar kingdoms on his demise. They represented the 'gods', and returning after death to reside with the 'god' was part of their religious beliefs. But suppose this was not part of an after-death experience, but one in which the living pharaoh could enter into at special ceremonial times. By renewing his communion with the 'gods', he could rekindle his vision, incorporating a deeper wisdom for the guidance of his people.

What if the assumed mortuary temples outside of the pyramids were used instead by the living pharaoh for purification and dedication rituals before entering the pyramid? The sarcophagus in the King's Chamber might then have only been used by the living pharaohs to access the realms of wisdom to which the 'air-vent' stargates directed him. Maybe also the chambers of each of the other pyramids, despite missing the ventilation shafts, could have been established for similar purposes. Through such places, time and inter-dimensional mind travel could be undertaken through to levels of consciousness beyond this Earth because the 'path kept straight on' through the circle of the heavens to the stars. Let us also suppose that such portals allowed for a two way communication, that the energy from the cosmos could be focused down on to the Earth, that sites such as Avebury and Stonehenge provided gateways for life-enhancing energy. Perhaps this was the vision that impelled Neolithic peoples to build their monuments in patterns that reflected this concept.

The Excalibur of Arthur

In Chapter 9 there was an excerpt from a channelled communication about the final days of Atlantis. This suggested that the chief high priest of Atlantis called forth all the spiritual powers of that civilisation and, through the power of his consciousness, located and buried these in different parts of the world as time-capsules for a future age. The key, we are told, symbolised by the Excalibur of King Arthur, was placed in England. From this we might infer that some of this Atlantean power was woven into the landscape of the British Isles. We might conjecture also that those Atlantean refugees, finding themselves in 'spiritually' barren lands and deprived of their portals to these other realms of consciousness, would set about establishing new gateways. So, the stone circle sites might have nothing to do with earth energies, but everything to do with the energies from the stars. I do not mean the physical energies of the star systems, but something infinitely more subtle – dimensions of consciousness higher than those that could be assessed through the mind alone.

A grouping of sites might therefore have been constructed symbolically to link to a pattern of stars within a particular constellation. Not because there is intelligent life in these stellar realms, but because that area of space acted as a gateway into another realm of reality. Each site might provide one facet of experience, like the individual colours of a rainbow, but all of them together are required to make the complete pattern.

This picture fits my own experiences at these sacred places. The 'energy' there is one that appeals to the spiritual aspirations within us. This happens, not in a blind dogmatic way, but one that is infinitely liberating, unfettered by the chains of restricted religious practice that holds so much of the world's population in its grip. The interlinking of these sites allows for those finer impulses to feed into the whole system so that all is renewed, to the benefit of all. The Earth too responds, for the spiritual realms that surround this sphere can participate in and experience this interconnection. By accessing the infinity of the cosmos at sacred places we access the infinity of our own souls.

Whatever the achievements of that ancient continent of Atlantis, it finally became unbalanced and was destroyed. Perhaps the Atlantean priests and priestesses reached too high into the stars and, like Icarus, forgot their connection with mother Earth. Perhaps they unleashed forces that rent their world asunder. On a symbolic level, the link between heaven and Earth is crucial to our survival into the twenty-first century if we are to come to terms with the excesses of materialism. We need to be able to renew our vision from the higher realms of consciousness, while remaining with one foot firmly on the ground. This I believe is the legacy bequeathed to us by the landscape temple I found on the Marlborough Downs.

Perhaps those from Atlantis, like the latter day Tibetans, were forced from their homes and obliged to take their knowledge into the world around them. A wisdom and an ability to open up channels of communication to higher realms of consciousness were then fixed at specific locations in the landscape. These sites are once more starting to communicate their messages to us. Merlin is awake calling us forth. We only have to stop and listen.

Appendix 1
DESCRIPTION OF THE
MARLBOROUGH DOWNS
CIRCLE SITES

Rather than simply giving the bare details of each site, I have set out a journey that can be followed by car and on foot. Most sites are within easy access of roads. A few have to be walked to; sometimes the walk is more than a mile. One or two sites, such as the long barrow at East Kennett, are on private land and no access should be made without consent of the owners.

Eastern circle

59 kilometres (37 miles) total circuit
A suitable starting point for a journey around the different sites of the eastern circle is the henge monument at **Avebury**. Covering more than 33 acres and having an overall diameter of about 427 metres (1400 feet), Avebury is the largest henge monument in Britain. In addition to a massive bank and ditch, which was more than 6 metres (20 feet) deep, it boasted an outer circle of sarsen stones, with two inner circles each with a diameter of about 100 metres (328 feet). Little now remains of these inner circles and many stones from the outer ring, particularly in the eastern segment have now gone, removed at a time when it was fashionable to

break up the stones. Some of the megaliths at Avebury are among the largest ever erected; these range between 60 and 90 tonnes, making them nearly twice the weight of the biggest trilithon pillars at Stonehenge. Transporting and putting up these stones would have been an enormous undertaking, requiring hundreds of people. The excavation of the ditch would also have been a mammoth task and it has been variously estimated that it would have taken around 250 people working continuously for about 20 years to complete. The circumference of the Marlborough Circle passes through the western side of the monument at the approximate position of the public car park opposite the post office. This part of the henge still retains many large stones which give a good impression of how it might have looked in times past.

The next group of church sites which led to my discovery of the circles lie close to the small brook that eventually merges into the Kennett river. Leaving the henge by its northern gateway via the A4361 and travelling north, the first point after Avebury is the ancient church of **Winterbourne Monkton**. This is found by turning left at the sign about 2 kilometres (1.2 miles) from the henge and following through to the car park alongside the farm buildings. The small church is dedicated to St Mary Magdalene and was built around 1133. There is a suggestion that it is on the site of an earlier chapel founded by monks from Glastonbury in 928. Inside there are two unusual timber pillars which support a square bell tower with an inset pitched roof. Outside, at its eastern end, there is a large recumbent Sarsen stone which marks the grave of Revd Brinsden who died in 1710. This was taken from an ancient barrow just north of the church. At the western end of the church, old undressed foundation stones can be clearly seen at ground level. Such stones are found in many churches and are so obvious that they suggest that it was the deliberate intention of the builders to incorporate stones from pagan sites into the structure of the building. Inside there is an ancient font which gives clues to the antiquity of the church. It carries a carved chevron design and has an ancient fertility symbol on its northern face.

Leave the church and turn left at the junction with the A4361. The next site can be found by a left turn just prior to a sharp right-hand bend in the road. On entering the hamlet of **Berwick Bassett**, you will see a sign marking the footpath way to the church on the right hand side of the road. This straight trackway is covered over by trees and you get the impression of walking through a tunnel before emerging in front of the small fourteenth century church of Berwick Bassett, dedicated to St Nicholas. When I first saw this church 20 years ago it was derelict, having been abandoned in 1972. It has recently been restored by the Redundant Churches Conservation Trust. Part stone and part brick, the building has an unusual small tower. Close by are some standing stones drilled to take gate posts. Whether there are old or recent I cannot tell, but an information leaflet on the church states that Sarsen stones were used for grave stones at this site. The church has a thirteenth century font, suggesting that it was built on the site of an earlier church.

Continuing back along the A4361, the church of **Winterbourne Bassett** can be found from another signposted left turn 2 kilometres (1.2 miles) from the turning to Berwick Bassett. On entering the village, the church can be found down a short roadway on the left-hand side. Built in stone with the earliest parts dating from around 1100, it has a light airy feeling with resplendent deep red and purple stained glass windows. The church was originally dedicated to St Katherine. St Peter was added at a later date. A gently curving trackway leads from this church and follows the exact line of the circumference of the circle for a distance of about one mile to the next church at Broad Hinton.

If you are travelling by car, drive back to the A4361 and turn left. Take the next turning left, signposted to **Broad Hinton**. The church is off this road on the left-hand side, the directions are signposted. Broad Hinton church, like the previous churches, is fairly small although it is used more frequently than the others. Surrounded by trees, including an ancient yew, the light in the church is much more sombre and brooding, reflected in the blackened oak panelling and intricate memorials to the dead. Outside there is a stone cross but its base does not suggest it is of great age. The footpath from Winterbourne Bassett can be found to the eastern side of the churchyard. Of all the churches, this is the greatest distance from the calculated line which here follows the footpath. The exact crossing point, which forms a 60° angle between the East Kennett long barrow and the centre of the eastern circle, is marked by a small pond close to the church way junction with the B4041.

Returning back to the main road, a white horse chalk figure can be clearly seen on the side of the downs opposite. The intersection point between the two circles lies just off the left-hand side of this road in the middle of a corn field. Access to it can be found from a bridleway about 4 kilometres (2.4 miles) along the road from the junction out of Broad Hinton.

Continuing towards **Wroughton** the church can be found shortly after the road dips down the escarpment on the left-hand side. This is a large church built prior to 965 and contains the remains of an ancient broken cross in the churchyard. There are also some old earthworks to the south-west of the churchyard which face out towards Swindon. Pieces of Roman pottery have been found in the field alongside the church.

The next site can be found by taking the B4005 to Chiseldon: passing through the village the road joins the A345 which is the main road to Marlborough. Turn right and then first left on to a road, which was originally part of the Ridgeway track. This will take you past the large hill-fort of Liddington Castle on your right. Cross the A419 and a short way on you will find a **crossroads** with Ermine Street, a Roman road. Watkins noted that crossroads were often found at significant ley crossing points. Turning right and then first left to the village of Blaydon, the road runs alongside the motorway. Just over half a mile up the road turn left again and cross over the motorway. A trackway will be found on the left-hand side just past the bridge which leads to the **tumulus** on Hinton Downs. This is about a third of a mile up the track on the right-hand side.

A fairly large gap now occurs of nearly a quarter of the circle before the next point. This can best be found by travelling back to Marlborough and then taking the A4 road towards Newbury. Just outside the town and up the hill, is a sign to Savernake Forest and Tottenham House. Turn right here. This will take you on to a straight road called the Grand Avenue, which coincides with an old Roman road. Just under 2 kilometres (1.2 miles) along this road there are some earthwork embankments which mark the edge of the western circle at this point. If you parked your car here and followed these embankments for a short distance on the left-hand side of the road, you would be walking along the circumference to the **earthworks** that lie next to the A4. In the other direction, two tumuli sites can be found about one mile away although the easiest access by road is from the A346.

Continuing on for 4 kilometres (2.2 miles) you come to a T-junction. Turn left here and a short way up the road a sign will indicate the way to the church. The church in **Savernake Forest**, dedicated to St Katherine, is of recent origin being built in 1860. Unusually the aisle of this church is oriented on a west-south-west axis, which coincides with the alignment of the circumference of the circle.

The next point is the church in the town of **Wootton Rivers**. There are a number of routes that can be taken from Savernake. The easiest route is probably found by turning left from the church and taking the road to Burbage. At the end of the town, turn right on to the B3087 to Pewsey. Turn right again about a mile and a half up the road at the signpost to Wootton Rivers. The church can be found, via a short road, on the left-hand side. Dedicated to St Andrew, it is of ancient origin, being modified and enlarged in a number of stages. Although not included in the western circle, this site lies very close to the intersection between the two circles which falls just to the east of the road, where it crosses the Kennett and Avon Canal. If there was once a marker at this point, it would undoubt-edly have been removed during the excavation of the canal. Running close by is the railway line between Great Bedwyn station and Pewsey. Effectively three great systems of transport – road, rail and water – come together at this point. The northern intersection has no markers either, being set in the middle of a corn field close to the A361.

The remaining sites all date from Neolithic times and are not easy to access. The first is the spectacular promontory of the hillfort called the **Giant's Grave**. This can be found by taking the Marlborough Road out of Wootton Rivers. At the junction with the A345, turn left towards Pewsey. You will have to park your car in the village of Oare and then make a fairly strenuous climb up to the hillfort. The effort is well worthwhile. From the top, the views are spectacular. (For those who wish to cut short their jour-ney, and access some of the sites in the western circle, move on from here to the sites at Pewsey and Manningford Bohune mentioned in the western circle section.)

The circumference line then passes along **Huish Hill**, moulding to the contour of the land and its earthworks, and then on to some more earthworks at **Gopher Wood**. Both of these sites can only be accessed by trackways. Next point is the **East Kennett** long barrow, which is on private land with no direct access. The barrow can best be viewed from the road that leads out of East Kennett. The barrow's axis aligns to the circumference of the circle.

The final point is a small group of tumuli on the northern summit of **Waden Hill**, which also boasts, on its lower eastern slopes, the stones of the Avenue. The tumuli are not readily accessible. They are on private farmland. From Waden Hill, you can return to Avebury.

Western circle

59 kilometres (37 miles) total circuit
The most appropriate starting point for the exploration of the Western Circle is the church of **Bishops Cannings**, built *circa* 1150 and dedicated to St Mary the Virgin. This site is on the direct alignment between the two centres which also goes through the West Kennett long barrow. Bishops Cannings can be found just off the A361 Avebury to Devizes road. It is the first turning left past the Beckhamton roundabout. The church is fairly large having a tall stone spire and a number of large undressed foundation stones which could indicate it was built on an older site, with the stones being incorporated into the church fabric.

Between Bishops Cannings and the next site of Calstone Wellington, you will find the impressive promontory of Morgan's Hill. I have not included this point as one of the sites of the western circle for no actual tumulus or mound is shown on the maps to pinpoint the precise position of the circumference. However, its position as a clear marker through to the opposite side of the circle makes it a likely candidate as a surveying key site. Here can be found two towering radio masts, an OS trig. point and the enigmatic copse of trees at Furze Knoll, all within 200 metres (656 feet) of the circumference, which cuts across the end of the hill.

Leaving Bishops Cannings by the same road, you need to cross the A361 and take the road to Calne. After 3.7 kilometres (2.3 miles) you will see a signposted road on the right to **Calstone Wellington**. The church can be found on the right-hand side just through the village. This church is also dedicated to St Mary and falls on a direct alignment between the centre of the western circle and Silbury Hill. The present church was erected in the fifteenth century but there is evidence of an earlier church dating to the twelfth century.

The next point is the church at **Compton Bassett**. To find this site, take the Calne road out of Calstone Wellington then take the first turning right which will take you through to the A4. Reaching this road, you will need to turn left then almost immediately right towards Compton Bassett. The church is about 3.2 kilometres (2 miles) along the road on the right-hand side. It is a large church dedicated to St Swithin and, like many others, built on ancient foundation stones. There is some evidence of a church from Saxon times.

Leaving Compton Bassett the circumference of the western circle then remarkably follows the sweep of the escarpment, between the downs and the plain below for over 7.24 kilometres (4.5 miles) through Highway Hill, Clevancy Hill and Clyffe Hanging. Leave Compton Bassett and follow the road along the bottom of the escarpment until the sign Clevancy, then turn right. The next site of **Townsend's Knoll** can be found at the end of the lane on the left-hand side. It is an ancient conical mound probably containing a burial site, but could equally well have been used for surveying by using transit markers as described in Chapter 11. In support of this, an alignment can be shown running from the Knoll to Bradenstoke Abbey–Rodbourne church with its ancient cross–Corston church–Foxley Green church–Leighterton church–Boxwell long barrow. This is a total of seven sites within a distance of 28 kilometres (16.53 miles) (see Fig. 102).

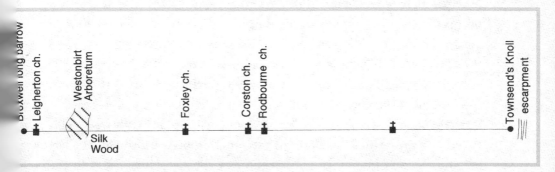

Fig. 102. Ley from Townsend's Knoll on the circumference of the western circle to the Broxwell long barrow

The next three sites can only be accessed by walking along the ridge foot-path that leads from Clevancy to Clyffe Pypard. They are shown as **tumuli and earthworks** on my old 1:25,000 scale map. However, the most recent Pathfinder series (1:25,000) has omitted them.

The next site, accessible by car, is the church at **Clyffe Pypard**. This can be found by leaving Townsend's Knoll and returning back to the minor road that leads to Bushton. Turn right at the T-junction and right again in Bushton, which is about 2.4 kilometres (1.5 miles) along the road. The road is signposted to Clyffe Pypard. The church can be found by taking a left turn after entering the village. Like many other churches in the area, ancient foundation stones can be seen, which suggest that the site was used before the church was erected. Dedicated to St Peter, the earliest parts of the present church date from the late thirteenth century. Close by there is an ornamental lake, which gives this site a special tran-quil atmosphere. This completes the marked sites in this sector of the circle.

The next place, **Ogbourne St George**, is nearly a quarter of the circle further on. The most attractive route to get to Ogbourne involves cross-ing the centre of the Marlborough Downs. Turn left on leaving the church at Clyffe Pypard and turn left again out of the village, taking the road to Winterbourne Bassett. The remains of a stone circle can be seen on the left-hand side of this road about 4.5 kilometres (2.8 miles) further on. Pass through Winterbourne and, at the junction with the A361, turn left towards Wroughton. Some 1.4 kilometres (0.9 miles) along the road you will come to a junction signposted to Rockley and Marlborough, where you will need to turn right. The road will take you up on to the highest points of the downs and provides access to **Temple Farm**. After 13.8 kilometres (8.5 miles) you will see a signpost to Rockley. Turn left here and follow along the road until it stops at the edge of a wood. There is no right of way for vehicles beyond this point, but you can walk along the farm road way to Temple Barn, a distance of just over a mile. There you will find a large clump of beech trees. This marks the approximate position of the junction between the St Michael ley and the axis joining the intersection of the two circles. Just to the north-east of this point a long barrow originally existed, but has now been completely destroyed.

The name Temple Farm stems from the Knight's Templar who were founded in 1119 to protect pilgrims on their way to the Holy Land. The order was finally destroyed in 1307 by Philip the Fair of France after it had attained great wealth and power. Many lands were donated to the Templars. Temple Farm was one of them. It was donated by John Marshall, an ancestor of the Earls of Pembroke.

Leaving Rockley, you turn right at the junction with the road to Marlborough. Within a few hundred yards there is a left turn to Ogbourne Maizey. Take this road through the village until it meets the A345, where you will need to turn left. This is a busy road, so care is needed, but about 2 kilometres (1.3 miles) along the road you will see a trackway opposite the turning to the village of Ogbourne St Andrew. Park here. The track takes you to the **centre of the eastern circle**. This lies close to where the track meets the abandoned railway embankment.

When you leave, turn right and take the road to Ogbourne St George, which is signposted on the left-hand side about 2.4 kilometres (1.5 miles) further on. Enter the village and take the next turning to the left. This will take you down a short road 1.3 kilometres (0.8 miles) to the church, which is signposted on the right-hand side. It is dedicated to St George. As well as being on the circumference of the western circle, it is on the Michael ley. The present church was built between the twelfth and fif-teenth centuries on the site of an earlier church. The church notes indicate that there was almost certainly a 'heathen temple' here before the original church was erected. Just back from the church in the village of Ogbourne there is a house which lies on the circumference. Built into the corner of this house is a large undressed mark stone which stands out clearly from the other coursed stonework.

From Ogbourne, access can be gained to the point where the alignment between the two centres intersects with the circumference of the western circle. To find this point, return to the centre of Ogbourne and turn left at the T-junction. The road will take you round the village and under the A345. Immediately after the bridge, you will see a roadway on the right-hand side. Take this road, which follows the alignment of an old Roman road. You will pass a trackway crossing and a short way further on you will see a farm gate entrance on the left. This is the approximate position of the intersection. From here, the East Kennett long barrow can be clearly seen, as can the alignment through to the West Kennett barrow. In the far distance, the radio masts and the clump of trees of Furze Knoll marking the approximate edge of the western circle are visible on the skyline. This is the only place that I have found in the whole pattern where it is very nearly possible to see right across one of the circles.

To reach the next point, you will need to retrace your steps back to the A345 and take the road through to Marlborough. The earthworks have already been mentioned in the description of the Eastern Circle, but the **tumuli** can be found by taking the A346 out of Marlborough. You will see a church on your left-hand side after about 2.7 kilometres (1.7 miles), and a further 2 kilometres (1.3 miles) along the road you will find a driveway access known as Sawpit Drive. Park here and walk up the drive until you meet a crossing with another trackway. Turn left here and a short walk of around 320 metres (350 yards) will take you to the site of a **tumulus** on the right-hand side of the track. To find the next group of tumuli, return to Sawpit Drive and turn left. At the next main pathway turn left again. About 800 metres (0.5 miles) along this path, you will come to another junction. At this point the group of **tumuli** are immediately in front of you in the 'v' made by the two trackways.

The last but one point on the circle, before returning back to Bishops Cannings, is the Wesleyan Chapel in Pewsey. The chapel is not ancient, being built in the nineteenth century, but shows how modern religious buildings can often be found on leys. This might of course be pure coincidence. With all the new developments over the past 150 years, some sites would align due to chance alone. I only mention this site here because it does fall on the circumference of the circle. Readers can make their own assessments on whether it should be included or not.

The last point is the de-consecrated church of **Manningford Bohune Common**, which has subsequently been turned into a private home. This can be found by taking the Woodborough road out of Pewsey. Just before this village, about 4.3 kilometres (2.7 miles) from Pewsey, there is a left turn over a railway bridge. Take this road and turn immediately left again over the bridge. Follow this road for a short distance and turn left again. The church site can be seen 270 metres (300 yards) up the road on the left-hand side. Built in the nineteenth century, the church does not appear to have ancient origins. However, when excavations were carried out to put in the septic tank for the new dwelling, a much older series of burial sites, dating from the middle ages, were discovered which had not been marked on the diocesan map. The site had therefore been used prior to the 1800s when the church was erected. The circle then returns to the church at Bishops Cannings, completing the circuit.

Appendix 2
Number Symbolism

Numbers over the millennia have acquired special attributes or principles which have become embodied in sacred tradition. But differences occur between cultures. For example, 6 is a number of evil to the aborigines, while to the Pythagoreans it was the perfect number because its factors also added up to 6 (1+2+3 = 6). In the Western esoteric tradition, odd numbers are regarded as masculine (yang) while even numbers are feminine (yin). Some of the associations are given below:

0 represents the divinity in the stage of becoming. The flow between 0 and 1 is the basic code for all computers. Some cultures do not use the zero, but in its circular form it represents infinity and the universe.

1 is the first principle, the fundamental upon which all other numbers are built. It is the number of unity and divinity and is associated with the sun.

2 represents duality, the yin/yang principle as understood in Taoist belief, representing the tension of opposites held in balance. Polarity is a fundamental principle which expresses itself through opposites – so we have life and death, the finite and the infinite, spirit and matter, positive and negative and so on. It is also reflected in the twin circles of the Marlborough Downs. The circles could be seen to represent these two polarities.

3 is the building block of the cosmos for two forces coming together to produce a third. The trinities of gods and goddesses found in many mythologies reflect this principle (for example Osiris, Isis and Horus) which finds echo in the Christian trinity of Father, Son and Holy Ghost. In numerology, it is a dynamic, creative number associated with the planet Jupiter which, in astrology, represents expansion. Within the pattern of the twin circles, it is depicted by the overlapping area where one finds its primary expression in the triangle of the pyramid. The symbolism of spirit, mind and body are expressed through the circle, triangle and square, which are the building blocks of all structures.

4 represents the physical plane and its manifestation through the elemental worlds of fire, air, water and earth. It is expressed through the four seasons, the four Evangelists, the four cardinal directions and is symbolised by the cross and the square.

5 was held sacred by the Chinese, as part of their five elements which form the basis of acupuncture. It is the pentagram and the pentangle, which incorporates the golden mean. It is sometimes said to be the number of man, so beautifully embodied in Leonardo's sketch. It finds expression through the five senses and is associated with communication and movement as portrayed by the god Hermes.

6 is the number of harmony and beauty expressed through the hexagon and the six pointed Star of David. Six held a prime place for the Pythagoreans. Its factors can be both added or multiplied to make six ($1 \times 2 \times 3 = 6$; $1 + 2 + 3 = 6$). It is often associated with the planet Venus.

7 was the number of the mystic. Its connection with the π (pi) proportion $^{22}/_{7}$ is obvious. It is the seven stars of the Great Bear, the seven days of the week and the seven known planets of the Old World. These are connected: Sunday to the sun; Monday to the moon; Tuesday, after the Norse God Tiw, to Mars; Wednesday, after the Norse God Woden, to Mercury; Thursday, after the Norse God Thor to Jupiter, Friday, after the Norse goddess Freya, to Venus; and Saturday after the Roman god Saturn to the planet of the same name.

8 is the number of completeness uniting spirit with matter. It is the 8 precepts of the Buddha, the 8 trigrams of the I Ching, the 8 noble trees, the

8 shrub trees and the 8 peasant trees of the Beth-Lois-Nuin alphabet. The 24 runes are made up of 3 groups with 8 runes in each. Tipped on its side it is the symbol for infinity that we use today.

9 is a pivotal number between the previous cycle and the next cycle of numbers starting with 10. It therefore stands for both evolution and involution depending how its energy is manifested. In this context, it is sometimes associated with the planet Mars.

10 completes the first part of the counting cycle. It is the 10 Sephiroth of the Kabbalists; the perfect triangle, made up of 10 dots, of the Pythagoreans. It is the number of God in the Hebrew system of Gematria. Its two symbols of 1 and 0 represent complete manifestation of the divinity. It is possibly for this reason that a factor of 10 was chosen for the division of the polar meridian into a million units. (In ancient Egypt, the number one million was symbolised by a scribe on one knee holding up both hands either in homage or astonishment.)

11 produces the first repetition of digits and as such was regarded as a master number. It would appear that in all cases repetition of digits 22, 33 (the highest grade in Freemasonry), 55 and so on, held some special meaning. The value of the number 11 in surveying and proportional terms would have given it a similar position to the number 7.

12 is the number of completeness and is connected with the 12 months of the year, the 12 signs of the zodiac, the 12 Apostles and so on. Multiplied by itself to produce 144, it becomes one of the numbers of the Fibonacci series. This number or tenfold multiples of it was extensively mentioned by St John in the *Book of Revelation*.

Appendix 3
ANGLE GENERATOR AND
DEGREE MEASURES

Angles	Main Ratios		Exact Equivalent	Reciprocal Angle	Other Ratios
1°	57	1	1.01	89°	
2°	28.5	1	2.01	88°	
3°	19	1	3.01	87°	
4°	28.5	2	4.01	86°	
5°	23	2	4.97	85°	
6°	19	2	6.01	84°	
7°	24.5	3	6.98	83°	
8°	28.5	4	7.99	82°	
9°	19	3	8.97	81°	
10°	17	3	10.01	80°	
11°	36	7	11.00	79°	
12°	23.5	5	12.01	78°	
13°	13	3	12.99	77°	
14°	4	1	14.04	76°	
15°	15	4	14.93	75°	
16°	7	2	15.95	74°	
17°	18	5.5	16.99	73°	
18°	21.5	7	18.03	72°	
19°	14.5	5	19.03	71°	
20°	11	4	19.98	70°	

Angles	Main Ratios		Exact Equivalent	Reciprocal Angle	Other Ratios	
21°	13	5	21.04	69°		
22°	5	2	21.80	68°		
23°	16.5	7	22.99	67°		
24°	9	4	23.96	66°		
25°	15	7	25.02	65°		
26°	20.5	10	26.00	64°		
27°	25.5	13	27.01	63°		
28°	15	8	28.07	62°		
29°	9	5	29.05	61°		
30°	19	11	30.07	60°		
31°	5	3	30.96	59°		
32°	8	5	32.01	58°		
33°	20	13	33.02	57°		
34°	20	13.5	34.02	56°		
35°	10	7	34.99	55°		
36°	11	8	36.03	54°		
37°	26.5	20	37.04	53°		
38°	20.5	16	37.97	52°	11	7
39°	18.5	15	39.04	51°		
40°	31	26	39.99	50°	6	5
41°	23	20	41.01	49°		
42°	10	9	41.99	48°		
43°	15	7	25.02	47°		
44°	29	28	43.99	46°		
45°	1	1	45.00	45°		

Deg.	Metres	Meg. Yds	Furlong(s)	11.55	Royal Cubit	Pyk Belady
1	110,573	133,413	551.29	9,573	210,615	191,468
2	110,574	133,415	551.30	9,574	210,617	191,470
3	110,575	133,416	551.30	9,574	210,619	191,472
4	110,577	133,418	551.31	9,574	210,623	191,475
5	110,579	133,421	551.32	9,574	210,627	191,479
6	110,582	133,424	551.34	9,574	210,632	191,484
7	110,586	133,429	551.36	9,575	210,640	191,491
8	110,591	133,435	551.38	9,575	210,650	191,500
9	110,596	133,441	551.41	9,575	210,659	191,508
10	110,602	133,448	551.44	9,576	210,670	191,519
11	110,609	133,457	551.47	9,577	210,684	191,531
12	110,616	133,465	551.51	9,577	210,697	191,543
13	110,624	133,475	551.55	9,578	210,712	191,557
14	110,633	133,486	551.59	9,579	210,730	191,572
15	110,642	133,497	551.64	9,579	210,747	191,588
16	110,652	133,509	551.69	9,580	210,766	191,605
17	110,662	133,521	551.74	9,581	210,785	191,623
18	110,673	133,534	551.79	9,582	210,806	191,642
19	110,684	133,547	551.84	9,583	210,827	191,661
20	110,696	133,562	551.90	9,584	210,850	191,681
21	110,709	133,577	551.97	9,585	210,874	191,704
22	110,722	133,593	552.03	9,586	210,899	191,726
23	110,736	133,610	552.10	9,588	210,926	191,751
24	110,750	133,627	552.17	9,589	210,952	191,775
25	110,764	133,644	552.24	9,590	210,979	191,799
26	110,779	133,662	552.32	9,591	211,008	191,825
27	110,794	133,680	552.39	9,593	211,036	191,851
28	110,810	133,699	552.47	9,594	211,067	191,879
29	110,826	133,719	552.55	9,595	211,097	191,906
30	110,843	133,739	552.64	9,597	211,130	191,936
31	110,861	133,761	552.73	9,598	211,164	191,967
32	110,878	133,781	552.81	9,600	211,196	191,997
33	110,895	133,802	552.90	9,601	211,229	192,026
34	110,913	133,824	552.99	9,603	211,263	192,057
35	110,931	133,845	553.08	9,604	211,297	192,088
36	110,949	133,867	553.17	9,606	211,331	192,119
37	110,968	133,890	553.26	9,608	211,368	192,152
38	110,987	133,913	553.36	9,609	211,404	192,185
39	111,006	133,936	553.45	9,611	211,440	192,218
40	111,025	133,959	553.54	9,613	211,476	192,251
41	111,044	133,982	553.64	9,614	211,512	192,284
42	111,063	134,005	553.73	9,616	211,549	192,317
43	111,083	134,029	553.83	9,618	211,587	192,352
44	111,103	134,053	553.93	9,619	211,625	192,386
45	111,122	134,076	554.03	9,621	211,661	192,419

Ancient measurements in each degree of latitiude

Ancient measurements in each degree of latitiude					
Deg.	Metres	Meg. Yds	Furlongs(s)	11.55	Royal Cubit	Pyk Belady
46	111,142	134,100	554.13	9,623	211,699	192,454
47	111,162	134,124	554.23	9,624	211,737	192,488
48	111,181	134,147	554.32	9,626	211,773	192,521
49	111,201	134,171	554.42	9,628	211,811	192,556
50	111,220	134,194	554.52	9,629	211,848	192,589
51	111,239	134,217	554.61	9,631	211,884	192,622
52	111,258	134,240	554.71	9,633	211,920	192,655
53	111,277	134,263	554.80	9,634	211,956	192,687
54	111,296	134,286	554.90	9,636	211,992	192,720
55	111,315	134,309	554.99	9,638	212,029	192,753
56	111,334	134,332	555.09	9,639	212,065	192,786
57	111,352	134,353	555.18	9,641	212,099	192,817
58	111,370	134,375	555.26	9,642	212,133	192,848
59	111,388	134,397	555.35	9,644	212,168	192,880
60	111,405	134,417	555.44	9,645	212,200	192,909
61	111,422	134,438	555.52	9,647	212,232	192,939
62	111,439	134,458	555.61	9,648	212,265	192,968
63	111,455	134,478	555.69	9,650	212,295	192,996
64	111,471	134,497	555.77	9,651	212,326	193,023
65	111,487	134,516	555.85	9,653	212,356	193,051
66	111,502	134,534	555.92	9,654	212,385	193,077
67	111,517	134,552	556.00	9,655	212,413	193,103
68	111,531	134,569	556.07	9,656	212,440	193,127
69	111,544	134,585	556.13	9,657	212,465	193,150
70	111,557	134,601	556.20	9,659	212,490	193,172
71	111,570	134,616	556.26	9,660	212,514	193,195
72	111,582	134,631	556.32	9,661	212,537	193,216
73	111,594	134,645	556.38	9,662	212,560	193,236
74	111,605	134,659	556.44	9,663	212,581	193,255
75	111,616	134,672	556.49	9,664	212,602	193,274
76	111,626	134,684	556.54	9,665	212,621	193,292
77	111,635	134,695	556.59	9,665	212,638	193,307
78	111,643	134,704	556.63	9,666	212,653	193,321
79	111,651	134,714	556.67	9,667	212,669	193,335
80	111,659	134,724	556.71	9,667	212,684	193,349
81	111,666	134,732	556.74	9,668	212,697	193,361
82	111,672	134,739	556.77	9,669	212,709	193,371
83	111,677	134,745	556.80	9,669	212,718	193,380
84	111,682	134,751	556.82	9,669	212,728	193,389
85	111,686	134,756	556.84	9,670	212,735	193,396
86	111,690	134,761	556.86	9,670	212,743	193,403
87	111,693	134,765	556.88	9,670	212,749	193,408
88	111,695	134,767	556.89	9,671	212,752	193,411
89	111,696	134,768	556.89	9,671	212,754	193,413
90	111,697	134,770	556.90	9,671	212,756	193,415
	10,001,987	12,068,035	49,867.59	865,973	19,051,404	17,319,458

Appendix 4
CANON OF ANCIENT MEASURES

Throughout this text, measures have been reconstituted to fit into the cannon of proportions that harmonise with either the length of the meridian (Pole to Equator) or from the equatorial circumference of the Earth. The meridian measure was re-introduced with the metre which was taken as one ten millionth part the length of the meridian. Because of inaccuracies in the original calculations the metre as established is not precise for the Pole to Equator is actually 10,001,987 metres. It is demonstrated in this book that in past times this distance was initially divided into one million parts and then an equilateral triangle established in which the meridian division was the height of the triangle while the sides provided the base measurement from which a whole family of measures were taken. The length of each side can therefore be shown to be 11.5493 metres. This is the nominal base for the measure. In practice, as Stecchini has pointed out, slight adjustments were made to fit the latitude where the measure was being used. For example, the Egyptian Royal Cubit, which has a nominal value of 0.525m, is given in Richard Gillings' book *Mathematics in the Time of the Pharoahs* as 0.523m although other authorities make it a fraction longer. Egypt resides between latitudes 24° and 30° approximately and from the table in Appendix 3 we could take the average length of one degree between these latitudes as 110,797 metres. Multiplying this distance by 90, which is the number of degrees in the quadrant, gives a distance of 9,971,685 metres. The ratio between the nominal measure and the corrected measure for this exact latitude is therefore 1:0.997, as in the case of the Royal Cubit, which gives a precise length 0.52351 metres.

Imperial measures, I believe, have been derived not from the meridian but from the equatorial circumference. Through the passage of time these have become distorted so that modern imperial units no longer fit into an exact harmonious relationship with the Earth. However, the system of division can still be used and might be relevant for those architects and planners who wish to design their buildings to have a resonant harmony with the cannon of ancient proportions. To fit the Earth, the revised metric equivalent for the main units of the Imperial family can be shown as follows:

1 Short Furlong (SF) = 200.5708 metres
1 Short Yard (SY) = 0.9117 metres
1 Short Foot (SFt) = 0.3039 metres
1 Short Inch (SI) = 25.3 millimetres

[Note: (SF) after the unit denotes that this is a shortened version of the present imperial standards.]

It is possible that these measures were derived from the length of the meridian based at a latitude of 55°. I am however, of the opinion that the equatorial circumference is the correct base measure.

Professor Thom's Megalithic Yard can be derived both from the meridian (see Fig. 57) as well as from a proportion of the furlong, as there are 242 Megalithic Yards in one furlong. The metric equivalent for the Megalithic Yard is therefore:

1 Meg. Yard = 0.8288 metres

Thom claimed that he had discovered various divisions and multiplications of the Megalithic Yard. These can be shown as:

1 Megalithic Inch = 1 Megalithic Yard ÷ 40 = 20.72 millimetres
1 Megalithic Fathom = 1 Megalithic Yard × 2.5 = 2.072 metres
1 Megalithic Chain = 1 Megalithic Fathom × 10 = 20.72 metres

The two families of measures

Polar meridian

The combining measure for the polar meridian families is the stade of 184.8 metres for:

1 Stade	= 16 × (11.55 unit)
	= 100 Fathoms
	= 320 Pyk Beladys
	= 352 Royal Cubits
	= 400 Geographic Cubit
	= 500 Remens
	= 600 Geographic Feet
	= 616 Egyptian Feet

Equatorial circumference

The unit for Imperial measures is, I believe, based on the length of 1° longitude which equals 555 short furlongs (SF).

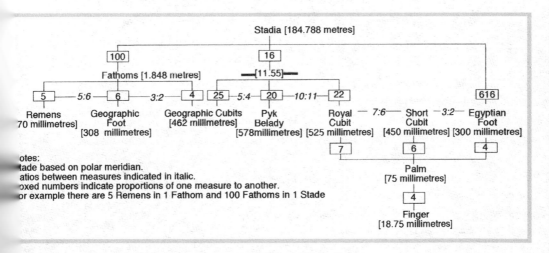

Fig. 103. Family group of measures related to Stadia

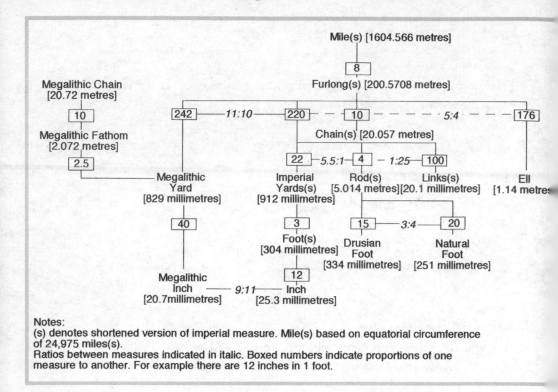

Notes:
(s) denotes shortened version of imperial measure. Mile(s) based on equatorial circumference of 24,975 miles(s).
Ratios between measures indicated in italic. Boxed numbers indicate proportions of one measure to another. For example there are 12 inches in 1 foot.

Fig. 104. Family group of measures derived from short furlong

BIBLIOGRAPHY

Aldred, Cyril, *Egypt to the End of the Old Kingdom*, Thames & Hudson, 1974

Balfour, Michael, *Stonehenge and Its Mysteries*, Macdonald and Jane's (Publishers) Ltd, 1979

Barnatt, John, *Prehistoric Cornwall*, Turnstone Press Limited, 1982

Bauval, Robert & Gilbert, Adrian, *The Orion Mystery*, William Heinemann, 1994

Berlitz, Charles, *Atlantis*, Fontana, 1985

Blavatsky, H. P., *Isis Unveiled*, J. W. Boulton (NY), 1889

Bord, Janet & Colin, *The Secret Country*, Paul Elek, London, 1976

Burl, Aubrey, *Prehistoric Avebury*, Yale University, 1979

Burl, Aubrey, *The Stone Circles of the British Isles*, Yale University Press, 1976

Burl, Aubrey, *The Stonehenge People*, J. M. Dent, 1987

Bushnell, G. H. S., *The First Americans*, Thames & Hudson, 1975

Cotterell, Arthur, *Illustrated Encyclopedia of Myths and Legends*, Cassell, 1989

Dames, Michael, *The Avebury Cycle*, Thames & Hudson, 1996

Devereux, Paul, *Earth Memory*, Quantum, 1991

Devereux, Paul, *Shamanism and the Mystery Lines*, Quantum, 1992

Devereux, Paul and Thompson, Ian, *The Ley Hunter's Companion*, Thames and Hudson, 1979

Donnelly, Ignatius, *Atlantis – The Antediluvian World* (revised edition), Sidgwick and Jackson, 1930

Dunbavin, Paul, *The Atlantis Researches*, Third Millennium, 1995

Edwards, I. E. S., *The Pyramids of Egypt*, Ebury Press and Michael Joseph, 1947

Ellul, Joseph, *Malta's Prediluvian Culture*, Printwell Ltd, 1988

Emery, Walter, *Archaic Egypt*, Penguin Books, 1971

Gilbert, Adrian and Cotterell, Maurice, *The Mayan Prophecies*, Element Books, 1995

Gillings, Richard, *Mathematics in the Time of the Pharaohs*, Dover Publications (NY), 1972

Gimbutas, Marija, *The Civilization of the Goddess*, HarperCollins, 1991

Hadingham, Evan, *Circles and Standing Stones*, William Heinemann, 1975

Haggar, Nicholas, *The Fire and the Stones*, Element Books, 1991

Hancock, Graham, *Fingerprints of the Gods*, Heinemann, 1995

Hancock, Graham and Bauval, Robert, *Keeper of Genesis*, Heinemann, 1996

Harbison, Peter, *Guide to the National Monuments of Ireland*, Gill & Macmillan, 1970

Hart, George, *Egyptian Myths*, British Museum Press, 1990

Hawkins, Gerald, *Stonehenge Decoded*, Fontana, 1970

Heath, Robin, *The Key to Stonehenge*, Bluestone Press, 1995

Hogben, Lancelot, *Mathematics for the Million*, Allen and Unwin, 1936

Hope, Murry, *Atlantis – Myth or Reality*, Arkana, 1991

Howarth, Stephen, *The Knight Templar*, Collins, 1982

Ivimy, John, *The Sphinx and the Megaliths*, Turnstone Press Limited, 1974

Lamb, H. H., *Climate, History and the Modern World*, Routledge, 1995

Lawlor, Robert, *Sacred Geometry*, Thames and Hudson, 1982

Lockyer, Sir Norman, *Stonehenge and Other British Stone Monuments Astronomically Considered*

MacCana, Proinsias, *Celtic Mythology*, Newnes Books, 1968

Mackie, Euan, *The Megalith Builders*, Phaidon Press, 1977

Mann, A. T., *Sacred Architecture*, Element Books, 1993

Michell, John, *City of Revelation*, Garnstone Press, 1972

Michell, John, *The View Over Atlantis*, Sago Press, 1969

Millar, Hamish and Broadhurst, Paul, *The Sun and the Serpent*, Pendragon Press, 1989

Muck, Otto, *The Secrets of Atlantis*, Collins & Sons, 1978

Nelson, Dee Jay and Coville, David, *Life Force in the Great Pyramid*, DeVorss & Company, 1977

Newham, C. A., *The Astronomical Significance of Stonehenge*, John Blackburn, 1972

Osborn, George, *Exploring Ancient Wiltshire*, Dorset Publishing Co, 1982

Pennick, Nigel, *Earth Harmony*, Century, 1987

Pennick, Nigel and Devereux, Paul, *Lines on the Landscape*, Robert Hale, 1989

Phillips, Patricia, *The Prehistory of Europe*, Penguin, 1980

Quinn, Bob, *Atlantean*, Quartet Books, 1986

Salter, Mike, *The Old Parish Churches of Worcestershire*, Folly Publications, 1990

Schultz, B. M., *Callanish*, B. M. Schultz, 1983

Sharkey, John, *Celtic Mysteries*, Thames & Hudson, 1975

Straffon, Cheryl, *The Earth Mysteries Guide to Bodmin Moor*, Meyn Mamvro Publications, 1995

Taylor, Stephen and Dee, Nerys, (ed) *Atlantis Past and to Come*, Atlanteans Association Ltd, 1968

Thom, Alexander, *Megalithic Luna Observatories*, Oxford University Press, 1973

Thom, Alexander, *Megalithic Sites in Britain*, Oxford University Press, 1967

Thoth, Max and Neilsen, Grey, *Pyramid Power*, Warner Destiny Book, 1974

Tompkins, Peter, *The Secret of the Great Pyramid*, Harper and Row, 1971

Watkins, Alfred, *The Old Straight Track*, Methuen & Co, 1923

Wood, David, *Genisis*, The Baton Press, 1985

The Larousse Encyclopedia of Mythology, Hamlyn, 1994

INDEX